A COLD WELCOME

Joseph Walker glared at me.

"I'm glad you came to the reopening." I flashed him the pageant smile again. It worked as well as it had the first time.

"Why are you here?" he asked.

I blinked. "Excuse me?"

"I would like to know your plans for this shop."

I felt myself bristle. "What do you mean?"

"Do you plan to stay here? To run this shop?" His voice was stern.

"Yes," I said. "That's what I moved here to do."

"That's what I was afraid of. You have no business running this shop. Rolling Brook is an Amish town. You should leave it to the Amish. The *Englischer* was right. What does a girl from Texas know about the Amish?"

My face grew warm. "I'm sorry you feel that way," I said, using the same uncompromising tone he'd used with me. "But I inherited this shop. Whether you like it or not, I'm here to stay."

"Why am I not surprised? You're proud, just like Eleanor was. She never knew her place either."

My blood boiled. Aunt Eleanor was the most unimposing, unassuming woman I had ever known. "Please don't talk about my *aenti* that way."

He snorted. "*Aenti?* Use your own *Englisch* words." He turned and stormed out of the shop.

I stood there for a full minute wondering what just happened.

Murder, Plain *and* Simple

AN AMISH QUILT SHOP MYSTERY

Isabella Alan

AN OBSIDIAN MYSTERY

OBSIDIAN
Published by the Penguin Group
Penguin Group (USA), 375 Hudson Street,
New York, New York 10014, USA

USA | Canada | UK | Ireland | Australia | New Zealand | India | South Africa | China

Penguin Books Ltd., Registered Offices: 80 Strand, London WC2R 0RL, England
For more information about the Penguin Group visit penguin.com.

First published by Obsidian, an imprint of New American Library,
a division of Penguin Group (USA)

First Printing, September 2013

ISBN 978-0-451-41363-5

Printed in the United States of America
10   9   8   7   6

PUBLISHER'S NOTE
This is a work of fiction. Names, characters, places, and incidents either are the
product of the author's imagination or are used fictitiously, and any resemblance
to actual persons, living or dead, business establishments, events, or locales is
entirely coincidental.
   The publisher does not have any control over and does not assume any respon-
sibility for author or third-party Web sites or their content.

For my namesakes
Isabella Flower
and
Thomas Alan Flower

ACKNOWLEDGMENTS

Danki to my editor, Talia Platz, who had a terrific idea and let me run with it, and to my agent, Nicole Resciniti, who I believe is a superhero in disguise.

Thank you to Molly MacRae, who graciously introduced me to her editor at Obsidian at Malice Domestic years ago. I know this book never would have happened without your generosity.

Special thanks to all of the wonderful people I've met in Holmes County while researching the novel, especially Anna Hochstetler, owner of Swiss Village Quilts and Crafts in Sugarcreek. Anna is always a kind hostess, and her shop is a lovely treasure tucked away in the heart of Amish Country.

Also special thanks to master quilter Charlotte Hennessey for trying to teach me to hand quilt and allowing me to mar her beautiful quilt with my clumsy stitches.

Love to my mother, Rev. Pamela Flower, who reads every manuscript more than once.

Finally, thank you to *Gott* in heaven.

Chapter One

There it was—the empty white bakery box. Just a light dusting of powdered sugar surrounded it on the blond wood kitchen table in my new home in Holmes County, Ohio. A streak of red jelly ran along its side with my fingerprint perfectly preserved in raspberry red. It was a crime scene.

My stomach ached as I remembered the enormous jelly doughnut that had been inside the box. Did I really eat the entire thing? After weeks of starving myself for my big Texas wedding that was not to be, I'd gone on a bender. I shivered when I thought about the two-week juice cleanse. What a waste.

Oliver, my black-and-white French bulldog, whimpered.

I grabbed the box off the table and shoved it into the wastebasket under the sink. "Don't judge. I was under extreme distress. Moving across the country is stressful, you know. Besides, lugging all the boxes into the house yesterday burned off the calories."

He butted the back of my knee with his head as if he understood. My überathletic ex-fiancé, Ryan Dickinson,

Esq., would not have been so sympathetic. But what Ryan thought shouldn't matter to me now. Unfortunately, it did—a lot.

I wanted to lie on the couch and take a nap. I could blame it on carb overload, but I knew the true cause of my lethargy was fear. What was I doing in Ohio? I'd quit my well-paying advertising job in Dallas, Texas, to move to Amish Country. Was I crazy? Had I finally hit my quarter-life crisis at thirty-four, almost ten years late, or was I experiencing a midlife crisis a few years early? I couldn't decide which of those would be worse.

On the heels of my broken engagement, I learned I'd inherited my Amish aunt's quilt shop, Running Stitch. I saw the inheritance as a divine sign to get out of Texas.

Aunt Eleanor had not grown up Amish. She had left her modern life when she fell in love with an Amish man. She gave up her culture to be baptized into the Amish church. The hopeless romantic in me wished someone would make such a sacrifice for me. Ryan could not. He'd called off the wedding because of "commitment issues." After six years of dating and one year of being engaged, you'd think he'd have been over those.

As a young child, I'd spent countless hours at my aunt's quilt shop, watching my aunt's quilting circle and learning the craft myself. When I was ten years old, my father got a high-powered executive job and we moved to Dallas, Texas. Until I reached high school and became too preoccupied with my own life, I returned to Holmes County every summer to quilt with my aunt and tramp around the Ohio countryside with my childhood friend Jo-Jo. Even after I stopped visiting Ohio, I kept quilting and looked forward to my aunt's letters, which always included a quilting tip or pattern inside. From hundreds of miles away, she continued to teach me the craft. I saw moving to Ohio as an opportunity to dedicate myself to the craft I loved. I might have thought this was an excellent idea, but my friends back in Dallas thought I was on the brink of a nervous breakdown. Standing in the middle of my Ohio kitchen, I wondered whether they were right.

This called for the big guns—er . . . boots, I meant. I hurried through the small two-bedroom house I rented in Millersburg. I opened box after box until finally I found them, my cowboy boots.

The boots were made of aged leather and the yellow daisy and blue cornflower pattern was stitched along the side of the foot and up the calf. The fine hand stitching reminded me of Aunt Eleanor's quilts. I think that's what drew me to the boots in the first place. It certainly wasn't the price, which had been a month's worth of my advertising salary. I didn't wear the boots often, only when I needed a boost of rawhide courage. Starting a brand-new career hundreds of miles away from any family and friends qualified.

Solemnly, Oliver watched me wrestle the boots onto my feet. He knew to respect the boots.

With the proper footwear intact, I felt ready to face the appointment that morning at my aunt's shop—my shop. Running Stitch was in Rolling Brook, a small, mostly Amish town two miles south on Ohio's Route 83, five minutes from my new home.

In front of Running Stitch, I climbed out of my little SUV to find my aunt's lawyer, Harvey Lemontop, waiting for me on the sidewalk. Martha Yoder, who had managed the shop during my aunt's illness, was with him. Harvey was a short man and resembled a pillow with arms because of the way his belly hung out over his belt. His dress shirt was open at the throat and his diamond-printed necktie hung crookedly from his neck.

Where Harvey was disheveled, Martha was as neat as could be in a plain navy dress, crisp black apron, and white prayer cap. I parked diagonally in the spot directly in front of the quilt shop and climbed out of the SUV.

Oliver hopped onto the pavement with a solid thump. He cocked his head at me, showing off his large batlike ears to their best advantage. They resembled antennae, one black and the other white, searching for a signal as they flicked back and forth.

The shop was on the center block of Sugartree Street, the main road going through Rolling Brook. Unlike Millersburg, which was dissected by Ohio 83 going north to south and Ohio 39 going east to west, Rolling Brook was off the state routes, so the traffic consisted of the Amish living nearby and English tourists. Running Stitch was a brick-faced shop that had been painted olive green. A darker green awning covered the entry. Several Amish-style quilts hung from quilt racks in the large picture window.

On the left side of Running Stitch was a bare redbrick woodworking shop. A fiftyish Amish man with a long gray beard was standing outside the shop, a black felt hat atop his head. His pose mimicked the life-sized black cutout lawn ornaments of Amish men I'd seen propped against trees and fences on my drive across Ohio's countryside. I smiled at him, but he didn't smile back.

"Ms. Braddock, I'm glad you made it here safely. How was your trip?" Harvey shook my hand. His was damp, and it reminded me of holding raw chicken.

"It was long but fine. Please, call me Angie."

He nodded. "You remember Martha Yoder."

"Yes, of course," I said.

Martha examined my feet. "Those are some boots you got there. I haven't seen anything like that before."

"Don't the farmers wear boots?" I asked.

"Work boots, sure, but nothing like those. Clearly, those boots are not for working."

Was that a dig? I shook it off.

"Thank you so much for taking care of the shop while *Aenti* was ill." I used the Pennsylvania Dutch word for "aunt." "And for agreeing to stay on. I know I will need your help as I get started."

Martha smoothed her hands over her apron. "It was my pleasure. I wished she had been well enough to visit the shop more often these last few months."

Oliver barked a greeting. Ignoring Martha, he waddle-walked over to Harvey for a head scratch. The lawyer obliged, and Oliver shook his stubby tail in doggy glee.

Harvey motioned to the door. "Shall we go in?"

Martha unlocked the shop's door. Inside, she flicked on the overhead lights, illuminating the store.

My eye was drawn to half a dozen quilts, each one in the geometric color-blocked Amish style, hung on the plain whitewashed walls. Four of the six quilts I recognized as my aunt's work. I walked over to the one closest to the front door and felt tiny stitches of the goosefoot-patterned quilt. Aunt Eleanor could fit as many as twenty stitches within an inch. Her stitches were far too tiny to count, but I knew they were there. A pang of sadness hit me, and I blinked rapidly.

"She did beautiful work," Martha said.

I nodded and forced myself to look at the rest of the shop. There was one large room with a short hallway in the back that led to the office, the restroom, and a small stockroom. Beside the stockroom, a door opened into the fenced backyard. I stepped across the wide-planked oak floors to a short wooden counter that sat at the front of the shop with a cash register. I ran my hand along its smooth surface and came back with fingers covered in a thin film of dust. Oliver's toenails clicked across the floor. I thought of Aunt Eleanor's welcoming smile and sure fingers as her needle worked its way in and out of a quilt. She never dropped a stitch and never scolded me when I did.

In the far corner, a quilt frame, which looked like a huge picture frame on its side balanced several feet above the floor by two sturdy table legs, held a four-patch quilt. Metal clamps held the four corners of the quilt tightly to the frame so the fabric wouldn't bunch up and the stitches would be flat and precise. The frame was pulled only four feet out from the middle of the quilt pattern. As the quilters moved out from the center, the frame could be adjusted to grow wider and wider, to the full size of the quilt. At the moment, the quilt was only half-finished. A light layer of dust coated the exposed fabric. On the wall opposite the cash register, shelving ran the entire length of the room. The shelves held bolts of dark fabric. On the opposite wall was the fabric to appeal to English shoppers. There were pastels, flower patterns, stripes, and bright colors.

Beyond the stockroom, I opened the door to the tiny backyard. Oliver made a beeline for an azalea bush. The yard was at a slant, as Rolling Brook was on a hillside. My aunt had planted a small garden there. It would need some weeding, but the gladiolas, hollyhocks, and other late-summer flowers flourished. I had a clear view of the green rolling hills and an Amish farm about a mile away. A tiny farmer hitched his horses to a buggy. Although I'd lived in Millersburg as a child, standing in my aunt's garden was the first time I realized how beautiful this part of the country was. As a kid, I'd taken its beauty for granted. This was the first time I really saw it with my adult eyes.

I tried to picture Ryan Dickinson, my former fiancé, standing next to me. In my mind's eye, I put him—with his fancy suits and expensive European leather shoes—into life in Rolling Brook. It didn't work. Ryan, an up-and-coming attorney, was a Dallas boy born and bred. He loved the traffic, fast pace, and intensity of the city. Nothing about Rolling Brook was intense. I smiled to myself. The only way I could be there at that moment was alone, and I realized being alone wasn't such a bad thing. Maybe the un-Ryan-ness of Rolling Brook was its true appeal. Then again, it might have been the boots working their magic.

Harvey stepped into the garden and stood beside me. He wiped his brow with a blue handkerchief.

"It's beautiful," I said, motioning to the view.

He smiled and a dimple appeared on his left cheek. "It is."

A cardinal landed on the wooden fence surrounding the garden. Oliver yipped and dashed under the closest bush, which was a little too small for him, leaving his hindquarters exposed. He held his black stubby tail completely still, as if he thought the cardinal wouldn't see him if he didn't move. I didn't bother to tell him it was a bird, not a tyrannosaurus. My Frenchie suffered from ornithophobia. We'd sought treatment from acupuncture to hypnotism. Nothing had worked.

"Is your dog okay?" Harvey asked.

"He's fine," I assured him.

He cleared his throat. "Are you sure you want to take the shop on, Ms. Braddock? It's a big job. I can still help you sell it if you've changed your mind."

I smiled at him. "I thought I told you to call me Angie."

The small lawyer blushed. "Yes, you did. I'm sorry, Ms.—I mean Angie."

"There's nothing to be sorry for. As for your question, my answer is yes. I do want to run the shop. I haven't been so sure of something in a long time."

"What's wrong with your dog?" Martha joined us and handed me a set of keys.

"He's afraid of birds," I said casually, as if this were a normal canine problem.

She laughed. "*Ach*, he's going to see a lot more of those in Holmes County."

That was my fear. The cardinal hopped along the fence as if he knew. Poor Oliver. His transition to country life was going to be much more difficult than mine.

"Can the cowgirl run the quilt shop?" Martha sounded dubious.

I shook the keys in my hand. "She's willing to try. The shop is perfect."

"Only the *gut* Lord is perfect." She winked at me. "But we'll get as close as we can. Now, you'd better saddle up. There's a lot of work to be done."

I cocked an eyebrow at her. "How do you know all these cowboy expressions?"

She grinned. "I may have watched a Western or two during my *rumspringa*."

The boots bolstered my courage. "Can I ask you a question?"

"Yes, of course."

"The man standing outside the woodworking shop. Who is he?"

Harvey's dimple disappeared. "You must mean Joseph Walker. He owns that shop and makes the best wooden furniture in the county. I have a few of his pieces in my home."

"He seemed"—I searched for the right word—"cold."

Harvey laughed nervously. "Oh, I'd hoped that we could talk about Joseph later."

Martha folded her arms. "You may as well tell her. She needs to be prepared."

"Prepared?" I looked from one to the other. "Prepared for what?"

Harvey pulled at his tie. "He claims he owns Running Stitch."

I waved my hands in the air. "Wait. Roll back. What?"

"He has a fifty-year-old deed for the property with his father's name on it. It clearly states the Walkers are the owners."

"Then my aunt and uncle must have bought the shop from Joseph's father at some point. Where is my aunt's deed to prove Joseph wrong?"

Harvey swallowed. "That's the problem. We can't find it anywhere."

Chapter Two

"What do you mean, you can't find it?" I asked.

Harvey loosened his tie. "I mean that we can't find it. We've looked everywhere. It wasn't with the will or any of her other papers."

"Did you search her house?"

Martha gave me an appraising look. "The quilting circle and I packed up and searched Eleanor's house and now it's empty. There is nothing there. The farm and land goes to one of Jacob's cousins."

My hands began to tingle. "Then it must be in the shop. Did you search the shop?" I took a step toward the back door. "Let's look for it now."

Martha shook her head. "We searched the shop too. Angie, it's not here."

"Okay, okay," I said, thinking aloud. "Someone somewhere must have a copy. Like the state or county."

"Typically the county clerk keeps a copy of all property deeds," Harvey said.

I waved them to the door. "Let's go there now and get it."

Harvey fumbled with the end of his tie. "I tried but it wasn't there either."

"How is that possible?"

"Thirty years ago, a frozen pipe burst in the basement of the clerk's office where the older files were stored. Hundreds of documents were destroyed. When the janitor cleaned up the mess, he just threw the sopping wet documents away without realizing their importance. After the flood, the clerk's office sent a letter to all the property owners who may have been affected, asking them to bring their deeds and other documents into the clerk's office to be copied. They didn't have anything other than the paper copies—the documents were too old to have a digital version. Many of the English folks in the county complied." He sighed. "However, because they want distance from the English government, many of the Amish didn't bother. They didn't see how it would be important to them. Your uncle must have been one of the Amish men who ignored the county's letter."

"You're her lawyer. Didn't you have a copy?"

He shook his head. "I wasn't her lawyer then, and the man who was is long dead."

"Are you saying that I don't own Running Stitch?"

"No, no, I'm not saying that. I'm certain Eleanor owned the shop. We just have to find the deed to prove it."

Hadn't he just told me he looked everywhere for it?

"In the meantime, I recommend that you stay away from Joseph Walker. You don't want to say or do anything that might hurt our case."

"Our case?"

He nodded. "If we can't find the deed, we might have to go to court over this."

I felt dizzy. At that moment, moving to Ohio seemed like the worst idea I'd ever had.

Joseph Walker scowled at me each morning as I unlocked the door to Running Stitch. I know Harvey warned me against talking to Joseph while the property was in dispute, but his glares were getting old.

Today was no different. I held the car door open, letting Oliver hop out, and slammed the car door after him. I snapped the leash onto Oliver's collar. Joseph watched our every move.

"This is ridiculous," I muttered to Oliver.

The dog snuffled in agreement.

I stepped on the sidewalk and gave him my best Texas pageant girl smile. When we moved to Texas, my mother suddenly discovered she was a Southern belle trapped in a Yankee's body and embraced everything she could of Southern living, including picking up a Southern drawl in her forties and, much to my horror, signing me up for Little Miss pageants across the Dallas–Fort Worth Metroplex.

My dazzling smile had not worked on the judges, nor did they work on Joseph Walker. His glare cut into me. I took a few steps toward Joseph and was jerked back by Oliver, who had wrapped his leash around the leg of a park bench. His round brown eyes popped out of his head.

"Come on, buddy, you're making me look bad in front of our new neighbor."

"You should have more control over your animal." Joseph's voice was hoarse from lack of use.

I turned to face him, and he glowered at us.

I cleared my throat. "My name is . . ."

"I know who you are."

I glowered back. Two could play at this game. "I know who you are too. You're Joseph Walker. I heard you are the best woodworker in town."

His black felt hat dipped down, hiding his eyes. "A person should not boast, not even about another's talents. Whoever told you that was in the wrong."

Oliver wiggled underneath the park bench.

"Animals are for work. They aren't pets."

Oliver whimpered as if he understood the woodworker's words.

"I'm sorry you feel that way." I gritted my teeth. Like me, like my dog. Don't like my dog, I don't like you. "I know there's been a little confusion over my aunt's shop."

His eyes narrowed into slits. "There is no confusion. I own the property."

My eye twitched. "The shop belonged to my aunt, and now it belongs to me."

"You have the deed?"

I licked my lips. "I'll find it."

"Hello?" A breathy voice broke into our conversation. I turned to find a woman with close-cropped silver hair. She stepped onto the walk and a man came out of the shop behind her. He appeared about ten years younger than the woman, maybe forty. His hair was slicked back in *Grease* style. Someone should have told him that hairstyle went the way of poodle skirts and monogrammed sweaters decades ago. He didn't wave at us but followed the woman across the street.

A purple crystal hanging from the woman's neck caught the sunlight and sparkled. They made an odd couple: one a 1950s throwback and the other a New Age princess.

I snuck a glance at Joseph. His lip curled as if he'd drunk sour milk.

"Angela Braddock! I'm so pleased to finally meet you." The woman wrapped her arms around me. Her puffy blouse ballooned into my face until she pulled away. "I told Farley that we need to get over to the Running Stitch and introduce ourselves."

"Nice to meet you . . ." I let the words hang in the air. Should I know who this woman was? She didn't look like one of my aunt's old friends, or a member of my aunt's Amish quilting circle. Did she know my parents before they flew South?

She lightly smacked her forehead with the heel of her hand. "It would help if I told you my name. I'm Willow Moon." She shot a thumb over her shoulder. "I run the Dutchman's Tea Shop across the street."

I stopped short of asking her if "Willow Moon" was the name on her birth certificate.

"This is township trustee Farley Jung," she declared proudly. She pronounced "Jung" with a hard "j" like in "jungle."

Farley held out his hand, and we shook. He grasped my hand for a few seconds longer than necessary and made eye contact with me until I looked away. Can we say creepy? In the seconds I had known Farley, I decided I would much rather be stuck on a deserted island with Joseph if forced. Joseph, who insulted my dog and claimed to own my shop, so that was saying something.

I discreetly wiped my hand on the back of my jeans. "I'm glad you both stopped by. I've been planning to visit the other shops on the street. I haven't met too many people in town yet."

Willow's eyes flitted to Joseph. "I see you've met Joseph."

Joseph scowled and leaned back against the brick facade of his shop.

Willow cleared her throat. "I'd be happy to take you around and introduce you to the rest of the shopkeepers." She clapped her hands, and for the first time I noticed her fingernails were painted rainbow colors. "You arrived in Rolling Brook at the perfect time."

I did?

"Why's that?" I asked.

"Because of the First Annual Watermelon Fest, of course. It's only a week and a half away! It will be the most exciting event Rolling Brook has ever seen."

"We do not need exciting," Joseph snapped, and pushed off the building. "No more than we need *Englischers* in our town. Rolling Brook is for the Amish, not for you." He dug his fists into his sides.

I stumbled back and knocked my calf against the park bench. Willow and Farley seemed unfazed by Joseph's outburst.

"Joseph, we know how you feel about the fest, but you're in the minority." Trustee Farley spoke for the first time.

The two men glared at each other in mutual disdain. If we were in a Western movie, someone would have shouted "Draw!"

Joseph straightened to his full six-feet-plus height and vibrated with barely restrained anger. He looked like a furious Pilgrim. "You plan to turn Rolling Brook into an *Englisch* circus. You have no concern for our ways. You use our culture for money. The Amish who go along with you have lost their way. They should speak with their elders to see what the *Ordnung* says about such things."

Willow trilled a laugh, sounding like a blue jay in a tree. "I doubt your Amish rule book has anything against watermelon, Joseph. Honestly, you're the most serious man I have ever met—and most of the men in Rolling Brook are Amish."

"*All* the men of Rolling Brook should be Amish. You *Englischers* don't have enough squalor in your cities that you must bring it here?"

Squalor? Really?

His dark eyes bored into me. "I suggest you go back to that big city you came from. You are not welcome." He spun on the heels of his thick work boots and walked through the front door of his shop.

"Well, that was"—she squinted into the sunlight— "awkward. Pay no mind to Joseph Walker. He's full of hot air."

Farley glared at the woodworker's shop. "He has caused nothing but problems for us since the moment we suggested the Watermelon Fest. He refuses to recognize how much business it will bring his shop. If he did, he'd be much happier."

Willow handed me a flyer for the festival. "We'd love it if you could hang this in the window of your shop."

I took the piece of paper and saw several other stores on the street had identical flyers displayed in their front windows, including the Amish bakery across the street, which is owned and run by my aunt's dear friends the Millers.

Movement in the display window of the woodworker's shop caught my eye. A figure stepped away from the front window. I couldn't tell if it was a woman or a man.

Farley cleared his throat. "We would also like to know if you can participate in the fest. As a new shopkeeper in town, it would give you the opportunity to promote your business and meet others in the community."

Any business I could drum up would be helpful. "I would be happy to help out. What would you like me to do?"

"We will think of something." Willow glanced at the CLOSED sign in Running Stitch's glass door. "When do you plan to reopen?"

"Tomorrow. We are having a grand reopening party. You both should come."

"We wouldn't miss it," Willow said.

Farley took a step closer to me. "As for Joseph Walker, ignore him, like Willow said. He will be silent on the topic of the Watermelon Fest soon enough."

I shivered at the trustee's intensity. He must *really* like watermelon.

The odd pair said their good-byes and headed down Sugartree, handing out flyers to tourists.

Oliver braced his two front paws on my leg. I scratched him between the ears. "It's because I didn't wear the boots. Had I worn the boots, Joseph would have been nicer."

Chapter Three

Later that morning, I stood in the middle of the shop, holding one of my aunt's heavy quilts in my arms, trying to decide the best place to display it. It was a double wedding ring pattern. Like most traditional Amish quilts, it was pieced together with geometric shapes of strong color. Her double wedding ring was purple, navy blue, black, olive green, and maroon. It was some of my aunt's finest work. I inhaled the quilt's scent, and it smelled like dusty cotton, which I found somehow comforting. There was nothing more comforting to me than the smell of a quilt or the act of quilting, but translating that passion into an occupation was turning out to be a greater challenge than I thought it would be. And Joseph Walker's claim to own Running Stitch made things even more complicated.

Oliver whimpered at my feet.

"What's wrong, buddy? Are you nervous about the reopening too?"

He pawed at my leg, and I leaned over to pet him. As I did, he buried his face in the quilt and growled softly.

I jerked the quilt away. "Oliver, don't try to bite that. It's Aunt Eleanor's quilt."

He slunk back to his bed pillow by the display window.

I was still wondering about Oliver's strange behavior when the shop door banged open. The bell nailed to the door jingled. Oliver perked up from his pillow. Seeing who it was, he rested his head back on the pillow with a snuffling sound.

Martha Yoder stood in the doorway with her quilting basket hooked over her arm. The basket rocked back and forth as she tugged at her bonnet ties and removed the hat from her head, revealing the white prayer cap underneath. "I see you've found the double wedding ring. Do you have a special person in mind for that?" Her blue eyes sparkled.

I blushed. "I'm going to hang it behind the cash register."

Behind her, Rachel Miller, a petite young woman, stepped into the room, balancing three-month-old Abram on her hip. Abram had a tuft of hair sticking up on his head. In Rachel's other arm, she held a basket from her family's bakery across the street. I hoped Rachel remembered to pack her county-fair-winning snickerdoodles. The cinnamon-covered cookies were my favorite. Silver-haired Anna Graber was a few steps behind her. All three Amish women were members of my aunt's quilt circle. We hoped to recruit more quilters during the grand reopening. My aunt started the circle over twenty years ago as a place where Amish women could have a break once a week to socialize with other women. She told me once that even Amish wives and mothers needed time away from the family and housework. Most of the quilts were made to be gifts, but some were sold in the shop.

Rachel placed her heavy basket on the cash register counter and switched Abram to her other hip. "I brought over some cookies for you to taste, Angie, for tomorrow's opening. My husband, Aaron, and I plan to make ten dozen. People always want a little bite to eat while they shop."

"Can I pay you for the cookies? Please?" This was the third time I had asked her this question in the last two days.

"Absolutely not. Consider it my family's welcome gift to you."

I grinned. "Okay. I won't argue with you about it any longer."

"*Gut.*"

Anna patted Oliver on the head. "I think behind the cash register is a fine place for the quilt."

"You don't want to keep it for yourself, Angie?" Martha asked. "Since this is *your* store. Everything in it belongs to you."

I noticed that Rachel and Anna shared a look at Martha's comment.

Rachel bounced her son on her hip. "It will be nice to quilt again. I've missed it."

"We all have," Anna agreed. "Eleanor would be pleased to know we are carrying on." One of the chairs held an opened cardboard box of fabric rotary cutters. All but one were still encased in their plastic packaging. I had bought them the day before from a big-box craft store's going-out-of-business sale. When I'd told the store manager I planned to use them in my quilting shop, she had given me the entire case for pocket change. I picked up the loose pair. It had a bright yellow handle. A red button released the safety holding the four-inch circular blade in place. A black plastic trigger freed the blade, so it could be rolled along a hard surface to cut fabric.

"That looks dangerous." Rachel stepped back. "I wouldn't want my children to touch those."

I admitted the blade was razor-sharp.

Anna's eyebrows knit together. "Silliest thing I ever saw. Why don't you use scissors?"

I grimaced. "These cut the fabric faster."

Martha rolled her eyes. "Faster is the *Englisch* way." I wondered whether she'd picked up the eye roll from watching television during her *rumspringa*. "You won't sell any of those to the Amish," Martha added.

"I'm sure the *Englischers* will buy them," Anna said. "Maybe I'll even give them a try."

Martha scowled at Anna.

"I'll put them away." I picked up the box of rotary cutters and carried them to the stockroom. I placed the box on a shelf next to piles of quilting squares. The shelf groaned under the weight, so I moved the box to the floor. I added "fix shelves" to my growing to-do list before returning to the main room.

"Aaron and the boys will bring the rest of the goodies tomorrow morning," Rachel said. Still balancing Abram on her hip, she placed the basket of cookies on the long folding table in front of the display window. Out of respect for Amish plainness, I had covered the long table with a simple navy blue tablecloth.

"Tomorrow's the big day, Angie. How do you feel?" Rachel's voice bubbled with excitement.

"Okay, I think. I hope we live up to Aunt Eleanor's memory." I removed the cookies from the basket and uncovered the plates. Snickerdoodles were the first cookies revealed. I resisted popping one into my mouth.

"The opening will be *gut*. Everyone in Rolling Brook will be here." She bounced from foot to foot. Abram wouldn't have gotten a better ride on a bucking bronco.

"Half of Millersburg too, and don't discount the out-of-town *Englischers* driving in. It's bus season." Rachel shook her head. "I suppose we should be grateful that the *Englischers* want to come here and spend their money. I'd think they would have everything they needed at home." She eyed me. "Including fancy fabric cutters."

"I know one person not coming." Martha waggled her eyebrows.

Rachel's green eyes widened. "Who?" She placed Abram in the oak cradle standing in the corner of the shop and used her foot to rock the cradle at a frenzied pace. He didn't stir. The kid must have a cast-iron stomach.

Martha adjusted the clamp on her side of the frame. "Joseph Walker."

Rachel wrinkled her small nose.

"I met him a couple of hours ago." I ran a cloth over the cash register counter.

Martha folded her arms. "Harvey Lemontop told you not to talk to him."

"I know," I said. "But I had to say something. The guy glares at me every morning like I'm a criminal. Maybe if he gets to know me, he will drop his claim on the shop."

"Until the deed is found, Angie, you should follow the lawyer's advice. No good will come of talking to Joseph Walker. He's a stubborn man," Anna said.

"You don't have to worry about me talking to him again. Clearly, he didn't want to talk to me, and I don't think he'll be coming to the reopening either," I replied.

Anna shook her head. "He'll be here. I can promise you that. And you better be prepared for when he shows up."

Chapter Four

The next morning, a half hour after Running Stitch officially reopened its doors, there was no sign of Joseph Walker, but he appeared to be the only person in Holmes County not interested in dropping by. A tour bus from Cleveland stopped in the middle of Sugartree Street, and two dozen elderly city folks climbed out of the bus. They wore shorts, souvenir T-shirts, and orthopedic shoes. A large potted plant propped open the shop's front door, and as the bus passengers disembarked, I waved to them with one hand while the other hand held a tray of snickerdoodles to lure them in my direction. "Grand reopening!" I called. Half the bus's occupants made a beeline for me.

In no time, my snickerdoodle tray was empty. I went back inside the shop to reload. A line of guests stood at the register. Martha rang up each purchase with a smile playing on the corners of her mouth. Both Amish neighbors and English guests admired my aunt's quilts hanging on the walls. The wedding ring quilt, proudly displayed on the wall behind the cash register, received the most attention. Much to my delight, I saw one of the women from the tour bus holding a basket-patterned quilt, which was one of the most expensive quilts on sale. Some of my fear about running my own business started to slip away when I heard the sound of the cash register drawer opening. After the shop closed, I would search again for the deed.

I walked over to the long table at the front of the store where the baked goods were going fast. As I refilled my tray with snickerdoodles, Rachel placed a hand on my arm. "Look at what a success this is, Angie. Your *aenti* would be so proud of you."

"I couldn't have done it without you. Thank you for providing the food."

She waved away my thanks. Her brow creased and a little of the sparkle went out of her eyes. "There's something I should tell you."

"Is something wrong?"

She held her bottom lip between her teeth as if she was considering something unpleasant.

"Rachel?" I asked.

She rearranged her fry pies on a platter. "I didn't know Sarah Leham has joined the quilting circle."

"I thought you knew. Martha invited her. She said Sarah was an excellent quilter."

"She is," Rachel insisted. "It's only . . ." She trailed off.

"What?" I asked as I watched another visitor walk to the register with a quilt. *Cha-ching* rang in my head.

"It's not right to gossip." Rachel moved on to rearrange the sugar cookies.

"If it's something I need to know, please tell me. I'm still new here, and I'm depending on you, Martha, and Anna to help me understand how Holmes County works."

"Just be careful what you say around Sarah." She glanced behind her to see her son Eli trying to climb one of the shop's display shelves. "Oh, I'd better stop him."

I didn't have time to worry over Rachel's words as a red-haired man close to my age dressed in jeans and a green polo shirt approached me. "Are you Angela Braddock?" he asked while chomping on a large piece of pink bubble gum.

"Yes." I placed my tray of snickerdoodles on the table. I know they were for the guests, but would anyone notice if I popped one into my mouth?

He held out his hand. "I'm Danny Nicolson. I run the Web site for the Holmes County Tourism Board and am interested in doing a piece about your shop for our next newsletter. We e-mail the newsletter to over five thousand subscribers. Most of those subscribers are in the state of Ohio, but it would be great exposure for your store."

After ten years working for an advertising agency, I knew how valuable this interview would be. I couldn't believe this was the first I'd thought about the tourism board. I had been so consumed with getting the shop back in order for the grand reopening and searching for the deed, it hadn't occurred to me to publicize beyond sending press releases about the reopening to all the local newspapers, including the large dailies in Akron, Canton, and Cleveland. "That would be great," I said.

"Excellent." He grinned, displaying a gap between his two front teeth. "Can I interview you tomorrow morning here at the shop, say, six thirty a.m.?"

I was surprised he wanted to meet so early, and my surprise must have shown on my face.

He cracked the gum in his mouth. "I know that's early,

but I have a meeting in Columbus at nine, and I wanted to get the interview in before I leave."

"Six thirty is fine. I look forward to it."

He handed me his card. "Running Stitch has always been a popular shop in Rolling Brook. I know an article about the grand reopening will be a huge hit on the Web site." With that, he grabbed an apple fry pie and wandered around the room making notes.

The card listed only Danny's name and phone number. There was no reference to the tourism board. I inwardly shrugged—maybe he was freelancing—and slipped the card into my jean skirt pocket. The interview would be an excellent opportunity I must take advantage of.

"Angie?" Anna called me from the quilting circle. Anna, Rachel, and a third woman I didn't know sat around the quilt frame. Their callused fingers worked their quilting needles with a speed and efficiency I doubted I'd ever achieve, no matter how many lessons Anna gave me.

Anna didn't look up from her needlework as I stood behind her chair.

Over the pieced-together blue and black quilt topper, the ladies stitched a tiny heart and tulip design set in perfectly symmetrical diamond-shaped boxes. I stared in amazement as Anna moved her quilting needle up and back along the curve of a heart at least ten times before pulling the thread through the quilt. When she finally tugged the thread through, her tiny stitches were identical and roughly the size of the tip of a ballpoint pen.

Anna tilted her head toward the third woman. "I'd like to introduce you to Sarah Leham."

Sarah was extremely thin and wore a pair of plain

wire-rim glasses. Her glass lenses were two perfect circles and gave her eyes an owl-like appearance.

"It's nice to meet you, Sarah," I said. "I'm glad you can be a part of the quilting circle."

Sarah wrapped a piece of thread around her needle three times and jerked it into a quilter's knot. She ran her fingers along the thread's length and snipped off the tail with a pair of tiny scissors. "*Gut* to meet you too. As for the circle, I wouldn't miss it. I'm just so happy and excited to be asked to join. I'm so sorry about your aunt. She was a wonderful woman. It's a terrible loss to the entire community." She took a breath.

I jumped in. "What are you ladies working on?" While I spoke, I shot a glance at Rachel, who was bent over her corner of the quilt, so I couldn't see her face.

"It's a quilt for my granddaughter," Anna said. "A wedding present."

I flinched and wondered if I would ever have a positive reaction to the word "wedding" again. "Is your granddaughter engaged?"

"No, but it shouldn't be long. She's already eighteen."

I blinked. If eighteen was the marrying age in Holmes County, I was way beyond an old maid. At thirty-four, I was prehistoric.

Sarah adjusted her glasses on the tip of her nose. "What brings you to Rolling Brook, Angie? It's hard for me to believe that an *Englischer* would leave her exciting life in a big city. We are much simpler here, but I do love living in the country. I don't think the city would suit me at all, and I know it wouldn't suit my husband. He's a farmer through and through."

"My aunt's shop brought me here," I said.

She inserted her needle off her pattern line and

brought it back up through the quilt at the precise spot where her last stitch ended. With a yank she buried the quilter's knot deep within the quilt, so that it looked like the thread magically appeared unbroken on the pattern. "Yes, yes, we know Eleanor left you the shop. I heard about the missing deed. I'm so, so sorry you are facing such a challenge already. Have you found it yet? Any clue to where it might be? I'm happy to help you look. I'm very good at finding things. Ask any of my children. When they can't find something, they come to their *mamm* to look for it, and sure enough, I usually do. When would you like me to start looking?"

"Ow!" Rachel cried.

"Don't bleed on the quilt," Anna gave Rachel an appraising glance.

Rachel jumped out of her seat. "Excuse me. I'll run this under cold water." She popped her left index finger into her mouth as she hurried away from the circle.

Out of the corner of my eye, I saw Martha waving at me from the cash register. "It was nice to see you, Sarah. I'm looking forward to getting to know you."

"We will chat later," Sarah said. "I have so much to tell you."

I'll bet she did. Her confident tone made my back stiffen.

Rachel winked at me. "All better," she mouthed.

I suspected Rachel was better with a needle than she led us to believe.

"Angie, we made it," Willow called as she floated over to me. The extra fabric of her gauzy silk blouse followed her in a wave. I wondered where she bought her clothes. Certainly not in Holmes County.

Greasy-haired Farley followed in her wake.

"The shop is doing well. Have you told folks about the Watermelon Fest?" He shared a lopsided smile that I pictured his high-school self practicing in the bathroom mirror to impress the ladies. It didn't work on me.

"I placed the flyer in the window. I've been too busy to speak more than a few words to anyone today."

"Completely understandable. This is a big day for you." Willow beamed.

Farley pursed his lip. "Monday we're having a final planning meeting for the Watermelon Fest. Can you join us?"

"Sure," I said. Martha would be here to watch the shop then.

"It's going to bring even more traffic to Rolling Brook," Farley said. "We placed advertisements about it online and in the papers. Danny Nicolson has been a tremendous help."

At the cash register, a woman in denim shorts bought a large stack of quilted place mats, and I smiled. "I just met Danny. He wants to interview me to do a piece on the store."

"You should," Willow said. "Danny has a talent for getting things noticed."

Behind Willow, Martha's waving for me to come to the cash register became more urgent.

"Excuse me."

"We will see you at the meeting," Willow said.

Martha scowled. "What were you doing talking to those two?"

My brow shot up in surprise. "They invited me to a meeting about the Watermelon Fest."

"If Running Stitch supports the Watermelon Fest, it will ruin your connection with the Amish in town."

"Like Joseph Walker?"

She nodded.

"Why?" I asked. "It sounds like a fun idea and should bring more business to town. That's always good for everyone. There's a festival poster in the window of Miller's Amish Bakery, so Rachel and Aaron must be fine with it."

"They might be." She grimaced. "But some think it's another sign that the *Englischers* are trying to take over the town. Rolling Brook is an Amish town, not an *Englisch* one."

I cocked my head. "If that's the case, why is the trustee English?"

She shook her head. "Amish would never run for office." Her eyes narrowed as she watched Willow and Farley move around the room. "I don't think you should do it. It is not what Eleanor would have wanted."

I blinked. "I don't know why my aunt would have a problem with it. She had both Amish and English customers for decades. It's great to advertise and grow the business. I think I should at least hear them out to see what it's all about."

"You promised that Running Stitch would remain an *Amish* quilt shop."

"It will." I gripped the side of the counter. "But the business must grow too."

Her jaw twitched. "It is your decision. You're the boss." She stepped around the counter. "Can you watch the cash register? I'd like to rejoin the circle."

I watched Martha take her place at the quilting circle with a knot growing in my gut. Apparently life in Rolling Brook wasn't all peace, tranquillity, and quilts.

A woman in her late forties, wearing a brightly colored

sweater, approached the cash register with a basketful of different-colored threads, needles, and patterns. "Are you a quilter?" I asked her.

"No, not really. I'm nothing like the ladies in the corner, that's for sure. I dabble mostly." She laughed, and her strawberry blond hair shook back and forth. "I probably won't use half of this stuff, but I can't resist buying every time I come into this store."

"That's fine with me." I smiled.

"You're Eleanor's niece, right?"

I nodded as I rang up her purchase.

She reached into her wallet. "I'm Jessica Nicolson. I own an antiques shop over in Millersburg."

I put her needles and thread in a small brown bag. "Nicolson? Are you related to Danny Nicolson?"

Jessica rolled her eyes. "That's my cousin. Let me guess. He asked you for an interview?"

I nodded.

"He thinks he's the next big reporter, if he only could catch a break." She rolled her eyes but had a good-natured smile on her face.

"He said he wanted to interview me for a tourism Web site."

She took her bag. "I'm sure he did, but what he really wants is a big story."

"I guess I'll be a disappointment, then. There's no big news around here," I said.

She grinned. "That's what I keep telling him." She picked up her shopping bags. "I'm sure I'll be back soon to buy more things I won't use. Stop at my shop sometime. It's called Out of Time. It's right on Route Eighty-three."

"I'll do that," I promised. I'd already planned to hit the rest of the shops in Rolling Brook and Millersburg.

Jessica headed for the door and ran smack into Joseph Walker, who was stepping into the shop at the same time she was leaving. The two stared at each other, and then, as if she were a horse poked in the rib with a cowboy's spur, Jessica fled. The woman walking a few steps behind Joseph tipped the edge of her bonnet with a pale hand. She watched Joseph as he glanced back at Jessica, who hurried up the sidewalk.

I rang up two more customers as Rachel approached the counter. "Let me take over for a while."

"Who is the woman who came in with Joseph Walker?"

Rachel scanned the room. "Oh, that's his wife, Abigail."

"She's so tiny."

Rachel nodded. "They are a bit of an odd couple."

"How's your finger?" I asked.

"As good as new." She beamed.

I grinned back and turned the cash register over to her. I watched Joseph move about the room. The way he examined everything from the needle display to the pine floors made me edgy. It was as if he was appraising the value of each, just like he owned the place, which he thought he did. His wife stopped at the quilting circle and chatted with the ladies. They all seemed happy to see her, but I noticed they were keeping a wary eye on her husband.

I heard Rachel's sons Eli and Isaiah giggling in the corner of the shop. I found them sneaking cubes of Amish cheese to Oliver.

"What's going on here?" I asked, trying to sound serious.

Oliver gulped down a piece of Swiss. He cocked his head as if to say, "I have no idea what you're talking about."

Eli and Isaiah giggled.

"Don't give him any more treats." I put my hands on my hips and gave them a mock glare.

They nodded and ran out the back door. Oliver waddled close on their heels.

"Are you the owner?" a male voice asked me.

I spun around and found myself face-to-face with a tourist. An Indians ball cap was pulled low over his eyes. "I am," I said.

His mustache twitched. "But you're not Amish. They assured us on the tour bus that we will be going to authentic Amish locations and they brought us here."

"I . . . well . . ." I was lost of words. Should I apologize for my non-Amishness?

"You'd think with the amount they charge for the tour that they'd take us to real Amish places. I wish my wife hadn't talked me into this. What a waste of money to drive around the boondocks in this heat and not see real Amish people," he grumbled. "What are you anyway? A cowgirl?"

I felt my face redden. Sheesh, you'd think a girl could wear her cowboy boots in peace. Did the guy even look around? I might not be Amish but there was no lack of Amish in my shop.

"*Ya*, you're right. She's not Amish," a gravelly voice chimed in.

I found myself staring into the angry eyes of Joseph Walker.

"That's what I'm saying," the man said. "Now, you're Amish, right?"

"*Ya*," Joseph sneered.

The man took a step back. "I—I think I'll go find my wife."

Having successfully terrorized the tourist, Joseph Walker glared at me.

"I'm glad you came to the reopening." I flashed him the pageant smile again. It worked as well as it had the first time. O-kay.

His eyes were dark brown and reminded me of the hide of the longhorns I'd seen while driving across Texas. His disposition reminded me of the same.

He glowered at me. "You had no right to reopen this store."

I blinked. "Excuse me?"

"This building and the land around it belong to me."

I felt myself bristle. "You're wrong."

Behind her husband, Abigail wrung her small white hands together, reminding me of Lady Macbeth.

"Do you plan to stay here? To run this shop?" His voice was stern.

Out of the corner of my eye, I saw Isaiah snatch another sugar cookie off the platter before running to the backyard again. I hoped he didn't feed it to Oliver. "Yes," I said. "That's what I moved here to do." I straightened my shoulders. "And I will take you to court over this dispute, if I have to."

"That is the *Englisch* way, isn't it? Get the government involved. You can never solve anything on your own."

I opened my mouth to make a smart remark, but Joseph was faster. "You have no business running this shop. Rolling Brook is an Amish town. You should leave it to the Amish. The *Englischer* was right. What does a girl from Texas know about the Amish?"

My face grew warm. Abigail fidgeted a few feet away. Sarah Leham patted her arm. Where had Sarah come from? Two seconds ago, I saw her at work around the quilting circle. The woodworker's wife had a pained expression on her face, and Sarah cocked her head as if to hear more clearly.

"I'm sorry you feel that way," I said, using the same uncompromising tone he'd used with me. "But I inherited this shop. Whether you like it or not, I'm here to stay."

"You'll be gone soon enough when I'm proven the rightful owner." He sniffed as if he caught a whiff of something unpleasant. "You're proud, just like Eleanor was. She never knew her place either."

My blood boiled. Aunt Eleanor was the most unimposing, unassuming woman I had ever known. "Please don't talk about my *aenti* that way."

He snorted. "*Aenti?* Use your own *Englisch* words." He turned and stormed out of the shop. Abigail whispered an apology to Sarah and followed a few steps behind him.

I stood there for a full minute wondering what had just happened.

"Pay no attention to him." Anna straightened the stacks of notions on the shelf behind me.

Until she spoke, I hadn't even noticed she was there. "How could he say that about Aunt Eleanor?"

"Joseph and his family are Old Order, much stricter than the order your *aenti* and I belong to. He doesn't approve of women running a business alone. In his mind, Eleanor should have closed the shop when your uncle died and settled into the quiet life of a widow. I would be surprised if he wasn't suspicious of Eleanor, since she grew up in an *Englisch* home."

"There are different kinds of Amish?"

She laughed. "Oh goodness, yes." She gestured to the room. "Right now in this room alone I see three different sects: Old Order, Dan, and New Order. There are many more than that. Now stop worrying over Joseph Walker," she ordered. "I saw you eyeing those snickerdoodles. Have you eaten anything yet?"

I shook my head. After my encounter with Joseph, the thought of food made me queasy.

"If you don't hurry, Rachel's boys are going to eat up every last one of her famous fry pies."

I smiled my thanks but had a sinking feeling Joseph Walker wasn't finished with me yet. *Where was that deed?*

Chapter Five

Early the next morning, the alarm clock on the milk crate serving as my bedside table went off, and I threw a pillow at it. The clock crashed against the closet door, but the noise stopped.

Three minutes later, the alarm clock on the dresser left by a previous tenant sounded. I opened one eye, took aim, and hurled another pillow. Silence. Three minutes after that, a third alarm clock rang. This one was inside the closet and set to a local oldies station. The volume was set to eardrum-bursting. I sat upright in bed.

Oliver was at my feet with his head buried under the comforter. I blinked. Why were all these alarms going off? Where was I? What day was it? Then, I remembered the shop's reopening. Although Running Stitch closed at seven, I'd stayed at the shop until almost midnight cleaning up, counting the money in the cash register, updating the shop's accounts, and looking for the shop's deed, which I never found. In general, I was a night person and worked better in the evening. I sent the quilting circle ladies home around nine despite their protests. They needed to be with their families and had given me too much of their time already. When I finally fell into bed, it was after one in the morning. Suddenly, I remembered Danny Nicolson and the six thirty a.m. interview. I was late, very late.

After throwing on the first passable outfit I could find, I let Oliver into the backyard. If he needed to escape any birds, he could wriggle through the doggy door, his favorite feature of our new home, cut into the bottom of the kitchen door. Then I flew from the house. I didn't even brush my hair. I hoped Danny didn't want to take pictures of me. The rat's nest on the top of my head would be bad for business. I jumped into my SUV and drove the five minutes to Running Stitch. When I pulled into the diagonal space in front of the store, Danny was tapping his foot on the sidewalk in front of the shop.

"You're late," he said by way of greeting.

"I'm so sorry. I overslept."

Danny's eyes dropped as if he had heard it all before. He probably had. "It's already a quarter till. I have to leave at eight, so let's get started."

"Of course," I said. With a shaky hand, I unlocked the front door to the shop. I willed myself to calm down. I'd overslept. It was no big deal. I flipped on the overhead lights. I paused in the doorway. "That's strange," I murmured. Aunt Eleanor's double wedding ring quilt wasn't hanging on the wall behind the register. Had we sold it? I felt a pang. It was the one quilt in the shop I hoped to keep for myself.

Danny cleared his throat. "Is it all right if I come in? I'm on a tight timetable."

I stepped out of the way. "Sure."

"The quilting circle looks like a good place to do the interview. How's that?" Danny asked.

"Good idea," I said, but my mind was still on the missing quilt. Maybe Martha put it somewhere for safekeeping.

He sat on one of the straight-backed chairs around the quilt frame. "Are you okay?"

"I'm fine." I dropped my purse on the counter. "Before we start, I need to run back to the stockroom to check on something."

He gave an exaggerated glance at his wristwatch. "Fine." He stopped just short of rolling his eyes.

I'd feel better during the interview if I knew where my aunt's quilt was. The only place it could be was the stockroom.

I opened the door to the small stockroom, pulled the string leading to the overhead light, and screamed.

Joseph Walker lay on the wood floor inches from my feet, and he wasn't moving. He was dead. My first clue was his blank eyes staring at the ceiling. My second tip-off was the ugly gash across his throat.

Just above his head, my aunt's quilt lay in tatters on the floor and spattered with blood. It was so mutilated that the pattern was unrecognizable. I wouldn't even have known it was my aunt's quilt but for the colors. The rotary cutters that the ladies teased me about lay in the middle of what was left of the destroyed quilt. The safety button was off and the blade was stained a brownish red.

I felt light-headed.

"What's going on?" Danny demanded, too close to my ear, and I stumbled. I reached for the shelf closest to me to catch my balance. The shelf broke and dozens of quilt squares fell to the floor and on top of Joseph, soaking up some of the blood puddle on the floor.

"Holy smokes," Danny whispered.

I came to my senses. "Call nine-one-one," I ordered.

"I can't. My cell phone is in my car. Do you have a phone here?"

"No, the phone company is coming Monday to set up a landline and the Internet."

I reached into my pocket and pulled out my cell phone. The display read NO SIGNAL.

Danny peered at my screen. "Oh, that carrier doesn't work here. Only one or two do."

I pushed him aside. "Maybe I can get a signal outside."

I unlocked the door to the garden and rushed outside. Bending at the waist, I braced my hands on my knees and gulped air. I had never seen anything so gruesome in my life. *Police. Call police.*

I held my phone in the air, waving it from side to side. "Come on! Come on!" Miraculously, a half of a bar appeared.

The operator picked up, and I told her my location and about my horrifying discovery.

"You found what?" she asked in disbelief as my cell dropped the call.

I tucked the useless device back into my jeans pocket and reentered the shop. Danny was just outside the stockroom, taking photographs of Joseph's body with a tiny digital camera. "What are you doing?" I demanded.

He snapped two more photos before responding. "Working on a story."

"This isn't the story you came here to write."

"No, it wasn't," he said with a glint in his eye. He held the camera up and snapped a picture of me.

"Don't do that." I grabbed for the camera, but he held it out of my reach. I was considering wrestling him for it when I heard sirens.

Within minutes my shop was overrun by police. It looked like they called in the entire sheriff's department. A young officer no more than eighteen introduced himself as Deputy Anderson. He asked Danny and me to stand outside the shop.

We stood just left of the shop's threshold when another sheriff's department's vehicle parked in the middle of the street.

"That's Sheriff Mitchell. He'll want to talk to you." Anderson's voice held a hint of awe.

When the sheriff stepped out of the vehicle, I winced. Just as I'd feared, it was the same officer I'd met the last time I visited my aunt, six months ago. I hoped he'd forgotten me because our meeting included the sheriff plucking me off the frozen sidewalk. Not one of my most graceful moments.

Sheriff Mitchell was a tall man, maybe even six-four. He wore a navy-colored department uniform like Deputy Anderson's. However, while the younger man played dress-up, the sheriff carried himself as if he were ready for a publicity shoot. Short tufts of salt-and-pepper hair stuck out from under his sheriff's department baseball cap. He gestured to Anderson to join him just out of Danny's and my earshot. The pair looked at us often.

"Think they are talking about us?" Danny asked.

As far as I was concerned, that question didn't deserve a response.

Anderson and the sheriff approached us. Mitchell's eyes moved from me to Danny and back again. I was startled by how bright blue his eyes were. They reminded me of a clear day in Texas. "Did either of you touch anything?" The blue eyes narrowed.

"I stumbled into the shelf and knocked fabric on top

of him. It was an accident." Despite the humid air, I wrapped my arms around my body.

He turned his gaze on the reporter. "What about you, Danny?"

"No, nothing."

I bit my lip. "What about the photos?"

Danny glared at me.

Mitchell's eyes zeroed back on me, blinding me. His eyes weren't blue, as I first thought, but a blue-green color like aquamarine.

"Photos? Photos of what?" the sheriff asked.

I blinked, breaking eye contact with the sheriff, and glanced at Danny, who looked like he wanted to strangle me. "Of Joseph. Danny took some."

Mitchell held out his large hand. "Camera."

"There's freedom of the press. You can't confiscate—"

"Camera. Now." Mitchell's tone didn't leave room for argument.

Danny fished the small digital camera from his pants pocket and handed it to Mitchell. The sheriff removed the camera's memory card and slipped it into the breast pocket of his uniform before returning the camera to Danny.

"I have other photographs on there I need!" Danny cried.

Mitchell shrugged. "Danny, Deputy Anderson will take down your statement."

"I have an important meeting in Columbus in only a few hours."

"The sooner you give your statement, the sooner you can leave," Mitchell replied.

Danny glared at me before he followed Anderson to his patrol car. If looks could kill, Danny put me six feet under.

Across the street outside Miller's Amish Bakery, Rachel and her husband stood with their arms wrapped around each other. Their eyes were as big as Rachel's famous apple pies. I nodded at them. Even at a distance, their presence comforted me.

Mitchell focused on me, and I felt myself squirm. "Tell me everything from the beginning."

So I did. I was just getting to the part where the police arrived when my pocket vibrated. *Bing! Bing! Bing!* my cell phone cried. Now it worked, of course. I removed it from my pocket and checked the display. A calendar reminder was in the middle of my screen. In capital letters, it read DRESS FITTING! I stared at it. Feeling the same amount of shock I felt when I discovered Joseph's body.

"What is it?" Mitchell asked in a kinder voice than he'd previously used.

"I . . . I . . ." was the best I could do.

He took the phone from my hand. His action shook me out of my stupor. "Hey! You can't take that."

"Sure, I can. It might be related to the case." His brow wrinkled. "Dress fitting? Are you going to be in a wedding or something?"

"Or something," I muttered.

"Want to talk about it?"

"Trust me. This has nothing to do with Joseph."

"Uh-huh." His tone dripped with doubt. He stared at me, and for a second time, I felt myself fidget under his blue-green-eyed gaze. I gritted my teeth and stared him back in the eye. I wasn't going to let some small-time sheriff intimidate me.

Mitchell reached into the breast pocket of his uniform and removed a white business card. "You think of anything else, you call me anytime."

Without examining it, I stuffed it into my purse.

He seemed to recognize the defiance in my expression and smiled. "Against my better judgment, you're free for now, even if you are a prime flight risk."

"Flight risk?"

"You have no friends or family here. There's nothing keeping you here."

I straightened my spine. "I do have friends in Holmes County. You don't know anything about me."

"I will soon enough."

"I'm not a flight risk," I muttered.

"Prove it. Don't leave town."

I glared at him.

"And watch where you're walking, too. I don't want to have to pick you up off of the ground again." With that, Mitchell went inside the shop and left me with my mouth hanging open.

Heat rushed to my face. Ugh. He *did* remember.

As soon as Mitchell disappeared into the house, Rachel ran across the street, dodging officers as she went. "Angie, what's going on? When my husband told me there were police cars outside your shop, I couldn't believe it." She gave me a big hug. "Did someone break into Running Stitch?"

"Yes, but it's more than that." I pursed my lips. "It's Joseph Walker. He's dead."

She gasped. "Dead?"

"I found him in the stockroom."

"What was he doing there?"

"I have no idea," I murmured. "It only gets worse, Rachel. Joseph Walker was murdered."

"Murdered," she whispered. "That can't be possible."

I glanced at the shop door. "I think the sheriff believes I killed him."

"He couldn't possibly think that," she insisted.

I didn't bother to argue with her.

Rachel wrapped her arm around me. "Do you need anything?"

"Do you make doughnuts in your bakery?"

She was taken aback by the question. I had to admit it wasn't an obvious transition to anyone but me.

"Not usually, but we can," Rachel said.

"Could you make one as big as my head?"

The EMTs wheeled the body bag out of the shop on a stretcher. The coroner followed close behind.

I swallowed the lump in my throat. "I'm changing my order. I think I need two head-sized doughnuts."

Chapter Six

The sheriff followed the stretcher out of the shop. His jaw set as he held a clear plastic evidence bag in his hand. The rotary cutters were inside the bag.

Rachel stared wide-eyed at the bag. "Aren't those yours, Angela?"

Her comment got Mitchell's attention, and a chill ran down my back.

He held up the bag in his left hand, and I noted the lack of a wedding ring. I gave myself a mental head smack. *Why is my brain even registering the mundane fact that the sheriff isn't married at a time like this?*

He let the bag dangle from his long piano-player fingers. "Is this yours, Miss Braddock?"

I swallowed. "Yes, but then again, everything in the shop's mine. It's my shop."

He nodded. "What are these?"

"Rotary cutters. They're used to cut fabric more quickly along a straightedge."

"Have you touched them?"

"Yes, but not since the day before the party."

"What party?"

I told him about the grand reopening.

"Who else might have touched the cutters?"

"No one."

He cocked an eyebrow at me.

"I mean no one except whoever did that to poor Joseph Walker. I put the whole box of the cutters in the stockroom the day before the party and didn't think about them again until—" The image of Joseph's wound sprang into my mind, and I had the urge to stick my head between my knees. Rachel gripped me by the upper arm as if she thought I might keel over. She might have been right.

Mitchell lowered the evidence bag and gave me a half smile. "Was the stockroom locked all night?" he asked.

It was already in the lower eighties and the humidity climbed steadily with the heat. Despite the damp heat surrounding me, I wrapped my arms around myself for warmth as I thought. "No, it doesn't have a lock. We went in and out of the room many times after the party, and I never noticed the cutters."

"Who is 'we'?"

I inwardly groaned. I shouldn't have gotten them involved. "My quilting circle was helping me clean up."

Rachel straightened to her full height. "I was there." In her Amish clothes, she looked like a Pilgrim about to tell off the governor of Plymouth. The only difference was she wasn't wearing buckle shoes. She wore plain white sneakers.

He smiled. "Anyone else?"

"Martha Yoder, Anna Graber, and Sarah Leham. They are all members of the quilting circle."

"Any one of them had access to the stockroom."

"Yes," I said, trying to keep the frustration out of my voice.

"I'm going to have to talk to them."

"But they had nothing to do with Mr. Walker's—er—condition. They left hours before I did."

A gleam caught in the sheriff's eyes. "You were in the shop alone."

Now I'd stepped into it, I thought.

"It's my shop. Of course, I was the last one out."

"What time did the quilters leave, Mrs. Miller?"

Rachel fingered the edge of her apron. "Nine."

His aquamarine eyes zeroed in on me. "And what time did you leave?"

I sighed. "Midnight."

"You were alone in the shop for three hours in the middle of the night. No one else was with you?"

"Does my dog count?"

A smile flashed across Mitchell's face and disappeared. "No. Why did you stay so late by yourself?"

"I work better at night and wanted to finish up some things before I went home." I shifted my weight from foot to foot, missing my cowboy boots, which were at home with Oliver.

"What things?"

I threw up my hands. "Filing, accounting, mundane work like that."

"Who waited for you at home?"

I fidgeted. "No one. I live alone."

He nodded as if he suspected that was the answer. "Who has keys to the shop?"

"I do, and so does Martha Yoder. She works for me."

"Anyone else?"

I shook my head. "Unless my aunt's lawyer kept a copy."

"Who's that?"

"Harvey Lemontop."

He nodded. "I know him." He tapped his pen to his cheek as he considered the information.

I could almost hear the gears click in his head as he processed what I'd told him. It was as if I could see the thoughts running through his head. The case was a done deal. I was the killer. I had means and opportunity. All that was left was motive.

"How well did you know Mr. Walker?"

Ahh, and now we get to that motive question. I felt light-headed.

"Not well at all. His woodworking shop is right next door, but we hadn't had much chance to speak since I took over Running Stitch. We are both so busy." Even to my own ears, the excuse for not knowing Joseph sounded lame, but I certainly wasn't going to tell the sheriff that the woodworker thought he owned Running Stitch.

"Do you know anyone who might have an issue with Mr. Walker?"

Farley Jung's thin face and greasy hair popped into my head. What had he said the day I'd met him? *He will be silent on the topic of the Watermelon Fest soon enough.*

"You do know someone." The sheriff took a step closer to me.

"I know that he and those organizing the Watermelon Fest had a disagreement over the event, but it can't be that," I insisted. "No one would kill another person over watermelon."

"You'd be surprised. You must mean Willow Moon and Farley Jung, then."

I nodded.

"Okay, do you know if anyone has an issue with you?"

"With me? Why me?" The light-headedness was getting worse. *This can't really be happening. It just can't.*

"He was killed in your stockroom. Maybe someone was sending you a message."

I shivered. "I just moved here. I couldn't possibly have made an enemy already."

The only person who came to mind was Joseph Walker, but certainly he'd thought of me more as an annoyance than an enemy. Weren't the Amish pacifists anyway?

"You need to stop by the sheriff's department today to get fingerprinted. The address for the department is on the card I gave you."

"Fingerprinted?" I squeaked.

"You said that you touched the murder weapon. We need your fingerprints to rule you out."

Or convict me, I thought with a lump in my throat. "Can I go back into the shop?" I asked. I needed to change the subject immediately. It was either that or crash to the sidewalk in a dead faint. Mitchell had already picked me up off the sidewalk once. We didn't need a reprise of that embarrassment.

Mitchell shook his head. "Not today. Maybe not until the end of next week either. You're going to want to have your stockroom professionally cleaned. Your insurance should cover that."

I winced. I hadn't even thought of the condition of the stockroom. Did my aunt have insurance on the shop? I made a mental note to ask Harvey Lemontop.

"Now what do I do?" The rhetorical question popped out of my mouth.

I felt Rachel's small hand on my shoulder. "Come

over to the bakery. A strong cup of coffee will do you good."

Amish coffee was the best choice I had.

Sheriff Mitchell watched me, making me feel like a bug under a microscope. I wondered if he had learned that stare down in cop school or came by it naturally.

"Am I free to go?" Unsuccessfully, I tried to keep the edge out of my voice.

He nodded with a peculiar expression on his face. "I know where you live."

Chapter Seven

I let Rachel guide me across the street as the ambulance with Joseph's body drove away. No sirens. I was surprised he was taken by ambulance. Didn't the Amish want to take the body themselves? Then I remembered this was a homicide and everything must be handled differently.

Did Abigail know? I felt queasy at the thought of the quiet Amish woman with milky skin hearing the news. Her sweet demeanor gave the impression that there wasn't much she could handle. Would her husband's death topple her completely?

Miller's Amish Bakery smelled like fresh-baked bread with a hint of lemon oil and vinegar. The scent reminded me of my aunt Eleanor's house, as they were my aunt's main staples to clean her home. Oiled oak shelves supported loaves of fresh-baked Amish bread in clear plastic sacks held closed with bright yellow twist ties.

Directly across from the front door, a long glass display case ran the length of the room. Fry pies, Amish cookies, and fruit pies filled the case. Rachel's frowning husband stood behind the counter. A young Amish girl no more than twenty with chestnut hair worn Amish-style—parted down the middle and secured at the nape of her neck into a bun—busied herself cleaning the display case with water and vinegar from a plastic spray bottle. Within the hour, the bakery would be overrun with English tourists, who were there to buy a piece of Amish life and feel wistful about simpler times. Considering Joseph's death, Amish life might not be as simple as it seemed. The Amish forgo electricity and automobiles, but they still had problems too—big problems that led to murder, apparently.

I winced when I thought of all the business Running Stitch would lose during that day and over the next week. I hoped the sheriff would let me reopen by the following weekend or I could be in real trouble. It was already August; summer was the height of tourist season in Holmes County, and I desperately wanted to be open for the Watermelon Fest. As soon as the thought about the Watermelon Fest crossed my mind, guilt washed over me. How could I even think that when a man was dead, leaving behind a wife and children?

"Have a seat, Angie. I'll bring you a cinnamon roll." Rachel hurried over to her husband. He walked through the swinging door to the back of the bakery, and Rachel followed him.

Four small round tables were nestled in the corner of the room. Each table could seat two people at a time. It wasn't much of a dining room, but it was a nice place to enjoy a cup of coffee and a piece of pie. Apparently, I wasn't the only one who thought so. There were two elderly Amish men with long white beards and navy shirts sitting at one table. They eyed me. I touched the top of my head and tried to tame the growing cocoon of blond curls. There was a stainless steel freezer in the corner of the room that held frozen treats. I examined my warped reflection in the freezer's lid. I looked as if I had been electrocuted. Choosing not to brush my hair that morning had been a bad move. That would teach me to be late. Another idea struck me. Had I been on time, would I have run into the killer? When had Joseph been murdered? I had so many questions running through my head. The one weighing most heavily on my mind being, would I go to jail?

"Is something wrong with the freezer, Angela?" Rachel's sweet voice asked.

I yelped and turned around.

Her cheeks pinkened prettily. "I'm sorry I scared you. Would you like some ice cream from the freezer?"

Actually a vat of ice cream sounded like what the doctor ordered right then, but I never indulged before noon. The cinnamon roll was different. It was breakfast ... sort of.

Behind her the younger Amish woman watched me. I flashed her a smile. She turned away and concentrated on polishing the spotless counter. The two men at the table spoke in the low rumbling German-sounding Pennsylvania Dutch. Rachel turned her neck to look at them, silencing them immediately.

"What were they talking about?"

Her cheeks turned even redder. "You."

"What did they say?" Her frankness made me smile.

"It's no matter."

I let it drop for the time being. "Who is that at the counter?"

"That's Aaron's sister, Mattie."

Rachel set the plate of rolls on the table farthest away

from the two old-timers. "I'll get you some *kaffi*. Mattie made a fresh pot."

When Rachel went back into the kitchen, I walked to the corner of the room on the pretense of perusing the bread selection. As I surveyed the loaves of dense Amish friendship bread, it hit me full force what a tremendous mistake I'd made by leaving Dallas. Who was I to think that I could run a quilt shop? I left behind a good-paying job with a pension, health insurance, and a dental plan. I also left behind Ryan Dickinson. Sure, he didn't want to marry me, but maybe he would have changed his mind if I stayed in Texas.

I gave myself a mental kick in the head and slid into one of the two chairs at the table. I was letting the post-traumatic stress of finding a dead body rule my thoughts. Ryan was the biggest reason to *leave* Dallas, not to stay.

Rachel returned with two steaming white mugs of coffee as the cowbell on the bakery's front door clanked against the glass. Sarah Leham rushed into the room. "Angie, there you are. Thank heavens you're safe. As soon as I heard the news, I rushed straight to the shop. When I saw the police there and couldn't find you, I suspected the worst." Sarah's prayer cap was slightly askew. "Are you all right?"

"I'm fine, Sarah. You didn't have to come all the way into town."

"Of course I did. All of us in the quilting circle feel responsible for you, especially now."

I winced. If Sarah knew about Joseph's death, there was a good chance all the Amish in Rolling Brook knew. Despite the Amish aversion to gossip, Joseph's murder was enough to keep tongues wagging in the county for weeks. Add in a newcomer from Texas like me and the talk could last months.

I stifled a grimace. "What was the worst?"

Her eyes widened. "What do you mean?"

"You said you feared the worst. What was it? Joseph's death?"

Her eyes sparkled with barely restrained excitement. "Oh no, I already knew about that. I thought you had been arrested."

Suddenly, the cinnamon roll didn't look as tasty as it had a minute ago.

Screech! One of the old-timers scratched the bottom of his chair across the wide-planked pine boards. He tipped his chair in our direction. I was surprised he didn't cup his ear to hear our conversation more clearly.

"Why did you think that?" I lowered my voice.

Sarah either was unaware of the eavesdropper or didn't care. "Because Joseph was murdered in your shop. The sheriff must think you did it." She leaned in. "Especially if you consider the missing deed. What better motive is there than that? With Joseph gone, you don't have to argue with anyone over who's the rightful owner of Running Stitch."

He must. She was right. Sheriff Mitchell seemed nice enough, but what if he put up a front to get my guard down? I bet a lot of women confessed to all sorts of indiscretions when faced with those aquamarine eyes. I wiped my sweaty palms on my jeans.

Rachel said something in their language, and Sarah glared at her. In English, Rachel added, "Angie's done nothing wrong. The sheriff will know this."

I wasn't as sure. I plastered a brave smile on my face

even though I felt the itch of tears in the corners of my eyes. "As you can see, I'm free. I'm fine, Sarah, really. Joseph is the one who is not."

Sarah cleaned her glasses on the hem of her apron. "You're right. What a terrible loss. Poor Abigail. She's so sensitive. Who knows how she will take this news?"

A knot twisted in my stomach as Abigail's pale face came to mind again. "Do they have any children?"

Sarah nodded. "Five girls, ages four to twelve. Each one is prettier than the last, but like most Amish men, Joseph always had hoped for a son to inherit his business."

I tried to put Joseph's children out of my mind. It was too painful. "How did you hear the news?"

"The buggy telegraph. It's faster than one of your telephones." She took a chair from a neighboring table and set it next to me. "That's for sure."

Reluctantly, Rachel took the other empty chair at the table and sat.

Sarah reached for one of the mugs of coffee.

Rachel pulled it away from her. "That's for Angie."

I waved her concern away. "It's all right. I appreciate it, Rachel, but I'm feeling a little queasy. I don't think I could drink it."

Rachel squeezed my hand. "It's the shock." She stood up. "I should have thought of that. Let me make you some tea."

Before I could stop her, she jumped from the chair and left me alone with Sarah. Sarah sipped my coffee. "Rachel Miller needs to learn not to be such a mother hen. She thinks everyone needs some mothering all the time. Folks need to learn how to stand on their own two feet."

I felt the same way in principle, but I also believed if a person found a dead body, a little mothering was permissible. Was there something more to the tension between Rachel and Sarah? I thought about the warning about Sarah that Rachel whispered to me at the grand reopening party. Had the warning really been for my sake, or was there more to the story?

"Now, tell me. If the police didn't arrest you, who did they arrest?"

"No one, at least no one yet. It's only been"—I pulled my cell phone from my purse—"two hours since I found him."

"And you were alone when you discovered the body?"

I glanced at the kitchen door. Where was Rachel? How long did it take to brew Amish tea anyway? "No. Danny Nicolson was with me. He was going to interview me for the tourism board Web site."

"Did the police question Danny?"

Rachel returned with the mug of tea. "Sarah Leham, I hope you weren't interrogating Angie. We need to care for her now. She's had a frightful morning."

Sarah grimaced. "Do the police have a list of suspects?"

Rachel sighed.

Out of the corner of my eye, I saw the two elderly Amish men lean forward even more. I hoped they wouldn't break their hips if they fell out of their chairs. I discovered the source of the buggy telegraph. I lowered my voice. "Not yet."

"Sarah, you keep this up and I will have to ask you to leave." Rachel lifted her chin. "Angie, you haven't touched your cinnamon roll. It's fresh from the oven."

The nausea that started with Sarah's inquisition

wouldn't go away. *I'm a murder suspect.* How did that happen? "Rachel, thank you, but I want to go home. I need to check on Oliver anyway. I hadn't thought I would be gone this long. I'm sure he's wondering where I am." I stood quickly and knocked over my chair. Just as fast I picked it up and tucked it under the table.

"You can't leave yet, Angie," Sarah said, giving no heed to Rachel's warning. "We have so much to talk about."

That was all the encouragement I needed. Rachel seemed to think so too. She turned to the counter. "Mattie, bring me a bakery box."

A strand of chestnut hair fell from the younger woman's prayer cap. Quietly, she tucked it back into place and did what her sister-in-law asked. Mattie handed Rachel the box while keeping her eyes trained on the wooden floor.

"Mattie, how are you, dear?" Sarah asked. "I saw you chatting with Zeph Shetler at the general store not long ago. Did you have a nice talk?"

Mattie's face turned the deepest shade of red I'd ever seen. It was close to eggplant purple. Without a word, she spun on her heels and walked through the kitchen door.

On the bright side, it seemed that Sarah's interest in my life wasn't some kind of special treatment. She was an equal-opportunity gossip, which might explain Rachel's dislike of her. I wondered if Sarah had any close friends in the Amish community. I knew they must frown upon her rumormongering.

"Sarah," Rachel admonished. "You embarrassed the poor girl." Rachel slid the cinnamon roll from the plate to the bakery box.

"I did see her with Zeph Shetler. Do you think the two will marry in the fall?"

Rachel's jaw twitched. She turned her back on Sarah and spoke to me. "The roll's not a head-sized doughnut, but I hope it will work in a pinch."

I gave her a wobbly smile. "Thank you, Rachel."

I took the bakery box from her hand. Sarah followed me to the door. "If you need anything, don't be afraid to call on us."

I nodded and stepped outside. The humidity hit me like a wall. Several of the police cars were now gone. I noted that Sheriff Mitchell's car was still there and three other sheriff's department vehicles. Luckily, none blocked my little SUV in. I hurried over to the car and hopped in the driver's seat. As I pulled away from the curb, Sheriff Mitchell stepped outside of Running Stitch and watched me drive away.

Chapter Eight

Gravel crunched under my tires as I parked in my new driveway. I hopped out of the car. The first thing I planned to do when I got inside was take a shower and slip into my University of Texas sweats. With the buggy telegraph on high alert, I had no plans to leave the house the rest of the day.

I climbed the three steps to the porch as if I wore lead shoes. *I'm a murder suspect? That's just my luck. I get dumped, and then this happens, which is so much worse.* The sheriff's blue-green eyes came to mind. Did he think I killed Joseph? For some reason, I didn't want the sheriff thinking badly of me. I blamed this concern on stress. I did just find a dead body in my beloved aunt's quilt shop, a shop that would go under if the sheriff's department didn't let me open back up soon. Anyone would be under distress in those circumstances. The box from Rachel's bakery felt heavy in my hand. It wouldn't last long thanks to the stress I was currently under.

I walked through the small living room into the large eat-in kitchen, which was my favorite room in the house. It was twice the size of the living room. All the appliances were vintage apple green. My landlords, the Goodings, assured me that everything worked. I secretly loved the retro appliances and hoped that was true. In the corner of the room stood a round Amish-built oak table with four paddle-back chairs around it. It had been left by the previous tenant. The appliances and table would have been ridiculous in my modern, streamlined Dallas high-rise apartment. Here in Millersburg, they charmed me. Blue flower-patterned curtains decorated the window over the sink.

I rooted through the boxes on the kitchen counter in search of a glass. Finally, I found one in the third box. The one labeled "glasses." Go figure. I filled the glass with water from the faucet and looked out into the backyard.

"Oliver?" I called, and then remembered that I let him out in the backyard before racing to the shop. Surely, if he'd entered the house through the doggy door, he would be at my feet in the kitchen, begging for a treat.

Through the window, I was startled to see a man bent at the waist and peering into the doghouse Mr. Gooding had made for Oliver. My heart constricted. I grabbed an old broom that leaned against the wall and threw the back door open. "Get away from him!"

The man placed a hand on his back and groaned as he straightened up. "Watch what you're doing with that thing. You could really wallop someone."

I lowered the broom. "Mr. Gooding?"

His silver tumbleweed eyebrows knit together. "Course it's me. Who'd you think it was?" He placed a hand to his chest.

Oliver ran out of the doghouse and braced his paws on my legs. I rubbed his ears between my fingers.

Oh no, I gave the poor guy a heart attack. I took a step closer. "Are you all right?"

"I'm fine, I'm fine. It's indigestion." His jowls jiggled as he talked, reminding me of a Saint Bernard. "I came over because I heard about Joseph Walker."

Already? Did the buggy telegraph cross with an English cell phone tower?

"I wasn't sure when you would be getting home. Mrs. Gooding thought the sheriff might have arrested you, so I dropped by to check on Oliver."

My face felt hot. The Goodings thought I was a criminal. Would they kick me out on the street? I took a deep breath. "As you can see, I'm free."

He nodded. "Good. Both Mrs. Gooding and I know you wouldn't do anything wrong. You're such a nice girl."

That was a relief—even if it was a ridiculous assumption on the Goodings' part. Niceness did not negate the ability to commit murder. I wasn't going to argue the point. "What did you hear about Joseph's death?" I asked. I realized it might be helpful to know exactly what the rumors floating about the county were.

He pulled at his long eyebrows. "Well, they said that he was found dead in the middle of the shop and wrapped up in a quilt. The Amish say it must have been an English person who did it because the Amish know better than to ruin a perfectly good quilt."

"He wasn't found dead in the middle of the shop." I went on to tell him what I had discovered in Running Stitch's stockroom.

I left out the part about my aunt's quilt being shredded, because something about that clue felt important. I planned to keep it to myself until the police mentioned it or someone on the buggy telegraph heard the news. I also left out the detail of the murder weapon, because it was covered with my fingerprints. I internally groaned as I remembered the sheriff asked me to stop by the sheriff's department to get fingerprinted.

Mr. Gooding clicked his tongue. "Just awful. I don't imagine you expected to find something like that since moving to Holmes County."

"No, I didn't."

Oliver dropped to the ground and snuffled the grass. A Dallas pooch born and bred, he wasn't used to all this lush green open space.

"I'm glad to see you're okay. That will ease Mrs. Gooding's mind." He walked over to the gate in the white picket fence. "If there is a way we can help you, you let us know."

"I will," I promised.

He disappeared around the side of the house.

Oliver and I went back inside and I locked all the doors and windows. Oliver cocked his head at me. "Just being cautious," I told the Frenchie. "You don't want to know about my morning."

The house was without air-conditioning and was stifling with the windows closed. I didn't care. I wasn't taking any chances. Dozens of questions ran through my head. Who could have killed Joseph in such a brutal fashion? What was Joseph doing in my shop? Why was my aunt's beautiful quilt destroyed?

I needed to do something, or I would lose my mind. Going to the sheriff's department to get the fingerprinting over with was the best option. First, though, I needed a shower badly. I groaned when I thought of the condition of my hair. The sheriff probably thought I was part of some refugee program.

After I'd showered and tamed my curls, I debated taking Oliver with me. I didn't like the idea of leaving him home alone with a murderer on the loose. In the end, I left him at home because I didn't think the sheriff would appreciate it if I showed up with my dog. I squatted in front of the little Frenchie. "Now, if anyone tries to come in here, you hide."

He licked my face.

The Holmes County Sheriff's Department was ten minutes north of Millersburg in Holmesville. The building itself looked like a tan brick fortress with sharp triangular shapes. I wondered if the architect built it that way to intimidate criminals. It worked on me.

Taking a deep breath, I stepped through the glass doors and gave my name to the stony officer at the desk. Without a word, she took me in a windowless back room.

"Do you fingerprint a lot of people?" I asked. It was a dumb question, and I knew it. However, her silence made me nervous.

She grunted in reply. "Place your right hand here." She pointed to a flat touch screen on the countertop. The touch screen sat in front of a computer monitor. I watched my fingerprint be recorded on the monitor while she pressed down hard on each digit. "Left hand," she barked.

Giving up on any conversation, I gave her my left hand.

"Take a seat." She motioned to a metal folding chair and handed me a clipboard. "Record your statement and sign it."

Taking a deep breath, I sat on the uncomfortable chair and wrote down what I had found that morning. When I was done, I handed her the clipboard.

She flipped through the pages. "You're free to go."

I fled before she changed her mind. When I stepped outside, I closed my eyes and inhaled the sweet country air. *I cannot go back in there.*

"Glad to see you stopped by so quickly," a voice in front of me said.

My eyes popped open to find Sheriff Mitchell studying me. I swallowed.

"You changed your hair."

Self-consciously, my hand flew to my blond curls. Ugh. At least I no longer looked like I used a hand mixer on my hair.

"Did you get fingerprinted?"

"Yes. Your desk officer isn't the chatty type, is she?"

He barked a laugh. "I've worked with Nadine for ten years, and I think she's said maybe fourteen words to me."

I gave him a small smile. "Do you know how Joseph got into my shop? I'm sure I locked both doors before I left."

"We think the person came through the back door. The front has two dead bolts, and the culprit would have risked being seen from passersby. There was no sign of forced entry. The killer may have had a key."

"Oh," I said, disappointed. Forced entry would have gotten me off. A key? That meant the only suspects were Martha and me. What would Martha have against Joseph Walker? I was the more likely suspect between the two of us. There had to be other options.

"That said, the back door is flimsy. An amateur could have broken in with a credit card. Like many of the Amish, your aunt had not been concerned with security. I suggest you have a new lock installed with a dead bolt on that door."

"I will."

His expression softened. "I'm going to drop by your house tomorrow to check things out."

"Check out my house?"

He shrugged as if it were no big deal. "I'd like to take a look around as part of the investigation."

My back stiffened. "Don't you need a warrant to do that?"

"Sure, I can get one. Do you have anything to hide?"

"No. Nothing." I licked my lips. "Do I need a lawyer?"

His eyes shifted to a dark shade of blue. "You are entitled to one."

I took that as a "yes."

Chapter Nine

I returned home with the full knowledge that I was a murder suspect. And not just any suspect—I was the prime suspect. What could I do about it? I had to do something. I needed to give Sheriff Mitchell some other options. The only way to do that was find out who killed Joseph Walker for myself. Even though Joseph wasn't the nicest guy in the world, he didn't deserve to die, nor did his family deserve this tragedy. The real killer should be brought to justice. That would not happen if the police fixated on me.

When I turned the SUV onto my street, I saw a horse and buggy parked on the curb in front of my house. Anna Graber sat on a resin chair on my front porch and stood when I turned into the driveway.

I climbed out of the car.

Anna adjusted her glasses. "Where have you been?"

I swallowed. "I was at the sheriff's department."

Her face was somber. "I've heard the news."

I let out a breath. There was no need to ask her what the news was.

She inspected my face. "Are you all right?"

"I don't know." I swallowed a lump in my throat.

She clicked her tongue. "Joseph was a stern man, but honest. This is a tragedy for the entire community."

"The sheriff thinks I killed him." The lump in my throat grew bigger.

Her eyes went round behind her glasses. "I never heard anything so ridiculous. I'm sure the sheriff doesn't really feel that way. He had to ask you questions because it's your shop."

My shop? That still sounded strange to my ears. Had I already ruined everything that my aunt had spent decades creating? The murder wasn't my fault, but I still felt like I let Aunt Eleanor down somehow. "Thank you for stopping by and checking on me. That was nice of you."

"You're coming with me. Do you think I would leave Eleanor's niece alone on a day like this?"

I hedged. Having settled on my hermit plan, I wasn't eager to give it up. "I really should stay home and unpack. I don't know where anything is. I'm going to run out of clean socks."

She arched an eyebrow at me. "The best excuse you've got is dirty socks. You're coming to the farm with me. A visit to the country will do you good."

I raised an eyebrow. "We aren't in the country now?"

"Course not. We're in town, an *Englisch* town at that. Now, go fetch your quilting basket and Oliver, and we will be off."

Ten minutes later, I stepped out of my house with my quilting basket and my dog. Before I left the house, I checked that the door was locked three times. As I was about to check one more time, Anna said, "That locked door isn't going to protect you from whoever hurt Joseph. Only *Gott* can."

I let my hand fall from the doorknob and joined Anna and Oliver at the buggy. I smacked the floor of the buggy with my hand. "Up, Oliver."

He eyed Anna's horse and glanced back to me as if to ask, "Are you serious?"

Anna's horse blew air out of his mouth, fluttering his lips and showing off his large square teeth.

Oliver's brown eyes bulged as he moonwalked back onto the lawn.

"I'll get him to hop up here." Anna rooted around in a basket beside her on the bench seat and came up with a six-inch-long piece of beef jerky. She shook the jerky at my dog, and he hopped into the buggy and lay on the floor with the piece of dried meat between his front paws.

She smiled triumphantly. "Works every time."

"You keep jerky in your buggy?" I asked.

"Buggy rides are long. You never know when you need a bite to eat." She climbed into the buggy with the ease of someone who did it every day of her life.

I laughed and climbed inside, falling into the seat like a bag of sand. I hoped the dismount would go more smoothly.

Anna clicked at the horse, and we rocked into motion. The childhood memories of riding in my uncle's buggy came to my mind. The pleasant rattle of the carriage and the rocking back and forth were like being in an adult-sized cradle. In my mind's eye, I could see *Aenti* in the front of the buggy working on a lap quilt. If she was seated, she was always quilting. Her mind was barely occupied by her stitches. Despite her lack of attention, she never dropped a stitch or strayed from the quilting pattern.

Anna turned on Clay Street, and I pretended to be fascinated with the Holmes County Courthouse, which was a beautiful sandstone building with enormous arched windows on all four sides. A blindfolded lady of justice held scales over the public entrance, and a clock tower was perched on the roof. In front of the courthouse, where Jackson Street and Clay intersected, was a large green courtyard. In the middle of the courtyard was a nineteenth-century American soldier statue, austerely surveying downtown Millersburg. To the north side of the courtyard was a brick building, the Holmes County Old Jail, which now housed civil servant offices even though jailhouse bars remained on many of the windows. I suspect they left them on for historical purposes, but I wondered how the civil servants felt looking through barred windows each day. Was it a view I would come to know well because of Joseph's murder?

Anna lifted a hand from the reins and squeezed mine, which were folded in my lap. "I miss her too."

Surprised, I turned to her. How did Anna know I was thinking about my aunt?

She adjusted the reins in her hands. "I miss her every day, but no more than when I sit down to quilt. Your *aenti* was the best quilter in the county. No one else in the circle can come close to her talent."

I bit the inside of my lip. "What can you tell me about the wedding quilt that was in the shop?"

"It was some of Eleanor's best work. She made it a few years back. It was one of the last quilts she pieced and quilted herself before she became too ill to do it."

I winced as I thought of it in tatters and spattered with blood on the stockroom floor.

"What's wrong?" she asked as a minivan whizzed past us.

I squirmed on the hard seat. "The quilt was with Joseph."

"You mean he took it?"

"No, I mean . . ." I hadn't considered that Joseph may have been the one to take the quilt off the wall before, but I guessed it was possible. "No, I don't think so."

"Then what?" Her dark brown eyes magnified by her glasses bored holes into me.

I swallowed. "It was with his body, covered in blood and torn to pieces."

"But it was on the wall." Her face paled.

"It wasn't when I went into the shop this morning. I can assure you of that."

She took a deep breath. This seemed to come as more of a shock to her than Joseph's death. "But that's one of her best quilts. It's priceless."

Anna's change of mood wasn't making me feel any better about the loss of the quilt. "I know."

She shook her head. "There must be a reason that the quilt was there. Someone had to have made an effort to get it down off the wall. Those quilt hooks aren't easy to work. Whoever got it down did it for a reason."

I hadn't thought about it. "You think it was a message." The morbid thought brought a sour taste to my mouth.

She nodded and the ties of her prayer cap waved back and forth.

If it was some kind of message, it was meant for me.

Chapter Ten

The gentle rock of the buggy on pavement turned into a spine-tingling rattle on the loose gravel as Anna turned into a driveway leading to her farm.

"I'm sorry that I didn't visit more often," I blurted out. "I mean that I didn't come and visit Aunt Eleanor more often. I should have."

She smiled. "Your *aenti* understood. She loved you like a daughter. She wouldn't have left you her shop otherwise."

Her comment only made me feel worse. "I forgot how pretty it was here in the summer. Everything is green and full of life. It's so different from Dallas."

Anna pulled back on her horse a tad to slow his pace as we made our way up the long drive. "I've never been, but I don't doubt that. I don't think I would care much to live in a big city."

I tried to place Anna, or any of the ladies from the quilting circle, in Dallas. It didn't work. Just like placing Ryan in Holmes County didn't work. Some folks needed to stay in their part of the world. Was I different because I could navigate in both, or was I a different person in one place than I was in the other? Neither Anna nor Ryan could mask their true selves. Maybe I was a chameleon.

Anna parked the buggy beside a two-story farmhouse that belonged to her son, Jo-Jo, who had been my partner in crime as a child.

Any further discussion was drowned out by the squawking of geese. A flock of thirty domestic geese clustered in a pen beside a large whitewashed barn.

I peered under the seat at Oliver. He heard them. His nails scratched at the buggy's floor as he tried to further conceal himself under the bench.

"Ollie, they aren't flying." I looked up at Anna. "They can't fly, can they?"

She laughed. "No."

Oliver whimpered.

Anna wrinkled her nose. "The geese are Jonah's latest experiment. He wants the farm to succeed. That's not an easy task with all the corporate farms producing mass crops." She placed a hand to her head. "You would not believe the squawking. I have to sleep with three pillows over my head to find any rest, and I can still hear them. I wish my son had chosen a quieter animal to farm, like rabbits."

Oliver agreed.

The screen door of the farmhouse opened, and a young, handsome Amish man in a straw hat with his shirtsleeves rolled up to the elbows stepped out. "*Mamm*, what are you doing here? I thought you were off to the quilt shop this morning."

"So did I, son." She turned to me. "You remember Angie, don't you? Eleanor's niece. She inherited the quilt shop."

Jo-Jo grinned. "Sure do."

A memory of a towheaded boy whom I played with as a child tickled the back of my mind. I'd hated to leave him almost as much as I hated to leave my aunt and her quilters. "Jo-Jo, it's so good to see you."

Jo-Jo's face turned impossibly red. "I don't go by that name anymore."

Anna smiled. "It's been nearly twenty years since you two played together as children, hasn't it?"

Jonah, Anna's youngest child, who was a year older than me, grimaced. "That was a long time ago. Much has changed."

I started to move my arm to offer a handshake but thought better of it. "It's nice to see you again. Congratulations about the family and farm. It looks like you have done well for yourself."

His mouth tilted up at the corner. "I've done all right."

Anna jerked a thumb in the direction of the geese. "I wished you could have done all right without the addition of those monsters."

The geese seemed to understand Anna's insult and began squawking with increased gusto.

The second corner of Jonah's mouth turned up.

Anna pushed her glasses up her short nose. "One of them chased Ezra into the house. If I didn't know better, I would have thought the goose was herding the poor child."

He had a full-on grin now and looked so much like the blond boy I remembered. "It's *gut* for children to learn how to behave around the animals the hard way. That will make them remember better than anything I say to them will." He ground the toe of his work boot in the dirt. "I heard you are engaged. Congratulations."

"I was." I paused. "I'm not anymore."

"Oh." Jonah cleared his throat. "I'm headed over to the Walker place. The family is taking it hard."

My mental trip down memory lane came to an abrupt halt. "Have you seen Abigail?" The question rushed out of my mouth.

"No, but her brother, Elijah Knepp, stopped by the farm earlier. He said she was in a bad way. My wife, Miriam, is over there now sitting with her. I'm going over to do the chores." He tapped the dirt off his boot.

Anna sniffed. "Elijah should be the one who is doing the chores."

Jonah's mouth twitched. "He said he had business in town, and I offered to step in."

Stepping in and offering help was so like the Jo-Jo I remembered.

"I must go. Since the buggy's already out, can I take it?" Jonah asked.

Anna nodded. "Of course."

"Danki." Jonah stepped up into the buggy. "I have the family buggy hitched behind the barn if you need it."

Then, I remembered something. "Wait."

Jonah turned around, as if he knew what was coming next. *"Ya?"* He had one leg suspended in the air like he was about to stomp out a line dance.

Before I could answer, Oliver stuck his nose out from under the front seat of the buggy.

"Who's this?" Jonah asked.

"That's Oliver." I slapped my leg. "Come out, boy."

The cowardly canine wiggled backward.

I stepped around Jonah and stuck my hands under the seat. I grabbed Oliver by both shoulders and pulled. He barely moved an inch. I put my hands on my hip.

"Oliver." I felt my face turn red. Of course, the dog would misbehave at a time like this.

Jonah peeked under the bench. "He's shivering." He wrinkled his brow. "What's wrong with him?"

I grimaced. "It's your geese. He's afraid of birds."

"How can a dog be afraid of birds?" Jonah asked with some of the Jo-Jo twinkle I remembered in his eye.

I shrugged.

A grin spread across my old friend's face. "I'll get him out."

"Don't hurt him." My eyes went wide.

"Don't worry." He reached under the seat, and after a few grunts came up with the dog. He placed Oliver into my arms. The dog promptly buried his head in my armpit. "Life must be different in the big city. I never met a dog afraid of birds before. I've met plenty of birds afraid of dogs, though." He hopped up into the buggy. "*Mamm*, I should be home with Miriam and the children this afternoon."

"Where are the children now?" Anna asked.

"Miriam has the baby with her, and we sent the others to her sister's home for the day."

Anna nodded.

"I told Elijah about the Watermelon Fest in Rolling Brook next weekend. I don't know if he will help mend the barn." Jonah looked down at us from his seat in the buggy.

Anna adjusted her glasses on her nose. "Some folks are still uncomfortable with him being back home."

"I suspect Sheriff Mitchell will want to talk to him," he trailed off.

My heart gave a little flip when Sheriff Mitchell was mentioned.

Anna and I watched as Jonah rode away in the buggy. "He's a good boy. I'm glad that you got to see him again. He moped for days after your family moved to Texas and looked forward to seeing you each summer. It was hard for him when you stopped coming." The next part she whispered under her breath. "But it was for the best."

I wanted to ask her why but decided I didn't need to. It was for the best because Jonah was Amish, and I was not. Maybe as children our friendship was innocent, but as teenagers, it was a recipe for disaster.

I placed Oliver on the ground and he hid behind my leg. I wondered if there was a dog therapist in town I could take him to. I suspected Anna wouldn't know of any. "Who is Elijah Knepp?"

Her mouth twisted as if she didn't like the taste of the words that she was about to say. "He's Abigail's younger brother. I hope he will be there to support his sister like she has supported him after all these years."

"Why did you think it was a good thing he wouldn't be at the Watermelon Fest?"

She sighed. "Elijah has had a tough time with the law. He just got out of prison."

I stepped back and nearly tripped over Oliver. I leaned down and picked him up. He was going to be as active as a rock as long as there were birds in the vicinity. "What did he go to prison for?"

"It is no secret. He burned down a barn. It was—" She stopped herself.

"What?"

She ran a hand over her apron. "It was not important."

I gasped. "Was it an accident?"

She shook her head. "And the police would have

never found Elijah if Joseph hadn't turned in his brother-in-law."

My eyes widened. "He must be a suspect for Joseph's murder, then."

Not that I wished any ill will toward a man trying to get back on his feet, but this was great news for me. Elijah had a real, plausible motivation for murder. It was much better than the one the police suspected of me, which was not being welcome to the neighborhood. Elijah couldn't be the only one either. In fact, there must be dozens of folks in Holmes County with a motive to hurt the woodworker. I shivered to think that there could be more than one person capable of what I saw in the stockroom. However, I had to believe that to solve the murder, and it was worse to imagine myself in an orange jumpsuit with a six-foot woman named Big Bertha as my cell mate. If the police had a viable suspect, then they wouldn't concentrate on me so much. Maybe the shop would open sooner too. Financial ruin wasn't around the corner after all. I winced. How could I think of the shop and myself when Abigail and her children were in so much pain?

Anna studied me. "Why are you making that face?"

I forced a smile. "What face?" I cleared my throat. "It was nice to see Jonah again. It brought back a lot of memories."

She smiled. "Have you eaten anything today?"

Forlornly, I thought about the enormous uneaten cinnamon bun back at my rented house in Millersburg. "No."

She clicked her tongue. "I didn't think so. Let me make you something as we wait for the rest of the ladies to get here."

"The rest of the ladies?"

"I called an emergency quilting circle meeting. We shouldn't sit around and worry with idle hands. The best action to do at a time like this is quilt. I promised you a lesson after all. It will give us the peace we seek."

Oliver ran after Anna as if his tail were on fire. I wasn't sure if it was the sound of the geese that spurred him on or the promise of food.

Chapter Eleven

Rachel knocked on the screen door's frame just as Oliver and I finished our meal of roasted turkey, biscuits, and fresh milk. Oliver had everything but the coffee. As the last bite of biscuit melted in my mouth, I decided diets were *way* overrated. Oliver gave a contented sigh in agreement.

Rachel stepped into the kitchen with Abram on her hip. "Am I the first one here?"

The older woman nodded. "But everyone is coming."

A frown formed on Rachel's delicate features. "Everyone?"

Anna arched an eyebrow. "Sarah is coming too." She returned to the kitchen to prepare the coffee.

Rachel blushed, and again, I wondered if there was something more to Rachel's mistrust of Sarah. Rachel pulled a lap quilt from her blanket and laid it on the floor. She placed Abram on his tummy on top of it and removed a handful of wooden blocks from her basket for him to play with. The baby closed his fists over one of the blocks and gurgled at us as if to ask if we saw his accomplishment.

Rachel perched on the oak rocking chair closest to

her son. "You must think me awful for not wanting Sarah to be here. She—"

Anna poked her head through the doorway that led into the kitchen. "Angie, can you carry this tray for me into the living room?"

I glanced back to Rachel. Relief was clearly visible on her face. "Go on," she whispered.

In the kitchen, Anna had a pewter tray set out with five steaming mugs of coffee, a creamer of milk, and bowls of white and brown sugar. "Put it on the end table beside the couch. The ladies can help themselves from there."

Oliver lay on the blanket next to Abram. His tongue hung out of his mouth and his stubby tail wagged back and forth.

I placed the tray on the end table as instructed. "I'm so sorry Oliver climbed on your quilt. I can put him outside." As I said that, I cringed. The last place Oliver would want to be was outside with the geese, and I didn't like the idea of the dog being out of my sight. If Joseph's murder was really a message for me, wouldn't my dog be an easy target?

Rachel laughed. "Don't even think about it. Abram is completely taken by him."

I examined the plump pair on the floor and saw that she was right. Abram held on to one of Oliver's batlike ears as if it were the edge of his favorite blanket. My little dog grinned, clearly enjoying the attention. I was about to ask her what she'd wanted to say about Sarah when I heard the rattle of a buggy outside the house. More members of the quilting circle arrived. My questions for Rachel would have to wait.

The screen door creaked open, and Martha loosened

her prayer cap tie as she stepped into the house. "Anna, I can smell your sweet *kaffi* from my buggy. I would love a cup. Maybe it will clear all of our heads." She turned her blue eyes on me. "Terrible news for the shop and, of course, Joseph, *Gott* rest his soul. I'm glad to see you in one piece."

I handed Martha a cup of coffee.

She placed her quilting basket on the floor next to a rocker identical to the one Rachel sat in and took the white mug from me. "When will the shop reopen?"

I cleared my throat. "I don't know. It's not likely to be this week."

Martha sat on the rocking chair. "How could this have happened?"

"I don't know." I selected a cup of coffee for myself.

"Didn't you remember to lock up the shop last night?" The sharpness of her voice was unexpected.

I nearly dropped the mug of coffee I held. "Y-yes. Of course, I remembered to lock up."

Martha leaned back in the rocker. Her expression was hooded. "Maybe you forgot. How else could anyone have gotten inside the shop?"

I remembered the sheriff's questions about the keys. Martha had the only other key. Unless Harvey Lemontop kept a spare. I would be sure to ask him.

Rachel's forehead creased. "If Angie says that she locked it, then she did. Maybe someone broke the lock. It wouldn't have been that hard to do." She removed fabric from her basket. "Did the police say how Joseph and"—she searched for the right word—"the other person got inside the shop?"

A flush crept up my neck. "The sheriff thinks whoever

broke in either had a key or used a credit card on the back door."

Martha flushed. "Had a key? That's ridiculous. You and I are the only ones with keys."

"Maybe there is another key we don't know about. Aunt Eleanor was sick a long time—maybe she gave it to someone and forgot to get it back."

"Absolutely not. She would not have done that without telling me. If there was another key to Running Stitch, I would know about it." Martha scowled into her coffee. "You must have left the door unlocked."

"I didn't," I said, but doubt crept into my voice. *Had I locked the door?* I thought that I had, but I couldn't remember with one hundred percent certainty. I remembered letting Oliver into the backyard for a potty break after the quilters left. Did I lock it when he came back inside the store? I must have.

"Did Joseph and his killer enter the store together?" Anna asked.

"What?" I asked.

"Did they go in together or separately? Who was there first?"

"I—I don't know," I said.

"How did Joseph die?" Martha sipped her coffee.

The room grew warmer, and I placed my mug of coffee back on the end table. It was too hot to hold in this humidity. The Amish didn't air-condition their homes, and little breeze came through the screen door and open windows. I didn't want to tell them the fabric cutters they teased me about had been used as the murder weapon.

"Gude mariye!" Sarah Leham's shrill voice rang through the front door. Despite Rachel's obvious misgiv-

ings about the nosy quilter, I couldn't be more relieved to see her.

The screen door smacked against its frame as Sarah hurried into the room, carrying an enormous basket. She set the basket by the door. "I didn't know which project we'd be working on, so I brought everything."

Martha arched an eyebrow. "Since the quilt frame is stuck in the shop, we will be piecing today."

Sarah grinned. "*Gut.* I brought two projects that need piecing. It's always so difficult to decide which one to work on. My husband says that I should stick to one project to the end, but when I think of a new pattern or see a new bolt of fabric, I want to jump into a fresh project right away. My husband says I'm far too impulsive for an Amish woman, but that is just my way." She took a breath.

Martha pursed her lips. "Your husband is right. If you start something, you should finish it."

Sarah shrugged off Martha's criticism as Anna stepped into the room. "Fix your *kaffi* and find a place. The Lord said idle hands can lead to trouble."

Sarah picked up a cup of coffee and added cream and sugar. "I'm glad you called this meeting, Anna. There is so much we need to discuss. I think we should get right to it."

I didn't like the sound of that.

Rachel kept her head bent down over her fabric pieces. Oliver belly-crawled over to her and lay on her right foot. Oliver loved feet almost as much as he feared birds. I smiled to myself as I remembered the way he would lick Ryan's toes, much to my former fiancé's disdain. At the time, I had been embarrassed by Oliver's behavior. Now I relished the memory.

Sarah settled on one end of the sofa closest to the coffee tray. "What makes you smile, Angie?"

It sounded like an innocent question, but considering its source, I doubted it. "Oliver likes Abram and Rachel. I'm glad he's making friends. It's been a tough adjustment for him."

Martha glanced at Oliver, who had fallen asleep the second his head hit Rachel's big toe. "He's a dog. Why would he need adjusting?"

I bit my tongue. Literally.

Anna sat on a small easy chair and began to remove dozens of two-inch-by-one-inch lavender, cornflower blue, and cream diamond fabric from her basket. "Angie sees her dog as a member of the family."

Martha pulled four shoofly quilt squares from her basket. They were already pieced together. She began pinning the squares to one another, so that she could sew them together. "With managing Running Stitch these last two years, I haven't had much time to spend with animals."

My brow creased. Was that what this was about? Martha was upset about working at the quilt shop? I opened my mouth to ask, but Sarah was much faster with the tongue. "I can imagine that caring for the shop while Eleanor was ill was difficult. You must be happy Angie is here now to take that burden. Why, I can see her making all kinds of improvements. Maybe Angie being here will attract even more *Englischers* to the shop." She turned to me. "Surely, you will know what appeals to them better than we would."

Martha concentrated on the pieces of cloth in her lap, but I didn't get the impression that Sarah's declaration brought her much comfort.

Anna gathered up her pieces and pulled up the bottom of her black apron so they were cradled into its fold. "Sarah, switch places with me, so that I can instruct Angie how to piece."

Sarah stood without complaint and moved her enormous basket beside the chair Anna vacated.

The older woman sat next to me on the sofa and laid small diamond pieces out on the cushion between us.

I picked up two of the diamonds and placed one on top of the other. They were perfectly cut and exactly the same size. Many times when I cut fabric, there were frayed edges that I didn't mind because i knew they would disappear into the quilt when the pieces were sewn together. I had a suspicion that every one of Anna's quilts was perfect, inside and out. "Ever since I moved to Texas, I've done all my piecing on my sewing machine."

"Some Amish in Holmes County do it that way on a treadle sewing machine, but your *aenti* was a firm believer in keeping the traditional hand-quilting ways alive. She only made hand-pieced and hand-stitched quilts. She said that doing it by machine would make a quilter lazy."

I thought of the dozens of frayed edges that were buried in the middle of the many quilts I had made for family and friends back in Texas. Was I a lazy quilter? Apparently.

Anna handed me a tiny plastic box of straight pins. "Start pinning and then we will work on stitches."

Rachel gave Abram a sandwich bag of animal crackers. He removed one and crushed it into the quilt. I winced, but Rachel seemed unconcerned that her son marred such a beautiful piece of art. To the Amish, quilts were first and foremost practical items, only extremely beautiful practical items.

Martha, Sarah, and Rachel all worked on new piecing projects too. While I pinned, Anna removed a twelve-inch-by-twelve-inch wall quilt from her basket. It was pieced in the bear-paw pattern and basted together. Basting was a way to hold the quilt's three layers, the top, the batting, and the bottom, with long pieces of loose thread. The thread typically was a bright color so that it could be removed with little trouble when the quilting was done.

Anna had basted her quilt with bright orange thread. Barely glancing at the tiny quilter's needle between her left thumb and forefinger, she threaded her quilting needle by feel. "This is a size eight quilter's needle. I like to use a small-sized needle because it's easier to keep your stitches small if the needle is smaller."

"Size eight. Got it." The needle was much smaller than any I had used before. I wondered how many I would lose in the couch cushions, and who the unlucky ones would be who would find them when they sat on Anna's couch.

Anna set her needle to the fabric and eyed me. "Why aren't you pinning?"

My hands had stilled on my lap as I watched Anna work. "I was paying attention to you."

"You can do that and pin at the same time. Isn't that what you *Englischers* call multitasking?"

I gathered another handful of fabric diamonds from the middle cushion.

She nodded approval. "Just like on a sewing machine, you follow the line from the quilt pattern." She traced a finger along the drawn-on blue line on the fabric. "This looks dark, but it will wash out after the quilt is complete like it was never there. My eyes aren't as good as they used to be, so I use bright blue to make my stitch lines. You can see from the blue line that this quilt is set for a wave pattern. I chose that because it's one of the easiest and a good place for you to start. Just follow the curve of the wave."

Anna dipped her needle in and out of the fabric five times before she pulled the needle through slowly. I knew she decreased her pace for my benefit. When the thread was taut, there were five identical millimeter-long stitches.

"That's amazing," I said, knowing my own stitches would never be that uniform.

"Nee," Anna said. "Only the Lord is amazing. This is a mere skill. Your stitches will be the same in time. Place those pieces back on the cushion."

I did as instructed, and she placed the small quilt on my lap. Handing me the needle, she said, "Your turn."

Carefully, I smoothed the quilt over my lap and found the place where the next stitch should begin.

Rachel pinned a goosefoot-patterned square together. "You will be a fine hand quilter when Anna is done with you, Angie."

I shot her a quick smile and returned my attention to the quilt.

I held my top lip between my teeth as I adjusted the needle in my hand. "Do I need a thimble?"

"Thimbles are for sissies." Anna winked at me.

I chuckled. "Sissies?"

"I hear how the *Englisch* teenagers in Millersburg talk."

If "sissy" was the only phrase Anna picked up from the teens in Millersburg, it must be a mild town. I bowed my head again to focus on my stitches. Everything else fell away as I concentrated on moving the needle through the fabric. At the age of ten, I quilted like this the night before my family left for Texas. I had begged my parents to let me visit Aunt Eleanor's shop one last time. They agreed, and now that I was older, I suspected that they were glad to have a ten-year-old out of their hair as they did their last-minute packing. When my father came to pick me up at the shop later, Aunt Eleanor and I clung to each other with tears running down our faces. I promised I would be back in the summer, and I did return to Holmes County each summer. As an adult my visits became less and less frequent. Anna said that Aunt Eleanor understood why I stopped coming, but guilt gnawed at me. A good niece would have visited at least once a year. I could have given my *aenti* that.

My mother had been thrilled over the idea of leaving Ohio. She grew up in Millersburg and married my father, her high school sweetheart, but always felt like she was meant for something bigger. There wasn't anything much bigger than the Big D. When we settled into the Lone Star State, she fully embraced Dallas society life, got highlights, Botox, and a Texas drawl. Meanwhile, her older sister continued her quiet life married to a New Order Amish man. Sometimes it was hard to believe that the two women were sisters, or that they grew up in the same house in Millersburg. They couldn't be more different if they tried.

Chapter Twelve

I fumbled with the tiny needle, dropping it onto the couch cushion. Luckily, it was tethered to the quilt by the thread. No one would be skewered by my needle, at least not yet.

"You're having a bit of trouble, Angie," Sarah said. "Maybe you'd do better with a bigger needle. Those small ones can be difficult to manage for beginners. You should have seen the needle my mother gave me to start with. It was the size of a fork."

"I doubt it was that big," Anna snorted. "Like anything, this takes time and practice. Quilting teaches patience."

After my first few clumsy stitches, the motorized memory of my last visit to Aunt Eleanor when she taught me hand stitching came back to me. I heard the murmur of the ladies around me, but I was preoccupied with my work and the memories of my aunt's hands moving swiftly across the fabric of a quilt. My own pace was considerably slower.

"Were you scared, Angie?" Sarah asked.

I blinked at her. "Scared?"

She scooted forward in her seat. "When you found Joseph? Were you afraid? I'm sure I would be. In fact, I would have run screaming from the shop. Is that what you did?"

I had been so consumed by the quilt that I forgot about Joseph. Well, I almost forgot about Joseph. With Sarah's questions, the memories of his body in the stockroom popped to the forefront of my mind like a burnt piece of toast.

I bit back the urge to snap at her for interrupting my moment of peace, one in which murder wasn't an invited guest. "I didn't do anything that dramatic. I was too shocked to be afraid. According to the police, the murder happened sometime late at night, so by the time Danny and I got there, the murderer was long gone." At least, I hoped he was, I mentally added.

"Danny was with you?" Martha's tone was sharp.

"Y-yes. He wanted to interview me for the tourism board newsletter. We made plans at the opening yesterday to meet at the shop this morning."

Abram emptied the bag of animal crackers on the wide planks of Anna's floor. He carefully selected which one to eat first. The baby sucked a giraffe's head.

Rachel clucked her tongue. "What a mess."

The infant's antics gave Martha time to compose herself, but I didn't forget her reaction so quickly. "Does it surprise you that Danny was with me?" I asked.

"No—I mean—yes, it does. You need to be careful around Danny Nicolson. He is a worse gossip than Sarah."

"Martha!" Sarah cried. "That was completely uncalled for."

Martha shrugged as if unconcerned that she offended the other Amish woman.

I tucked the needle into the quilt for safekeeping. "What can you tell me about Danny? He seems determined to be a success."

"He's a pest." Martha gripped her needle in her left hand. "If anything happens in the Amish community, he's right there wanting to know about it."

I plucked the needle from the quilt and rolled it back and forth between my fingers. "His cousin Jessica told me that he would like to write for a large paper."

"I've heard that too," Sarah said, giving Martha a triumphant smile.

"When did you talk to Jessica?" Rachel asked her in a quiet way. She set her quilt aside and knelt on the floor next to Abram. She began picking up the animal crackers and placing them back in the bag.

"She stopped by the shop during the grand opening and bought a few things. She said that she has an antiques shop in Millersburg called Out of Time." I smoothed wrinkles out of the quilt top on my lap. "She seemed perfectly nice, much different from Danny, but . . ."

Sarah leaned forward. "But what?"

I twisted my mouth, wondering whether I should say anything, especially considering Sarah was in the room ready to pounce on any piece of tidbit I let slip. However at the same time, I was new to Holmes County. I didn't know Jessica. Maybe one or all of these women did and could give me insight into her. I let out a breath. "When she saw Joseph Walker come into Running Stitch, she seemed upset."

Martha leaned forward. "What do you mean?"

"The two physically ran into each other as Jessica was leaving the shop and Joseph was coming in."

Rachel picked crumbs off the quilt as Abram threw two more cookies on the floor. "If she ran into him, she was probably embarrassed. I know I would be."

Martha snipped the end of her thread with a pair of tiny scissors. "She probably knew how he felt about *Englischers*. Joseph made no secret about disapproving of anyone who wasn't Amish."

"He disapproved of anyone who wasn't Old Order Amish." Anna shook her head. "He thought that New Orders like us break the *Ordnung*."

I didn't argue with them, but I thought there was something more to Jessica's reaction. It seemed personal. I decided to change the subject away from the Nicolsons as it was clear the Amish women knew next to nothing about them. "Do you know of anyone who may have wanted to hurt Joseph or didn't like him?"

Sarah rubbed her hands together. "*Gut.* We need to discuss this."

Rachel cringed at the other woman's comment.

Anna merely shook her head. "Didn't like him? Half of the county didn't like him. He wasn't a likable man. Everyone was shocked when sweet Abigail Knepp agreed to marry him. They were such an odd pairing."

Abram threw more crackers on the floor, and Rachel sighed.

"What about Benjamin Hershberger?" Sarah asked. "He can't be sad Joseph is out of the way."

My head snapped up. "Who is Benjamin Hershberger?"

Anna shot Sarah an annoyed glance. "He's another woodworker in Rolling Brook. Joseph was his biggest competition. He's a kind old man. He wouldn't hurt anyone."

"It wasn't much of a competition," Sarah said, unfazed by Anna's glares. "Joseph's work was far superior to Ben's."

"Ben's work is *gut* too," Rachel said. "He is a friend of my husband's and a *gut* man."

Sarah seemed unconvinced.

Trying not to sound overly curious, I asked, "Where is his shop?"

"Just a block away from Joseph's," Martha said.

That meant it was just a block away from the quilt shop too. Ben could have easily gone to the quilt shop, killed Joseph, and returned to his own store before anyone would know. Not that this explained how either man entered *my* store. *What was Joseph doing in there so late at night?* The Amish were early-to-bed, early-to-rise people. They weren't traipsing around town after midnight.

"Aren't there a lot of woodworkers in Holmes County?" I ran my index finger along my stitches. "Why is there bad blood between these two?"

Rachel knelt on the floor again to collect the animal crackers Abram dumped. Sarah watched her for a second before answering. "Joseph was Ben's apprentice. Now he is—was—better than his teacher. Ben's business has been cut by two-thirds since Joseph opened his doors."

"Sarah Leham." Anna's tone was stern. "How could you possibly know that?"

She held a superior gaze. "You should pay closer attention to what people say, Anna Graber."

Anna opened her mouth to say something and thought better of it.

Trying to bring the ladies back on track, I said, "Then, Ben has a clear motive for murder."

First Elijah, now Ben. How many Amish in Rolling Brook wanted to take out the austere woodworker? It was looking better and better for me. I needed to convince the sheriff that these other men were better suspects than I was. Probably not the nicest thought I ever had, but I kept picturing a six-by-six cement room and bad prison food. Plus, there was Oliver to think about. Who would care for my Frenchie if I got hauled off to the Big House?

"Did the sheriff say who he thought did it?" Martha asked. Her voice was calm and she seemed to be in control of the churlish mood that hit when she first arrived. If my wild curls were an indication, it was muggy outside. Maybe Martha's temper could be attributed to the heat. Or perhaps I was giving her too much credit.

"He did."

Sarah's eyes gleamed behind her glasses. This must be better than Christmas morning for her. "Who?"

"Me," I said simply.

The women gasped. Startled, Oliver darted around the room on the lookout for a rogue pigeon.

"There aren't any birds in here, Ollie," I said soothingly.

Sarah's forehead creased. "What does that mean?"

I just shook my head.

Tears threatened to fall from Rachel's eyes. "The sheriff can't think it was you. You didn't even know Joseph, not really."

Sarah threaded her needle. "We're here for you, Angie. Tell us how we can help."

Irritation flashed across Rachel's face. "Sarah, you're looking at Angie as if you were a cat ready to attack a mouse."

Sarah leaned back in her paddle-backed chair. "Rachel Miller, you need to mind your own business."

Rachel's face turned deep red. "That's a strange thing for you to say."

Martha folded her hands on her lap. "It's no surprise the sheriff suspects Angie. It's because of the missing deed."

My stomach tightened into a painful knot, more painful than the stomachache I had after the juice cleanse. *Does Mitchell know about the deed yet? He must.*

Anna placed her sewing basket on her lap and began to pack up her kit. "I think that's enough quilting for the day. Angie must be tired, and I need to take her back home."

I couldn't agree more.

Chapter Thirteen

Oliver ran into the house as if he were Quasimodo returning to the safety of Notre-Dame. Our rented house was a bird-free sanctuary of sorts.

A light blinked on my answering machine. The phone company gave me service just two days ago, and I had yet to give anyone my number, except . . . I knew who it was.

I pressed the play button. "Miss Braddock. This is Sheriff Mitchell from the Holmes County Sheriff's Department. Thank you for stopping by the department for fingerprinting and to give your statement. I have a few more questions to ask you about the case." His voice was stern. "There seems to be some information you neglected to share with me. We can discuss this when I drop by. By the way, you're not answering your phone, which means either you aren't home or you are screening your calls. I hope it's the second one because, remember, I told you not to leave town."

I pressed the erase button. *Could I be wrong, or was the sheriff teasing me?*

I must have imagined the teasing. Yep, that's what

happened. "I'm cracking up, Ollie. I guess that's what happens when you find a dead guy."

"Woof!"

I let Oliver outside. He peered left and then right, sniffing the wind for birds. Seeing and smelling none, he ventured out.

Going over the conversation with the quilting circle in my head, I decided I needed to get a lawyer. Ryan's handsome face instantly came to mind. He wasn't a criminal lawyer, but his expertise would certainly be helpful in this situation. I grimaced. However, he was partly responsible, wasn't he? Had he not dumped me, I would never have moved to Ohio, taken over my aunt's shop, and met Joseph Walker. It's funny how I had the ability to pin everything back on Ryan. Surely, it wasn't fair to him, but it made me feel a touch better about my circumstances.

I did know one lawyer in Holmes County, and that was better than nothing, and I needed to ask Harvey about the shop key. I opened the back door and called Oliver. He dug in the garden with his rear end sticking high in the air. "Oliver! Come!"

Nothing.

"Oliver! Incoming robin!"

His head popped up. He ran for the door, almost knocking me over in the process. The bird fear came in handy at times.

Harvey Lemontop's office was in an old house that looked as if it could double as a barn. His wasn't the only office in the building. A dog groomer also shared the converted home. The groomer was on the first floor, and Harvey was on the second. Since the building seemed pooch-friendly,

I decided to bring Oliver inside with me. He wiggled his stubby tail and started toward the sound of the barking emanating from the groomer's door.

"Sorry, buddy. Maybe we can come back later to make some friends." I noted the dirt on his paws from digging in the garden. "You could use a bath too." Considering my new business was about to go under because the quilt shop was closed, the only bath he would be getting was a hose-down in the backyard.

My hand trailed along the ornately carved banister as we walked up the rose-patterned carpeted steps. On the second floor, a door flew open and an Amish man rushed through it. He nearly collided with me as he pushed his way down the stairs. Oliver ran down the steps to get out of the way and ducked behind a huge potted plant. The man muttered an apology but didn't stop to see if he'd knocked me onto my behind.

The front door slammed closed after him, and the dogs in the groomer's office began to howl and bark at the commotion. Oliver's quivering nose appeared around the plant.

Harvey stepped out of the door holding a black felt hat. "Elijah?" he called, only to find me standing gap-mouthed on the stairs. "Oh." He pulled up short. "Hello, Angela. Can I help you with something?"

Elijah?

I stared as the front door swung open on its hinges and turned back to the lawyer. "Was that Elijah Knepp?"

The lawyer cleared his throat. "Umm, yes. Do you know Elijah?"

"No," I said. Mentally adding that I planned to meet him. He was my best chance of clearing my name. Benjamin Hershberger was a good option too, but Elijah had a record, making him the much more appealing murder suspect. If Aunt Eleanor could hear me now. Contemplating murder suspects, looking to clear my name. I was sure this wasn't what she expected to happen when she left me the shop.

"Can I help you with something?" The lawyer didn't act eager to talk about Elijah, but I wasn't going to let him off that easy.

"What was he doing here?" I moved up one step.

He frowned.

"Was he here about Joseph's death?"

He removed a white handkerchief from his pocket and wiped his brow. "Now, Angela, I'm sure you know, since I'm an attorney-at-law, that I can't share my conversations with my clients with others."

I did know that. Ryan crammed it down my throat when we were together whenever I would ask him about his cases. He never appreciated my curious nature. That should have been another warning sign. It was funny how all the warning signs against him were finally coming to light when he was hundreds of miles away.

Harvey pointed at Oliver half-hidden behind the potted plant. "Is that your dog?"

I slapped my thigh. "Oliver, come."

The Frenchie wiggled out of his hiding place and looked around. Seeing no Amish men or renegade birds, he galloped up the stairs and sat on the step next to my feet.

The lawyer pursed his lip. "Animals aren't supposed to be in the building."

I gave him a *you're kidding me, right?* look. "You have a groomer in the downstairs office."

"I know. That's why I don't allow it."

Oliver gave the attorney his best poor-me face.

The lawyer shoved the handkerchief back into the pocket of his polyester pants. "I suppose I can make an exception in Oliver's case. He seems well behaved, if a little excitable. Are you here to see me?"

"Yes." I nodded.

He rested his hand on his office's doorknob. "What can I do for you?"

"I think I need a lawyer."

He nodded as if he'd been expecting this. "Step into my office."

Oliver and I walked up the final two steps and followed Harvey through a doorway. It opened into an attractive waiting room decorated in what my mother would call Victorian chic. It had been one of her many design phases between ranch elegant and modern country. I couldn't remember what style my mother was currently showing off in her Dallas home. It may have even changed twice since I moved. It was hard to keep track.

"My secretary's not here today. She only works three days a week." He nodded at the empty receptionist's desk. He opened the white door behind the receptionist's desk. It opened into a spacious office, which was also decorated in Victorian style. "Please sit."

I perched on the edge of a red velvet chair. If I had such a chair in my house, it would be covered with dog hair in seconds. I could see why Harvey didn't want any animals in his office.

Oliver eyed the matching chair eagerly.

I pointed to the floor. "Oliver, down."

He lay down with an annoyed snuffle that said, "You never let me have any fun."

"Why do you think you need a lawyer?" Harvey walked around his ornately carved desk.

"I assume you heard about what happened to Joseph by now."

He nodded.

I shifted in my seat. "That's why Elijah was here, wasn't it?"

He pursed his lip. "Angela, I said I would not answer questions about Mr. Knepp, and I haven't changed my mind in the last three minutes."

It had been worth a shot.

"I found the body," I blurted out.

His eyes widened. "I knew he'd been found in your shop, but I didn't know you'd made the gruesome discovery. Are you all right?"

I closed my eyes, trying to put the image of Joseph far back in my mind. *Am I all right? Nope.* "It was a shock." I took a breath. "The sheriff didn't come right out and say it, but he thinks I did it. This is why I need a lawyer. I need help."

"Mitchell is a good man. He would never think that of you."

What was it with this town and thinking the sheriff was the end-all and be-all? Sure, he seemed nice enough, but if he had a viable suspect, I guessed he would arrest him or *her* just like any other cop. Then again, he did let me go this morning. That's probably because he didn't have all his evidence gathered, I reminded myself. He'd arrest me when everything was in order. I inwardly groaned. What a cheerful thought. "What are my options? I need to know someone will get me out if I'm thrown in the slammer."

He wrinkled his button nose at my choice of words. "I don't think that will happen." He held up his hand before I could protest. "But if it does, give me a call."

Excellent. I have my one phone call from the Big House lined up.

The velvet chair felt itchy against my bare arms. "Would it be a conflict of interest if you represented me and Elijah?"

"Why would you say that?" He settled back into his captain's chair, which was also upholstered with velvet fabric. Apparently, the fabric didn't bother him in the least.

"Isn't he a suspect too? Was that why he was here, because he was scared the police will want to talk to him?"

Harvey pursed his lips. He was taking this confidentiality thing a little too far in my opinion.

"If you're not comfortable with me being your representation, I can recommend the names of other attorneys in Millersburg to you."

How would I know another attorney would fight for me? Truthfully, I didn't even know if Harvey would, but he was my aunt's lawyer. If Aunt Eleanor, who was an excellent judge of character, trusted him, then he must be a good guy. "No referral necessary." I bit my lip. "About payment."

He waved away the concern before I could fully express it. "Don't worry about that. Your aunt was a good friend. I'm doing this for her. I know you didn't kill Joseph Walker."

I let out a big sigh of relief. Ryan said it didn't matter if he believed the clients he represented were guilty or not. He just had to convince the jury to doubt the client's guilt. However, it meant a lot to me that Harvey believed me. "Thank you," I murmured. "Sheriff Mitchell said there was no sign of forced entry into the shop. Joseph

Walker and his murderer either got in with a credit card or with a key. Do you know of any other copies of the shop key?"

"No. I gave you the only key I had."

That left only Martha and me as key holders, just as I'd suspected, which meant I had to put my employee, and my aunt's friend, on my list of suspects along with Benjamin and Elijah.

I leaned forward. "The best way to keep me out of jail is to prove my innocence. Then, we will never have to worry about an arrest or trial."

Harvey looked a tad green. "I don't recommend that, Angela. Mitchell is a good cop. He won't arrest an innocent woman."

Thinking about the message on my answering machine at home, I wasn't so sure about that.

Chapter Fourteen

Back at home, Oliver and I stared at the pile of boxes in the corner of the living room. Was it even worth unpacking them at this rate? If I was sent to prison, I wouldn't need those things. And if I had to go back to Texas with my tail between my legs after leading the quilt shop into financial ruin, it would be awfully depressing to repack them all. I'd admit that was the better option over a black-and-white striped jumpsuit.

Oliver barked at me.

"Okay, maybe, just maybe I'm being a tad overdramatic, but I have good reason to be."

He bumped his head against my calf. I took it as a show of support. Before I could come to a conclusion about the boxes, my cell phone rang. The readout display showed my parents' home number. I showed it to Oliver. "Should I answer it?"

He barked softly.

"Yeah, I don't think so either." Ignoring my instinct, I said, "Hi, Mom."

"Sugar." My mother's adopted Texas drawl rang in my

ear. "How are you, darlin'? How are things back in little old Millersburg?"

Peachy, I thought. I found out I may not own Running Stitch, discovered a dead Amish man in Aunt Eleanor's shop this morning, and may be arrested for the crime. Of course I didn't say that, but she went on, like I knew she would, before I could come up with a milder response.

She sighed. "I do miss Millersburg sometimes. It looks like a postcard. You would not believe how many ladies here read those Amish romance novels they sell at Cracker Barrel. They love to hear stories about my Amish sister."

I highly doubted my mother missed Millersburg, but I knew she did love sharing stories. In her mind, any time she was the center of attention was a good one. The one and only time Mom had come back to Millersburg since we moved to Texas over twenty years ago was to attend her sister's funeral a few weeks ago. I doubt she would ever return to the county again.

"How's the shop?" she asked. "I'm sure Eleanor left everything in order. She was always so neat."

Except for the missing deed . . .

"It's coming along." I learned long ago, it was easier for everyone if I was vague with my mother. It's what she wanted. It was what I wanted too.

"Have you found a Realtor yet? I've been searching online for recommendations in Holmes County."

"A Realtor? Why would I need one of those?" I sat on the kitchen stool and looked out the window into the backyard. A cardinal hopped along the white picket fence. I'd wait until he left before letting Oliver outside.

She sniffed. "To sell the shop. That's what you went there to do, wasn't it?"

I ground my teeth. "I'm not selling the shop."

She gasped. "Don't tell me you plan to stay in Ohio for good."

"I told you that was my plan when I left."

She chuckled. "You tease your mother. Both you and your father love to do that."

My jaw started to ache from clenching it too tightly. "I'm not teasing. Why would I go back to Texas?"

"For the wedding, of course." All the mirth left her voice.

I felt a migraine beginning to tickle at the base of my skull. "There is no wedding."

"No wedding?" She gave a sharp intake of breath. "You only need a break after your little spat with Ryan."

"Mom, it wasn't a little spat. The wedding is off. The engagement is over."

"Sweetie, it can't be. The wedding is three months away. Surely, you two can patch things up by then. I took the liberty of mailing your wedding invitations."

"You did what?" I grabbed the side of my head just in case it started to spin in place.

"Don't take that tone with me." Her flat Midwestern accent came out when she was upset.

I closed my eyes and counted to eight in Spanish. Slowly, I opened my eyes. "Mother, why would you do that?"

She sniffed. "I was only trying to help. People have to make plans to come, book hotels and flights. Things like that. I wouldn't have to go to such extreme measures if you had sent Save the Date cards months ago like I asked you to."

I winced because I knew that she really thought she was helping. "Everything's been canceled."

She gasped. "No, it hasn't."

"Yes, it has. The caterer, the reception hall, the music, everything. Not to mention, the groom has no intention of showing up." I put a hand to my left eye. It would start twitching any second now. I could feel the beginnings of the twitch deep inside my cornea. "What am I going to do about the invitations? We have to tell the guests the wedding is off." This was the exact situation I wanted to avoid. The one mercy Ryan gave me during our breakup was he dumped me before I took the invitations to the post office. Now I didn't even have that.

"No, we don't. You and Ryan must get back together in time for the wedding. I can get the caterer and reception hall back. I just need to make some calls. They will pull everything together for me. I give them enough business with all those charities and dinner parties I hosted over the years."

I may have stopped breathing. "Mom, let me make this crystal clear. Ryan and I are *never* getting married."

"But . . . but he's perfect."

Yep, that's what I used to think too.

"What did you do to upset him?" Her voice was sharp.

She might as well have punched me in the gut. "Nothing. I did nothing."

"Maybe that was the problem. By doing nothing, you didn't keep his interest." She moaned. "I knew you should have gotten married years ago, like I wanted. Now you two would be getting a divorce and this would be so less embarrassing."

The eye twitch showed up right on schedule.

She sniffled.

"Are you crying?" I knew my tone was accusatory, but I was the one with the license to cry in this situation.

"I knew I should have sent you to those debutante classes when I had the chance. Instead you were able to convince your father to let you take drawing classes. What a waste. What good is drawing going to do you?" She whimpered. "There must be a way to win Ryan back."

"I don't want to win Ryan back." For the first time I realized I meant it. "Mom, I've got to go." I glanced at Oliver. "Oliver has to go outside."

He cocked his head and started doing the potty dance. I swear the Frenchie understood me better than anyone.

"I'll think of a way to get you two back together—don't worry." She hung up.

I stared at the cell phone in my hand. What just happened? Could this day possibly get worse? It started with my finding a dead body, and now this? I knew the dead-body thing was the worse of the two, but the invitation nightmare rocked me to my very core.

I paced the first floor of my little house. What was I going to do? I needed my computer. I thought the wedding guest list must still be on there. In a rage, I did delete most of the files pertaining to the wedding. Could I re-create the guest list? I knew my mother had a copy, but she might become suspicious if I asked for it. I could feign renewed interest in the wedding. That could work. It had to work.

My cell rang again, causing me to jump. It was my parents' house number again. Mom was calling back to cover more wedding details. Did Ryan know about this? After our seven years together, he certainly knew how my mother operated, so it wouldn't be much of a surprise to him. But oh, the humiliation!

"Mom, I—"

"Your mother is in the other room." In contrast to my mother, Dad had never lost his flat Midwestern accent.

I sighed with relief. "Dad! Thank goodness it's you."

He chuckled.

"Do you know what she did?" My voice was just short of a screech.

"Yes, I know about the invitations."

"I am going to die. Was being dumped not mortification enough?"

"Angie—"

I gripped the cell in my hand. "What am I going to do? Can you get on her computer and grab the guest list? I suppose I can send a mass e-mail or something like that. You know, one that said 'just kidding, happy April Fools'.'"

"It's August," my father replied.

"Well, yeah, but these are desperate times. I have to say something!" My hand began to ache from holding the phone so tightly.

"Angie . . ."

"I have to do something before this goes too far. What if people RSVP?"

"Angie!" he bellowed. My father was not a yeller.

"What?" I asked, startled by his outburst.

"It's going to be fine. I promise."

"But she said she sent the invitations."

"Don't you worry about a thing, sweetheart. Your mother thinks she sent the invitations. I offered to mail them."

"You? You were the one who sent them." I felt like I had been keelhauled. Dad had always been the one on my side. He'd been the one who had my back.

"No." He laughed a deep tummy laugh. I could almost

see his round belly jiggling as it hung over the brown leather belt holding up his khakis. "Never fear. They are safely hidden away in my office. They will never be mailed. They will never see the light of day again. They sleep with the fishes."

I laughed at my father's jokes and suddenly felt terribly homesick. "Thank you, Daddy."

"I love you, and your mother loves you too in her own way. She misses you desperately — we both do — this was her attempt to convince you to move back here."

Tears sprang in my eyes. Before I could check it, a question popped out of my mouth. "Do you think I did something to drive Ryan away?"

"You? Never. I never cared much for that Ryan."

I knew that wasn't true. My father and Ryan had been close. They bonded over corporate America and golf. Ryan was the son my dad never had. However, it made me feel better hearing him lie to me.

"Don't worry about anything down here. I can manage your mother. I've been doing it for nearly forty years. You enjoy yourself in Holmes County. To be selfish, I don't like how far away you are, but if that's where you need to be right now, then all right. I want you to be happy." There was a pause. "Ouch."

"What's wrong?" I asked quickly.

"Oh, it's just my bum knee. I'm having surgery on it Monday."

"I didn't know that." Worry laced my voice. My father had hurt his knee over fifty years ago playing Little League baseball.

"Don't you worry. It is nothing. It's only laparoscopic surgery. I have had that before. I'm sure one day the doc will have the whole knee replaced." He laughed.

"I wish you would have told me," I said.

"You have enough to worry about. Now, put this invitation mess with your mother out of your head."

I hung up without breathing a word about the murder to either of my parents. What they didn't know wouldn't hurt them, I hoped.

Chapter Fifteen

Sunday in Millersburg was a lazy day. Half the population was in church and the other half was still in bed or watching Sunday morning cartoons. Businesses didn't open until one. After a restless night's sleep, even quilting couldn't calm me, and I put away the twelve-inch practice square Anna had given me yesterday. I didn't have the patience to concentrate on those tiny stitches. I needed to stretch my legs, and Oliver needed to work off all the treats he'd eaten since moving to Amish Country. All right, we both needed some exercise for the same reason.

I clicked the leash on Oliver's collar, and he wagged his stubby tail with excitement so hard his entire rump wiggled back and forth. I hadn't realized how much he'd missed our walks. Back in Dallas we'd walked twice a day, every day. Mostly because I lived in a high-rise apartment building with no backyard, and I needed to accommodate his potty breaks. However, since moving to Ohio, I hadn't taken him on a real walk. I'd been too consumed with getting the store up and running and then yesterday there was Joseph's death. I was a horrible doggy mama.

I walked out of the house and turned south toward the center of town. It was slow going as Oliver had to stop every five feet to sniff the ground and inhale all those foreign but lovely country smells. Before long, Oliver and I were in the center of Millersburg where Clay, also known as Route 83, and Jackson, also known as Route 39, intersected. If I drove due east on 39, I would end up in Berlin, one of the most visited Amish communities in the county. Rolling Brook was half of Berlin's size, but it was still a regular stop on the Amish bus tour circuit. I inwardly groaned as I thought about all the business I would miss. Though I had to admit that I was much better off than Joseph Walker, who was out of business permanently.

Oliver and I stopped beneath the nineteenth-century soldier's statue on the side etched with Grant's name, in front of the sandstone Holmes County Courthouse. Ulysses S. Grant was a Civil War hero, the eighteenth president, and an all-around Ohio superstar. Even though it was still early morning, the air was thick. My curls were out of control again today. I needed to invest in some Frizz-Ease fast.

As Oliver snuffled the ground, I considered my options. Sunday wasn't a good day to investigate any of my Amish leads. All of the Amish were at a church meeting in someone's house. I didn't know which house, as the location changed weekly, and it wasn't a good idea to storm into Amish services, making accusations.

I considered my suspects. Both Elijah and Benjamin were Amish and unavailable. Monday, I would talk to Benjamin at his shop. Elijah was more difficult to find. I suspected that his sister knew where he could be found if I had the chance to speak to her. After my uncle Jacob died, my aunt Eleanor was not left alone for a moment as the Amish community surrounded her. Abigail would be no different. I decided to talk to Rachel about it. I also wanted to ask her for the scoop on Sarah. There was a definite tension between the two Amish women that had more to it than Sarah's love of gossip.

While I was deep in thought, a dog barked at us from the sidewalk. Oliver stopped his snuffling and stared at the newcomer, a Boston terrier. The little but solid black-and-white dog shook with excitement as he spotted Oliver. Oliver barked a greeting. For all his fears, Oliver wasn't afraid of other dogs—at least he wasn't afraid of other dogs smaller than he was.

As cute as the Boston was, it was his human on the other end of the leash who caught my attention. Sheriff Mitchell in perfectly faded jeans and a Millersburg High School T-shirt smiled back at me. The sun reflected on the silver flecks in his hair. I believe my heart literally stopped for a second as all the moisture in my mouth evaporated. The urge to tamp down my unruly hair was almost overpowering.

"Good morning, Miss Braddock," the sheriff said as he and the little dog walked onto the courthouse green to join us.

Unable to speak, I grunted back. What, I'd lost use of speech? *Get it together, woman. This is the man who thinks you are a killer.* "Hi," I squeaked. At least it was a start.

A hint of a smile played on the sheriff's lips. "Is this your dog?"

I blinked. "My dog?"

He pointed at Oliver. "The Frenchie. Is he yours?"

"Oh, oh, yes. This is Oliver."

Mitchell took three big steps and was within an arm's length of me. He held out his hand to Oliver, and my dog buried his nose in his palm. *Stocky traitor.*

The Boston jumped up and down, and the two animals circled each other, sniffed, and touched pushed-in noses.

"I think they like each other," Mitchell said.

"Looks like it," I muttered. "What's your dog's name?"

"Tux."

I couldn't help myself. "What a cute name for a Boston."

He grinned. "I think so." He cleared his throat. "How are you doing after yesterday?"

I sighed. "Okay." I chewed on the inside of my lip. "How is Abigail?"

His face fell. "She's devastated."

I dropped my eyes as I thought how Joseph's widow must feel. Joseph was grumpy, but Abigail must have loved him. "I'm sorry to hear that."

He nodded. "The community will support her. That's the one thing about the Amish. They have the ability to come together in tragedy."

I thought about all the Amish people who were there to comfort me during Aunt Eleanor's funeral, many of whom I'd never met before and I suspected would never meet again. "I remember what an Amish funeral is like."

"That's right. Your aunt was Amish."

"Yes. The quilt shop was hers. The ruined quilt was hers." I looked down. I didn't want him to see me tear up over a quilt. It felt wrong to be so emotional about it, a material object, when a man was dead.

"So, was your family Amish?"

Either Mitchell took mercy on me or he didn't notice talk of the quilt choked me up. I bet it was the former. I doubted the seasoned law enforcement officer missed much of anything.

I tried to focus on his question. "No, my mom and Aunt Eleanor were raised in a regular English home. There is a ten-year difference between the sisters. My mother is the younger of the two. My aunt met my uncle Jacob when she was in her thirties and left her English life to marry him."

"She left everything to be with him." His voice held awe.

I met his blue-green eyes for the first time. "She really loved him. Everyone did. He was the sweetest, gentlest man you'd ever have the pleasure of meeting."

"They sound like a wonderful couple."

I broke eye contact. "They were." I frowned. "Aunt Eleanor worked so long to make the shop a success. I only had it open for one day, and it's a disaster. Maybe I should follow my mother's advice and move back to Texas."

"First of all, you can't go back to Texas while the investigation is in progress."

My skin grew hot as my head slammed back in reality. What was I doing telling the sheriff all this stuff about me? He wasn't a friend; he wasn't even an acquaintance. He was a cop who wanted to throw me behind bars.

"Second of all, you should give Holmes County a fair try before you leave," he added quickly.

"I want to, but it hasn't been the best of starts."

He laughed. "I'll give you that."

I gave him a small smile. I needed to get back on

track, which was steering the sheriff to other suspects. "Have you spoken to Abigail's brother, Elijah Knepp?"

His gaze sharpened. "Elijah?"

"He just got out of prison, didn't he? Joseph was the person responsible for him being there. Maybe he was plotting revenge all these years."

He watched me carefully. "How do you know all that?"

"I didn't get the impression that it was a secret."

He removed sunglasses from the breast pocket of his shirt and slipped them on, his beautiful aquamarine eyes hidden from sight. The neighbor with the dog was gone, and the cop was firmly back in control. "You got my message on your answering machine?"

"Yes. You said there was something I left out of my statement. I don't know what that could be. I told you everything I knew."

"Seems you were in a fight with Walker at your shop's grand reopening."

"A fight?" I yelped. "That's ridiculous. Who told you we had a fight?"

"People attending the party. They all agreed that you had an argument with Joseph Walker right in the middle of the shop."

"An argument is not a fight." I threw up my hands. "You make it sound like we started duking it out in the middle of Running Stitch."

He shrugged. "Fight, argument—it's all the same. It's motive."

My heart constricted. He *did* think I killed the woodworker. I wished he'd take those stupid sunglasses off, so I could see his eyes, and I wished I had sunglasses with me, so that I could hide mine. "How could I have killed

Joseph Walker like that? He was huge and built like a lumberjack. I'm no Minnie Mouse, but he had six inches on me and fifty pounds."

Mitchell folded his arms. "We already determined that the assailant was smaller than Walker because the cut in his throat angled up. That means it came from below."

"Well," I argued, "everyone was smaller than him, so that doesn't help much."

"It helps to know from the direction of the cut and blood spatter that the assailant was right-handed."

Reflexively, I hid my hand behind my back. "Right."

He held up his hand. "Before you say it, I will. Most people are right-handed."

"Elijah Knepp is smaller than Joseph and went to prison for arson for burning down a barn."

Mitchell sighed.

"Was anyone hurt in the barn fire?"

"No." He crossed his arms. "Some livestock was lost."

"Why did he do it?"

The sheriff grimaced. "That we never fully discovered. He claimed it was an accident. He said he knocked over a lantern on a hay bale. It's possible. It's happened before within the Amish communities."

"If it was an accident, then why was he sent to prison?"

"Because the place was doused with kerosene before the fire."

"The fire was deliberate." I paused. "How long was he in prison?"

"Thirty months," Mitchell clipped.

"That's a long time," I said.

Mitchell stuck his hands in his jeans pockets. "It is."

"Then why are you talking to me? You should be talking to Elijah. He has a *much* better motive than I do."

"I plan on speaking with him." His jaw twitched.

I gave a little sigh of relief. So I wasn't Mitchell's only suspect. That was excellent news. "What about Benjamin Hershberger?"

Mitchell removed his sunglasses and stared at me. His blue-green eyes were like electric beams, which I couldn't look away from even if they burned my retina. "What are you up to? Are you meddling in my investigation?"

Meddling? Me?

I cleared my throat. "Of course not." I paused. "But I thought you may need some help finding more suspect options. You know, other than me."

"Miss Braddock, I have been the sheriff of Holmes County for ten years. Before that, I was a chief of the Millersburg Police Department. I know what I'm doing."

I stepped back and butted into the cement mount holding the stone soldier in place. "There's no reason to take it personally."

Mitchell tugged on Tux's leash. "Come, Tux."

The dog gave Oliver a forlorn look, and the two touched noses one more time. I wish it were that easy for humans.

"Hey," I said. "When are you bringing the statement by my house?"

He checked his watch. "I'll be there in two hours. Do me a favor," the county sheriff said. "You worry about quilts, and I will worry about who killed Joseph Walker." He led a disappointed Tux away from Oliver and me. Oliver whimpered as he watched his new playmate go.

"I'll stop worrying about Joseph Walker if you promise not to arrest me!" I cried after Mitchell.

He appraised me over his shoulder. "That, Angela Braddock, formerly of Dallas, Texas, I cannot do."

I watched Mitchell and Tux cross the street and make their way up Jackson. I gritted my teeth. "If that's the case," I said barely above a whisper, "then, you have given me no choice but to meddle."

Chapter Sixteen

At last Tux and Mitchell were completely out of sight. Oliver gave a long doggy sigh.

I patted the top of his head. "Sorry, buddy. I chased your new friend away by asking too many questions."

He barked softly.

I marched down Clay Street, playing my conversation with the sheriff over and over again in my head. Why wouldn't he admit that it was *very* unlikely that I killed Joseph Walker? I guessed he learned to take the hard line in cop school. At least I had the foresight to talk to Harvey the day before. The next time Mitchell got on my nerves, I'd tell him to "talk to my lawyer." I'd always wanted to say that anyway.

I paused at a bookshop and peered into the window. Next to the bookstore, a refinished park bench with ivy vines stenciled along the back sat in front of the neighboring shop's display window, along with a wheelbarrow full of odds and ends, a small wooden ladder, and an old push mower. A plastic container of metal weather vanes stood next to the shop's front door. It was an antiques shop called Out of Time, Jessica Nicolson's shop.

The sign in the window said that hours were one to five on Sundays. It wasn't even ten in the morning yet. I peeked through the window and saw a very fat gray cat lying next to the cash register across the counter. Jessica was at the counter counting out bills. I tapped on the glass. She jumped and dollar bills went flying into the air.

This perked up the cat some. At least she opened her eyes for half a second to watch the money flutter to the floor. With hurried motions, Jessica collected the bills and shoved them back into the cash drawer. Then, she strode across the shop, weaving in and around the maze of antiques toward the front door.

I heard the lock turn.

"I'm so sorry I startled you like that," I said in a rush. "Oliver and I were out for a walk and came upon your store. I remembered you asked me to stop by sometime. I can come back when you open."

"No, no reason for that." She sniffled.

I squinted at her. Her eyes were red rimmed and her cheeks pasty white. "Are you okay?"

She stepped back and let Oliver and me into the shop. Upon entering I was almost skewered by a suit of armor holding an ax.

"Don't mind Knight Richard here." She removed a crumpled tissue from her pocket and touched it to her eye.

My mouth hung open. "Where did you come across that?" There were no medieval castles in Holmes County, that was for sure.

"Oh, I bought it at an estate sale in Akron. It belonged to one of those old tire tycoons that used to run the big rubber plants up there. It cost me a bundle too, but I always wanted a suit of armor. I doubt I'd ever have another chance to have one." She patted Knight Richard on the arm.

"So it's not for sale?"

She smiled more broadly. "Everything in the shop is for sale for the right price. Are you interested in my knight? He's no trouble, probably the best man you can find in Holmes County."

"No thanks," I said, thinking that I had enough man trouble in my life as it was, if I counted Ryan and Sheriff Mitchell. I grimaced to myself. Sheriff Mitchell wasn't man trouble. He wasn't to be thought of like a man, as in someone who might spark my interest. He was a cop ready to send me to the pokey.

"Did I say something wrong?" she asked.

I stepped all the way into the shop, edging away from the knight while Oliver disappeared under a coffee table. "Oliver, you come back here."

"He's all right." She closed the door. "My cats weave in and out of the antiques all the time."

I wasn't so sure. Ever heard of a bull in a china shop? I didn't think a bulldog in an antiques shop could have that much better of an effect. "Will my dog upset your cats by being here in the store?"

"They will hide from him. Is he used to cats?"

I nodded. "He's been around them since he was a puppy. My parents back in Texas have two Persians. Oliver gets along with them fine."

"Persians are gorgeous cats." Jessica's eyes glanced back and forth around the room. "I wish I had a place for you to sit, but there was a big estate sale last weekend in Canton, and I'm still unpacking everything. So things are" — she paused — "tight. You will have to excuse the mess."

I sidestepped a rocking chair that was full of cast-iron pots. "If you need help organizing, I'm happy to pitch in. There's not much else I can do for the next few days."

Her expression was pinched, and her eyes watered. "Yes, I heard about that."

"Are you all right?" I asked.

"Oh, it's just allergies. It's always so dusty in here." She laughed halfheartedly.

Allergies? I wasn't buying it.

"If you don't mind standing, I can pour you a cup of coffee. I made a fresh pot. I'll never be able to drink it all."

"I'd love some." Mentally, I added, *I'd love some information too.*

Jessica wove between and around the antiques with practiced ease. I took two steps and an ornate candelabra stabbed me in the hip. I winced as I edged around the sharp metal piece.

Jessica's coffeepot was on a small card table behind the cash counter. A collection of porcelain clown dolls was also on the table. I did my best to ignore the creepy-happy smiles and painted faces. I liked clowns as much as Oliver liked birds, maybe less. Jessica poured coffee into a mug shaped like a cow. She slid it across the counter to me and filled her own mug, a chicken. At least it wasn't a clown mug.

"If you think this is bad, you should see the back room. It's even worse in there but worth it. I bought some lovely pieces, and they should move quickly out of the store if I can find the place to show them off. Thank you for your offer of help. I may take you up on it."

"Does your shop get a lot of business?"

"The shop does all right, especially in the summer and weekends when folks are in town to visit the Amish shops and businesses. But I do most of my sales online through my Web site."

I perked up. "How does it work? I'm hoping to do that same thing. I think it would be a great way to sell quilts."

She nodded. "It would be. I'm sure there are a lot of customers across the country that would love to have Amish-made quilts but can't make it to an Amish community to purchase them. Occasionally, I run across an antique quilt that I can sell at Out of Time. The antique Amish quilts always get a nice price. They can be hard to come by too. Most of the old Amish quilts are rags today. Before the tourists came, quilts were made for the practical purpose to keep the owner warm. Selling through your Web site is an excellent idea."

I nodded. "I think so too."

"When you are ready to set up your Web site, let me know, and I can show you what I did."

"Thank you. I'd really appreciate that." I smiled.

The gray cat opened one eye and closed it. "Who's this?"

"That's Cherry Cat. As you can see, she's very pregnant. I have two other cats, Melon and Berry. You might not see them while you're here. They are more reclusive than Cherry." She waved her arms around. "As your Oliver discovered, there are many places to hide in the shop. I've only had Cherry for two weeks, and she thinks that she runs the place and somehow convinced Melon and Berry of that too." She laughed.

I scratched the cat between the ears. Her fur was short and soft; it felt like velvet. "She's beautiful."

"I think she is a Russian Blue, or at least part Russian Blue. She doesn't have any papers, so I will never know for sure."

The cat leaned into my touch and purred so loudly I wondered if a passerby would hear her out on the street.

"I'm part of the foster kitty program with the shelter here in Millersburg. They found Cherry a few weeks ago hiding under a bush beside the courthouse. I'm one of the few foster homes willing to take a pregnant mother in. She's such a good girl, though, I plan to adopt her for good. That's how I got Berry and Melon too. They started as foster kitties."

"When are the kittens due?"

"The vet said any day now. I've been keeping my eye on her to see if she starts building a nest somewhere. I have a box in the back where she can have the kittens. Hopefully, I can catch her when it's the time. There are a lot of places in this shop to hide a kitten. If she has her babies somewhere on the floor of the shop, it will be nearly impossible for me to find them until she is good and ready to show me where they are."

I believed her. Plastic crates of vinyl records sat on top of Art Deco tables, fishing poles leaned against an old-fashioned gumball machine, and a lady's bicycle circa 1930 hung from the ceiling, held by thick steel hooks. "I can see why you wouldn't want her to wander off. I think I could get lost in here too."

"You wouldn't want a kitten, would you?" Despite the redness around her eyes, they twinkled with the prospect of finding one of her wards a good home.

I shook my head. "No, Oliver is more than enough for me."

Jessica nodded, but I got the impression that she wouldn't give up that easily in finding Cherry Cat's babies good homes.

I cleared my throat. "Really, I can't take on a new pet

right now. I assume you heard what happened at my quilt shop yesterday."

Tears gathered in the corners of her eyes. "I did." She wiped at her eyes with the back of her hand.

"Jessica, there's something wrong. You can't tell me your reaction is just allergies."

A tear rolled down her cheek and fell from her chin. She didn't bother to wipe this one away. "I'm sorry."

I was taken aback. "There's nothing to be sorry for."

She clutched her coffee mug in her hands. It was a wonder she didn't burn her palms. "It's such a horrible, horrible thing to happen here of all places."

Was Jessica upset because of the shock or was it something more? I suspected the latter. "I found Joseph."

Her eyes doubled in size. "I didn't know that. I'm so sorry."

My gruesome discovery yesterday flashed across my mind's eye once again. I hoped one day I would be able to forget it. "Danny was with me when I found the body."

"My cousin Danny?" She wrinkled her nose. "I hope he behaved himself."

I arched my brow. "For the most part. Do you expect him to misbehave?"

Jessica sighed. "I hate to speak ill of him, and our grandmother would wallop me a good one if she thought I was demeaning Danny—he always was her favorite— but I would watch what you say around him. That's all."

Between Sarah and Danny, I had to watch what I said around several people in Holmes County. Before it popped out of my mouth, I stopped myself from telling Jessica about the photos that Danny took of Joseph's body. I bet the sheriff would not appreciate if I shared that information, and I'd like to stay on his good side as much as possible.

"I'm sure Danny is chomping at the bit to follow this story. And the biggest story ever to come out of Rolling Brook. He might even get the attention from the big daily newspapers that he wants so badly." Her tone was surprisingly bitter. "He doesn't care about the family involved."

"You mean Abigail and her daughters?" I asked.

She looked at me with a start. "Y-yes, that's who I meant."

"His wife is devastated."

"I imagine so." She took a tissue from the box sitting on the counter. "And those poor girls."

I set a mug of coffee on a tabletop pool table. "How do you know Joseph?"

She straightened a line of porcelain clown dolls. I could hardly look at them. They freaked me out that much.

She smoothed a clown's shirt. "I know him as well as anyone else in the county."

"I think you know him better than that," I said.

One the clowns toppled forward on its face and she righted it. "What do you mean? Holmes County is small. After you've lived here a while, you will know everyone knows everyone else."

"When you left the quilt shop and almost ran into Joseph, you looked upset."

"I hate to run into anyone like that. I could have knocked him down."

I cocked an eyebrow at her. Joseph was twice her size. If anyone was going to get knocked down on impact, it would be her. "Most people aren't as visibly upset when they run into a neighbor about town."

She abandoned the clowns and crossed her arms. "I thought you were raised in the South. Shouldn't you be more polite, then? Or are things different where you come from?"

I took a step back, away from her hostility. An icy feeling crawled up my back. Could Jessica be involved in the murder? "I never fit in all that well in the South." My voice was matter-of-fact.

Much to my relief, she chuckled. "I'm sorry. I don't know what came over me."

"I think Joseph came over you," I said, relieved that the counter was between us. I could make a dash for the door if need be, but what about Oliver?

"I think you should go. I need to get ready for the shop to open." She reopened the cash drawer and began smoothing out the bills that had flown into the air when I rapped on the window.

"Did he hurt you somehow?" I asked.

She spun around. "No, never. Joseph would never hurt anyone. He was an upright man. He always did the right thing. Always. Some may not have liked his methods."

"What methods would those be?"

"Joseph believed firmly in his order's rules. He thought they were the only way to live. Anyone who didn't obey the rules was judged."

"He sounds rigid—I mean more rigid than even an average Amish man."

She squeezed the dollar bill in her hand. "He wasn't always that way. When he was younger and in *rumspringa*, he was different. We—we were friends. We spent many happy hours together. He was interested in my English ways."

Hmmm, interested in her English ways? I wondered. "Were you a couple?"

She winced and resumed straightening the money. "We were, but it was such a long time ago."

"Was it serious?"

Tears gathered in her eyes. "I thought so, and maybe he even thought so for a while. He even talked about leaving the Amish so we could be together."

"Why did he change his mind?" I tried to keep my tone gentle. I didn't want to break our rapport and lose this newest bit of information about the stern Amish man I found with my aunt's ruined quilt.

"One night, his mother was lost. One of the cows on the farm got loose. No one was home. Joseph's father was in another town on a construction job, and Joseph was with me. The other children were too small. She went after the cow. It was during the blizzard and she lost her way." A tear ran down Jess's cheek. "They found her three days later. She died in the storm."

"I'm so sorry."

She laughed bitterly. "The cow had come back the same night it ran away." Her voice became choked. "His mother died that night, and he was with me."

"You can't blame yourself for that."

"Joseph blamed himself. He wasn't there when his mother needed him. He never forgave himself for that. He was baptized the next week and never spoke to me again. Everything changed in an instant. I had no idea what was going on." She pressed the crumpled tissue to her eyes again. "I finally found out from one of his Amish friends what had happened. By that time he was already baptized, and it was too late."

"That's terrible."

"I can't blame him. He followed his convictions." She straightened her shoulders. "It showed me the kind of man he was. He put his family and culture before himself."

I shifted uncomfortably. "You haven't spoken to him after all these years."

"It's been over thirty years. He hadn't spoken a word to me since the day his mother died."

"Does Danny know about your past relationship with Joseph?"

"He's so much younger than me. He was only a small child during that time." She dusted the counter with a dry rag. "No one in my family knew. No one in his family knew. We both kept it a secret. Neither family would have approved."

I thought for a minute. That had to be painful, and I thought about a motive for murder. Thirty years of abandonment and resentment brewing could have caused Jessica to lash out. Maybe seeing Joseph at the grand reopening was the last straw. It sent her over the edge. I set my mug on the counter and stepped back.

Cherry Cat sighed contently. Then again, it was hard for me to see anyone who would agree to be a foster cat owner to be a cold-blooded killer. I had to ask the question. "I take it the police don't know your history with Joseph either."

She looked up sharply. "No, they don't. Do you plan to tell them?"

I avoided the question. "Where were you the night that Joseph was murdered?"

Her face fell as if she decided something about me and didn't like it. "I was at the Millersburg No Kill Shelter. It was my turn to spend the night there with the animals."

"Was anyone there with you?"

She sighed. "Do the animals count?"

I sighed. "No."

"Then, no." She blew her nose. "I'm sorry. I didn't know that I'd react this way. I hadn't seen Joseph face-to-face in such a long time until I visited Running Stitch—we'd avoided each other for years—and then I find out the next day he died in the same store. It's too much."

Suddenly a yowl that could have awakened the dead cut through the silence in the shop. Oliver barked. Then, a crash as a vase fell from its precarious perch on the top of a bookshelf.

Woof! Woof!

An orange streak jumped over an urn sitting on a chest of drawers and flew into the back of the shop. Oliver was in pursuit. I grabbed him by the collar. "Oliver Braddock! Look at the mess you made."

Jessica hurried around the corner and pushed the urn back from the edge of the chest of drawers with her finger.

The orange cat reappeared and leapt to the top of another bookcase. He glared at Oliver and hissed. Oliver fainted dead away.

"Is your dog okay?"

I sighed. "He does this when he gets too worked up. The vet insists that it's nothing to worry about. There's nothing physically wrong with him. Do you have any water?"

She skirted back around the counter and handed me a half-full bottle of spring water. I opened the bottle and splashed some on Oliver's face.

He blinked at me, and then shook his face. His jowls sent water flying in all directions, including on me. I squatted next to him. "It's okay, boy. The kitty's not going to hurt you."

He examined my face as if unconvinced and closed his eyes.

The orange cat hissed from his perch.

Jessica laughed. "Oliver found Melon after all." Watching the animals' antics seemed to lighten her mood.

I tapped Oliver's cheeks. He opened one eye. He hadn't fainted. He faked it in the name of self-preservation. He played possum. I stood. "I'm so sorry about that. I can pay for the vase."

She shook her head. "Don't worry about it. It wasn't a real Ming."

Thank heavens for that.

She blushed. "Thank you for listening. It helped to tell someone about Joseph and me after all this time. You're right. I have to be more careful and not show his death has affected me. If you, who I just met, picked up on it, others are bound to too."

"You're welcome," I said, feeling guilt tickle at my heart. I hadn't asked those questions to comfort her. I'd asked them to find yet another viable suspect to hand on a silver platter to Sheriff Mitchell with a nice calligraphically written note that said, "See all these people who wanted to knock off Joseph Walker, and you're wasting your time on little old me."

Chapter Seventeen

As I left Out of Time, I wondered, *Will I still be pining over Ryan thirty years from now?* The idea made me nauseous. Maybe that was another good reason I left Texas. Maybe if I had still been in Dallas and saw Ryan often, he would be harder to get over. My mother would love it if I died of a broken heart. The funeral would be the event of the season. She could easily cross out "wedding" on all the invitations and replace it with "memorial." It would have the flair of the dramatic that she desired.

When Oliver and I got back home, he wiggled out the doggy door into the backyard.

I watched him through the kitchen window for a few minutes. He snuffled at the ground. The cinnamon roll sat inside its box on the counter. I still hadn't eaten it. Sounded like a good lunch to me. I poured myself a glass of milk, opened the box, and froze. There was a huge bite out of the bun. I hadn't bitten into it—and neither had Oliver. There was no way that he could reach the box on the counter and the bite was from a human's mouth, not a dog's. Someone had been inside my house.

Oliver. I grabbed the broom and rushed into the

backyard. Nothing appeared out of the ordinary in the yard, but I still walked around the perimeter with my broom held in attack position. My next-door neighbor, an elderly woman I'd yet to meet, trimmed her roses. Her eyes widened, and she scurried into her house as I stomped by. Good. Maybe she would spread the word that I was armed and dangerous.

I sat on the concrete steps leading into the kitchen and watched Oliver dig in the garden. I half turned and pushed in on his doggy door. It moved easily. I needed to do something about it. *Was this how the pastry mangler entered?* It would have to be a very small person, but I wasn't taking any chances. I could call Mr. Gooding to take care of it, but I was unwilling to wait. The problem had to be fixed immediately.

I stood and pulled my tool kit out from under the kitchen sink. The kit was a moving gift from my father, since he'd said he wouldn't be close by to be my handyman. The toolbox was pink, the tape measure was pink, and all the tools had pink handles. I removed the hammer and a box of nails from the toolbox and carried them outside. Leaving the door all the way open, I sat back on the step.

Thwack! Thwack! Thwack! I sent the nail through the rubber doggy door into the wooden door itself. The nail bent and fell on the concrete block.

Oliver barked.

"I know you like your doggy door, but it's not safe. When the killer's in the slammer, we can reopen it."

He whimpered.

I sighed and picked another nail from the box. Thwack! Thwack! That nail bent too.

Oliver barked sharply, and I glanced up from my DIY project, convinced I would find a wild man with a rotary cutter in my backyard. Instead I saw Sheriff Mitchell standing at the gate. His faded jeans were gone and he was back in cop clothes, although he didn't look any less handsome. "What are you doing?" He carried a clipboard in his hand.

I jumped up from the cement step. "I'm trying to close Oliver's doggy door."

"Why?"

"You may know there is a murderer on the loose, and he might be coming after me." Tears threatened at the corners of my eyes. Some were from fear of a cold-blooded killer, and some were the result of my incompetence with a hammer. "And he ate my cinnamon bun."

"Your what?"

"My cinnamon bun. Rachel gave it to me yesterday after I found—well, you know—and I just opened the box. There's a huge bite out of it."

"Are you sure you didn't eat it? No midnight snacking?"

"Of course, I'm sure," I snapped.

"Show it to me."

I led him into the house and pointed at the bakery box on the counter like it was exhibit A in a murder case. Who knew? Maybe it would be. Conviction by sugary pastry.

"I'm going to take this with me when I leave."

"Are you going to test it for DNA or something?"

He stopped short of rolling his eyes. "Or something." Mitchell held out his hand. "Give me the hammer."

I handed it to him and followed him back outside.

He squatted in front of the door, placed his clipboard on the ground, and pulled four nails from the box. Mitchell held up the nails for me to see. "These are to hang pictures, not for major construction."

"I doubt my dad thought I would need to fortify a doggy door when he bought them."

Mitchell grimaced and held three of the nails in his mouth. With one thwack of the hammer he drove the first nail home. The three other nails were in place with three more strikes of the hammer. He stood and gave the hammer back to me.

Oliver barked. Mitchell scratched him between the ears. "I bet you didn't like that, did you, buddy?"

I tried to tear my eyes away from Mitchell, but I watched his every move. He caught me staring and smiled. He picked up the clipboard. "I brought you a copy of your statement. You can read through it while I check out your house." He gazed at me with those aquamarine eyes.

"Yes," I murmured with my legs feeling like molded Jell-O. *Get a grip, Angie.* I cleared my throat. "Yes, I have nothing to hide."

He nodded. "Good."

I stepped around him and opened the door to the kitchen. Oliver shot through and landed on his pillow under the table. Mitchell laughed.

"How long will this take?" I asked.

"Just a few minutes. I'll start on the second floor."

I sat at the kitchen table to read over my statement. As I reviewed it, I was distracted by the sound of Mitchell moving around in the rooms upstairs.

When he came into the kitchen, I stood up. "Find anything?"

He shook his head. "That's good news for you."

"What were you looking for?"

"Why didn't you tell me about the deed?" he countered with his own question.

"Deed?" I squeaked.

Mitchell folded his arms across his chest. "Don't pretend you don't know what I'm talking about."

I tilted my chin up. "I wasn't pretending. How did you find out about it?"

"Since you haven't been that forthcoming as to why Joseph Walker was inside your shop, I asked other sources."

"Who?"

"That's not important. What is important is we have a plausible reason as to why Joseph was inside Running Stitch in the middle of the night when the rest of the county was asleep."

"You think he went in there looking for the deed?"

"It's still missing, isn't it?"

Reluctantly, I nodded.

"Have you been searching for it?"

"Yes. The quilting ladies have too. We can't find it anywhere. If that's why Joseph went into the store, it was for nothing. I searched every nook and cranny of that shop. The deed's not there."

"If Joseph found it first, what would that mean?"

I squirmed. "I guess it depended on how honest he was."

The corners of the sheriff's mouth tilted up into an ironic smile. "In my experience, if someone is breaking into another person's place of business in the middle of the night, they aren't doing it to do that person any favors."

"So Joseph was there to find the deed," I paused, "and destroy it. Without the deed, I can't prove the shop is really mine."

"Right."

"That still doesn't explain the other person, the killer, in the shop."

He swallowed. "It would if that other person was you."

A chill ran the length of my body. "It wasn't."

He frowned as if considering what to say next.

I had to convince the sheriff there were other options. "Did you find any other fingerprints in the stockroom?"

He frowned. "No, and there were no fingerprints on the back door or murder weapon. The killer wore gloves and wiped the cutters clean for good measure."

My face fell. "Can I get back into the store? I left some items I need inside Running Stitch. It would only take me a minute to go inside and grab them."

He sighed. "What would that be?"

I thought quickly. "Some business files. I'm expecting some deliveries this week, and I want to call the companies and make arrangements for them to deliver them to my house."

He was quiet for a full minute.

"Well?"

"I'm mulling this over."

Mulling, really?

"Not getting these files will be detrimental to my business," I said, shooting for a concerned business owner.

That wasn't entirely true. I could probably find everything I needed online at home, but I wasn't going to tell the sheriff that. I needed to get inside Running Stitch.

"I won't be able to let you in today." He paused. "I have a prior engagement."

Was that code for date?

"That's okay," I said, trying to keep my voice light. "I can go in myself. I have my key, and it's clo—"

"No." His voice sharpened. "You can't go into Running Stitch alone. If you do, you will be in serious trouble."

O-kay.

"Then, what am I supposed to do, Sheriff?" The lightness was gone from my voice. "I need those files."

He sighed. I had a feeling he had been doing that a lot more since he met me. He continued, "Deputy Anderson is on duty today. I will give him a call, and he'll meet you in front of the shop. Depending on where he is in the county, it may take him up to an hour to get there. Do not go inside until he gets there. Understood?"

"Understood," I said.

"Good," he said. "When Anderson lets you inside, you're banned from the stockroom. That area is strictly off-limits. I hope your *files* aren't inside there, because if they are, that's tough."

He said *files* as if he didn't believe my excuse for reentering the shop. The nerve of him, to doubt me. "Thank you, Sheriff." I handed him the clipboard.

"You're welcome," he said.

"Thank you for fixing the doggy door too."

He watched me. "I won't let anything happen to you, Angie. I promise."

Before I could react, he slipped out of the back door with the bakery box in hand.

After Mitchell left, Oliver and I went straight to Running Stitch. Rolling Brook's main drag was completely still. There wasn't a car, a buggy, or even another human being on the street. All the shops were closed on Sunday, including Miller's Amish Bakery. I parked my car in the spot in front of the quilt shop. I glanced at Oliver. "We could have totally been in and out of the shop by now.

We will remember for next time we have the hankering to break and enter, okay?"

He barked agreement.

Sugartree Street wasn't completely peaceful, I decided as I climbed out of the car, and Oliver hopped onto the pavement beside me. Yellow crime-scene tape crisscrossed the front door of Running Stitch in an angry yellow *X*. I wondered if I should have brought my broom with me.

Oliver whimpered. His sympathetic pushed-in face always cheered me up. "I don't think this is what Aunt Eleanor thought would happen when she left me the shop."

Part of me wanted to sit safely inside my SUV until Officer Anderson showed up, but a stronger part of me knew this might be my only chance to get a peek inside Joseph's shop. I snuck around the side of the store through a narrow alley between my quilt shop and the woodworking shop that was only the width of a person.

A waist-high white fence surrounded the back of the quilt shop's property, but there was no such fence behind the woodworker's place. An eave connected to the woodworker's building hung back about ten feet into the yard; it was held up by two thick wooden posts. Underneath the eave was the outdoor version of Joseph's workshop. Sawdust covered the cement block floor, and lathes, sanders, and table saws waited at the ready. A vise held a half-completed chair leg in a death grip. A piece of sandpaper lay on the workbench beside the vise, as if the user only stepped away from the project for a minute with every intention of coming back. Had Joseph been sanding the chair leg before he went into my shop and met his end?

Was Mitchell right? Was Joseph searching for the deed? I had to admit it was the only reason I could think of that explained why Joseph was inside the quilt shop. Did he meet someone there? Did that someone kill him?

I let Oliver into Running Stitch's yard through the gate. "Stay," I told him.

He seemed unconcerned and ran off to dig up Aunt Eleanor's flower garden.

I stood still and listened for the sound of Deputy Anderson's approaching patrol car. Hearing nothing, I inched on the woodworker's property. I walked under the eave to the back door of the shop. Cupping my hands beside my eyes, I peered inside. It was too dark to see anything. Disappointed, I stepped back.

Bang! Something fell to the ground to my left. I jumped three feet in the air and knocked over a half-completed end table. The table couldn't hold my weight, and one of its legs broke off as it crashed to the ground with me on top of it.

I caught my breath as I rolled onto my back. I froze at the sounds of footsteps running down the alley.

Chapter Eighteen

My heart pounded so loudly in my ears, I didn't hear other footsteps approaching. "Miss Braddock, what on earth are you doing?"

I blinked from my position flat on my back to find Deputy Anderson standing above me with his gun drawn. Slowly, I sat up. "Can you help me up?"

He lowered the gun and seemed to consider my request.

"What are you going to do? Shoot me? Put the gun away, please."

The young officer holstered his gun and gave me his hand.

I wiped the sawdust from my backside. "Did you see the guy running away?"

Anderson's eyes flicked around as if he expected the bogeyman to jump out. "Guy? What guy?"

"The guy that was just here two seconds ago."

"Did you see someone?"

My face grew hot. "No, but I heard the person run away back down the alley."

He crossed his arms. "I came from the alley and I didn't see anyone."

I gritted my teeth. "I know I heard something."

"Maybe it was a raccoon."

"I don't think so. Unless it was a raccoon on steroids," I muttered.

His eyes narrowed. "What are you doing over here? The sheriff said you'd be waiting for me out front."

Think fast, Angie.

"I, well, I came over here to see if anyone was in the woodworker's shop. I wanted to give my condolences to the family." I smiled sweetly.

His brow furrowed. "It's Sunday. There ain't anyone in Rolling Brook on Sunday."

As if I didn't know, I laughed. "I'm from Texas, remember?"

"Isn't that the Bible Belt? Wouldn't you know about keeping the Sabbath?"

"Well, sure, but that doesn't stop us from going shopping."

The young officer watched me for a minute, and then, his shoulders relaxed as he seemed to accept my answer. I realized that it was a very good thing that the sheriff had another engagement because he never would have bought my story.

"Can we go into Running Stitch?" I asked.

"All right. The sheriff said you needed some files."

"That's right."

"And you are not going into the stockroom."

What, the sheriff didn't trust me, so he had to tell his officer about my no-stockroom order? Huh.

Rustling came from the quilt shop's garden. Anderson put his hand on his holster.

"Calm down, cowboy. It's my dog." I walked over to the white picket fence. "Oliver!"

My little black-and-white dog backed out of the bushes rear end first.

Anderson relaxed.

I opened the back gate. "Let's go in this way."

Anderson hesitated. "You don't want to go in the front."

"Won't that disturb the crime-scene tape? You would have to fix it after we go inside. Back here," I said reasonably, "you don't have to worry about that."

"Oh, you're right," he said.

I walked through the gate, and Anderson followed while I rifled through my purse for the shop key.

"Your dog is going to have to stay outside."

"I think he's happier out here." I pointed to Oliver's rump sticking out from under the azalea bush.

Anderson smiled. He wasn't so bad. Having a gullible cop around in this case was a bonus.

I removed the key from my purse and unlocked the door. It swung inward.

"Wait," Anderson said. "Let me go in first."

"Of course." I stepped out of his way.

The officer went into the shop. I stood on the threshold. From my vantage point, I could see the door to the stockroom was closed. It was so close, if I reached out my hand, I would touch it.

"Come on in," he said.

I moved inside. The short hall was dark, but I could see the light coming in from the front window in the main part of the shop. It took all I had not to throw open the stockroom door and look inside. Not because I wanted to see the place Joseph died or remember what he looked like in death, but so that I could search for clues. There had to be something in that stockroom that would give me a clue to who the killer was.

In the semidarkness of the shop, shadows danced on the floor. "Can we turn on the overhead light?" I asked.

"Oh, yeah, I guess so," the deputy replied. He flicked on the switch by the front door. The shadows disappeared as the room was bathed in electric light. I wondered how the Amish functioned without electric lighting. Were they unafraid of shadows?

The shop looked undisturbed. There was no evidence that the police, EMTs, and goodness knew who else were inside the shop the day before. The sheriff ran a neat ship.

"We can't stay in here very long, Miss Braddock," Anderson said.

"Right." I hurried over to the cash register and opened one of the drawers under the counter. Inside was my calendar and address book. I sighed as I glanced at all the appointments that would have to be canceled for the next week: the phone guy, the Internet, and even the quilting circle. Perhaps we could move the quilting circle to another location, like Anna's house again or maybe even my own house.

Officer Anderson's radio crackled. "Anderson? This is dispatch."

"I need to take this," he said.

The radio crackled again. "The reception is bad inside here. I need to take this outside. Are you almost done?"

"Yes, I need a few more files."

He hesitated, but the voice on the radio was sharp. "Anderson, do you copy?"

He removed the radio from his belt. "I copy. Go ahead, dispatch."

He hurried down the hall and outside into the tiny back garden. I grabbed the rest of the files from the drawer, and anything else I thought I might need, and shoved them in my large hobo-style purse. I hurried back to the hallway. Through the open back door, I saw Anderson pacing as he spoke to dispatch. It was an opportunity, but I wouldn't have much time. I got my phone from my purse and opened the stockroom door. The sheriff's department already collected the fingerprints they needed from the scene—mine. I turned on the light. Joseph, the destroyed quilt, and the entire box of fabric cutters were gone. There was a deep red stain in the middle of the hardwood floor. I didn't have enough time to take it all in. I held up my smartphone, and I snapped as many photos as I could.

"Miss Braddock?" Anderson's voice floated through the back door.

In one motion, I hit the stockroom lights and shut the door. I backed up and stumbled into the closest hiding place I could find: the bathroom.

Anderson stepped into the shop. "Miss Braddock?" he called again. This time his voice had a hint of urgency.

I took a deep breath, dropped my cell phone to the bottom of my purse, and turned on the faucet. There was a fine layer of fingerprinting powder on my hands from touching the door. I pumped soap onto my hands. "I'm in the bathroom," I called. I opened the door with a big smile. "I'm so sorry. Nature called."

The deputy's face turned the color of a beet. "Oh, oh, I'm sorry."

"Ready to go?"

He seemed relieved that I dropped the bathroom talk. "Are you? Did you get everything that you need?"

I patted the side of my purse. "Yep. Thanks so much for coming out here to do this. I really appreciate it."

He nodded. "Okay, then."

We stepped back into the garden. I slapped my thigh. "Oliver."

The dog ran over, and I pulled his leash from the enormous purse and snapped it onto his collar. Officer Anderson held the gate open for us. "If you need anything else from the shop, don't hesitate to call the department."

I smiled brightly. "The sheriff will be the first person I call." *When I find the real killer.*

That night, I downloaded the pictures I'd taken in the stockroom onto my computer. They were grainy and dark when blown up to the full size of the computer screen. Other than a good shot of the large bloodstain in the middle of the floor, I couldn't make anything out. I powered down the laptop in frustration. The only thing I accomplished by going into Running Stitch Sunday was making the sheriff more suspicious of me. That I didn't need to do—he was plenty suspicious on his own.

Chapter Nineteen

I spent four hours Monday morning on the phone with delivery companies, the phone company, and my suppliers. Each and every one put me on call waiting for an average of twenty minutes. If I heard one more note of smooth jazz, I would scream.

After the last frustrating call was made and all my appointments or deliveries were rescheduled or suspended—at least I hoped that they were—I was ready to venture out. So was Oliver.

"Ollie, you're going to have to stay home today," I told the Frenchie. "Mommy needs to do some sleuthing, and I don't want you to be in any danger. No one can get you in here."

He pawed at the doggy door. "I know you want that to open, but I can't do it. Something might happen to you."

Oliver cocked his head in an obvious plea for me to change my mind. That was not going to happen. It was after eleven in the morning, and the first stop I planned to make was Benjamin Hershberger's woodworking shop in Rolling Brook. If he was anything like his protégé, Joseph Walker, I knew he would not approve of a canine on his property.

I rolled my little SUV down Sugartree Street and parked in the community parking lot. Sunday the town had dozed through the hot summer afternoon. Now on Monday, Amish shopkeepers and English tourists strolled up and down the street. Buggies and minivans parked in the diagonal parking spaces that lined either side of the road. Rachel's sister-in-law Mattie stood outside the bakery shaking crumbs out of a white linen tablecloth. As I strolled up the street from the parking lot, I waved at her. She eyed me but did not return my wave.

Running Stitch was the one place that ruined the picturesque landscape, as the yellow crime-scene tape was still firmly in place. Two elderly ladies in Capri pants, flowered blouses, and walking shoes stood in front of the quilt shop.

"This is a disappointment," the lady wearing the teal visor said. "We made special plans to come to Rolling Brook today because we heard that it had reopened."

I winced.

"I know, Opal." Her companion patted her arm.

Part of me was tempted to slink away, but the business owner in me gave that part a swift kick in the pants. These were potential customers, and I needed to pay attention to them. I straightened my shoulders. "Can I help you, ladies?"

The pair turned in my direction. Opal nodded. "Yes, we want to know why this shop is closed. What is the crime-scene tape across the door? We drove all the way here from Akron to buy more fabric and thread for our quilts and our trip is wasted."

"I'm Angela Braddock, the shop owner."

"You're not Amish," the one holding the large cat-face-printed purse said.

"No. I inherited the shop from my aunt. She was Amish."

Opal squinted at me. "You're Eleanor's niece?"

I nodded.

Opal stepped closer to me and examined my face. "I guess I do see some resemblance around the eyes."

"Maybe," her friend agreed. "What happened?"

"There was an accident," I said. "Unfortunately, we will be closed for a few days because of it. I'm so sorry you drove all this way to be disappointed." I reached into my purse for a pad of paper. "Let me write you out a note so that the next time you visit, you will get a discount."

Quickly, I wrote a twenty percent coupon for each of them, dated it, and signed my name at the bottom. I handed them each one of my on-the-fly coupons and a business card.

Cat Purse wrinkled her nose. "Will these coupons work?"

I plastered a friendly smile on my face. "It's my shop, so they most definitely will. I do hope that you will come back."

Opal examined the card in her hand. "We just might."

That was the most I could hope for, I decided as I watched them shuffle across the street toward the bakery. Mattie was still outside. Now she swept the walk with a flat broom. She greeted the ladies as they approached.

I started down the street in the direction of Benjamin Hershberger's shop. Anna said that it was only a block from Running Stitch. I passed a yarn shop, and out of the corner of my eye, I caught movement down one of the narrow alleys between the yarn shop and the next building. I turned my head sharply, but there was nothing there. Perhaps I really didn't see anything, and I was still spooked over the sound of running feet from yesterday.

I hoped Deputy Anderson had been right and my encounter yesterday had been with a raccoon. They grew their raccoons big in Ohio. To tell the truth, I didn't find it much more comforting to be stalked by an enormous raccoon.

I shook off my anxiety when I saw Benjamin's shop. It was across the street. A hand-carved wooden sign hung over the front door that read ROLLING BROOK WOODSHOP. Two white wooden rockers sat on either side of the door. I waited as a horse and buggy trotted down Sugartree before I crossed the road.

In the shop's display window there was a beautifully hand-carved rocking horse and cradle.

Wooden chimes clanged together as I opened the door. The shop smelled like sawdust, wood oil, and stain. I felt like I had been transported back in time.

An elderly Amish man with a grizzled beard, which fell to his chest, sat on a three-legged stool by the cash register. *"Gude mariye."*

"Good morning." I returned his greeting.

"Is there anything I can help you find?" His Pennsylvania Dutch accent was thicker than that of most of the Amish I had met in Rolling Brook.

"Are you Benjamin Hershberger?"

He arched one eyebrow. *"Ya*, I am. Can I help you?"

"I hope so. I'm Angela Braddock. I—"

He pulled on the end of his beard. "You're Eleanor's niece, then. She talked about you all the time."

My eyes widened. "You knew my aunt?"

"Course I did. Rolling Brook is a small place and all the shopkeepers know each other. Your *aenti* and I had shops on this road for years and years. My shop has been here for nearly fifty years." He knocked wood shavings out of his hair.

"You may have noticed Running Stitch is closed."

"I did note that as my old horse and I rode down the street today."

"There was an accident."

A knowing expression crossed his face. "Ahh, so you've come to talk about Joseph."

I nodded. "Yes."

"It seems to me that the Amish telegraph spread the news. You're not the first one who has stopped by with questions about my former apprentice."

I sidestepped a three-foot-tall metal tool cabinet.

"The sheriff was here already with the same questions."

So Mitchell was considering other suspects. This cheered me up even though it was impossible for me to believe this kind old man would hurt anyone. "What did you tell him?"

"Ahh, you want the easy road. A summary, perhaps? It's going to take more time than that." He stood and stepped around the counter. He picked up an identical three-legged stool to his own and set it across from his. "Have a seat now and ask your questions. Who knows? You might ask something that the sheriff didn't think of."

"Okay," I said with some hesitation. This was not how I expected my questions to be accepted. Weren't the Amish typically guarded people with outsiders?

"First things first. You can call me Old Ben. Everyone

else does, so you might as well too. It's what I hear most and answer to best."

I smiled.

"Now, what's your first question?"

I sat on the stool. "Joseph was your apprentice. Did the two of you get along?"

"Not one bit. Joseph was a cranky apprentice and the older he got, the fouler his mood became. He could find fault with anyone about anything."

That pretty much summed up my assessment of the slain woodworker.

"But," Old Ben went on, "he was a fine woodworker. The best man at the craft I ever trained. He surpassed me with his skill and talent years ago."

"How did that make you feel?" I winced at the Dr. Philesque question, though I suspected that Old Ben had no framework for pop psychology and wouldn't notice the cliché phrasing.

"I felt proud of him, of course. He was my student, and I taught him the trade. It was a *gut* reflection on me as a teacher. Not that I was prideful about it, mind you."

I held my purse in my lap. "So it didn't upset you at all?"

"I was angry at first, especially when he decided to open his shop on the same street. There are a lot of locations in Holmes County to open a woodworker shop. Why did he do it here?" He went on without waiting for an answer. "It was his way of telling me that he was better. My business was cut by two-thirds when Joseph opened his shop."

"Your shop is still open," I said.

"Yes, it is still open because I have a lot of standing contracts with local gift shops to keep them in the trinkets, like toys and jewelry boxes, and small furniture, like these kitchen stools we're sitting on. Most of those contracts are about to run out, though."

"Does that mean the shops will be looking around for other woodworkers to fill their orders?"

"That's right," he said.

I tried to keep my expression neutral. Did Old Ben know that he had given me a perfect and timely motive for him to have murdered Joseph?

The next question was a little more difficult to ask. "Where were you Friday night?"

He arched a grizzled eyebrow. "Is that when Joseph died?"

I swallowed hard. "Yes."

"What time exactly?"

"After midnight."

He harrumphed. "What respectable Amish man would be out after midnight? My shop closes at five on Friday. I was home by six in the evening. My dear wife had dinner on the table for me. Pan-fried chicken. My favorite."

"Oh," I said. So much for the perfect motive.

"Don't be so hard on yourself. I know folks are talking about Joseph's death. I'm not surprised my name came up. Everyone knew we didn't care for each other. However, he was a child of God, and I pray his soul finds peace in the hereafter."

I smiled. "Thank you for talking to me. I know it's not easy to talk about these things with a stranger."

He shook his head and his beard moved back and forth in a wave. "You're not a stranger. You're Eleanor's niece."

I smiled.

"I remember you, you know?"

"Me?" I paused.

"Oh yes, you used to be in the quilt shop during the summer visiting Eleanor. I remember you spent a *gut* deal of your time with Jonah Graber."

I felt my cheeks flush.

A wide grin spread across the old man's face. "Ahh."

"It was nice to meet you," I said quickly.

"Please visit again."

"I will," I promised, and fled.

Outside on the sidewalk, I mentally kicked myself. Why did I blush when Old Ben mentioned Jonah? Jonah and I had nothing in common anymore except our childhood. Maybe the memory of that was what caused my embarrassment. Yes, that must be it.

Chapter Twenty

It was strange not needing to be anywhere on a Monday morning. At my old job at the Star of Texas, I would have been at work for three or four hours by now, cranking out advertisements for everything from a Dallas restaurant to toilet bowl cleaner. I considered my options. I could go back home and take Oliver for a walk or continue the investigation.

My feet decided what direction they wanted to go and I found myself in front of Miller's Amish Bakery. Mattie was no longer outside the shop. Instead two English customers sat at a small table outside the door eating blueberry fry pies. The blueberry filling dripped from their chins.

The bell sounded when I went inside the bakery. Mattie stood behind the counter and refused to acknowledge me. It was clear that I was not a favorite of the young Amish woman. What wasn't clear was why.

An Amish woman and man lingered in the store. The man carried a huge bag of flour and set it on the other side of the counter. It was Jonah Graber.

"Hi, Jonah," I said.

He smiled when he saw me. "*Gude mariye*, Angie. You are visiting the bakery for some sweets. I remember how much you liked those when we were *kinner*."

The woman in a white cap and a dark purple plain dress and apron examined me. "Nice to meet you, Angie. I'm Miriam, Jonah's wife. My husband has spoken of you many times."

He has?

I returned her greeting, and Rachel came out of the kitchen and her pretty face broke into a smile. "Angie, I'm so happy you're here. I so would like to visit with you. Hello, Miriam and Jonah. Thank you for bringing the flour."

"It was no trouble," Jonah said.

Rachel looked from Jonah to me and back again. "Do you two know each other?"

I adjusted my purse strap on my shoulder. "Jonah and I knew each other as children."

"I didn't know that." Rachel smiled. "How nice."

If the scowl on her face was an indication, Miriam did not agree with Rachel. Jonah's wife held the bakery's glass door open with an expectant expression.

"*Ya*, it is. We have other deliveries to make. I'm sure we will see you again, Angie. I'm glad you're back." He shot me a lopsided grin and resembled his fourteen-year-old self.

"Thanks," I said, noting that Jonah was being much friendlier this morning than he had when I visited his family farm the day before. What had changed between then and now?

"Mattie, I'm going to go out for a minute. Do you mind watching the shop?" Rachel asked.

"*Nee*," the younger woman said barely above a whisper.

Rachel placed a hand on my shoulder. "This is a quiet time in the bakery. Let's walk a bit."

I followed Rachel outside. A group of English tourists walked by us. One pointed and said, "There's an Amish now. Don't those clothes look uncomfortable?" The woman doing the asking was wearing four-inch spike heels and skintight jeans. Not the typical Amish Country tour attire.

When we were out of hearing range, I said, "I don't think she should be the one talking about uncomfortable clothes."

Rachel barked a laugh and covered her mouth. "It's not right to laugh at others like that."

"Do tourists say stuff like that very often?"

She wrinkled her nose. "All the time. We deal with it because tourism is the big business in Holmes County. I didn't mind, considering her outfit." She giggled.

"She should be careful. These sidewalks were not made for heels."

Rachel examined my feet. I wore sandals today. "No cowboy boots?"

I laughed. "No, I'm trying to save them for special occasions."

Rachel's face became serious. "Does the sheriff really think you were the one who . . . hurt Joseph?"

I pursed my lips. "Mitchell is difficult to read. He seems friendly enough, but as soon as I think he is on my side, he reminds me I'm a suspect, and not just any suspect, but the main one."

"I can't believe he would think that of you." She pressed her hands together. "I want to apologize about how I acted around Sarah on Saturday. I should not have behaved that way."

"You don't need to apologize to me."

"I know Sarah is the one I should apologize to." She focused on a crack in the sidewalk. "She can be difficult. You may have noticed she doesn't listen much."

A courting buggy clomped down the street. The young couple sitting inside had nearly a foot of space between each other on the front seat. If the girl moved any farther away from the young man, she would fall off.

The sun was high in the sky now. I stepped into the shade of a young tree. "Is there another reason the two of you don't get along, other than her love of gossip?"

Rachel watched the buggy make its way down Sugartree. "Sarah has spread rumors about my family. They have hurt my sister-in-law."

"Mattie?"

She nodded. "When Elijah was arrested, it was difficult for Mattie."

My ears perked up. "Why?"

She swallowed. "Elijah and Mattie were courting then." She added quickly, "They aren't anymore. My husband and I are glad for that."

"Aaron didn't like Elijah?"

"*Nee.* Elijah was not like most Amish men. He rarely went to church services or even socials with the young people. It made me uneasy." She lowered her voice.

"He's a loner?"

She shrugged. "That might be the *Englisch* word for it." She paused for a moment. "I suspected that he hit Mattie a time or two. She denies it, but I saw her bruises. There have been no bruises since Elijah went to prison."

"Poor Mattie. Is she happier now?"

"I don't know. You can understand how devastated Mattie was when Elijah went to prison. She's still not fully recovered and refuses to consider any other young man as her beau. There have been many who have volunteered."

"Has Mattie seen Elijah since he has gotten out of prison?" I asked.

"Oh no. She doesn't want anything to do with him."

"Did she say she doesn't want anything to do with him?"

Rachel began walking again. "She doesn't have to. Her brother, my husband, would be furious if she saw Elijah. Aaron and Mattie's parents are both gone now, and she lives with us. She is always so helpful with the *kinner*, especially the boys." She cleared her throat. "Elijah's family was most hurt by Sarah, but our family was hurt too."

"By Sarah's gossip?"

Rachel played with the tie of her prayer cap, twisting it around and around her index finger. "*Ya.* She wasn't the only one who spoke of Mattie, but she kept the gossip going. You heard what she said to Mattie in the shop about Zeph."

"What exactly did she say about Mattie and Elijah?"

Rachel sidestepped an English woman pushing a stroller. "She said the fire was as much Mattie's fault as it was Elijah's."

I stopped in the sidewalk. We were almost in front of Old Ben's shop now. Beyond it, I could see the old barn where the Watermelon Fest would be held that weekend. Several Amish men were mending the roof and walls. "Why?"

She turned to me. "Because Mattie, as Elijah's betrothed, should have known what Elijah was up to and told someone."

I turned around and started back to the bakery. "That doesn't seem fair. She may not have known. Did she know?"

"I—I don't know. She doesn't talk about it. She hasn't spoken much at all since Elijah's arrest."

"Do you know where I can find Elijah?"

Her eyes were twice their normal size. "No, and please don't ask Mattie. It will only upset her. We don't speak of Elijah in our home. It is Aaron's rule." She worried her lip. "You aren't going to go looking for him, are you?"

"He does have the best motive for the murder," I said evasively.

A shadow moved in the corner of my eye as we passed another gap between the buildings. I spun around. "Did you see that?"

She grabbed my arm. "See what?"

"It was nothing."

She laughed. "It was probably a raccoon."

This was the second time something like this was blamed on a raccoon. "Are there a lot of raccoons in Rolling Brook?"

She shrugged. "No more than normal, I would say."

I forced a laugh. "I'm jumpy."

"Anyone would be, Angie. I would be a mess if I were in your shoes. I will pray for you."

I hugged her. "Thank you."

Rachel and I walked back to the bakery. Before I crossed the street toward the quilt shop, she grabbed my arm. "You won't try to do anything foolish like talking to Elijah Knepp on your own, will you? He is an angry and dangerous man."

"So angry and dangerous that he would kill his brother-in-law?"

She dropped her hand. "I—I don't know. I can't think that about someone who was once so close to my family." Her eyes widened. "You will be careful, won't you?"

"I promise to be careful," I said.

The Amish woman gave me a hug. "*Gut*, because I think you and I are going to be very *gut* friends, Angela Braddock."

My face broke into a smile. "I would like that."

Rachel went through the bakery door. As the door shut, I felt a prickling on the back of my neck. My foot was midair as I was about to cross Sugartree Street when someone grabbed me by the arm and pulled me back on the sidewalk. I stumbled back and my heart pounded against my chest.

Chapter Twenty-one

"Angie, there you are!" Willow Moon wrapped her arm around my shoulders, catching me before I fell onto the sidewalk.

I caught my breath. "Willow, you scared me half to death."

She trilled a laugh. "Where have you been? We've been waiting for you."

Is Willow the one who has been following me?

"You were waiting for me?"

She guided me up the street toward her tea shop. Her gauzy top floated behind her. "The Watermelon Fest meeting is starting in a matter of minutes. You didn't forget about it, did you?"

Actually, I had completely forgotten. Being accused of murder drove other concerns from my mind. I pushed the flimsy fabric aside. "I know that I'd agreed to come, but this isn't really a good time."

"Why not? Your shop's closed. Where else could you possibly have to go?"

"I . . . well . . ." I couldn't tell her that I was trying to find the real killer to clear my good name, now, could I?

"I thought so. Trust me. The fest will take your mind off of your troubles."

The wind chimes hanging from the tea shop's eaves jangled together. Mattie scowled at us from the sidewalk in front of Miller's Bakery. Rachel insisted that Mattie had not seen Elijah since he was released from prison, but I had my doubts. How could the two not have seen each other in a place as small as Rolling Brook? And if the former couple had seen each other, Mattie might know about Elijah's relationship with his brother-in-law Joseph, or maybe even where Elijah was the night Joseph died. I needed to talk to her. Considering her sour expression every time I saw her, would she talk to me?

Willow opened the glass door. All the tables were filled with tourists off the latest bus. They drank tea and ate cucumber sandwiches and blueberry scones. Trustee Jung and two women I'd yet to meet sat at a table by the window.

I sidestepped a toddler waddling around the room. "It looks like business is good."

"It's never been better. Not everyone coming to Holmes County wants the five-kinds-of-meat dinner that they serve at all the Amish restaurants." She waved at the trio at the table and skirted around the tables. Farley stood as we approached and the two women remained seated.

Farley pulled out a chair. "Please sit here, Angela."

"Umm, thank you," I murmured as I slipped into the chair. He patted my shoulder before he took the seat next to me.

"Hillary Mitchell, Wanda Hunt, this is Angela Braddock. She's the new owner of the Running Stitch."

Wanda held her teacup with a plump bejeweled hand.

"Glad to see another non-Amish business move into town."

"Actually, the business is Amish." I picked up the cloth napkin from my plate and placed it on my lap. "I inherited it from my aunt Eleanor, and she was Amish. Everyone in my quilting circle is Amish. I want to keep the shop in that tradition."

Wanda buttered her scone and appraised me. "But you're not Amish."

I glanced down at my jeans. *What was your first guess?*

"No, I'm not."

"Good." Wanda sipped her tea from a dainty flowered teacup. "The Amish bring the tourists here, but at the same time they can be rigid. They are unwilling to try anything new. It can be incredibly frustrating when we want to plan an event like the Watermelon Fest, which will benefit everyone, English and Amish."

Considering they still drove horses and buggies, I couldn't dispute the Amish reluctance to change.

The younger of the two women, Hillary, was seated on my other side. Her face was a perfect oval and her cheekbones were so pronounced, they could cut paper. She had long, perfectly straight black hair. She was beautiful enough to be a hit on the pageant scene. She was the daughter my mother wished I could be. "We all have a lot of respect for the Amish. How could you live in this county and not? But the resistance to the Watermelon Fest among those in the Amish community is without cause."

"She's right." Wanda placed her teacup back on its saucer. "You would think the Amish would welcome anything that brings more business to Rolling Brook. Many of the neighboring towns have similar events.

Sugarcreek has Swiss Days and Berlin has the Christmas parade."

A teenage waitress placed a silver-plated three-tiered server with cookies and tea sandwiches in the middle of the table. Willow thanked her. "The issue is Rolling Brook was almost exclusively an Amish town until ten years ago. Now it has several of the storefronts like my tea shop managed by English folk." A pot of tea sat in the middle of the table. Without asking, Willow poured me a cup. "Angie, you're going to love this. It's a special recipe I came up with just for the fest."

The tea smelled strange, like sweetgrass. "Oh?"

"Go ahead and try it."

The tea had a pinkish color. I hesitated. "What kind of tea is it?"

"Watermelon tea, of course. I know it will be a huge hit."

It sounded awful.

"Go on and take a sip."

I lifted the delicate teacup to my lips. It was worse than awful. It was like drinking a watermelon Dum Dum sucker. "Mmmm," I murmured.

She beamed.

I noted that Hillary's and Farley's teacups were almost full. Apparently, I wasn't the only one with a gag reflex. I held the teacup in my hand. Wanda refilled her cup. I hoped she'd finished the pot.

"The Amish are territorial." Wanda *tsk*ed, going back to the conversation about the Amish in town. She selected a ham salad sandwich from the server.

"Not all the Amish," I said, thinking of Jonah and the Millers. "Aren't some of them helping out?"

"Some are," Willow admitted.

Farley placed a pile of cookies on his plate. "When the Amish see what a success the Watermelon Fest is, they will wonder why they ever fought it."

"At least we don't have to worry about Joseph Walker meddling in it anymore." Hillary covered her mouth with her hand. "I'm so sorry. That's a terrible comment to make."

Wanda drained her cup of watermelon tea. "It's nothing to be ashamed of. Joseph Walker was the reason all the other Amish were set against the fest. He talked about it constantly at their church meetings. He didn't like anything English in Rolling Brook."

I thought of my not-so-warm reception from Joseph. Now, knowing his history with his mother's death and Jessica, I wondered if guilt motivated his anger at the English. Another thought entered my head. Joseph gave the watermelon folks trouble about the fest and now he was dead. That could only mean I was at a table surrounded by prime suspects in his murder. Time to start asking some questions. "How did Joseph meddle?"

Hillary patted a napkin to her mouth. "He used every opportunity to bad-mouth the fest to the Amish in town."

Wanda broke a cookie in half. "It wasn't just the Amish. A group of English tourists told me that Joseph said the fest was a crime against the Amish way of life. He said that we wanted to turn Rolling Brook into an amusement park. Can you believe that?"

"I witnessed him tearing down the fest posters," Willow added.

"Did any of the people he complained to take him seriously?" I popped a bit of peanut butter cookie in my mouth. It was heavenly.

"Some did, I'm sure. The most conservative Swartzentruber and Old Order Amish took his warnings to heart. They wouldn't be involved with the fest anyway." Willow refilled her teacup with the watermelon tea. How could she drink it?

My brow wrinkled. "If those Amish would not have helped with the fest anyway, it doesn't seem as much of a loss."

Hillary shook her head. "It is. This is the first year of the fest, and we need good press to make it an annual event." Hillary clenched her jaw. "Joseph went so far as to put an ad in the Amish paper condemning it. In my opinion, all the Amish should get behind the fest. They are being stubborn, but what can you expect from a people who haven't changed for hundreds of years? Sometimes I walk around Rolling Brook and feel like I'm back in the eighteen hundreds."

"Is that such a bad thing?" I asked.

Her hazel eyes turned to me. "They hold us back with their ways."

"The worst part is how he spoke badly of it to the tourists. That's unforgivable," Farley said.

Unforgivable? That seemed a little harsh to me. "But don't the Amish bring the tourists here? You wouldn't have much business in rural Ohio without them. You didn't have to open a business here."

Willow laughed nervously. "Oh, Angie, you are simplifying it too much."

Was I?

Hillary's face looked pinched. "You're new and don't know what you're talking about."

I was about to argue with her, when Farley leaned closer to me. "Do the police have any idea who did it?"

I scooted my chair away from him as I selected a

cheese sandwich from the tray. "The sheriff hasn't shared that with me."

Willow placed a scone on my plate. "I hope the police don't think you did it."

"They must think Angela is the killer," Wanda said, going back for some more butter. "He was found dead in her store." She eyed me. "I wouldn't be surprised if the police weren't doing a thorough background check on you right now. Do you have anything to hide?"

The piece of dry scone lodged in my throat and the only option to wash it down was the watermelon tea. I took a huge gulp, figuring the faster I drank, the less I would taste it. Wrong.

Willow laughed nervously. "Don't mind Wanda; she's suspicious by nature."

"I'm not suspicious, just realistic."

"I think we should focus on the fest. That's why we are all here, isn't it?" Willow asked.

Farley selected one of the small tea sandwiches to add to his plate. "The fest begins on Friday, and there are still so many more arrangements to be made."

Hillary had a checklist at the ready. "I disagree, Farley. Everything seems to be well in hand." She tapped her pen on the list. "We have the watermelon carving and watermelon eating set and ready to go. The watermelon weigh-in order too."

"Watermelon weigh-in?" I asked.

Farley grew serious. "Farmers have been babying their watermelon patches for a month trying to grow the biggest and best watermelon."

I set the cup back on its saucer. "What still needs to be done?" I asked, hoping to move the meeting's agenda along. "What do you need me to do?"

Willow refilled my teacup. "We will find a job for you."

That sounded ominous.

Wanda leaned toward me. "Just think of all the traffic your involvement in the Watermelon Fest will bring to Running Stitch."

I shifted away from the aggressive woman with a grimace. "But Running Stitch is closed. Indefinitely. I have no idea if it will be open by the beginning of the fest."

Farley reached a hand across the table and squeezed my wrist. "Just leave that to me, Angela. I will talk to the sheriff."

I slipped my hand out of his grasp on the pretense of wanting a sip of the awful tea. "You can talk the sheriff into letting me back into my shop?"

"Yes. I'm the township trustee, after all."

I resisted the urge to wipe my hand on my jeans. "I would appreciate it." I thought for a moment. I knew it would infuriate Martha if I participated in the fest, but I had to think of what was best for the business. "I'm happy to help out."

Willow grinned from ear to ear. "I knew when I heard you were coming, Angie, you'd be great for the town."

Great for the town? The only newsworthy event that had occurred since I arrived was the death of Joseph Walker. That wasn't great—it was a nightmare.

Chapter Twenty-two

As I left the tea shop, I again felt that prickly sensation on the back of my neck like I was being watched. I didn't believe the culprit was a raccoon. Since Willow was still inside the tea shop hammering out final details about the Watermelon Fest, it wasn't her. My heart constricted. Could it be Elijah Knepp? After Rachel's warning, I wasn't keen on meeting him alone—even in broad daylight in the middle of Rolling Brook with English tourists and Amish folks milling around.

I ambled away from the bakery on the pretense of looking into shop windows, but at the same time, I made sure to always keep close to a group of tourists. There was safety in numbers. I paused in front of the yarn shop. The sunlight hit the window just right to mirror my reflection back at me. Behind me, I could clearly make out the figure of a man on the other side of the street. The image was warped, but the color of the hair unmistakably red. Danny Nicolson. I should have known. Hadn't several people warned me about his desire for a big story? Even his cousin Jessica took the time to caution me.

Slowly, I turned my head as if to watch a buggy park

in front of the bakery. The reporter jumped into the alley. He was following me. Relief washed over me that it wasn't Elijah Knepp. But my relief was almost immediately replaced by irritation.

I went inside the yarn shop, where three English women were comparing different shades of Amish yarn. The shopkeeper, a middle-aged Amish woman, sat in a wooden rocker crocheting an afghan. I stepped behind a display where I could see out of the window, but I couldn't be seen from the street.

"Can I help you, miss?" the Amish woman asked.

The back of my neck flushed red. "Umm, no, I'm just looking."

She eyed me over her silver-rimmed reading glasses. "You're hiding, not looking."

I winced. "Am I that obvious?"

She smiled. "Yes, but if you want to hide out in my shop for a little while, that's fine with me."

"Thank you." I smiled. "I'm Angie Braddock."

"You're Eleanor's niece." She began a new row. The crochet hook moved in and around the yarn with little attention from her. "There's been a lot of talk since you moved here to take over your *aenti*'s shop."

I glanced through the window. Danny was still across the street eyeing the yarn shop. He seemed to be trying to decide what he should do next. Should he stay or should he go? I was weighing the same options.

The woman rocked and crocheted in perfect rhythm. "There's been even more talk since Joseph Walker was found in Running Stitch. What a terrible thing to have happened."

I winced. It was time to change the subject. "I didn't catch your name."

"Fannie Springer. I was a *gut* friend of your *aenti*. Many times when business was slow, we'd pass the time chatting and having a cup of *kaffi* together."

Everyone loved Aunt Eleanor. I hoped their love for her would be enough to convince them I was innocent.

"I'd like to visit your shop again."

"I would love to have you over for a cup of coffee." I paused. "Just as soon as the police remove the crime-scene tape."

"Oh, *gut*, I haven't been in the shop in several years."

"You haven't?"

"Nee." Her rocking slowed, and she set her crochet hook and blanket on her lap. "It wasn't the same after your *aenti* became ill. Martha Yoder didn't have time for quiet cups of coffee."

"Martha is a hard worker," I said, coming to her defense.

"That I know," Fannie said. Her tone told me it wasn't a compliment. This surprised me, as the Amish were big into hard work. "You be careful around Martha."

"Martha?"

"Yes. She is an ambitious woman. She does not work so hard because it's the right thing to do. She does so because of what she wants."

I didn't see anything wrong with that, but I knew ambition was not a trait held in high regard among the Amish. However, it was par for the course in the English world.

Through the window, I saw Danny slip out of the alley and move down the street. How was I going to catch him red-handed? I needed to act fast. I hurried to the door. "I will see you later, Fannie, and we will make plans for that coffee."

She nodded and returned to her crocheting.

I jumped onto the sidewalk and saw Danny heading north toward the old barn where the Watermelon Fest would be held. The sound of construction resounded from that direction as Amish men made final repairs to the dilapidated structure before Friday's opening.

Two could play at this game, I thought as I followed Danny down Sugartree. I hung back twenty yards and stayed close to groups of English tourists whenever I could, hoping I could blend in and he wouldn't see me. We walked almost all the way back to Old Ben's wood-shop when Danny suddenly made an about-face and turned in my direction.

In the nick of time, I slipped into an alleyway between two of the brick buildings. I peeked out just enough to see Danny glance in both directions. Did he know he was being followed? As if he were a scent hound who caught a whiff of the lure on the breeze, he headed in my direction. I jerked back and knocked my funny bone on the Dumpster behind me.

"Oww," I softly moaned.

I heard Danny's quick steps approach. I stuck my foot out of the alley. "Ahh!" Danny went sprawling face-first onto the sidewalk.

"Are you okay?" I asked, shooting for sympathy and falling short.

He moved to all fours and brushed the grit off his palms. "You tripped me."

I held out my hand to help him up. He glared at my gesture but grudgingly took my hand.

"Sorry," I said. "He's fine," I told a cluster of English tourists who walked by us. "Just a little clumsy."

Danny scowled. "Sorry?" He brushed dirt off his

knees and hands. He had red abrasions on the heels of his hand where he caught himself. He wasn't bleeding, so I didn't feel too guilty about it. Danny noticed. "You don't look sorry."

I placed my hands on my hips. "Maybe I would be sorry if you weren't following me all over town."

Danny's face turned the same color as his hair. "I'm not following you."

"Give me a break. I can prove you were following me. I bet that camera you're holding is full of photos of me from yesterday and today. Let me see your camera."

He hid it behind his back. "No way."

"Seriously, I don't want this to get ugly. I'm from Texas, remember?"

He snorted. "I lost a camera memory card because of you. I'm not risking another."

"I didn't take it. The sheriff did."

"Because of you. Because you told him I took photos of Joseph."

"Why would you do that? It's disgusting. Don't you have any respect for his family? What if they had seen those photos on the Internet?"

He laughed. "First of all, they are Amish, so there's no chance that they would have seen those on the Internet, and second of all, I wasn't planning to publish the photos. I wanted them to help me write my story."

The first part might be true, but the second part I didn't believe for a millisecond. Even Danny's own cousin Jessica said that Danny dreamed about a big break that would get him noticed by one of the larger papers in the region. A photograph of a murdered Amish man might be just the ticket. "Why are you following me?"

He snapped a photo in my face.

"Hey!" I grabbed at his camera.

He laughed. "Test shot. Sorry."

I gritted my teeth and lowered my voice. I noticed that both English and Amish on the street were staring at us. "Now, spill it."

He gave a dramatic sigh. "You will lead me to the killer."

"I'll what?" I practically yelled.

An elderly couple in board shorts and matching T-shirts stared at us as they passed. I felt myself blush.

Danny's smile was sly. "Careful. You don't want to scare the tourists away."

"Talk," I said through gritted teeth.

He shrugged. "You're either the murderer or you're trying to find the person who did it to clear your name."

I felt unbelievably hot. I could blame my rise in temperature on the humidity. "I didn't kill anyone."

"Okay," he said as if it were no concern of his. "Then, you're tracking down who did. That means I keep following you."

"You can't follow me."

"Why not? It's a free country. In fact, I can help you. You're new. You don't know your way around."

"I'll figure it out."

"Admit it. You need my help." His smile widened. "Or are you going to be able to find Elijah Knepp on your own?"

My face turned hot. "How . . ."

"How did I know you're looking for him? Because he's the obvious choice. No one has a better motive to off the woodworker than his brother-in-law."

"Do you know where to find him?"

He grinned, knowing that he had won. "I do."

"Then tell me."

"No way. We have to talk to him together. You want to clear your name, and I want the story about it."

I looked heavenward. I couldn't believe what I was about to say. "I guess I could use some help."

He clapped his hands. "Excellent. Meet me behind Running Stitch in an hour."

"Running Stitch is closed," I said. "We can't even go inside."

"Do you want to solve this case or not? You might not look bad in orange. That's the color the inmates wear around here."

"We can meet in the back in the garden. Why can't we go there now? It's a block away."

"I need to make a stop first."

"Where?"

"Don't worry about that." He winked at me and started back up the street.

I hoped my new partnership with the hungry reporter wouldn't fall into the category "it seemed like a good idea at the time." I had a sinking suspicion it just might.

Chapter Twenty-three

It wasn't worth driving home to Millersburg if I was going to meet Danny in an hour behind Running Stitch. Since I was on that edge of town, I decided to walk the rest of the way to where the Watermelon Fest would be held on Friday and Saturday.

Would Farley really be able to talk the sheriff into letting me open Running Stitch? He gave the impression he had a lot of pull as a trustee of the township, but Sheriff Mitchell did not strike me as a man who was easily swayed.

Elijah was still my number one suspect, but Farley and the Watermelon Fest folks had a pretty good motive too. Even Willow did, although I hated to think she was involved. I'd grown to like the eccentric tea shop mistress.

Beyond Old Ben's shop and the retail district of Rolling Brook, the barn came into full view as Sugartree Street curved to the east. The structure sat roughly twenty yards back from the road. An Amish man rode a lawn tractor and mowed the overgrown grass around the barn, an acceptable use of modern technology, I presumed. The barn itself was a small building perhaps for a hobby farm and roughly the size of a small colonial-style home. The weathered sides were gray from decades of wind, rain, and snow. The foundation was cinder block cement. The twenty-foot-tall sliding barn door was opened wide. Sawing and hammering sounds became louder as I approached the open barn.

Ten Amish men occupied different spots in the barn, mending cracks in the boards and stabilizing beams. They all worked with a confident air and every movement was meaningful. The man closest to me drove a nail into the wooden support beam with one strike of his hammer on the nailhead. It reminded me of the sheriff fixing Oliver's doggy door.

Despite the barn's open door, it was dim in the barn with no electric lights. Then Jonah came into view carrying a hammer.

His face broke into a smile. "Angie, what are you doing here?"

"I wanted to see the place where the fest will be. I came from a meeting with Willow about it."

"I see. She was able to talk you into helping. Willow is enthusiastic."

"Is she the one you've been working with about the barn?"

"I think so. I've only been able to help as I can. One of the other men here is in charge of making sure it's finished. I am in charge of everything on my farm. Sometimes it is nice not to be the boss."

"Everything? Even the geese?"

He snorted. "I'm not much of a boss of them. My *mamm* may have been right. Maybe we should have gotten a quieter animal to farm. We have not had a solid night's sleep since they arrived. After I leave here, I'm starting to work on a geese barn for them that will be out of earshot."

"Anna will be happy."

"Ahh, she has already complained to you, then? My *mamm* says what she thinks." He removed a bandanna from his pocket. "What will you be doing for the Watermelon Fest?"

"I'm not sure yet. Everything is up in the air with Running Stitch closed down."

"Will the shop be open by then?" He set the hammer in a wheelbarrow parked by the door.

I frowned. "I hope so." I gestured toward the barn. "Will it be ready in time?"

"We should finish today. It's a *gut* thing. Willow is anxious to get to work for her watermelon party." He walked through the barn door and blinked against the bright sunlight. "The guys are working on a platform to place the enormous watermelons on."

"Are you going to the Watermelon Fest?"

"*Ya.* I told them I would help out even if it is a party more for the *Englischers*."

"So you're not against it, like some of the Amish are."

He raised one eyebrow at me. It was like looking into his ten-year-old face. That expression used to infuriate me as a child because I could never get it down, as much as I practiced in the mirror. From the smirk forming on Jonah's face, I could tell he remembered too. "I wouldn't be here helping prepare the barn for the party if I thought the party was wrong. Watching *Englischers* eat watermelon until they get sick is not my idea of a *gut* way to pass the time when there is so much work to be done."

I laughed. "It doesn't sound like much fun when you put it like that."

He wiped his hands on a blue bandanna. "It will be *gut* for Rolling Brook to have such an event, no matter what some of the Amish in town say. It will bring more notice and tourists. Maybe more buses will come here instead of Berlin."

"Joseph Walker didn't feel that way."

"No, he didn't. Joseph wanted life to go back fifty years to when only a few *Englischers* knew about Rolling Brook. He would have been happy if every bus passed our little town by."

The sun felt hot on the top of my head, so I stepped into the shade. "If that were the case, it would destroy his business. Weren't most of his customers English?"

He shoved the bandanna into his back pocket. "*Ya*, they were, but I don't think Joseph would have minded the loss of business if there were fewer *Englischers* around." He laughed at my confused expression. "I know it's hard for you or a non-Amish person to understand, but it is how he felt."

"Did you know Joseph well?"

"Well enough. I certainly heard him speak about how he thought life in Rolling Brook should be. Joseph wasn't the only one who felt that way, but he was the most vocal about it." He leaned against the barn. "Some Amish are worried about the Watermelon Fest. They worry Rolling Brook will become like parts of Lancaster and lose its Amish authenticity."

"Amish authenticity? What's that?"

He laughed. "In other Amish towns it can be about appearing Amish for the *Englischers* and not being Amish like we are. The fear we can lose sight of the way we choose to live when we recognize that our lives can turn us a profit as business folk."

I smiled. "You don't want to become Amish Disney World. I got it."

He barked a laugh. "That's about right."

"When Anna brought me to your farm on Saturday, you said that you saw Elijah Knepp at the Walker farm."

Jonah's jovial expression faded.

"Is he there now?"

"I believe so."

"Where is the Walker farm?"

"Why?" He folded his arms.

"I would like to talk to him about Joseph."

"Why?"

I sighed. "He may know something about Joseph's death."

"Elijah Knepp is not someone that you should be talking to."

It was my turn to ask the questions. "Why not?"

"Elijah Knepp is my friend, but he has made some bad choices in his life. Now he is a confused and angry man. He's just been released from prison, and I told him he must look for *Gotte*'s will in his life." He cleared his throat. "But you should not speak to him. He has not found his way yet."

"He's the most likely person to have killed Joseph."

"That is true," Jonah said in his usual Amish candor. "Which is more reason you should stay away from him."

I couldn't promise Jonah that I could or would do that.

"I know you are afraid the police will blame you for Joseph's death."

"How do you know that?"

"Is it not true?"

"It's true." I sighed.

"Although twenty years have passed, I can still read your face."

I rolled my eyes. "What am I thinking now?"

He grinned. "How annoying I am."

"That's true too."

He laughed. "Sheriff Mitchell is a *gut* man. He knows how the Amish way works and doesn't try to change us. We are happy to have him in the county." Jonah frowned. "The sheriff before wasn't nearly as understanding. He will know you're innocent. He will find who did this."

I wished I had Jonah's faith and confidence.

"You have not changed, Angela Braddock. You worried far too much as a child, and you worry now. You fretted for days over moving to Texas when we were kids instead of enjoying your last few weeks here. *Gott* will settle the loss of Joseph's life. Leave that to him."

That was easy for Jonah to say. He wasn't the one who might be measured for an orange jumpsuit.

"I see you don't believe me." He smiled. "I'm glad you've come back. Texas was never right for you. Holmes County is your home."

Before Joseph's murder, I would have agreed with him.

Chapter Twenty-four

I paced the backyard of Running Stitch. I already had been there twenty minutes, and Danny was nowhere in sight. Where was he? What was taking him so long? What was the stop he had to make before meeting me?

Footsteps came down the alleyway. I leaned over the fence, expecting to see Danny. Instead I found Sheriff Mitchell. There was no time to run away and hide in one of the bushes like Oliver.

"Angie," the sheriff said. "I didn't expect to find you back here." He was back in his uniform and looking fine.

"I'm gardening. There's not much else I can do today since I can't get into my shop." I gave him a pointed look.

A small smile played on the sheriff's face. "What are you planting?"

"Umm . . ."

"Where are your garden tools?"

"Well, right now, I'm taking a survey. You know, to see what needs to be done and what I should plant."

He removed sunglasses from his pocket and placed them over his eyes. "You're making a list."

"Yep," I said, relieved.

"Where's your pen and paper?"

I tapped the side of my head with my index finger. "It's all up here. I have an excellent memory."

"Good to know," Mitchell said.

"What are you doing here?" I asked, happy for a chance to put him on the defensive.

"I thought I would stop by and have another go at the scene. See if we missed anything."

"Like what?" I asked.

He eyed me with suspicion. "I will know it when I see it."

I jerked a thumb in the direction of Running Stitch's back door. "Are you planning to go in there?"

"I was, but maybe I will come back later."

Because I was there. He didn't say it because he didn't have to.

"Can you do something about the crime-scene tape out in front? Tourists are taking pictures of themselves outside of the shop because it's a place where someone got killed. I don't want that to be the reason why someone visits my store."

His expression softened. "I will see about removing the tape, or at least making it a little less obvious. Deputy Anderson may have gotten carried away with it."

"You think?" I asked sarcastically.

Behind the sheriff, Danny stepped around the other side of the woodworker's shop. His eyes widened when he saw the sheriff, and he darted back behind the other building. Mitchell brushed imaginary dirt from his pant leg. "I'll return later to walk the scene. I trust you won't be here all day *gardening*, then."

"No, I'm almost done."

"Good." He walked through the gate and down the alleyway.

I waited a full thirty seconds before I hissed at Danny. "Danny, come out already. The sheriff's gone."

Danny's head peeked around the woodworker's property. "Doesn't look good for you, Braddock. The sheriff's going to send you upriver."

I rolled my eyes even though a large part of me thought Danny might be right. "Why did you hide from him?"

"Mitchell and I don't see eye to eye about the freedom of the press."

"That doesn't surprise me in the least. Since your idea of freedom of the press is taking photos of a dead man."

Danny unlatched the gate and walked inside. "Why did you tell the sheriff that you were gardening?"

"I don't know. It was the first thing that came to mind. Would you rather I had said I was waiting for you?"

He smiled. "Aw, see, Braddock, you and I aren't as different from each other as you think."

I grimaced. "What took so long?"

He shrugged. "The Walker murder isn't the only story I'm covering right now, you know?"

"What? You had a pie tasting to document?"

He scolded, "I came here to help you, and you're giving me attitude."

I folded my arms. "How exactly are you going to help me out? You'd better talk fast. I have things to do."

He snorted and leaned against the fence. "I know where Elijah Knepp is."

"So do I. He's on the Walker farm."

"Ahh, look out, Miss Super Sleuth. You've been doing your homework." He crossed his arms. "So you're going to drive to the Walker farm and talk to him?"

"No." I frowned. "Number one, I doubt he will talk to me. Number two, his sister and her daughters are there and are grieving, and number three, he's not someone I want to meet by myself."

"Bright girl. Knepp is one angry Amish man. I think all that time in the Big House with hardened English criminals only made him worse."

"Have you spoken to him?"

"No," he admitted. "But I've seen him many times while on the story."

"Where? How?"

"At the Walker farm."

"You just sauntered up to the Walker farmhouse and asked to speak to Elijah?"

"He's not in the farmhouse. He's hiding in the outbuildings. He knows the sheriff's deputies are watching the place for any signs of him."

I tapped the large hollyhock blossom next to me and watched it bob back and forth on its long giraffelike stem. "How do you know that?"

"I saw him on surveillance."

"You *spied* on the family?"

"You call it spying. I call it working a story."

It wasn't worth arguing with him over that point. "You saw him, but Mitchell's deputies didn't."

"Trust me, Knepp could walk by Barney Fife Anderson with Walker's blood on his hands and that guy would never notice."

I had to agree with him, as Anderson left me unattended in the quilt shop yesterday and bought my "I was in the bathroom" story.

"You need to come with me." He pushed off the fence.

I took a step back. "Where?"

"To the Walker farm, so you can see Knepp for yourself."

"You want me to spy on Abigail and her girls?"

"Do you want to find the killer, or would you rather go to prison?"

That sobered me. "The family must not think he's the killer if he's living on the property."

"Just because the family thinks that doesn't make it true. Knepp still has the best motive." He swallowed. "He hasn't lost his interest in fire either."

"I know about the barn fire, but not the details. He used kerosene. Whose barn was it?"

He cocked his head. "I'm surprised you don't know."

"Why's that?"

"I thought you were close to the Grabers."

My stomach dropped. "He burned down the Grabers' barn?"

Danny nodded as if he relished being the bearer of this news.

"But why? Jonah said they were friends."

He shrugged. "I guess Jonah Graber is the forgive-and-forget type. It would be very Amish of him to react that way."

Jonah not telling me was one thing, but Anna hadn't said a word either. Or Rachel, who must know. "Why did he do it?"

"Knepp never answered that question during the trial. The prosecutor asked and he refused to answer. If Elijah's the killer and I can tie Elijah's past into this story, it will be golden. The Canton paper is considering running it, but they don't want anything that is not one hundred percent true. The media is always afraid of getting sued." He glowered.

"It's highly unlikely that the Amish will sue you in this case. That's not their typical reaction."

"I know that," he snapped. "But the newspaper won't budge, so I have to be one hundred percent certain of Elijah's guilt before I submit my story."

I gritted my teeth. "I guess I could check the farm out to see where it is. I'm not calling it surveillance—I'm calling it locating."

"Whatever helps you sleep at night." He shook his head. "But sorry, no can do."

"What? You spent the last twenty minutes trying to convince me to go with you to the Walker farm."

"If I take you, we have to be partners. I tell you everything I know about the case, and you tell me everything you know. That's the only way I will do it."

I didn't like the sound of Danny's offer, but what choice did I have? "Fine."

He slapped me on the shoulder. "That's the spirit. I'll pick you up in front of the Millersburg courthouse at nine tomorrow morning."

"Why wait? I thought you were in a rush to get this story."

He ignored my question. "Remember. Nine sharp in front of the soldier's statue." He used his finger to pretend to fire a gun at me.

Why did I have the sneaking suspicion that I felt a lot like Faust must have when he made a deal with the devil?

Chapter Twenty-five

Oliver barked at me as I tied my tennis shoes the next morning.

"Sorry, buddy, but I can't take you for a walk this morning. I promise we will go for an extra-extra-long one when I get home."

He flopped onto his dog bed in the middle of the living room and pouted. He was an expert at making me feel guilty.

"I won't be long."

He flicked his ears.

Outside the midmorning air was heavy with moisture, and I practically felt my blond curls become larger. I half hoped and half feared that Danny wouldn't show up. The thought of spying on the grieving Walker family didn't sit well with me. I shivered to think what Anna and Martha would say if they ever found out. I would make sure they never would.

It was a three-minute walk from my house to the statue in front of the courthouse. In the bright sun I squinted at the perfectly straight soldier on top of the story-high monument.

I checked my cell phone. I was fifteen minutes early. That was fine with me. I wanted to beat Danny there. I didn't want him jumping out of the bushes in an attempt to scare me. There was a park bench in the shade by a small stand of trees. It was a good place to sit because I could see anyone approaching the statue from either direction.

I heard a dog bark, and then saw Tux, free of his leash, running toward me. He pulled up short, probably on the lookout for Oliver.

"Funny seeing you here again," Sheriff Mitchell said as he strode toward us. Tux ran back to his master and whined softly. "He's disappointed Oliver is not here. Where is he?"

"He's at home. I promised him a big walk later." I sat on my hands.

"What are you doing out here?"

"Just enjoying the day. I might as well explore Millersburg if I have all this extra time." I hoped the sheriff would be gone by the time Danny arrived.

My cell phone rang. I removed it from my shorts pocket and checked the readout. I grimaced and silenced the phone.

"Someone you don't want to talk to?" He peeked at the screen.

I showed it to him.

"You don't want to talk to your mother?"

I slipped the phone back into my pocket. "Not right now."

"Why not?"

His bold question made me laugh, and he smiled. "She wants me to return to Texas." I left off the part about wanting me to marry Ryan. She might be calling me about my dad's knee surgery, but I doubted it. I'd spoken

with my father the night before and everything had gone
well.

"And do you want to?"

"No."

His eyes fell to my naked left hand. "Does that have
something to do with your broken engagement?"

My mouth fell open. "How do you know about that?"
Then, I remembered Danny's warning that the police
would do a thorough background check on me. "Never
mind. It was part of your investigation, right?"

To my surprise, Mitchell blushed.

Tux rolled on his back in the middle of the green lawn.

"If my store doesn't open soon, I may not have much
choice about moving back to Texas. You don't know about
any jobs for graphic designers who can quilt around
here, do you?"

"There's not much call for that in Holmes County." A
smile crossed his face. "I have good news for you, though.
You can reopen Running Stitch tomorrow. We are finished with it."

I jumped off the bench and threw my arms around the
sheriff. "Really?" I dropped my arms. "I'm so sorry."

He grinned. "It's okay. I don't often get to share such
good news, so it's my pleasure."

"Does this mean I'm not a suspect in Joseph's murder
anymore?" The question popped out of my mouth before I could stop it.

He frowned. "No, it doesn't."

I couldn't help but wonder if Farley came through as
promised and talked the sheriff into letting me back into
the shop, but I thought better of asking Mitchell. I
cleared my throat. "I have a few more people that you
could talk to."

His demeanor changed from curious neighbor to cop in a half second. "Like who?"

"Willow Moon and Farley Jung. They both have an excellent motive."

"What's that?"

"The Watermelon Fest. Joseph was trying to raise Amish support against it. Maybe the organizers got mad."

He unsuccessfully tried to hide a smile. "You think that Joseph was murdered over watermelon?"

I glared at him. "I don't know why Joseph was murdered. I want you to see there are other options. Other than me."

More quietly, he said, "I know that, Angie. I have more than enough suspects, but the fact still remains that Joseph was killed in your store. Why was he there? Was it for the deed?"

"I have no idea."

"You didn't have plans to meet him?"

"Of course not. Joseph was barely on speaking terms with me." I watched cars stop at the main intersection in front of the courthouse. It was quickly approaching nine o'clock. Nothing good could come from the sheriff seeing Danny and me together. It would only make him suspicious of me. "Have you spoken to Elijah Knepp?"

He grimaced. "Not yet."

"He has to be a main suspect, doesn't he?"

"He's a person of interest. I would be more inclined to believe he was involved if there had been a fire."

"He burned down the Graber barn."

Mitchell sighed. "Anna Graber told you that."

I didn't correct him. Behind the sheriff, a ten-year-old silver coupe pulled up to the curb in front of the soldier's statue.

"Have you spoken to the Grabers?"

"No," was his short answer. "I have investigated a major crime like this before. I know what I'm doing." He took a step closer to me. "You need to stop talking about Elijah Knepp to people. If it had been up to me, he would still be in prison." He paused. "And he might not be the only one that you need to worry about. Do I need to remind you there is a killer loose in Holmes County?"

"You don't need to remind me of that," I said softly.

"Good." He whistled. The piercing sound broke through the rumble of traffic. "Let's go, Tux."

Thankfully, the sheriff and Tux walked off in the opposite direction of the silver coupe. I waited until the pair was out of sight before walking over to Danny's car. I reached for the door handle and peered into the car. It was a mess. The backseat was piled high with files and fast-food wrappers. There was a mark on the fabric ceiling. I told myself that it had to be ketchup. I sighed, slipped into the passenger seat, and buckled up.

He laughed. "Seems like every time I see you, you're in the middle of a tête-à-tête with the sheriff."

"If you would show up on time, you wouldn't have the problem."

He grinned. "After this murder gig is on the books, the Holmes County sheriff's budding romance might be my next story. I prefer to write more hard-hitting stories, but whatever pays the rent, you know."

I gritted my teeth. "Is the Walker farm very far?"

"No, it will take about ten more minutes to get there."

"Remember, I just want to see where it is. No spying."

He laughed. "Right. No spying."

Danny's laughter was beginning to grate on my nerves.

Chapter Twenty-six

The silver coupe rocked onto a loose gravel road. I held on to my seat. "I don't think this car was meant for country driving."

"It's only a few yards on this road." He pointed at the homestead that came into view. "That's the Walker place."

The house was a two-story gray and white farmhouse with a large white barn behind it. Three outbuildings sat around the property. Twenty or so brown chickens pecked at the ground in the fenced-in yard around a chicken coop. Good thing Oliver wasn't along. The amount of bird encounters in Holmes County was startling.

Four horses, each with its own buggy, waited in the grass in front of the house. I guessed they belonged to family and neighbors visiting the grieving widow. Sadness washed over me. I couldn't imagine how much pain Abigail and her children were in at that moment. I remembered how upset Jessica was over Joseph's death. Their pain must be a hundred times that.

To the right of the farmhouse was a small apple orchard. Danny drove past the house and turned into a dirt road on the other side of the orchard. He shifted his coupe into park and removed the keys from the ignition.

"What are you doing? I see where the house is. I saw it. Let's head back to Millersburg."

"No way. I told you this was a surveillance mission." He pocketed the keys and got out of the car.

I had two choices. I could sit in the car until he got back—who knew when that would be?—or I could follow him.

I climbed out of the car. "Danny?" I hissed. He had disappeared into the orchard.

Bees buzzed around my ears, and I shivered. I hated bees, wasps, and anything with a stinger. If I got stung, Danny was going to hear about it.

"Danny?"

He popped out from behind a tree. "Be quiet."

I placed a hand to my chest. "Cripes! Don't scare someone like that."

"Come on, Texas girl. Follow me." He disappeared back behind the tree, and I crept after him.

Down one of the orchard rows, I saw Danny crouched behind some overgrown bushes. He waved me over. I glanced at the bits of the Walker property I could see from the orchard. If anyone inside the Walker house looked closely at the apple trees, he or she would see me standing there. I ran over to Danny. "This is a bad idea."

"Stop complaining. We won't stay long. We came all the way here. We might as well see if we can catch a glimpse of Elijah."

"What are the odds he will be on the side of the house?"

He put a finger to his lips. "Just be quiet."

Another bee buzzed by me. I crouched down next to

Danny and tried to remain as still as possible. We were at the back of the house, closest to a small outbuilding, perhaps a storage shed or a workshop. The side door to the structure stood open, but we couldn't see inside from our angle.

The back door to the farmhouse swung against the house. A plainly dressed girl stepped outside. "I'll only be a moment," she called over her shoulder to whoever was inside.

Danny straightened to get a better look.

"Get down," I hissed, yanking him back down by the arm.

The girl's eyes glanced in our direction and just as quickly looked away. When she faced us, I saw it was Mattie Miller.

"I think I've seen her in Rolling Brook," Danny whispered. "I can't place her."

I kept my mouth shut.

Mattie glanced back at the farmhouse one more time before she ran over to the shed with the open door. She said something in Pennsylvania Dutch in a hoarse whisper.

Like Lazarus coming from his tomb, a form appeared. Elijah Knepp. Mattie threw herself into the Amish man's arms and began to cry. He patted her head and shushed her.

"Holy crap," Danny said. "This is like *As the Amish World Turns*. What a soap opera."

"Shh!" I shoved him back into the bushes.

Through a break in the limbs, I watched Elijah place a hand on Mattie's cheek and wipe away her tears with his thumb. The two spoke to each other in their language, and I didn't understand a word.

"What are they saying? Do you know any of the

words?" I hissed as I pulled down a branch blocking my view.

"No." Danny poked the camera into my side. "I can't get a clear shot of the girl. Move over."

"Shh!"

He dug the edge of the camera deeper into my side. "At least take a picture of him. We need it."

I took the camera from him on the pretense of taking a photo, but I wasn't going to take any pictures as long as Mattie was in the shot. Rachel had been too good a friend to me since I showed up in Rolling Brook. If Danny submitted the photo to the Canton paper, it would hurt the Miller family.

Elijah spoke again, and even though the words were foreign, his tone had finality to it. He touched her cheek one last time and strode away in the direction of the orchard.

Next to me, Danny forced his way into the middle of the bushes. "Get in here!"

"In the bush?"

"Yes. Hurry."

I crawled under the bush and ignored the sound of buzzing all around. The sharp spiny limbs cut into my exposed skin, but finally, I was concealed. Just in time, because I could hear and feel the vibrations of Elijah's approaching footsteps.

"Angie," Danny hissed.

"Don't breathe a word," I whispered. "He's here."

"Angie, there's a . . ."

"Shh!"

"Something is really wrong." He began to move toward me.

"Don't move," I breathed.

Elijah paused by our bush, staring back at the house. He removed his black felt hat and slapped it against his leg in anger. I felt the breeze the hat made on my face. He replaced the hat and continued down the orchard path.

Danny and I remained crouched in the bush for another minute. My legs began to fall asleep, and something tickled at the back of my neck. I mentally swore. If Danny was taking this opportunity to get fresh, he'd leave the Walker farm with a broken wrist. "You'd better not be touching my neck."

"It's not me. It's a spider."

"What!" I squealed. I burst out of the bush clawing at the back of my neck.

The back door of the farmhouse slammed open, and I hit the dirt on my stomach. Jonah, who was the last person I wanted to catch me spying, stood in the doorway, surveying the yard. Finally, he shook his head and went back into the house.

Danny crawled out of the bushes.

"Is the spider gone?" I shivered. I could feel its creepy little legs all over my body.

Danny smirked. "Yeah, I think you gave it a heart attack."

I loved nature, but this expedition was a little too much of a good thing in my opinion. I needed a shower. Stat.

Danny started to hop around like he was receiving electroshock treatment.

"What's wrong with you?" I demanded.

"I think the spider got on my back." He ran in place.

"Hold still and turn around."

Danny turned and twenty-some ants were crawling around on the back of his khakis.

"Umm, good news. It's not a spider. Bad news, they're ants. Lots of ants. I think you sat in a nest."

His jerking got worse. "Get them off of me!"

"Stop making so much noise. Someone will hear you."

He waved his hands as if in an attempt to rid himself of the ants. It wasn't working. "Get. Them. Off."

There was no way I was touching Danny. I picked up a dead limb from one of the apple trees.

His eyes grew wide. "What's that for?"

"The ants."

"Are you going to beat them to death?" He jumped a few feet away. "Never mind." He swiped his hands on his back end. He turned around again. "Are they gone?"

"Pretty much. There are two on your right pocket, but that's it."

He swatted the last two creepy-crawlies.

I grinned. "On the bright side, they aren't fire ants. If that happened in Texas, you'd be crying for your mama right now."

He scowled at me. "I'm crying for my mama anyway. I have ants in my pants. Real ants. I have to get out of here." He shook out his pant leg, and several ants flew in my direction.

Jumping out of the way, I stifled a laugh.

"I'm glad you find this so amusing." He stomped his feet to shake more of the creepy-crawlies loose. "I'm leaving."

"That sounds like an excellent idea," I said, trying to fight back a snicker.

"I'll get you back for this, Braddock."

"Get me back. For what?"

"You were the one who made me sit on the anthill."
His voice shook with anger.

"Quiet down. Do you want Elijah to see you?"

"No," he said grumpily. "Ouch!" he cried, and rubbed
his calf. "It bit me." He ran for the street in the direction
of his car.

"Hey, wait!" I ran after him.

Danny had already shifted into reverse by the time I
got to the car. Dust settled back onto the dirt road where
his car had been seconds before. The birds twittered in
the apple trees and the bees buzzed some more. Danny
got back at me after all.

Chapter Twenty-seven

I reached into my pocket for my smartphone. I hit the GPS. The device blinked twice and went out. I smacked it against my forehead. I forgot to charge it the night before. Now what was I going to do?

I looked back at the Walker farm. Jonah was there. He could give me a ride back to Millersburg. Did I have a choice? I didn't know my way back to town, and if it was fifteen minutes by car going fifty miles per hour, which was the speed limit for most of the back county roads, it would take me hours to get home.

I walked to the road. I thought that was a better way to approach the house than from the apple orchard.

I was close to the road when Elijah stepped in front of me. "Who are you?"

My mind went completely blank as my annoyance at Danny was replaced by ice-cold fear. "I'm, umm, I'm—"

I wanted to question Elijah, but not like this, alone on a country road. I gritted my teeth. Danny Nicolson would be sorry when I got my hands on him, if I lived so long.

"I'm Angie Braddock. I'm the new owner of Running Stitch, the quilt shop in Rolling Brook," I managed.

"I know where it is," he snapped. "You're the *Englischer* who killed my brother-in-law."

I shook my head. "Oh no, no, I didn't do it. I promise."

He shrugged as if it made no difference to him. "You're a long way from town."

"I enjoy walking. I may have wandered farther than I planned."

He's never going to buy that.

"You're like the rest of the *Englischers*. You lie."

I bit the inside of my lip. "I'm sorry for your loss."

"My loss? What are you talking about, *Englischer*? Joseph is no loss of mine. My sister is upset, but in the end, it will be better for her. She can make her own choices now. Joseph was too controlling of her."

"That's too bad." I took a step closer to the road. "I guess I'll see you around." All the questions in my head about Joseph and Elijah and how he felt about his brother-in-law would have to wait until I had some witnesses around and maybe an armed bodyguard.

Elijah stuck his hand into his pocket and pulled out a metal lighter. From his other pocket, he removed a hand-rolled cigarette. He flicked the light to life with his thumbnail, which would be an impressive trick had it not reminded me why Elijah went to jail in the first place. He set the flame against the end of the cigarette. He inhaled deeply.

What did Mattie see in this guy?

"You enjoy your smoke," I said lamely. Up the street, dust shot up into the air from an approaching car. Danny was coming back to get me. Thank goodness.

Elijah noted the dust too. "Stay away from my family.

I won't ask you again." He threw his half-smoked cigarette on the ground and disappeared into the orchard. I stomped on the smoldering butt.

The car came into view. To my disappointment, it wasn't Danny. It was a monster-sized SUV instead of his little silver coupe. The driver stopped and powered down the driver-side window. Trustee Jung in an ill-fitted business suit and greasy hair sat behind the wheel. He grinned. "What are you doing all the way out here, Angela?"

"Out for a walk," I said quickly. "I lost my way." At least that part was true, because I had no idea how to get back home.

"You're ten miles from Millersburg. You must really enjoy walking."

"I love it," I said enthusiastically.

"Do you need a lift back to town?"

Get into a car with a murder suspect. I don't think so. "No, I'm good. I love walking."

He glowered. "You already said that." He searched my face. "Are you going to tell me what you were doing so close to the Walker farm?"

"I'm near the Walker farm?" I feigned ignorance. "What are you doing out here?"

He smiled coldly. "Just out for a drive."

Yeah, right.

"At the Watermelon Fest meeting, you and some of the other members seemed upset with Joseph Walker and the more conservative Amish's resistance to the fest."

He raised his brow, and it touched his greasy hairline. "We are. The fest is important for the economy, both the Amish and non-Amish economy."

"Was anyone extremely upset? Upset to the point of anger?"

"Like angry enough to kill Joseph?" He barked a laugh that sounded eerily similar to a honk of a goose. "Are you insinuating someone killed Joseph over watermelon?"

"I'm making conversation." I shrugged as if it didn't matter to me. "The sheriff told me I could have my shop back tomorrow, so the Watermelon Fest should be no problem."

A smile curled his thin lips. "Excellent. You can go ahead and thank me."

"Thank you?"

"I told you I would talk to the sheriff about your shop. I did yesterday afternoon and now you will open tomorrow."

"Mitchell said I could reopen because they had finished processing the scene."

He waved the comment away. His pinkie ring caught the sunlight beaming in through the windshield. "He was saving face." He smiled to himself. "The Watermelon Fest was my brainchild. Since I have been trustee of Rolling Brook, I have done a lot of good for the town."

"I know Willow is excited about the Watermelon Fest," I said lamely.

"Of course she is. All the English shopkeepers are. It's the Amish I always have to worry about. The smallest of changes seem to offend them."

I thought about my aunt and uncle and about their graciousness and flexibility toward me when I would visit in the summers. They never expected me to dress plain and let me use the shed phone they shared with their neighbors to call my parents once per week. "I don't think all Amish are that way. They're people too, and they are all different from each other."

Farley snorted. "When push comes to shove, they will band together against us. Are you sure you wouldn't like a ride back to town?"

"Nope. I'm good."

He looked me up and down. "Good luck reopening the quilt shop tomorrow, Angela. I might drop in." He powered up his window and sped away, spraying a cloud of dust into my face.

Finally, I made it to the top of the Walkers' long driveway. A buggy rolled in my direction. I stepped to the side as the driver pulled the horse to a stop next to me. "Hello, Angie."

I recognized Rachel's husband, Aaron.

I waved. "Can you give me a ride back to Millersburg?"

"*Ya.*"

I climbed into the buggy. "Thanks."

"You have a stick in your hair." Aaron was a man of few words, and I was relieved that he didn't ask what I was doing wandering around the Walker farm.

I removed the stick and tossed it out of the buggy. At least it wasn't a spider.

Chapter Twenty-eight

I washed my hair three times in an attempt to remove the spider cooties. I wondered how Danny dealt with the ants and winced, though after he left me stranded in the apple orchard, my sympathy for him was at an all-time low.

Oliver followed me around the house as I towel dried my hair. I scratched him behind the ear. "I'm sorry, boy. That took much longer than I thought it would." He pawed at his doggy door, and I let him into the backyard.

The small lap quilt Anna had given me to practice my hand stitch on hung over the arm of my couch. I stared at it. I needed to get back to it. The shop and the quilting circle—these were the reasons I moved back. And if I happened upon another clue to the mystery of the woodworker's death while returning to my true purpose, all the better.

Oliver barked from the other side of the door. A sparrow perched on the fence and he wanted in. Now. I opened the door and the Frenchie nearly knocked me over. I needed to go out again. I had left the dog alone so much over the last two days, it seemed cruel to do it again so soon, even considering where we were headed. I slapped my thigh. "Oliver, let's go."

His stubby tail wagged with excitement. He wouldn't be that happy when he learned we were going back to the home of the geese.

Oliver peeked over the edge of the passenger's side window as my tires crunched over Anna's gravel driveway. The sound of the geese squawking was deafening. My pooch turned a forlorn face to me that clearly read "Traitor."

"If I left you back at the house, you wouldn't have been happy about that either." I patted his head.

His big brown eyes told me that this was much worse than an afternoon home alone.

"Okay, I will let you stay home next time."

Through my windshield, I spied Miriam among the geese, gently tapping their plump sides with a thin stick and shooing them to the other side of the pen. There were three children with her. I realized that these must be Jonah's children. There were two boys and a girl. The girl was the oldest.

I climbed out of the car, and let Oliver out too. He jumped to the ground and promptly snuck under the vehicle. I leaned over. My wild curls fell into my eyes as I did. "Ollie, I won't let the geese hurt you. I promise."

The two youngest children whooped and ran toward the car. They ignored the reprimands of their mother.

The two squatted beside me, and I noticed that they were twins. The duo looked so much like their father had when we were children, it took my breath away.

"Is that your dog?" one of the boys asked.

"Yes, his name is Oliver."

"What's he doing under the car?" his brother asked.

"Hiding. Who are you?"

The first boy pointed a thumb at his chest. "I'm Ethan, and that's Ezra."

"Nee." His brother shoved him out of the way. "I'm Ethan, and he's Ezra."

I put my hands on my hips. "Who is telling the truth?"

"I am," both boys said in unison.

I laughed. "Do you two play this prank on your teacher?"

They giggled.

I grinned. "Maybe I will call you both E. It's so much easier to remember."

"You can't do that. You have to call us by our names."

I folded my arms and gave them a mock stern face. "I would if I knew who was who."

The first boy sighed. "Fine. I'm Ezra and this is Ethan."

His twin shook his head again. *"Nee,* I'm Ezra and this is Ethan."

Miriam and her daughter gave up on the geese and stepped through the gate. Miriam said something in Pennsylvania Dutch to the twins. The boys exchanged a look before running off to the barn.

Jonah's wife gave me the once-over. "My mother-in-law isn't here. She went to visit a sick friend."

I stepped back to avoid getting frostbite from her chilly voice. "Do you know when she will be back?"

She held tightly on to the side of her black apron. *"Nee."*

The girl, who was about ten, stood behind her mother

and watched me with large brown eyes. I waved to her. "I'm Angie."

"I'm Emma. I know who you are. *Daed* said you were his *gut* friend from when he was my age."

"That's right." I smiled, happy that Jonah would share that with his daughter. However, my smile disappeared when I saw the pinched expression on Miriam's face. The Amish woman said something in their language to the girl. Emma ran after her brothers toward the barn.

"Please tell Anna I'm sorry I missed her." When Miriam didn't respond, I went on, "Is Jonah here?"

"Why?" she snapped.

"I'd like to talk to him." I swallowed. "You must know Joseph Walker died in my quilt shop. I wanted to talk to Jonah about it."

She narrowed her eyes to mere slits. "My husband knows nothing about Joseph Walker."

"I—"

Miriam glared at me. "Stay away from my husband."

I blinked. "Why?"

"He doesn't want to talk to you."

I didn't believe her. I had seen Jonah the day before, and he had been chatty, happy to see me. "How do you know that?"

"Because he is married, and married Amish men don't talk to unmarried *Englisch* women." She started toward the barn where the children had gone.

"Jo-Jo is my friend," I burst out.

Her head snapped around. "His name is Jonah. He is an adult. It's time to put away childish names. You will lead him to trouble."

"I would never do anything to hurt him or your family."

"I hope that's true." She continued on her way.

I reached for the door handle of my car. Did Miriam honestly think I wanted to harm her family? Had Jonah said something that made her think that?

I slapped my leg. "Come on, Oliver. Time to go."

The little black-and-white dog didn't appear.

"Oliver! Let's go!" I peeked under the SUV, but the dog wasn't there.

Suddenly, Oliver shot out from behind the barn with a gray goose in hot pursuit. The bird's wings were spread wide while it honked and squawked at my dog. The twins were two strides behind the goose, and they laughed and squealed.

Oliver as a white and black blur flew by me. I jumped in front of the goose. "Stop!"

The bird shook to a sudden stop. The twins pounced onto the goose. Oliver kept going and dashed for the pigpen. He wriggled his body under the fence and began running in a circle. The four pigs squealed and huddled in the farthest corner of the pen.

Miriam and Emma emerged from the barn. Emma ran over to help the boys with the angry goose, while their mother yelled at them in their language. The boys left the goose with Emma and ran for the pigpen. They clambered over the fence and chased Oliver. The boys' squeals were as loud as those of the pigs. Oliver and the twins were covered in mud.

I dashed over to the pen. "Oliver!"

The dog stopped dead in his tracks, so abruptly that the boys weren't ready, and they fell face-first into the mud. They splashed even more mud on themselves as they tried to stand up. Oliver wriggled under a gap in the fence and disappeared behind the barn.

Miriam placed her hands on her hips and yelled at them in Pennsylvania Dutch. The boys righted themselves and climbed over the fence. The pigs grunted approval. They were happy to have their pen back.

A male voice said something in their language. I turned to see Jonah striding toward us. His brow shot up when he saw me and he frowned when he saw Ethan and Ezra (or was it Ezra and Ethan?) covered in mud. "What is going on here?"

The boys talked over each other in a hurry to explain. "The lady's dog got loose," one said.

The other added, "And we were trying to catch him. He was too fast, and we fell into the pigpen."

Jonah folded his arms. "Dog? I don't see any dog."

I hurried over to Jonah's side. "It's my dog, Oliver. We have to find him. He's a city dog. He doesn't know how to behave on a farm."

The twins ran around the barn whistling and calling Oliver's name. Emma herded the runaway goose back into its pen with her flock. The geese squawked. Miriam walked up to her husband after firing a glare in my direction. The couple consulted for a minute.

Jonah shook his head. He waved me over. "Let's look for Oliver."

I went one way, he went the other. The twins were running their own search, but I think mostly they were enjoying running around covered in mud, and covering everything they came in contact with in mud too.

I searched under bushes and behind feeding troughs. I knew that Oliver would be hiding. The best place to hide was the barn, so I went there.

Emma sat on a milking stool in the barn. She pointed to the hay bale. "He's in there," she whispered.

Oliver's stubby tail was the only piece of him showing. I smiled at her and crept up on my dog. I knocked the hay off the top of his head. He shot a soulful look at me. I laughed. "Come on, Ollie. I think we've both had enough country life for one day."

"You have a funny dog." The girl pulled at a loose black thread in her apron.

"I know."

"I like your dog. I wish we could have one like that. Does he sleep in your house?" Emma asked over the screeches of the twins outside.

I pulled up a second milking stool. "He sleeps in my bed with me."

She sighed. "*Mamm* says dogs aren't meant to be in the house."

"I suppose that's true about some dogs, but Oliver wouldn't last one night outside."

She smiled. "You are the *Englischer* who owns the quilt shop in town."

"I am."

"My *grossmammi* said you were coming here, and we had to be nice to you because you are Eleanor's niece. Eleanor was *Grossmammi*'s favorite friend."

I smiled.

"My favorite friend is Ginny Walker."

Walker?

I was about to ask her if Ginny was related to Joseph, when she said, "Her *daed* died in your shop."

"I know," I said quietly. "How is Ginny?"

"Sad." She twirled a piece of hay between her fingers. The simple answer broke my heart.

"And scared."

"Why is she scared?"

She threw the strand of hay back onto the hay bale. "She thinks her uncle will come back now."

I gave a sharp intake of breath. "Elijah?"

She nodded. "A week ago her uncle came to their home wanting a place to stay, and her *daed* turned Elijah away. Elijah was very mad."

"How was he mad?"

She wrapped her bare arms around her waist. "He told Ginny's *daed* he would be sorry for turning his back on family."

My mind flashed back to the image of Elijah Knepp on the Walker farm. He had been hiding in the outbuilding. Did Abigail at least know that he was there? Was she hiding it from her daughters? "Thank you for telling me this, Emma."

Outside the boys and Jonah continued to call Oliver's name. I knew we should go out and tell them we found Oliver safe and sound, but I did not want to interrupt our conversation. I knew it was important.

Emma leaned forward. "Maybe you can find Elijah. I've told my *daed* to find him, but he will not. He said it is not our business."

My brow wrinkled. "Why do you want me to find Elijah? You just said that Ginny didn't want her uncle to come back."

"Because I hate to see my friend so afraid. Because he's the one who killed Ginny's *daed*."

My mouth went dry. "Are you sure? How do you know that?"

"Because that's what Ginny said. She would not say that of her own uncle if it were not the truth."

I had to agree. Would a little girl's suspicion be enough to convince Sheriff Mitchell? I wasn't so sure about that.

"Emma," Jonah's voice called from outside of the barn door.

"I have to go." She jumped off her stool and shot out of the barn before I could ask her any more questions, although I had dozens sitting at the tip of my tongue.

"Oliver?"

His stubby tail slithered into the pile of hay. After several minutes of searching, I managed to pull Oliver out from the hay and carried him from the barn.

When the Frenchie and I emerged from the barn, the mud-covered twins ran to us. "I've never seen a dog be so scared like that before."

"The goose was bigger than he was," I said in Oliver's defense.

The dog buried his wet nose into my elbow.

Ethan/Ezra laughed. "And she was mad too."

Jonah gripped his suspenders. "You two are filthy. Go wash up. Don't go in the house. Use the hose on the other side of the barn."

The boys' eyes gleamed at this suggestion. The air was humid as the hot afternoon sun seemed to be stuck in high-noon position despite the lateness in the day. They ran around the barn. Within seconds we heard shrieks of delight and the sound of the water hose.

Miriam and Jonah spoke in their language. The Pennsylvania Dutch words I knew as a child when I spent the summers with my aunt had been wiped from my memory. Maybe Rachel or Anna could teach me some. I'm sure they would come in handy at the shop.

I carried Oliver to my car. With one hand, I spread an old towel I kept for wet-dog emergencies on the backseat, and Oliver curled up on top of it. He was more than ready to go home.

Jonah was at my side. "Did you want to talk to my mother? She's calling on Abigail today."

I nodded. "I'm having a quilting circle meeting at my house at three and would like her to come. I'm here for another reason too, though."

He cocked his head and waited.

"I'm looking for Elijah Knepp. I need to talk to him. He's hiding out at the Walker farm in one of the outbuildings. Will you come with me?"

"How would you know where he is?"

"People talk," was my vague answer.

"I will not go with you to talk to Elijah." Jonah's eyes narrowed. "I already told you that was a bad idea."

"It's important." I thought it was even more important now that I heard what Ginny had told Emma about her uncle. If I couldn't talk to Elijah, maybe Ginny would talk to me.

"Angie, you don't want to get involved with Elijah Knepp."

"Why didn't you tell me that Elijah burned down your barn?"

A pained expression crossed Jonah's face. "Because it is in the past. I have forgiven him. When you forgive, you do not speak of the injury again. Would we want *Gott* to remind us of everything we've done wrong?"

"But—"

He cut me off. "I have told my wife she need not worry about you. We are *friends*; that is all. Because you're my old friend, I do not want you to be hurt. That means staying away from Elijah Knepp." His tone had finality to it. I would need to reach Elijah another way.

"Thank you for being my friend," I murmured as I

climbed in. I shifted the car into reverse and backed away.

One of the twins raced around the barn brandishing a bucket of water to throw on the other. Jonah shouted at them. Miriam ignored the boys and glared me down as I drove off the farm.

Chapter Twenty-nine

Unlike my Amish friends, I didn't have any wonderful homemade treats to serve my guests. I dumped a bag of potato chips into a ceramic bowl and set crackers on a plate. When this murder thing was over, I would take more time to cook, I promised myself as I artfully arranged pieces of cellophane-wrapped American cheese on the cracker plate.

A knock sounded on the front door. I left my calcium-rich masterpiece and let Rachel into the house. "Angie, your house is so cute."

"Thanks. Sorry about all the boxes everywhere. I haven't finished unpacking," I said. *And if Mitchell throws me in jail I won't need to,* I thought.

Rachel followed me into the kitchen and placed a hand to her mouth. "Angie, is that what you're serving?"

I eyed her. "Are you laughing at me?"

"No." She giggled. She held up a basket. "I brought some cookies from the bakery."

"You did?" I grinned. "Bless you!" I tossed the last piece of American cheese onto the plate. "My options are pathetic."

"I knew that you wouldn't have time to make anything." She placed the basket on the counter, and I began putting away the cheese.

Rachel removed a perfect plate of Amish-made cookies from her basket. "Can I do anything else?"

"Could you grab the iced tea from the refrigerator?"

She nodded and placed the iced tea pitcher on the counter.

I returned the cheese to the refrigerator and removed the lemonade. Between the iced tea and lemonade, at least I had decent summer beverages to serve my guests. "There's something I need to talk to you about before the other women arrive."

There was a second knock on the front door. *So much for that plan.*

I turned around to find Rachel holding the bowl of chips, the pitcher of iced tea, and seven glasses. All were perfectly balanced in her arms without a tray. "How did you do that?"

She laughed. "I'm from a big Amish family, remember? I'm used to carrying a lot. Also I have three *kinner*."

"Well, I'm impressed."

"Do you have time to tell me now?"

I couldn't talk to her about Mattie and Elijah now that the other ladies were here. "We can talk about it later."

Another knock rapped on the door. Rachel breezed out of the kitchen. "I'll get that. You put that cheese away before someone else sees it."

I laughed. After I tucked the cheese back into the refrigerator and picked up the pitcher of lemonade, I went into the living room.

Anna and Sarah sat on the couch. Abram was on the

floor pulling on Oliver's ear. The little dog didn't seem to mind. Mattie perched in one of the armchairs. I almost dropped the pitcher.

Rachel bumped into my back. "I hope you don't mind that Mattie came with me. She asked to come." She stepped around me.

"Absolutely okay," I said, regaining my composure. "I was just surprised that she didn't come in with you."

Rachel smiled her sweet smile. "She wanted to look at your garden. Mattie loves flowers. This is the first time Mattie has shown an interest in quilting. I've been trying to get her to join for years. You should see her cross-stitch. It's gorgeous."

The younger Amish woman blushed. "I do enjoy it."

"Have you quilted before?" Anna asked.

"A little," Mattie said barely above a whisper. "My *mamm* taught me, of course. We never had much time to dedicate to it because of the bakery."

Anna nodded. "Yes, I know your family works hard at the bakery, but then it's one of the biggest draws to Rolling Brook."

Sarah laid pieces of a bear-claw quilt on her skirted lap. "Where's Martha? Is she coming?"

I peeked out my front window as I passed it. Three Amish buggies were parked outside my window. I wondered what all my young professional friends back home in Dallas would think if they saw me now. What would Ryan think of it? I started. It was the first time that I had thought of Ryan all day. Did that mean I'd recovered from my broken heart? Or was I simply distracted by murder? "I don't know if she will be here. I couldn't find her today, but I left a message on the shed phone closest to her house."

"I'm certain she knows about it, then." Anna pursed her lips together. "If she's not here, there must be a *gut* reason."

Sarah leaned forward. "That's strange. With Running Stitch closed, you would think she would have time to come. She doesn't have a husband or children to tend to like the rest of us."

"I'm sure the next time we meet, she will tell us why she wasn't here," Anna said, ending the conversation about Martha.

I felt Sarah watching me as I set the lemonade in the middle of the coffee table next to the iced tea and cookies Rachel already put there. I cleared my throat. "Speaking of Running Stitch, the sheriff told me today that the shop can reopen tomorrow morning."

Rachel clasped her hands together as she lowered herself to a stool. "Angie, that's wonderful news. Truly." Abram played with blocks on his blanket a few inches from Oliver, who was the self-appointed babysitter.

I smiled. "I'm looking forward to opening up, especially considering the upcoming event this weekend."

Anna frowned. "You mean the watermelons."

I nodded.

The ladies all grew very quiet.

"Do the Amish not like watermelons or something?"

Anna snorted. "No, no, Angie. Watermelons are fine. Some are afraid that if too many tourists come to Rolling Brook, we will lose our true identity."

My brow wrinkled. "Is that how you feel?"

Anna smiled. "No, but I don't want you to put yourself in a position that might offend some in the community."

"I don't know how this little fest will make that much of a difference," I said.

Sarah poured herself a glass of iced tea. "Have you ever been to Lancaster County?"

"No," I admitted.

"We are not judging, but the Amish there run a few of the towns like a Walt Disney World attraction. Billboards everywhere, fifteen companies giving buggy rides, countless inns and hotels."

"Is that bad?" I asked.

Anna removed quilt pieces from her basket. "*Nee*, of course not, but neither is it bad not to want to be like that. To be an authentic Amish town with Amish shopkeepers doing the work they've done for generations."

"I see your point, but Holmes County is already one of the most popular tourist destinations in Ohio. Shouldn't Rolling Brook benefit from that?"

Sarah replaced her iced tea on the table and took up her piecing. "I agree with Angie. We shouldn't be afraid of something that will bring business to Rolling Brook. We will never grow as large as Intercourse in Lancaster, or even Berlin down the road. I think all the worry will be for nothing."

Anna wrapped thread around the tip of her needle for the quilter's knot. "I think most Amish will come around. The biggest naysayer was Joseph Walker, and he's gone now."

Again, I wondered if Willow and Farley were viable suspects.

"My brother doesn't like the idea either." Mattie spoke up for the first time. Her breathy voice was low.

Rachel blushed. "My husband will be happy when it brings new customers into the bakery, which it surely will."

I picked up my own sewing basket and removed the

crazy quilt I had started in Texas right after Ryan dumped me. A crazy quilt can be just about any quilt made without a pattern and with different kinds of fabric, very different from the way Amish make quilts. The Texas night sky was my inspiration, and I was just winging it as I went along. The colors were royal purple, navy, gold, bronze, and silver. Seeing it gave me a stab of homesickness.

"What's that?" Anna said, leaning forward.

I blushed and handed it to her. "A quilt I started right before I moved."

Anna stretched the quilt topper over her lap. "You made this?"

I nodded. "It's my own design. A crazy quilt. It's supposed to be the night sky over Texas."

Rachel stood off and examined the quilt on Anna's lap. "Angie, it's beautiful. A work of art."

"Let me see." Sarah adjusted her wire-rimmed glasses. Anna handed the topper to her.

Sarah ran her hand along the stitches.

I blushed. "I machine stitched it."

"That doesn't matter. The color choices and pattern are *schee*, beautiful," Sarah said.

Now my cheeks were red-hot. "Thank you," I murmured.

Sarah handed the quilt to Anna.

She inspected it more closely than the other two women. "Angie, you have the potential to be as *gut* a quilter as Eleanor. You have the eye. You only need to practice your hand stitching."

I tried to stifle the grin growing on my face. I knew the Amish believed in humility, but I couldn't hold it back. "Really?"

Rachel returned to her stool. "Really."

"I hope so, and I want this circle for teaching techniques too." I cleared my throat. "I think the circle can help lots of women. I would love to have three or four classes running out of the shop for different groups. Maybe a machine-quilting group for English women, and a hand-stitching group for beginners. Running Stitch has so much potential. We could also teach classes and give demonstrations." My ideas came out in a rush.

They were silent. Remembering the conversation of the Amish desire to keep Rolling Brook small, I worried that maybe these ideas were more than the ladies bargained for. Here I was some English upstart from Texas, trying to teach them something about running a business in Holmes County.

Anna slipped her reading glasses onto her nose. "Even though *Gott* tells us not to be prideful, Eleanor would be so proud of you right now."

I grinned. "Do you know other ladies who would be interested in quilting?"

"Of course," Sarah said. "Almost all Amish women quilt at least a little, and it's popular among the *Englischers* too."

"Do you think Abigail would like to join the circle now?" I let the question hang in the air. They all knew that I was going to add, "now that Joseph is dead."

Sarah selected a butterscotch cookie. "Abigail has wanted to join the circle for years. You should see her work. It's exquisite. Almost as *gut* as Eleanor's was. She didn't join because of her husband. He didn't approve of Eleanor running the shop on her own."

Anna leaned over and patted my knee. "I think it's a nice gesture that you want to ask her, but we should wait a few weeks. She needs time to adjust to her new life."

I chose a snickerdoodle from the tray. "That's what I was thinking. Maybe I will ask her in the fall."

"A fine idea," Anna said. "Have you mentioned any of your big ideas for Running Stitch to Martha?"

I looked up from my quilt. "No. We haven't had the time to discuss it with everything that has happened. I was hoping to tell her tonight before I told all of you. I know I should have spoken to her first about it, but I couldn't help myself."

Sarah and Rachel shared a look.

"What?" I asked.

"Martha won't be happy we know about this before she does," Rachel said quietly.

"Why?" I asked.

"Don't you know that she considered Running Stitch her store?" Sarah said. "She did from the moment Eleanor became ill."

Anna folded her hands on top of her quilt. "Martha thought she was the one who would inherit the quilt shop when Eleanor died. She talked about it often. She was upset when she learned it was going to you."

I felt a pang in my chest.

Sarah broke her cookie in half. "That's the real reason why she's not here," Sarah said, which only made me feel worse.

Chapter Thirty

The ladies and I quilted in silence for a few minutes. Learning how Martha really felt about my owning the shop was a shock. Perhaps she changed her mind about me since I moved to Holmes County? Again I remembered she was the only other person with a key to the shop.

Rachel laughed. "We are almost out of cookies. I have more in my basket in the kitchen." She started to stand.

"I will get it." Mattie jumped up from her seat.

"Danki," her sister-in-law said.

Mattie picked up the plate and hurried into the kitchen. After a moment, I excused myself and followed her. Before I left the living room, I saw Sarah's eyebrows shoot up.

In the kitchen, Mattie arranged the cookies onto the plate. "Thank you for holding the circle in your home. My sister-in-law is right; I do enjoy quilting. I love to do anything I can with my hands." She frowned. "Just not baking."

"You don't like working at the bakery?"

"*Nee*. The hours are long and every day is the same. We must get up at the same time every morning to make sure everything is ready to open at eight. That means getting to the shop at four. I would love to sleep in until five someday." She blushed. "I should not complain. There are many without such a job or a family to care for them. My brother and Rachel took me in when my parents died. They both have been very *gut* to me."

"I'm an only child. While growing up, I always wanted a brother or sister to play with, someone to take some of my mother's attention off of me."

Mattie laughed.

I bit the inside of my lip. "Have you seen Elijah Knepp lately?"

Her smile disappeared as she wiped her hands on her dark purple skirt and smoothed her black apron on top. "Why would I know anything about him?"

"He was your sweetheart."

She snapped the basket lid closed. "Did Rachel tell you that?"

"Yes."

Her eyes began to water in the corners.

"She had good intentions for telling me. She wanted to warn me about him. She knows that I would like to talk to him."

"About what?" Mattie asked.

"Joseph."

The name hung in the air between us for a moment.

She gripped the counter. "I have not seen him. My brother would not allow it."

"Mattie, I saw you with him this very morning." I tried to keep my voice gentle.

Her face flushed. "That's not possible."

"You were at the Walker farm and met him in an out-building close to the orchard."

Mattie gasped. "How could you have seen us? You were not there." She covered her mouth with her hand as she realized she'd admitted she was with Elijah that morning.

"Did he tell you anything about Joseph?"

Tears gathered in her eyes. "He said Joseph was the reason he went to jail, but that he did not kill him." Her voice dropped to a whisper as a tear slid down her pale cheek. "He promised me he didn't do it."

"You believe him."

"You do not understand him. I'm the only one who does."

"Didn't he burn down the Grabers' barn?"

Her eyes flashed. "It was an accident."

I wasn't sure how dousing the barn with kerosene could be an accident, but I didn't say that because I didn't want her to storm out of the house.

"Elijah has had a difficult life."

"Other than going to ⎣rison?"

She glared at me. "*Ya.* His father was a harsh man." She lowered her voice. "He hit his wife, Elijah and Abigail's mother, many times in front of the children. Elijah told the bishop, who did nothing. Many Amish don't see why this is wrong. Elijah said the best thing that ever happened to his family was his father's death."

"When did he die?"

"We were in our last year of school, when Elijah and I were in the eighth grade."

"Did you ever tell anyone about Elijah's father?"

"*Nee*, he asked me not to, and I keep my word." She

frowned. "Until now. But I am telling you because Elijah believed Abigail married someone like their father."

"Did Joseph hit Abigail?"

"I don't know. Elijah only said that he was cruel to her. I never pressed him. That is not the Amish way."

Clearly, I would make a terrible Amish person because I was always pressing people for more information. Mattie might not know it, but she gave me another reason Elijah might have killed Joseph—to protect his sister.

She nodded. "Please don't tell Rachel or Aaron about this."

"Rachel is—"

"I know Rachel is your *gut* friend, but I promised myself that I would not see Elijah again, and not for my family, but for me. Seeing him today was so difficult, and I know in my heart this is what *Gott* wants me to do." She wiped another tear from her eye. "Will you tell?"

"I won't tell."

She gave me a watery smile. "*Gut.* I did not come here to talk about Elijah. I came here to escape thinking about Elijah."

I patted her arm. "I can tell you from firsthand experience that quilting helps heal wounds from a broken heart."

"Is your heart broken?"

"It was, but every day it gets a little better."

Sarah stepped into the kitchen. "Is anything wrong?" she asked eagerly as if she hoped we would say yes. "You two are taking an awful long time in here."

Mattie spun around to hide her tears.

I picked up the tray of cookies. "Nothing's wrong."

"Mattie looks upset." Sarah took a step closer to the younger Amish woman.

"Allergies," I said.

Sarah squinted at me through her glasses. "I've never known Mattie to have allergies."

"Well, she does," I said.

"Do you have allergies, Mattie?"

"Something here has made my eyes water." She touched the corner of her right eye. "Excuse me." Mattie hurried past Sarah in the direction of the bathroom.

Sarah placed her hands on her hips. "I don't buy the allergies bit for a second. You said something to Mattie to make her cry. It was about Elijah Knepp, wasn't it? The two were promised to each other before Elijah went upriver."

I snorted a laugh. "Upriver? That doesn't sound like an Amish phrase."

"Well, I watched some television during my *rumspringa*." She placed her hand on my arm. "You won't tell me what was really going on in here, will you?"

I shook my head.

She dropped her hand. "Fair enough. I always find out, one way or another." She left the kitchen. Sarah missed her calling. She should have been a gossip columnist. I wondered if the Amish *Budget* had such a column.

As I followed Mattie into the living room, Anna said to Mattie, "What kept you two so long?"

Mattie sat and began her quilting again. "I don't wish to speak of it."

Anna smiled at her. "It's *gut* you're taking up quilting, then. Eleanor always said a quilt was the best keeper of a woman's secrets."

I nearly dropped the cookie tray.

Mattie took it from me. "Are you all right, Angie?"

"Yes, I'm fine. I—"

Sarah watched me over her cup of tea.

I shut my mouth. My heart thumped in my chest. That was it, why the quilt was torn to bits. That was where my aunt hid the deed. That wedding ring quilt was her favorite quilt she made. It would make perfect sense that she would place the deed there for safekeeping.

"Angie, you are as white as a sheet," Rachel said.

I felt the women's eyes on me. "I'm just worried about Martha. That's all."

Anna frowned. She wasn't buying it but didn't contradict me. She folded her quilt squares. "Ladies, I think it's time to go. Angie needs some rest."

The women packed up their quilting baskets. "No, stay. I'll be fine."

Rachel picked Abram off the floor. "Anna's right, and I should get home to start supper."

Mattie would not meet my gaze.

Anna placed a hand to her back as she straightened up too. "I'll stop by the shop tomorrow, Angie, to see if you need any help."

"I'm sure Martha will be there. When I left the message on the shed phone answering machine before you arrived, I told her the shop would open at the normal time tomorrow."

Anna patted my arm. "I will still stop by."

I watched the buggies roll away and wondered if Anna made that last comment to be nice or because she thought Martha would not show up for work the next day.

As the last buggy disappeared around the corner, my cell phone rang. I followed the sound into the kitchen. I was expecting to see my mother's number in the read-out, but instead it was Mitchell's cell. I knew because I had programmed the number into my phone and listed it under "paddy wagon." I twisted my mouth. I wasn't sure of the two whom I wanted to talk to least.

I answered the call, hoping that the sheriff wasn't about to tell me that he changed his mind and I wasn't allowed to open my store tomorrow morning after all.

"Angie, this is Sheriff Mitchell. I'm calling to tell you I made arrangements for a professional cleaning company to meet you at your shop tomorrow morning." He paused. "They are licensed to clean up crime scenes."

I grimaced. In my eagerness to reopen the quilt shop, I had forgotten the little issue of the stockroom. The red stain on the wood floor flashed across my mind's eye. I didn't know of any cleaning solution that would get that out. "Can I do it myself?" Throwing an area rug over the stain was always an option.

"No. You want a professional doing the stockroom." His tone left no room for discussion.

"Is it very expensive?"

"Your insurance company should cover it."

"They would if I knew Aunt Eleanor had insurance."

"She would have had to have insurance to run a business to sell wares in Ohio. Talk to her lawyer. I'm sure he has all that information. I lined up a locksmith to put a dead bolt on your back door."

"Thank you." The sheriff was going way above the call of duty. Was this how law enforcement worked in the country?

"Don't mention it."

I sat on the couch, and Oliver lay across my lap. "There's something I need to tell you."

"What's that?" The sheriff sounded wary.

"I know why the quilt was shredded." I went on to tell him my theory about the hidden deed.

"But then where's the deed?" he asked. "We didn't find it at the scene."

"Maybe the killer took it with him."

"That's possible." He was quiet for a moment. "If it was there in the first place."

"I know it was there," I said. "I know my aunt, and it makes perfect sense. And Joseph Walker would want the deed. He could destroy it, and I'd have no proof that the quilt shop was mine."

"So you think Joseph Walker went into the shop first."

"Yes, or maybe he and the killer went in together," I said.

"Okay, but that still doesn't explain how he got in."

"I thought you said that anyone could break in through the back door with a credit card."

"I did, but Amish don't have credit cards, or driver's licenses for that matter. I went through Joseph's wallet. He didn't have any card that would work."

"So the killer is English," I mused.

"I didn't say that."

"But Harvey said that Martha and I are the only ones with copies of keys."

Mitchell was quiet.

"You don't think Martha gave him the key, do you?"

"It's worth asking her."

I nearly dropped my phone. Oliver sat up and licked my chin.

I heard a child's voice in the background, and then Mitchell said, "Angie, I have to go. I will meet you in front of Running Stitch at nine sharp with the cleaning guys." He hung up.

I stared at the cell after he hung up. Why did the sheriff need to be there for the cleanup? Didn't he have better things to do, like finding Elijah Knepp? What was I going to say to Martha?

Chapter Thirty-one

When I arrived at Running Stitch the next morning, a white paneled van with huge red lettering on the side sat in the diagonal spot in front of Running Stitch. The lettering read "Crime Moppers." The tagline beneath the company's name was "We specialize in blood and gunpowder."

I groaned. This was just what the out-of-towners wanted to see when they visited Amish Country. I hoped the van would be gone before the tourists started showing up in an hour. Oliver sat in the backseat. I tied Oliver's leash to the park bench. "You stay. I want to make sure it's safe for you in the shop first."

He curled up under the bench. After the goose incident, he wasn't taking any chances.

As I approached the van, two men in white biohazard suits exited the van. An elderly couple strolled by. "It's nothing to be concerned about," I told them.

The man pointed a crooked finger at the shop. "You've got gunpowder that they need to clean up in there?"

"No," I said, happy to answer a question honestly.

"Herbert, don't you know that's the place an Amish

man's throat was slashed? It was in the paper," his friend said.

"Oh." He lifted his circa 1960 camera to his eye with shaky hands and snapped a photo of the van, the shop, the guys in suits, and me. "Who knew a weekend in Amish Country would be so exciting?"

"The shop opens at ten if you want to come back then."

The old guy's eyes gleamed. "You bet."

I felt a little guilty for drumming up business with the murder angle, but a girl's got to make a living.

I followed one of the suited men into the shop. "How'd you guys get in here?"

One of the men, who didn't look like he weighed more than a hundred pounds, said, "The sheriff let us in an hour ago. You must be Angie. I hope you don't mind that he did that. He let the locksmith in too. That guy has already come and gone. He put a really strong lock on your back door." He handed me a key. "That's the key to the back door now. The sheriff couldn't stay because he got a call out right after and had to leave. He wanted me to tell you that."

"It's fine," I said, wondering why the sheriff thought I would need to know that.

He hopped from foot to foot. "He said we need to be out of here by ten."

"That's right. That's when the shop opens."

"We should be able to do it. This is a standard job."

I tried to wrap my mind around the cleaning of crime scenes as standard.

"I'm Gill." He pointed at his lumbering partner. "That's Mack. So far, we cleared the room and we're about to start the cleaning process. Want to take a look?"

"Yes." I followed them to the back of the shop. The stockroom door stood open. My eyes fell on the stain on the floor. "The stain is the biggest concern."

"This is no problem," Mack's voice rumbled. "We've seen a lot worse than this, haven't we, Gill?"

"Word," skinny Gill replied. "We need to do the paperwork first. You have insurance."

"Yes." I'd called Harvey last night to learn that Aunt Eleanor had an insurance policy on the shop. He gave me all the pertinent information to file a formal claim.

"Gill, why don't you do the papers, and I'll get started," Mack grunted.

"I have the insurance numbers in my purse." I patted the bag at my side. "We can fill it out at the front counter."

Gill followed me to the front of the store, and I removed the notebook with the insurance information from my bag. He pulled a stapled form from inside his hazmat suit. He smoothed it over the countertop. "Just need to fill this out. And sign here, here, and here."

I started the forms.

Gill leaned his elbows on the counter. "You know, we've been working with the county on jobs like this for a long time."

"Uh-huh," I murmured as I painstakingly filled in the dozens of tiny boxes.

"This is the first time ever Mitchell set up the appointment himself. I was real surprised to get his call. He said it was essential we finish the job this morning, so that your shop could open. He called in a couple of favors to get us here." He sucked on his teeth. "Like I said, we do this all the time. Course most of our work is up in Stark County. More city folks with handguns up that way."

I flipped to the next page. "That was nice of the sheriff to call. I don't know any of the companies."

"I'm sure that's what he was thinking. Just being neighborly to the new girl in town."

I was only half listening. "Right."

"Then again, now that I met you, I think it could be the old sheriff has a bit of a crush on you."

My head snapped up. "What?"

He smiled. "One more signature on the last page, and we are all set."

I signed, and he folded up the form again and tucked it back into his white suit.

What a ridiculous idea. Mitchell didn't have a crush on me. He thought I was a cold-blooded killer. "I have a dog. Will it be safe for him to come into the store today?"

"Don't let him in the stockroom, and you'll be fine." He sucked on his teeth. "In fact, I would leave the stockroom alone for, say, twenty-four hours. After that, you should be okay." He moseyed back to the stockroom. "Mack, we are good to go."

The pair walked out to the truck and rolled the largest Shop-Vac I had ever seen across the floor. Seconds later the sound of the hose rang in my ears. Now would be a good time to take Oliver for a walk.

When I got back outside, Oliver had wrapped his leash around all four legs of the park bench. "Come on, buddy. We need to get out of here." I spent five minutes untangling the mess.

When he was free, I knew exactly where the walk should start, because I owed someone an apology.

It didn't take much encouragement from me to get Oliver to walk across the street to the bakery. While the other shops on Sugartree opened at ten in the morning, the bakery opened at eight. All the tables in the tiny seating area were occupied with elderly Amish men or English tourists who arrived at Rolling Brook early to avoid the influx of tour buses that would descend within the hour. Both Mattie and Rachel were hard at work behind the counter. Rachel waved at me, but Mattie gave me no acknowledgment. An apology was definitely in order.

The visitor in front of me thanked Rachel for the pies he'd purchased and left the shop.

"I saw the van in front of the quilt shop," Rachel said.

"They promised to be done by opening."

Oliver bumped against my leg. "Is it okay I brought Oliver inside? He's afraid of the van."

She laughed. "No problem." She reached under the counter and came up with a dog biscuit and handed it to me.

Oliver climbed halfway up my leg before I even had a good grip on it.

I held out the biscuit. "Sit."

He gave me a look that said, "Really?"

"Sit."

He sat and I dropped the biscuit in his mouth. I smiled at Rachel. "Now you're in trouble. He's going to remember where to get the treats from."

Rachel tucked a piece of stray hair back with a hairpin. "We have plenty more where that came from." She shot a thumb behind her. "I thought you would notice our new item."

"What's that?"

I read the black chalkboard. "Eight-inch cinnamon rolls and doughnuts." I laughed.

"They are selling like crazy. I guess size matters to

Englischers, and you aren't the only one who wants a doughnut the size of her head. Want one now?"

"No, I'll wait till my next moment of crisis. If the sheriff arrests me, you can send me one while I'm in jail."

"The sheriff is not going to arrest you."

I rested my arms on the counter. "I think you might be right. Don't you think if he had enough on me, he would have done it by now?"

"Exactly. This means you can give up your search for Elijah Knepp." She lowered her voice when she said Elijah's name. I knew it was because Mattie was so close by.

Mattie came around the counter with the broom. "Rachel, I'm going outside to sweep."

Her sister-in-law nodded.

Mattie made eye contact with me before she went out of the door.

"Now that Oliver had an extra treat, we should get along on our walk."

Oliver shuffled to the end of the counter where Rachel could see him better and gave her his best puppy dog gaze. It always worked on me, and Rachel was a sucker too. "What about one more treat?"

"Oh fine. He's had a rough few days. Remind me to tell you about him being chased by a goose on the Graber farm."

She grinned. "I can imagine how that went."

As if he knew exactly what we were saying, Oliver gave a full-body shiver.

She dropped the treat into his mouth, and he gobbled it down.

"All right, that's enough," I told him as I dragged him from the bakery. Rachel's cheerful laughter floated after us.

I found Mattie holding her broom at the right side of the bakery's window. She was out of the view of anyone inside the bakery.

She leaned on her broom. "What is going on at Running Stitch?"

There wasn't a delicate way to put it, so I said, "Those men are cleaning up the stockroom."

Her eyes locked on the van. "Oh." She dropped her head. "I am grieved for the family. It may not appear so, but I am. Had I married Elijah, they would have been my family too. Before—" She paused. "Before the fire."

Oliver hid under the park bench in front of the bakery. Even across the street we could hear the commotion of the Shop-Vac inside the stockroom.

"Why did Elijah burn down the Graber barn?" I asked.

She sighed. "I asked him once. It was before Joseph told the police. Joseph wasn't the only one who knew. I did too." She began to sweep the dust from the sidewalk out onto the street. "He said he wanted to know if he could."

"That was the reason he gave you?" I asked. Clearly, the guy was insane. Mattie was much better off without him. I didn't say that. I didn't want to disturb the rapport we had going.

"That's what he said. I did not question him further. I—I was afraid to."

"I wanted to apologize to you yesterday. I should have been kinder when I asked you about seeing Elijah."

"I accept your apology." She stopped sweeping. "What I can't figure out is how you saw us."

I gave her a sheepish look. "Well, do you really want to know?"

She nodded.

I went over and told her about Danny, the spider, and the ants in his pants. She laughed so hard she had to grip onto the broom to hold her upright.

I smirked.

"Have you seen Danny since then?"

"Actually no." I smiled. "I should probably find out if he's okay."

"I'm sure he's fine. He can write a story about it."

"I've been thinking about your embroidery."

Her eyebrows went up. "Yes?"

"And I wondered if you'd like to teach some embroidery classes at Running Stitch. The classes would fit well with the quilt shop. I think a lot of tourists would be interested in it."

She began sweeping again. "Oh, I don't know."

"It could be a few classes a year. It doesn't have to be a lot. Whatever you were able and wanted to do. We'd have to work out the terms, but I would pay you for your time."

Her brows knit together. "I've never taught anyone to sew before." Her eyes darted to the store's front door. "It would be nice to do something different. I will have to talk to Aaron and Rachel."

"I understand. If you're ever interested, let me know."

"I will," she promised. "Have you heard from Martha yet?"

I frowned. "No, I haven't."

Chapter Thirty-two

Gill and Mack were gone on schedule, and Running Stitch was back in business. I dusted the shelves and counter and turned the sign in the front window to OPEN. There was no sign of Martha.

I went into Running Stitch's back garden, where I'd get a better signal, and I tried to call the number of the Amish shed phone I had for Martha a third time. No answer. Again. I didn't bother to leave yet another message.

"Miss," a woman in a flower-printed jumpsuit asked. "I'm trying to select some colors for my next quilt. Do you have any suggestions?"

I placed my cell phone back into my pocket. "No problem."

In the early afternoon, Anna walked into the shop. She nodded her head at the group of women admiring my aunt's quilts. "Business is *gut*."

"It's been pretty steady, especially considering this is the middle of the week. I don't know if they are coming in because they are interested in quilts or interested in visiting a real-life crime scene. Either way, it's been good business. Most have bought something even if it's only been a thimble, which reminds me—I need to reorder some. They seem to be more popular than I thought." I chewed on my lip. "I wonder if decorative thimbles would be a nice keepsake item to sell too. I noticed most of the people coming in aren't serious quilters—they want a reminder of their visit to Holmes County."

Oliver sauntered over to Anna and allowed her to scratch his head. "You are full of ideas," she mused.

I laughed. "I guess I'm bursting with ideas right now because I'm happy the shop is open and traffic is good."

She set her basket on the front counter. "Are you the only one here? Where is Martha?"

"I still haven't heard from or seen her. I know something is wrong." I wondered if I should tell Anna my suspicions about Martha and the shop key. But Anna and Martha were friends. I couldn't say anything until I was sure.

"Wrong how? You think she's hurt?"

"No, but after hearing Martha wants the shop as her own, I think she's upset. Wouldn't she be here by now if everything was all right? Wouldn't she have contacted me to see when the shop would open?" I forced a smile. "I can understand why the Amish don't have cell phones, but it can be frustrating to an English person like me when you need to talk to someone."

Anna patted my hand. "Don't worry, *kind*."

"Anna?" I asked.

"That sounds like a serious tone."

I laughed. "It is. Why didn't you tell me Elijah burned down your family's barn?"

Anna sighed. "You asked Jonah the same thing, I suppose. Miriam told me you were on the farm yesterday. She was not happy about it."

"I'm lucky she didn't chase me away with a broom. Although ask Oliver about her attack geese. They make impressive security." I paused. "Jonah said because he forgave Elijah, the past did not need repeating."

She beamed. "Then, I raised my son well because that's my answer too."

"But—"

"No buts. The past is forgiven. Do you know why *Gott* asks us to forgive?"

My religious upbringing was slight, and my memory of the few times I attended Sunday school was foggy. The most outstanding memory I had was of the felt board in the classroom with little felt cutouts of Jesus and the disciples. I had always been drawn to fabric.

"It's as much for the forgiver as for the one forgiven. Those who don't forgive are destroyed by their own hatred and bitterness. That's the last thing *Gott* wants for his children."

Unsolicited, Ryan came to mind. If what Anna said was true, I needed to forgive Ryan as much for myself as for him.

She grinned. "I see those wheels turning. That's all that I ask. That you think of these things, nothing more."

The front door of Running Stitch banged open, and Willow Moon floated inside. "Angie, the store looks fabulous. You wouldn't even know a man was murdered here a few days ago."

Two customers at the needle display gasped and hurried out of the shop empty-handed.

I gritted my teeth. "Thank you, Willow."

"I've the most fantastic idea." She wove about the display in the middle of the room.

Anna covered her mouth to hide a smile.

"What's that?" I asked.

"What if your quilting circle had a quilting bee during the festival? You could invite as many Amish quilters you like. We could set it up in the field outside of the barn."

I leaned on the counter. "That doesn't have much to do with watermelon."

"True, but it would give a wonderful opportunity to showcase your store, and it's a way to involve the Amish. It may show other Amish the Watermelon Fest is not the end of the world." Her eyes were bright.

"It would be a great opportunity for the store, and it would put something out there about Running Stitch other than Joseph's murder," I agreed.

Willow nodded. "Exactly. I think it's high time we made peace with the Amish and English shopkeepers. It is a shame Joseph died, but we can use this as an opportunity to bring the shopkeepers together."

Her comment again made me wonder if she or perhaps Farley had anything to do with Joseph's death.

Something caught Willow's eye. "What cute thimbles." She floated in that direction. "My mother used to collect antique thimbles."

While Willow was distracted, I stepped closer to Anna and lowered my voice. "Do you think the quilting circle would do it?"

Anna considered this. "Some will come, but there will be others who will not. They will feel like they are being put on display. A quilting bee is a time of togetherness and work, not promotion and demonstration."

My face fell.

"Don't worry. I can roust up enough quilters." She picked her basket up from the ground. "To do this, I need to make some visits."

"Are you sure you want to help? Yesterday you told me all the reasons the fest was a bad idea."

She smiled. "I am not against the fest, and I'm happy to help you because you are Eleanor's niece. Let me take on this project for you. You have enough worries between the shop, the murder, and Martha."

Truer words were never spoken.

Willow walked over to us. "So, can you do it?"

I glanced at Anna, who nodded. "We'll do it."

Willow clapped her hands. "Perfect. This will be perfect."

Anna adjusted her glasses. "I love a good sew-in. That's what we Amish call it. Eleanor and I used to host one once a year. We stopped of course when she got sick. I have missed them. Leave it to me." She walked to the front door. "And I had better get started," she said, and left.

Willow made her way toward the door, and then spun around. "I have been meaning to tell you, the night of the murder, I saw lights on in your shop late at night. You know my apartment is over the tea shop, and I can see everything that happens on this street."

My mouth fell open. "I didn't know that." I hurried around the counter. "When did you see the lights?"

She thought for a long minute. "Maybe one in the morning."

I was already gone. It was Joseph or the killer.

"Did you see anyone go in the shop?" My tone was harsh. "Did you tell the sheriff?"

She shook her head. "Is it important?"

Of course, it is important! I wanted to shake her.

"Was anyone else with you? Did anyone else see the lights?"

She shook her head. "I live alone." She placed a hand to her chest. "You don't think I—I would never hurt anyone."

I didn't say anything.

"Joseph was a stern man, but he wasn't going to stop the fest. That was my only dispute with him. I would never kill anyone, but I would most certainly never kill anyone over watermelon."

She wasn't the only one with the watermelon motive. "What about Farley?" I asked.

She cleared her throat. "Farley? I don't know."

If she didn't know, then I would have to find out.

Late in the afternoon after my last customer left, Martha strolled into the shop. The busloads of visitors who stopped by Running Stitch that day were headed back to the big cities and suburbs.

Oliver lay on his dog pillow beside the quilt frame. He opened one eye when Martha entered and then closed it again.

I stuffed the insurance paperwork on the counter into a folder. "Martha, I'm so glad to see you. Did you get my phone message?"

"*Ya.*" She frowned.

"Is something wrong?" I asked. "I was worried when I didn't hear from you. We had a quilting circle meeting last night. Everyone asked about you and wondered where you were."

"*Nee*, nothing is wrong." She set her basket on the floor by the door. "I'm sorry to make the women worry."

I cleared my throat. "Business has been steady today. I don't think being closed for the last few days has had as big an impact on the shop as I feared. When I've had downtime, I've been working on ideas about programs to offer and merchandise to sell in the shop. I would love to get your opinion on some of my thoughts."

"I'm not interested in your ideas." Her tone was sharp.

I stepped back. "Oh, well, maybe later? I should start closing up."

"I don't want to hear about them later either." She folded her arms. "I am here to tell you I'm resigning."

"What? Why?"

"I thought about this a long time, and I don't like that you're trying to make this store more *Englisch*. I kept the shop as Eleanor always did, and you want to change it."

"That's not true. We'll continue to have everything Eleanor sold. I only want to do more."

"That is the *Englisch* way, isn't it? To strive for more and better? There is never enough. I managed Running Stitch for two years after Eleanor was ill, and what I did was more than enough to keep the business going."

"This is what this is really about, then? You're upset Eleanor left me the store."

"*Gott* forgive me, but yes. I should have been given the store. I worked with her every day for the last ten years."

Her words stung like a slap in the face. "Martha, I need your help with the shop. You know it better than anyone."

"*Ya*, I know it better than anyone. That is why it should be mine."

I sucked in air. "I'm sorry you feel that way. Everything was going smoothly until . . ."

"Until Joseph was murdered," she finished for me, and picked up her basket.

I dropped my arms to my sides. "Martha, if you are quitting, I need your key."

She froze and then slowly turned around. "I don't have it."

"You left it at home?"

She refused to meet my eyes. "*Nee.*"

"Did you lose it?"

She stared at the ground. "*Nee.*"

I swallowed. "Did you give it to Joseph Walker?"

She glared at me but said nothing.

"You gave him the key so that he could search the shop for the deed."

Still she said nothing. What if I was wrong? But then again, Martha hadn't needed her key since the day before the grand reopening party. She hadn't opened or closed the shop since then.

"If I am wrong, where is the key?" I asked.

She took two steps to the door and turned. "You are not wrong. I gave him the key because I wanted him to find the deed. If I couldn't have the shop, it was better that he own it than you. He would have let me run it as I chose, in the Amish way."

"Was he going to search the shop alone? Who was with him?"

"I only gave the key to Joseph. The shop is small. He would not need any help."

I opened my mouth to ask another question.

She placed her left hand on the doorknob. I remembered Martha's quilting at Anna's house. Her left hand stitched. No matter what part she had played in the breaking and entering of Running Stitch, she did not kill Joseph Walker, as the sheriff had said the killer was right-handed.

"My part in his death is something that I must live with, but you and this shop are not."

The front door slammed closed after her. I immediately left a voice mail for the sheriff with this latest bit of news. Then I called a locksmith to have the lock to the front door changed.

Chapter Thirty-three

The shops in Rolling Brook closed at five on weekdays, but everything in Millersburg, being the county seat, stayed opened until six in the evening. After locking up Running Stitch, I headed straight for Out of Time.

The bell jangled when I stepped into Jessica's antiques shop.

Oliver snuffled the floor in search of Cherry Cat and the others.

Jessica closed the lid to her laptop. "Angie, you came back at the perfect time. I made a major sale." She pointed at a huge cedar wardrobe. "See that over there? I just sold it, for a nice price too. The buyer will be back tomorrow with a truck to pick it up."

"Congratulations." I smiled.

"I know. I'm already plotting what I can place there. It took up some serious real estate in the shop." Her smile widened. "I have even better news."

Oliver sniffed the suit of armor's feet, and I pulled him away from it by the collar. It would not do for the ax to fall on him. "Better than a big sale?"

She pulled back the cotton curtain that separated the

back of the store from the sales area. "Come to the back room, and I will show you."

Behind the counter, Oliver and I followed Jessica through the curtain that blocked the back room from view.

Dishes, knickknacks, and old books covered every surface in the tiny room. When Jessica said that she had enough stock to take the cedar closet's place, she had not been exaggerating.

Jessica held her finger to her lips and pointed to a laundry basket in the corner. Inside Cherry Cat lay on her side while four newborn kittens slept curled up close to her tummy.

Oliver peeked between my ankles as he stared at the kittens.

"They are adorable." I gasped.

The Frenchie crouched down and watched the basket. I think he fell a little in love too. Cherry Cat hissed at him softly. It was only a friendly warning, "Don't try anything, buster."

"Cherry is a good mom. The vet thinks she's only about a year old herself, so this is likely her first litter. After the kittens are weaned and the vet says enough time has passed, I'll have her spayed."

"Are you going to keep her?" I asked in a hushed voice. I didn't want to hurt the kittens' ears with any loud noises.

Jessica laughed. "I have to. She runs the shop."

Cherry Cat was as happy as could be as her four little kittens snuggled against her. A fifth kitten I hadn't noticed at first was off by himself shivering in the corner of the laundry basket. I sat on the floor and gently petted the dewy fur between his tiny ears. The gray and white kitten staggered over to me on wobbly legs, moving his head back and forth and finding me by scent as his tiny eyes weren't opened yet. Oliver grew very still. I cupped my hand and the creature curved his body into the shape of my hand. I felt his cool nose on my palm, and his shivers subsided.

Jessica laughed. "I think you have a new friend."

All the kittens were adorable, but the moment I saw him, I knew this little guy was special. I had felt the same way when I adopted Oliver. It was a little like falling in love. I remember telling Ryan that at the time. He had gone with me to pick up Oliver. He'd rolled his eyes at my romanticized view on pet adoption.

Oliver snuffled but made no move to touch mama or the kittens. Cherry seemed to note his restraint and closed her eyes.

"Does this one have a name?" I asked.

"Not yet. Why don't you name him?" Jessica said with a knowing smile.

I thought for a minute. "Dodger" popped out of my mouth.

"From *Oliver Twist*, right?"

I nodded. "It was one of my favorite books as a kid. My father used to read it to me with all the voices."

"I can tell he's an adventurous little guy, so Dodger is the perfect name."

"Does this kitten have a home?" I asked.

"Yes," Jessica said.

"Oh." My face fell. I started to remove my hand. The little creature mewed in protest.

"Yours," Jessica said.

I laughed. "Am I that obvious?"

"Yes. He will be weaned in six weeks, and then he is

all yours." She picked up the kitten and nestled him against Cherry with his brothers and sisters. "Let's give Cherry Cat and the kittens some space and go back into the shop."

Reluctantly, I stood.

Jessica pulled out a three-foot-high antique milk can for me to sit on before she perched on her stool. "What brings you back here? Since the kittens were born last night, you couldn't have known about them. It's about Joseph again, isn't it?"

"Yes and no. It's more about your cousin. Danny."

"What did he do now?"

"Yesterday, he took me to see the Walker farm. I haven't seen him since, and he had a little mishap." I went on to tell her about the ants.

Jessica doubled over in laughter. "I would give anything to see it. It's something we could play at family parties over and over and over again. The whole Nicolson clan would love it."

I grinned. "I wish I thought to video it with my cell phone. It would have gone viral online."

Jessica started to cough; she was laughing so hard. She reached under the counter for a bottle of water and took a long swig from it. After she recovered, she asked, "How's Danny now?"

"That's why I stopped by. I haven't seen him since."

"Don't worry about him. He's a guy. His ego was bruised. He's probably in his apartment wallowing for a bit. He'll be fine." Her jovial tone dissipated. "When you came in today, I was afraid you were going to ask me more questions about Joseph's death."

"I never really thought you did it. If you wanted to hurt Joseph for abandoning you, why wait thirty years?"

She barked a laugh. "I'm glad the passage of time saved me from further investigation."

"If you wanted to, you could have easily hurt him back then by telling his Amish family he was dating you. They would have been devastated by that. Instead, you protected him and kept the secret."

"I loved him," she said simply.

I smiled. "Plus, it's hard for me to imagine anyone who can love homeless stray cats so much could kill anyone. You don't have it in you."

"Thank you," she murmured. "If not me, then who do you think it was?"

"You're not going to talk to Danny about any of this, are you?"

"Please, Danny and I barely acknowledge each other. He's my cousin, but we have nothing in common other than the same paternal grandparents."

"I think Elijah Knepp is the killer. You know anything about him?"

"I know he's Abigail's brother and went to prison for burning down a barn."

I nodded. "The Graber barn. Sheriff Mitchell doubts my theory because there was no fire involved in Joseph's death."

"I always thought the sheriff was handsome," she mused with a faraway gaze.

I blinked. Did Jessica have a crush on Mitchell? If she did, that was fine. There was no reason why it should matter to *me*.

"I saw you talking to him the other day outside the courthouse." She tucked her water bottle back under the counter. "He couldn't take his eyes off you."

"Off of me?" I squeaked. I'd thought that she was

about to admit to a mad crush on the county sheriff. I blushed as I remembered Crime Mopper Gill's comment about the sheriff being sweet on me. "That's ridiculous. He watched me to make sure I didn't bolt."

"I don't think so," she said knowingly.

I laughed it off. "I'd better get going."

She frowned. "I didn't mean to scare you away."

"One more thing. I'm thinking of offering quilting classes out of my shop. Do you think I could drum up enough business for the classes?"

She grinned from ear to ear. "Yes. I'd sign up. I could finally make use of all of those bolts of fabric I seem to stockpile because they are so pretty."

Oliver lay beside the curtain that led into the back room. He sighed and rested his chin on his forepaws.

Jessica laughed. "He misses Dodger already."

I stepped around the counter to pat my dog's head. "I think you're right. I never realized how much he wanted a playmate."

I snapped on Oliver's leash. "Bye, Dodger!" I waved to Jessica, and dragged Oliver through the front door of Jessica's shop.

Oliver whimpered as we returned home.

"I know it was hard to leave him, but he's too small to leave his mom. It's only a few weeks, Ollie. Then, Dodger will come home with us. Who needs Ryan? We can make our own little family right here in Holmes County."

He wiggled his stubby tail in agreement.

For some reason it was Mitchell's face, not Ryan's, that came to mind when I thought about my new family. My feet were on autopilot until I collided with Elijah Knepp.

Chapter Thirty-four

"Excuse me," Elijah muttered as he realized who had almost plowed him down. His face grew red. "You. Get out of my way."

I stepped to the side, and he kept going.

I followed him. "Mr. Knepp, can I talk to you for a minute?"

He increased his stride.

"Mr. Knepp?" I picked up my pace. "Mr. Knepp?"

He whirled around. "*Nee.* Leave me be."

I stayed a few feet back, grateful for the busload of tourists dismounting across the street, which meant plenty of eyewitnesses in case Elijah tried anything.

"Mmmm," a woman with a walking stick said. "Can't you just smell that sweet country air?"

Her friend took a deep breath. "I want to find a present for my daughter-in-law. She's so difficult to shop for. She's picky. Everything in her house has to coordinate. It drives me up the wall. I mean, will a little orange kill you?"

The tourists' proximity made me brave and I jogged

after the Amish man. "Mr. Knepp, I'd like to speak to you about your brother-in-law."

Elijah glared at me over his shoulder and kept walking. "I thought I told you, stay away from my family."

I increased my pace. "You're right. You did. I want to talk to you about Joseph."

He came to an abrupt stop, and I tripped over my own feet to avoid running into him again.

Elijah folded his arms across his chest. "What do you want to know?"

Elijah was only a few inches taller than me, but his glare brought me to a dead stop. "I—I—"

His lip curled. "You have nothing to say? No questions for me?"

"Where were you the night Joseph died?" I blurted out.

His expression was hooded. "You're like everyone else. You believe that I have murdered my brother-in-law. It does not matter where I was. It does not matter what I say. I cannot change what you believe." He started walking again.

I called after him. "Give me a reason to change my mind."

He stopped this time on the corner across from the courthouse.

I took a few steps forward, leaving twenty feet between us. I had no desire to get any closer to him. "You wanted to stay with your sister's family, correct? And he turned you away?"

"*Ya.*"

"Then, where were you staying the night he was killed?"

"In an outbuilding on the farm. My sister knew I was there. I had nowhere else to go."

I didn't tell him I already knew about his outbuilding hiding place.

"Can your sister vouch for you being there?"

"Yes." He folded his arms.

"Have you told the police this?" I couldn't keep the disappointment out of my voice. If Elijah had an alibi, I was back to square one. The only viable suspects I had remaining were Farley and Willow. I couldn't completely count out Jessica, since she didn't have an airtight alibi like Old Ben. The only one I was certain was innocent was Martha.

He scowled. "The sheriff and I do not get along. To talk to me, Mitchell will have to find me first." His eyes flicked over to the tourists. "You think you're safe because they are here."

My breath caught.

He stepped closer to me. "There won't always be witnesses around." He looked down at Oliver, who hid behind my leg. "It would be a shame if such a cute little dog got hurt."

A group of tourists strolled up to us and stood at the crosswalk, waiting to cross to the green in front of the courthouse. The sound of tourists' laughter washed over me as their high-pitched voices echoed in my ears. "I'm going to buy my son an Amish checkers set. They make them from wood. They are darling."

"Does your son play checkers?" her friend asked.

"He would if he had such a beautiful set," the first woman said with certainty.

"What about chess?"

"That game is way too hard."

Elijah grinned and stalked away. I watched him until his form disappeared around the corner. The tourists from the bus crossed Clay Street and flowed around me like a tide. Oliver leaned heavily against the backs of my legs.

I scooped my Frenchie up into my arms and ran all the way back to my house. I raced up my front steps, threw open the door, and locked and bolted it behind me.

Inside the house Oliver jumped into his dog bed, tucking most of his body under the blanket on top of it.

My hands shook as I scrolled through my phone's directory, stopping on "paddy wagon."

"Sheriff Mitchell." The county sheriff's voice cut through the fog surrounding my thoughts.

"It's Angie Braddock. I think someone just threatened me."

"Who?" His voice was sharp.

"Elijah Knepp."

"Where are you?"

"At my home in Millersburg."

"I'll be there in ten minutes."

I hit the off button on the phone. "Maybe I should have thought this through, Oliver. Maybe calling the sheriff right away wasn't the right move," I said to Oliver's tail, which was the only part of him visible under the blue and green blanket. The Amish man's words played in my head again. *It would be a shame if such a cute little dog got hurt.* Truth be told, I probably would be able to handle the threat more if it was directed at me, not at my dog.

The doorbell rang. I peered through the peephole. Mitchell and Deputy Anderson stood on the other side. I let them in. "You didn't have to come over."

Mitchell ignored me and pointed to the stairs that led to the second floor. "Anderson, check the house."

The deputy nodded and took the stairs two at a time. Mitchell stalked around my living room, peering at the carpet. Was he looking for footprints or something?

"He didn't threaten me in here," I said.

Mitchell did not speak to me as he moved on to the kitchen, still with his neck bent, staring at the floor.

I felt a blush creeping up my neck. Why had I called Mitchell? I wasn't a damsel in distress, for goodness' sake. I should have reported the threat and left it at that. He acted like Elijah hid somewhere in the house. I knew that wasn't the case. Oliver would have warned me of that.

I followed him into the kitchen.

"That's not really necessary. I saw Elijah on Clay in the middle of town. He wasn't here."

Overhead I heard Anderson move from room to room. He sounded like a Texas longhorn stampede. I scowled.

"I see the doggy door is still nailed shut," the sheriff said.

"It's going to stay that way until the killer is behind bars."

"Good." The sheriff's face softened. "Poor guy." His eyes fell on Oliver's tail.

"He got spooked," I said with a laugh. "When we saw Elijah in town."

"He has every reason to be spooked. Elijah Knepp is a scary guy."

"If he's so scary, why is he back on the streets?"

"Not my choice, remember?" His mouth set in a grim line. "What led him to threaten you?"

"He didn't actually threaten me. He threatened Oliver."

Mitchell sighed. "What led him to threaten Oliver?"

"Well . . . I'm not sure."

"What did you say to him?" Clearly, Mitchell thought I was partly to blame here.

Now I regretted calling the sheriff. Reluctantly, I told him.

"This is not good. You questioned Elijah, and what do you have to show for it?"

"He told me that Abigail was his alibi."

"I already knew that. She told me the same thing."

"Do you believe her?"

He sighed. "I believe she loves her brother and wants to protect him."

"He's hiding out on the Walker farm," I added, hoping to prove how much I had learned. I don't know why I had this desire to impress the sheriff.

Mitchell snorted. "I could have told you that. In fact, anyone in the county could have told you that. Everyone knows that Abigail has a soft spot for her brother."

Anderson thundered down the stairs. "All clear, sir."

I found his official tone annoying, but I held my tongue.

Mitchell pointed a finger at me. "I want you to stop talking to people about Joseph Walker. I especially want you to leave Elijah Knepp alone. He's unstable. You should stay here until we find him."

I blew out a breath. "I can't stay under house arrest. I have to go to work tomorrow. The shop is open. Now that Martha quit, I have to be there."

Mitchell shook his head. "I should have never let Farley twist my arm into letting you open so soon. I knew I'd come to regret it."

"Sheriff, I'll check the backyard," Anderson volunteered. He stopped short of saluting his commander.

Mitchell nodded, and the young deputy launched into the kitchen. The back door slammed closed after him. "I thought if you were busy with Running Stitch, you'd stay out of trouble." His aquamarine eyes flashed. "Obviously, I was wrong."

I scowled.

He ran a hand through his salt-and-pepper hair. "You need to be careful. I don't want anything to happen to you."

Remembering what both Gill and Jessica said about the sheriff made me blush.

Mitchell ruined the moment when he added, "One murder in the county is one more than I need."

I grimaced.

He peered into my face. "Is something wrong?"

"A man was killed in my quilting shop. An Amish exconvict threatened my dog. Of course something is wrong."

"I don't know what I would do if anyone did that to Tux." He scowled. "I still think you should stay home."

"I can't—"

There was a knock at my front door. By this time, it was approaching eight in the evening.

Mitchell's head whipped around in the direction of the door. "Are you expecting anyone?" He placed his hand on the butt of his gun.

"No, but it's always possible one of the ladies from the quilting circle may stop by. They like to check on me." I walked to the front door and peered through the peephole. I made a face.

"Who is it?" Mitchell asked in my ear.

I felt his breath on the back of my neck and slid away. "It's Danny Nicolson."

Mitchell rolled his eyes. "What does he want?"

I opened the door. The reporter entered the house. He walked with his legs wide apart like a cowboy who'd ridden his horse far too long. All he needed was a pair of chaps and a set of spurs. I winced. Could the odd stance be attributed to the ants?

I glared at him. "Where have you been? I dropped by Jessica's antiques shop to ask if she's seen you."

"I know. I got a text from her about an hour ago asking how my ant farm was." He gave me a measured look.

"Did you get rid of all of them?" I bent down to pick up a throw pillow that had fallen on the floor, which doubled as an attempt to cover up my smile.

Danny's lip curled. "I had to go to the doctor over that. I will spare you the details."

"I appreciate it," I said.

Mitchell rested his hands on his utility belt. "Mind telling me what this ant business is about?"

"No," we said in unison.

Mitchell shook his head. "What are you doing here, Nicolson?"

"I heard the call on the police band and raced over. I knew if Angie was involved, it had to have something to do with the Walker murder."

Mitchell watched him. "The police band would not have revealed the person's name."

"No, but I recognized the address."

"My home address?"

He rolled his eyes. "It wasn't that hard to find out. I am an investigative reporter."

Somehow I didn't find that so comforting.

Danny clapped his hands. "So, does this involve the Walker case?"

"We can't answer that," the sheriff said.

"I'll take that as a 'yes.'" He mimicked shooting a gun at me with his fingers, which was clearly his signature gesture. "I want an exclusive. Whatever it is will be a great sidebar to go along with my main story about Joseph Walker's death. You owe me, Braddock."

"You think I'm going to give you a sidebar after you abandoned me on the side of the road? You're nuts."

Mitchell's brow shot up. "He abandoned you where? Does this have anything to do with the ant talk?"

"Never mind," I said quickly, wishing I'd kept my mouth shut in Mitchell's presence.

The radio crackled on the sheriff's utility belt. After giving a sidelong glance at Danny, he took the radio into the kitchen.

"Sheesh," Danny said. "You'd think the guy doesn't trust me." He shot a thumb in the direction of Oliver's exposed tail. "What's up with Lassie?"

"He's had a long day. We both have."

"I'd like to hear more about that day."

Anderson walked through the front door. "There's no one on—" The deputy pulled up short when he saw Danny standing with me in the living room. "How'd you get in here?"

Danny cocked his head. "Maybe it's time for a career change, Anderson. I wrote a piece on vocational schools in the region if you need some recommendations."

Mitchell walked into the room before Anderson could come up with a comeback, which promised to take a while by the confused expression on the deputy's face.

"Angie, the deputy and I have to go on another call."

The sheriff slipped the radio back onto his utility belt. "Are you sure you want to go back to the shop?"

"I'm sure. I'll be fine. Thank you for coming over."

Danny watched our exchange. "Since the sheriff is leaving, Angie, you have time for that interview."

"Danny, I'm not giving you an interview about this. By the way, you still haven't interviewed me for the tourism Web site like you promised."

"Sorry, I got a little sidetracked by murder."

"I think it's time for you to go too, Danny," I said.

"I'm not leaving without my interview," he shot back.

Mitchell stood between us. "Nicolson, she asked you to leave. Don't make me ask Anderson to throw you out." He clapped a hand on Danny's shoulder and squeezed.

Danny glared at me. "Fine." As he walked through the door, he said, "I will get my story, Braddock. I promise you that."

Anderson followed Danny out of the door. I wasn't sure if it was to make sure the reporter left or to give himself more time to come up with the comeback he mulled over.

Oliver backed out from under his blanket and gave Mitchell his best poor-me eyes. The sheriff smiled and crouched next to the dog, scratching him behind the ears.

Mitchell's radio crackled again. "I'll have Anderson do some extra patrols in your neighborhood tonight, and I will station him in Rolling Brook tomorrow close to Running Stitch."

"I appreciate the extra patrols, but Anderson doesn't have to hang around my shop all day. It will add to the gossip about the murder to see a deputy there."

"This is not up for debate." He took a step closer to me and stared at me with his piercing blue-green eyes. I would have taken a step back, but the backs of my legs were up against the couch. "Stay away from Elijah Knepp."

Remembering the anger on Elijah's face, I whispered, "I will."

Chapter Thirty-five

I promised myself that I would keep my word to Sheriff Mitchell. Not so much for his sake, but for Oliver's. There was little doubt in my mind that Elijah murdered his brother-in-law. If a man could threaten a dog like that, there was no telling what he was capable of.

All through Thursday morning, I kept a close eye on Oliver, even when we were inside the store. During lulls between customers, I tried to occupy my mind by composing a newspaper advertisement for Martha's replacement. I got nowhere with the ad; every time I had a good idea, Anderson ambled by the front window and peered inside, causing me to lose my train of thought.

After most of the visitors had left the downtown area in search of lunch in Holmes County restaurants, I taped a be-back-in-five-minutes sign on the glass front door.

Anderson appeared at my side. "Where are you going?"

"Easy, Deputy. I'm just going across the street to visit the bakery."

"If anything happens to you or your dog, the sheriff will never forgive me."

"Nothing is going to happen between here and the bakery." I pointed across the street. "It's less than twenty paces away."

He took a deep breath. "Still. I'd rather you stay inside the quilt shop."

"Anderson, you are supposed to watch the neighborhood, not put me under lockdown. Now, I've told you what I'm doing—I'm visiting my friends at the bakery. You're welcome to walk me over and pace back and forth in front of the bakery window if it will make you feel better."

He gave a sigh of relief. "It would make me feel much better."

Anderson, Oliver, and I walked across the street to the bakery.

Behind the counter, Mattie removed cookies from the display case and wrapped them in cellophane. Tomorrow, the bakery would sell them at a discount price as day-old cookies.

"Is Rachel here?" I asked.

She frowned. "Abram is sick today. She is home with him."

"Nothing serious, I hope."

"Just a cold, but she didn't want to bring it to the bakery and possibly expose customers. You've had a lot of business in your shop this morning."

I smiled. "It was a good day for business, even if most of them wanted to know about the murder."

She shook her head. "It must not help that the deputy's been hovering around the street all day. He followed you over here, you know."

"I know."

"*Englischers* find the oddest things fascinating. For

the Amish, death is a part of life. It is sad for the ones still on earth, but it is a blessing to whoever is passing on to be with the Lord. Sadly, the circumstances of Joseph's passing make this time a little different." She sprayed a vinegar and water solution on the glass-domed counter. "Can I help you with something, or can I tell Rachel you stopped by?"

"Maybe you can help me." I leaned on the counter. "I need to hire someone to work with me at the quilt shop. Do you have any friends looking for work?"

The bell on the door handle rang as three women in jeans and sparkly tank tops entered the bakery.

Mattie held up her finger to me. "Why don't you sit at one of the tables, and we can talk about this after they leave?"

My brow shot up. "Okay."

The women read the chalkboard that hung beside the kitchen door. It listed all the items the bakery sold. Many were crossed out at this time in the day.

One of the women's mouths fell open. "There isn't any cappuccino here. I'm exhausted. I need a cup."

Her friends in impossibly high heels surveyed the room. "I'm sure they have something we can drink, Ashley."

Mattie smoothed her apron. "We have black *kaffi*."

"Just black coffee?" Ashley asked. "I can't stand the stuff. It's like drinking crude oil."

Mattie tucked her spray bottle and cloth below the counter. "The tea shop next door has special tea and lattes that you might enjoy."

Ashley pouted. "But we want authentic Amish food."

Need I tell the woman that cappuccino wasn't an Amish delicacy? I sat at one of the round tables in the café area of the bakery. Oliver was perched beside me and placed a paw on my right foot. I guessed Deputy Anderson wasn't the only one around looking out for me. Oliver would protect me as long as my assailant didn't have wings. At least he might try to protect me.

"You can buy some things from the bakery here and take them to eat with your lattes at the tea shop. People do that all the time, and the owner of the tea shop doesn't mind." Mattie folded her hands on the glass countertop.

"The tea shop is a lovely place," I said.

The women conferred and, in the end, ordered fry pies to go and went next door to the tea shop. After the women left, Mattie sat across from me at the table. "I thought about what you said yesterday about offering embroidery classes at Running Stitch, and I would like to do it." She took a deep breath. "If you have an opening, I'd be interested in working at the quilt shop too."

My brow shot up. "You are?"

She blushed at my obvious surprise. "Yes, I enjoyed the quilting circle and would love to learn more." She waved her hand back to the bakery counter. "This is my family's business and not what I want to do."

I bit the inside of my lip. "Doesn't your family need you?"

"They can find someone else. I've worked here for so long. I'd like a change." She pressed her hands together in her lap. "Please," she whispered. "I thought I would be leaving here when Elijah and I were to marry. That was not to be. Three years later, I'm still here."

An Amish person who wanted change? Was that an oxymoron? I don't know why I was surprised. The Amish were people too, with dreams and goals, with dreams like Mattie's that didn't come true. I knew what that was like.

I spent seven years of my life in a relationship that ended in a twenty-minute conversation. Still, I was hesitant. "I wouldn't want to take you away from the bakery. I know that Rachel and Aaron rely on you."

"Please, Angie." Her tone was plaintive.

"I'd love to have you, but you should talk to your brother and Rachel first. I know they would miss you here at the bakery."

A large group of English tourists came into the bakery set on buying Mattie out of everything that she had left. I waved to her as I left the shop.

Across the street, an Amish woman waited outside Running Stitch. Her back was to me, and I couldn't make out her face because she wore a heavy black bonnet even though the temperature hovered at eight-five degrees.

I crossed the road. Anderson patrolled the area in front of the bakery and tea shop.

"Thank you for waiting," I told the woman.

She turned, and I found myself in front of tearful Abigail Walker, the late Joseph's wife. "Can I speak with you?"

"Yes, yes, of course." I fumbled in my jeans pocket for my keys to the shop. Finally, I got a good grip on the keys.

Anderson continued to march up and down the other side of the street like a wind-up toy soldier. Good. I didn't want him to report back to Mitchell about my conversation with Abigail.

I unlocked the shop door and let Abigail and Oliver inside. "Would you like to sit down? There are chairs by the quilt frame."

Oliver flopped on his dog pillow in the corner of the shop.

Abigail loosened the ties on her bonnet but didn't remove it. "I cannot stay long. My brother tells me that you believe he killed my husband."

I winced. "I think he is the most likely person, yes."

"My brother, Elijah, did not kill him."

"Given his history, how can you be so sure?"

"Because he was staying with us. He was on the farm when my husband was killed." She closed her eyes for a moment. "It is harder to be in this shop where it happened than I thought it would be."

"I'm sorry. Do you want to go outside? We could go to the bakery or tea shop."

"*Nee.* I cannot stay long," she repeated.

"Could Elijah have left the farm without you knowing?"

"How? Rolling Brook is five miles from our farm. He could not have walked there and back in the dark. By this time it was well after midnight. I would have noticed if someone had gone to the barn and taken one of the horses or the courting buggy. My husband had our family buggy.

"In this way, my husband's death is my fault. Just that night, Joseph discovered Elijah living on our land. My husband was furious. He didn't want my brother there, but I had let Elijah stay. How could I not? He is my only brother. Joseph and I argued over Elijah's being there. Finally, my husband told Elijah he could stay the night, but he wanted my brother gone in the morning. Joseph was a *gut* man but he liked to give orders. He was angry at me for disobeying him." She touched her apron pocket. "Joseph was too upset to go to bed, so he decided to go to his shop and work. He was finishing a table and chair set for our bishop."

The image of the chair leg sitting in the vise outside the woodworker's shop came to my mind. It was the last project that Joseph worked on. Surely, Martha had given Joseph her shop key by the time that Abigail and Joseph argued. Had he used the argument as an opportunity to search my shop for the deed?

Abigail held on to one of her bonnet ties as if it were some sort of lifeline. "I asked him not to go, to stay home because it was so late, but he was so angry, he would not listen. Had we not argued, he might still be alive."

"I'm so sorry, Abigail."

"I know my brother has made mistakes, but I was willing to give him another chance. My husband was not." She licked her lips. "You can do everything right as a parent. *Nee*, you can believe that you can do everything right as a parent, but there is no guarantee how your children will grow up one day. You can only pray for your children and hope that *Gott* is merciful about their path. This is how I feel about my girls, and I know this is how our parents felt about Elijah and me. My parents are gone now, and I feel I owed it to them to lead Elijah back on the right path."

As if my mouth had a mind of its own, I said, "I didn't kill your husband."

"I know this." She removed a wooden horse from her pocket. "Joseph made this for the girls. When the sheriff came to our home to tell me Joseph had died, I was tidying up the living room and putting away the girls' toys. I was holding this when the sheriff came to the door. For some reason, I cannot put it down. I carry it everywhere. Is that strange? I should not cling to a possession like this."

"If it brings you comfort, there is no harm in it."

Abigail ran her fingers over the smooth carved wood of the horse's back as if she was unsure whether she could believe me. "I must go." She replaced the wooden horse in her apron pocket.

As she pulled open the shop's glass door, I said, "We have space for you in the quilt circle whenever you are ready."

She bowed her head. "That's very kind of you. I will consider it. Now I only think of my daughters. Thank you for listening." She tied her bonnet ribbons and left.

Chapter Thirty-six

At closing time, I tugged on the front door several times to make sure it was secure. Deputy Anderson was at my side and walked Oliver and me to my car in the community lot. "Anderson, you can go home. Really. There's been no sign of Elijah all day long."

"Really. You think so?" he asked, sounding relieved.

I laughed. "Really."

He heaved a huge sigh of relief. "Okay." He lumbered off to his cruiser.

I opened the door to my little SUV as my cell phone rang in my purse. I checked the readout. It was my mother again. I twisted my mouth. She was bound to be angry that I didn't return her last call.

I glanced down at Oliver. "It's Grandma. Should I answer?"

He barked what I interpreted as yes. I helped Oliver in the car and then answered the call.

"Angela Kathryn Braddock, have you been ignoring my calls and e-mails?"

Yikes, she broke out the "Kathryn." This was serious.

"I haven't had the Internet installed in the shop or my

new house yet to hook up the computers for e-mail." Of course, I could get e-mail to my smartphone and I had been ignoring my mother's hourly messages, but she didn't need to know that. It would only upset her.

"What about the calls?"

"Last time you called, it was a bad time. I was conferring with a town official about the quilt shop." Translation, I was talking to the Holmes County sheriff about the murder.

"I heard all about the murder in Rolling Brook. It was in your shop, and you're a suspect. You didn't tell me!"

I slid into the driver's seat, put the key in the ignition, and powered down the windows. The car was like a sauna inside. The steering wheel was far too hot to touch. I cranked up the AC. "I didn't want to worry you."

"Well, consider us worried. Both your father and I are worried sick. He's already gone through a whole bottle of Tums—his heartburn has been so bad since we heard. We would have been on the next plane out of Dallas to come fetch you, but your father is not supposed to fly while his knee heals."

Poor Dad. "How is Dad feeling today?"

"Other than scared to death for his only child? He's fine."

"Really. Don't worry. The sheriff is investigating," I fibbed. "It was unfortunate that it occurred in my shop. I have no motive to hurt the Amish man who was killed. The sheriff doesn't think I did." I mentally added, *At least I don't think he believes that anymore.*

"Are you safe?"

"I'm fine. In fact, the sheriff assigned a deputy to keep an eye on me all day."

She let out a sigh of relief. "I'm glad to hear that someone is taking this seriously."

"How did you learn about it?" I grew curious. The only news my father knew about came from the Dallas paper, and my mother wasn't one to troll the Internet for news about Ohio.

"Ryan called me."

I almost dropped the phone. "How would he know?"

"He said he read it online."

"What? Has he been googling me?" I could not keep the bitterness from my voice.

"Oh, honey, he's concerned about you, and for good reason, it seems."

I gritted my teeth. "I'm glad to hear Ryan was so concerned that he called *you* about it and not me."

"He thought it would be awkward to call you under the circumstances."

You think? I tilted the AC vent so the cool air hit me directly in the face.

"He apologized for everything and said the breakup was his fault. He sounded so sorry."

"The breakup *was* his fault. He dumped me, remember?"

"I know, honey, but I know he regrets it now. He misses you." She sighed. "He did convince me that it was best to postpone the wedding. Ryan needs to do some soul-searching."

My right eye started to twitch. "You mean cancel the wedding, not postpone."

"Not cancel completely. Ryan needs some time. He will come around."

Apparently, our seven-year relationship wasn't a long

enough time to search his soul. As long as Mom knew the wedding wasn't happening, I didn't care about the word she chose to use.

"Mom, I do not want to talk about Ryan anymore."

"Maybe you need to do some soul-searching too."

"My soul is fine, thanks—"

"I'm worried about you and this crazy Amish murderer on the loose. Do I need to fly up there and straighten this all out? I can't believe anyone would think that you'd hurt anyone. There was that incident when you were in elementary school when you threw a little boy over your head in pursuit of a pink egg in the middle of an Easter egg hunt, but that was in the heat of the battle."

"No." As soon as I realized how much force was behind my answer, I quickly lowered my voice. "I mean no, there is no need for you to come here. Dad can't come, and he needs you at home."

An older Amish woman who was walking down the street with a basket of groceries from the tiny market on the corner crossed to get away from me, the crazy *Englischer*.

"I suppose you are right. If you need me to come, call me any hour of the day, and I will fly up to Ohio."

"I will."

"I'll even skip the Little Jewel of Texas benefit, if I need to."

I had no idea what the Little Jewel of Texas benefit was, but it sounded awful.

"I'm a judge this year."

Across the parking lot, Willow Moon climbed out of a compact car.

"Mom." I cut her off. "I appreciate your concern. I

really do, but I need to go. The town is having a festival tomorrow, and I just saw the organizer. I need to talk to her."

Her voice brightened. "A festival. That sounds like fun. What is it celebrating?"

"Watermelon."

"Oh." She sounded disappointed, and then her voice lifted again. "Will there be a watermelon princess crowned?"

"I don't know. Let me ask the organizer. Talk to you soon. Bye."

"Remember to call me if you need me."

I hit the off button on the phone as Willow crossed the parking lot toward my car. She paused, waiting for a courting buggy to pass. "Angie!" Her face brightened. "I wanted to talk to you, and there you are right in front of me."

"Oh?"

"I have a special job for you for tomorrow."

"Oh?" My voice dropped.

"You will love it," she said with the same expression my mother had when she insisted a dress needed an extra layer of crinoline. I had a feeling that I wasn't going to be nearly as excited about this special job as Willow was.

Chapter Thirty-seven

Willow wrapped the long strings of beads hanging from her neck around her index finger. "Well, are you coming?"

"I thought the special project starts tomorrow," I said through my car's open window.

She dropped the beads onto her chest. "It does, but that doesn't mean we have to wait until then to talk about it. Let's go. It's in the barn at the end of the road. It's better if I show you."

I grabbed the steering wheel, which was now cool to the touch. Mitchell wanted me to go to work and home. That was it. He would not approve of my walking about town with Willow, a suspect, out in the open where Elijah could see me.

"What's the holdup? You got something better to do?"

"Not really," I admitted, and I climbed out of the car. "Didn't think so."

I opened the door to the backseat and snapped the lead onto Oliver's collar. He snuffled. *You promised we were going home,* his expression said.

"Change of plans, buddy."

He buried his face under his paw.

Willow peered into the backseat of my car. "He wants to take a nap. Just leave him there. He will be fine."

I would have agreed with her before my face-to-face with Elijah Knepp. "The walk will do him good. He's lain around Running Stitch most of the day." I picked up Oliver and set him on the blacktop, careful to avoid the horse dropping left there earlier in the day by a passing horse and buggy.

Oliver held his nose in the air as if in disgust. He never had these types of problems in Dallas.

Willow waved us on and the strings of beads around her neck clattered against one another with her every step. "The weatherman predicts eighty percent chance of sunshine for tomorrow. I plan to hold him to it."

"How are you going to do that?" I laughed.

"I will drive to Cleveland and give him a piece of my mind if I feel one drop of rain."

Now that Oliver was out of the car and moving, his mood improved—he stopped every few yards to smell a tree or bench along the sidewalk.

Beyond Old Ben's woodworker's shop, which was closed for the day, the barn came into view. Fresh wood on the siding and shiny pieces of slate roof marked the places where Jonah and the other Amish men made repairs on the old structure. "It's a hundred times better," I said.

Willow nodded. "It is. Jonah Graber and his team did an excellent job." She pointed to the open grassy area, which had recently been mowed. "Because of the good weather, the quilting circle can go there. It shouldn't be too hot, because the barn will provide the ladies shade most of the day."

A sense of dread fell over me. "I forgot to check with Anna about the other ladies joining the quilting bee."

"I knew you were busy the last couple of days with the shop, so Anna Graber and I settled the whole event. All you have to do is allow us to use your quilt frame."

I gave a sigh of relief. "I'm glad. The quilt frame is heavy, though."

She waved my concern away. "There are plenty of strapping Amish men around here who can carry it up the street."

"I'm not sure how I'm going to be in two places at one time," I said. "I don't have any help in the quilt shop right now."

She held on to the longest of her beaded necklaces. "What about Martha?"

"She quit."

"Well, you need to be here for your special assignment. We'll find someone to watch Running Stitch," she said as we crossed the grass to the barn. "You might want some flyers to hand out to the folks watching the quilters. This will be a gold mine in PR as far as Running Stitch goes."

"I'll work on them tonight." I hoped my printer could handle spitting out two hundred flyers. Rolling Brook wasn't the kind of place you could find an all-night print shop.

The barn's doors were wide-open and volunteers were inside setting up tables and chairs for the next day's festivities.

"Running Stitch will get plenty of exposure with the quilting bee. Thank you again for including it."

"It's no problem. Anna and I discussed that the bee

needs a watermelon tie-in. We don't want it to be too out of place, so she proposed a watermelon quilt pattern."

"I've never heard of that." I sidestepped a teenager hurrying into the barn with a bunch of green and pink balloons.

"She's going to make it." Willow stepped inside the barn. Despite all the stall windows being opened to let light inside, the space was dim. "We are bringing in some barn lights to hang from the ceiling. They should be here any time."

"You still haven't told me what my special assignment is."

"We need a timekeeper for a watermelon-eating contest."

"Oh." That didn't sound that hard. Was there a catch?

Willow pointed to one corner where two teenagers set up chairs stadium-style. "That's where the watermelon-eating contest will be at eleven in the morning."

"How many people are entered?"

"Five." She sighed. "I was hoping for more, but I must remind myself this is the first Watermelon Fest. Next year, it will be bigger."

Not if the Amish like Joseph have anything to say about it, I thought. "What exactly will I have to do during the contest?"

"It's as easy as an Amish fry pie. You start the clock and stop it when the first person finishes eating all of his or her watermelon."

It sounded too easy, but I thought this was a situation in which not knowing everything might be best. "Okay, I'll do it."

She grinned. "I've wanted to bring an event like this

to Rolling Brook for years. You don't know how hard I had to push and lobby for it."

I stopped walking. "I thought the Watermelon Fest was Farley's idea."

"Pfft!" Willow snorted. "That's just what he tells people. Don't get me wrong, I have appreciated his help. Especially when trying to get it approved by the town trustees. But the Watermelon Fest has always been my idea."

The force with which Willow said this surprised me, as it wasn't the reaction that I'd expected from the mellow tea shop owner. Up to this point, I hadn't really considered Willow a viable suspect because of her relaxed demeanor. That had been a mistake. "I'm sorry if my comment upset you."

Her expression softened. "Sometimes Farley can get under my skin, which is not a small feat. He's a blowhard, but at the same time, I know I need him to get the job done."

Had Joseph gotten under her skin too? Clearly, she was passionate about the Watermelon Fest.

"Do you trust Farley?"

She stopped walking. "Of course. Why?"

"You seem upset with him." I cleared my throat. "Do you think that he could have killed Joseph?"

"Over watermelon?" She laughed. "Oh, Angie, that's the funniest thing I've heard in a long time. Who knew you were a comedian?"

Who said I was joking?

"The next thing you're going to ask is if I did it." She doubled over in mirth.

"I was thinking about it," I admitted.

She wiped a tear from her eye. "I can assure you I

didn't. I know some of the Amish aren't overjoyed at the idea, but it will bring so much business. If people come for the fest and see everything our little town has to offer, they are bound to return. We get our share of tourists, but nothing like what Berlin or Sugarcreek do. I think Rolling Brook is just as quaint as those towns and should attract the same number of visitors."

"Have preparations gone more smoothly now that Joseph is gone?"

"Not at all. In fact, the trustees were considering calling the whole thing off. They would have had it not been for Farley. How can we have all these tourists in town with a killer on the loose? Two of the trustees are especially nervous. It's one thing for an Amish shopkeeper to get murdered, but what if it's a tourist? That would ruin everything."

I winced. Abigail and her children would have a difference of opinion.

I opened my mouth, but Farley's oily voice broke into our conversation. "Willow, I'm so glad to see you. Tomorrow will be a day to remember for Rolling Brook. Ah! I see you found Angela." He grinned.

"I did, and she agreed to be timekeeper for the watermelon-eating contest."

To my relief, Willow said nothing of my suspicions toward Farley.

"Excellent." He eyed me. "I see you aren't wandering around the countryside."

I gave him a weak smile, feeling exposed. I should have gone straight home like Mitchell wanted me to. "It's getting late. I should head home. Oliver wants his dinner."

The Frenchie barked agreement.

Willow smoothed the sleeves of her thin blouse over her arms. "Remember, we need you in the barn at ten thirty sharp." She seemed to want to say something more, but her eye flitted in Farley's direction.

I hoped that my suspecting her of murder didn't ruin any chances I had of building a friendship with Willow. Despite everything, I really did like the tea shop owner. Trusting her was another story.

"I'll be there," I promised, wondering how I was going to find someone to watch the shop.

"I'm headed back to the tea shop," Farley said. "I'll walk you back to your car."

"That's not necessary," I said, and headed across the grass.

Farley didn't take the hint and followed me.

When we reached the sidewalk, Farley said, "I've heard that you have been about town, trying to find out who killed Joseph Walker. I must be a suspect."

I stepped as far away from Farley as I could while still not walking on the grass. *Had Farley overheard my conversation with Willow?* "I know the Watermelon Fest is important to you."

"It's important to Rolling Brook's survival. We need to make our mark in Holmes County. We need to be known for something."

The best theme you could come up with was watermelon? I wondered. Thankfully, I didn't voice my opinion on this.

"Sheriff Mitchell already spoke to me twice about the murder. As you can see, I haven't been arrested."

We walked by Old Ben's store and the yarn shop. The lights were off in every building and the doors locked up tight. The barn and everyone in it felt very far away. If

Farley could drive straight to the point, so could I. "Do you have an alibi?"

A thin smile pulled across his face. "I do."

"What is it?" We had almost reached the bakery. I wished Rachel, Aaron, or Mattie were still there. Why did everyone in Rolling Brook have to leave so early in the day? In Dallas, five o'clock wasn't even quitting time.

"That you don't need to know. I've told the sheriff to get him off my case. He verified that I told the truth. You can ask him about it."

"I will," I promised.

Farley squeezed my shoulder from behind me. "Just remember, Miss Angela, I don't need to kill someone to get what I want."

I jerked away from him before crossing the street in the direction of the community lot and my SUV. I unlocked the car and hopped in with Oliver on my lap. The question remained. What did Farley want?

Chapter Thirty-eight

Ryan and Mitchell stood in front of Miller's Bakery on Sugartree Street. I was across the road, in front of Running Stitch. The two men shouted at me, both scowling and angry. Their cries dissipated halfway across the street as if they hit an invisible wall. I fluffed the skirt of the poufy pink and green watermelon princess dress I wore. How did I end up in the getup? My mother appeared, clapping her manicured hands. "Finally, she will get married!"

Oliver whimpered into my ear, chasing the dream from my mind.

I batted him away. "Oliver, the sun isn't even up." I shivered, trying to forget the dream. I didn't know which was worse, the dress or Mitchell and Ryan in the same place. The image of them side by side was jarring.

He smacked his paw onto my cheek.

I grabbed his paw. "Oliver? What was that for?"

He barked in my ear and whimpered again.

I propped myself up on my elbows. A strange glow came from the window. I sat up in the bed. "What's that? Is someone in the backyard?"

He barked again and pushed me with his front paw. His claws dug into my back.

"Okay, I'm up." I stumbled to the window.

My hand flew to my mouth. The doghouse was a fireball. The flames licked the wooden fence at the far end of the back lawn. My feet got tangled in the end of my quilt. I landed on the hardwood floor with a thunk. I crawled to my bedside table and yanked my cell phone out of its charger.

"Nine-one-one. What's your emergency?"

"My doghouse is on fire!"

"What's your address?"

I rattled it off, vaguely aware of how high my voice was.

"Please, ma'am. Stay calm. Are you close to the fire?"

"I'm on the second story of my house."

"Is the doghouse close?"

"Forty feet away?"

"You should get out of the house as a precaution. The fire department will be there soon. Stay on—"

Oliver bolted out of the room.

"Oliver!" I cried.

"Ma'am?"

"I'm still here." I detangled myself from the quilt and left my bedroom, carrying the phone with me.

"Ma'am?" the dull voice said in my ear. "Are you still in the house?"

"Yes, I'm looking for my dog. He ran downstairs."

"I advise you to go out into the front yard."

"I'm not leaving my dog in here by himself," I bellowed. "Oliver!" I tripped down the stairs. The smell of smoke was pronounced on the first floor and became worse as I stepped into the kitchen. Tendrils of smoke floated through the half-open doggy door. Canine bite marks dug into the rubberized flab.

I stared at the broken doggy door and felt last night's dinner in my throat. Would Oliver have gone into the backyard? Why would my cowardly dog run headlong into a fire? I didn't have time to question. I had to act.

"Ma'am? Ma'am?" the dispatcher asked.

I ran out of the front door. My pajamas didn't have any pockets, so I dropped the phone on a small table on the porch. "Ma'am?" was the last I heard from the dispatcher.

If I couldn't find Oliver, I could hold the fire back. On the side of the house, I unraveled the knotted hose and pulled it toward the backyard. I gasped as I stepped through the gate. The heat of the flame made me feel like I stepped into a pizza oven. The back fence was on fire now. In my mind, I could see the flames traveling around the fence and onto the siding of my house. I turned the water nozzle to jet and doused the fence with water, soaking myself in the process. The flames on the fence were small and died back. I then turned the hose on the doghouse. The water there made little impact.

Sirens carried in the stillness of the rural night and came closer. I heard the sound of the fire truck screeching to a halt in front of my house. Men yelled at one another as they climbed out of the truck. Poor Oliver. He must be terrified by the noise, wherever he was. He was safe, I told myself. He was only hiding somewhere.

Four firemen crashed through the gate. One took the hose from my hand, and another pushed me out of the way as he trained the fire hose on the doghouse. My back pressed up against the door, which led into the kitchen.

The fire grew smaller. A third fireman ran at the dog-house with an ax and beat the structure to the ground. Within seconds, Oliver's beloved home was chunks of charred wood and smoking splinters.

My chest heaved up and down. The fireman who took the hose from me set it on the ground. "Miss, are you all right?"

"Yes," I whispered, but it was a lie.

I leaned on the back door for support.

The fireman removed his mask. "We will need to check you out."

"I can't find my dog."

The fireman glanced back at the demolished dog-house.

"He wasn't in there. He's hiding somewhere outside or inside. I don't know."

"Be careful where you walk. You don't have any shoes on."

I realized that he was right. I stood straighter and started for the gate.

Sheriff Mitchell pushed his way through the firemen. "I need a full report on what started this fire," he barked at the man closest to him.

"Sure, Sheriff," the young fireman replied. "The fire chief will want to do his own investigation, though."

Mitchell pointed at him. "This is my case. It's related to the Walker murder."

The fireman's Adam's apple bobbed. "I'll tell the chief, sir."

Mitchell nodded as if satisfied. "Where's Miss Brad-dock?"

He pointed at me. "Over there."

The security lights in the back of the house caught the

green in Mitchell's eyes, making them sparkle like emeralds.

Inwardly, I groaned as I imagined my appearance in soaking wet pajamas and a soot-covered face.

He stomped over to me.

"Is Oliver okay?" was the first question out of his mouth.

His concern for my dog made me want to cry. I fought back the tears. "I can't find him. He woke me up to tell me about the fire, but then he raced down the stairs. He's hiding somewhere." My chest heaved. "I thought maybe he ran outside because he bit through the doggy door."

Mitchell spun around to inspect the door and stuck his shoe through it.

Mitchell smiled. "The Frenchie has a little bit of Lassie in him."

I nodded, but I felt myself start to shake. The harder I tried to hold myself still, the worse the shaking became. "I need to go look for him."

"Hey, Mitchell." A fireman with a full beard approached us holding a galvanized canister roughly the size of a chili pot. "We found this in the neighbors' bushes."

Mitchell removed a handkerchief from his pocket and took the canister in his hand. He held it loosely against the white cloth. He sniffed the top. "Kerosene."

"That's right. I knew right away this wasn't a normal fire. It burned too hot and too fast." He pointed his thumb at the canister. "It's arson."

Arson. I felt sick.

"I was afraid of this," Mitchell said just above a whisper. "It's an Amish canister."

I knew the sheriff and I were thinking the same thing—Elijah Knepp.

A yelp went up over Mitchell's shoulder. "Angie!"

I tore my gaze from Mitchell's. "Mr. Gooding?"

"Thank goodness you are all right." The shirttails of Mr. Gooding's striped pajamas peeked out from under his red sweatshirt.

Mitchell placed a hand on my back. "Let's the three of us go inside, so that the firemen can do their jobs."

"I need to find Oliver."

Mitchell dropped his hand. "Go."

I ran around the side of the house. Two fire trucks, Mitchell's department car, and the fire chief's SUV overflowed from my driveway to the street. Up and down the street, neighbors I hadn't even met yet stood on their front porches, clutching their bathrobes tightly around their bodies.

I scanned the yard for Oliver. Since Oliver was mostly white, I could usually pick him out when my eyes adjusted. I didn't see him. I dropped to the ground beside the bushes and peered inside. He wasn't there. I prayed he was still inside the house.

I concentrated my search there, checking the living room, kitchen, and study. Nothing. Finally, I checked the laundry room, which was really a closet converted to a laundry room at one end of the kitchen. It had a small stacked washer and dryer.

"Oliver!" I called in a hoarse voice.

I heard a whimper coming from behind the washer and dryer unit. I dropped to the floor. Light reflected off Oliver's terrified eyes. I reached in and caressed his ear. "It's okay. You can come out now."

With effort, the Frenchie wriggled out of his hiding place. He launched himself into my lap and buried his muzzle into my stomach. I squinted to hold the tears back as I carried him into the living room.

An hour later, I rehashed my story for Mitchell a third time while Mr. Gooding wrung his hands. "Oh my, oh my! I'm so sorry this happened."

Oliver lay across my lap. "Mr. Gooding, it's not your fault, and no one was hurt."

"It's awful." He looked to Mitchell, who stood near the stairs leading to the second floor.

The sound of hammering came from the kitchen. One of the firemen had volunteered to close off Oliver's doggy door with a plank of wood on both sides. It would do for now, but I planned to ask Mr. Gooding to install a new door altogether. Tonight was not the night to make that request.

I glanced at the clock on the end table. It was almost two in the morning. "It's late. I promise, Mr. Gooding, tomorrow you can come back and assess the damage to the garden."

"I'm not worried about the garden."

"I know, but you need to go home. Mrs. Gooding must be worried about you."

He ran a hand down his cheek. "You're right. My poor wife." He squeezed my hand. "You take care of yourself, miss."

"I will," I promised.

He petted Oliver's head. "You are a hero. I promise to build you an even larger and better doghouse." Finally, Mr. Gooding started toward the front door as the fireman stepped into the room. He placed my pink-handled hammer on my coffee table. "That's the first time I used a pink hammer. I need to go watch ESPN and drink beer to salvage my manhood."

Mitchell snorted.

"Thank you for fixing the door," I said.

The fireman smiled. "Anytime. See you later, Mitchell." He wiggled his eyebrows at the sheriff.

After the fireman was outside, the sheriff said, "You can ignore half of what he says. He thinks he's a comedian."

"Thanks for coming over. You should go home too. Big day tomorrow . . . I mean today." I forced a laugh. "The Watermelon Fest."

He scratched Oliver behind the ear. "You're welcome." He stood and peered through the blinds in my front window. "The fire chief is about to leave. I have a few questions for him. I'll leave right after that, so I will say good night." He turned his head toward me. "Will you be okay here alone? I could stay or wake up Anderson and have him keep watch."

Like he'd be a lot of help.

"Go," I said. "It's only a few hours until daylight now. I'll be fine. Whoever it is won't come back tonight."

"Whoever," Mitchell muttered. "I know exactly who did this."

"Elijah?"

"Bingo."

"But why? If he's innocent of his brother-in-law's murder, why come after me like this?"

"A guy like Knepp doesn't need more reason than that." He rubbed his eyes with the back of his hand. "This was exactly why I didn't want you involved in the case."

"I had to be. I thought you were going to arrest me."

"I don't think you killed anyone. I never did," he said as he walked through the door.

"You could have told me that from the beginning," I called after him.

Chapter Thirty-nine

The next morning, Oliver and I surveyed the damage. Last night, it looked bad, but it was even worse in the light of day. Charred pieces of wood and a circle of burnt, withered grass were all that was left of Oliver's dream house. I picked up a piece of the doghouse that had hung over the door. It read "Ol." It was the beginning of Oliver's name and the last piece that was even partially intact. I tossed it back onto the pile. I stepped carefully to avoid getting soot on my cowboy boots. If any day called for the boots, it was the day after a fire. "Do you think I should click my heels together three times to go back to Texas? We never had to worry about crazy Amish pyromaniacs there."

He barked.

"Yeah, I don't want to hear Mom say 'I told you so' either." I tugged on Oliver's leash. "Come on, boy. Maybe eating watermelon will cheer you up." I led the Frenchie through the gate. To my relief, I didn't see Deputy Anderson or any other police detail watching the house. Maybe Mitchell finally had gotten the picture that I didn't like to be babysat.

Oliver and I parked in the community lot and walked up the street toward Running Stitch. We found Mattie standing outside the quilt shop in a light purple plain dress, white apron, and prayer cap. Immediately, I thought of Rachel. Was she all right? Were the children okay?

"What's wrong?" I asked.

Mattie wrapped her arms around her waist. "N-nothing's wrong. Why would you think that?"

"I'm sorry. I . . ." I stopped myself from completing the thought. I was going to tell her I was spooked by the fire at my home last night, but that would remind her of Elijah. "Never mind. Can I help you with something? I will be going to the Watermelon Fest soon, but I have a couple of minutes."

She dropped the sides of her apron that she held. "No, I don't need any help, but I can help you."

My brow shot up. "How?"

"I spoke to Rachel and Aaron. I told them that I didn't want to work at the bakery any longer. I told them that I wanted to work for you."

"What did they say?"

She examined the side of her apron again. "My brother wasn't pleased, but Rachel spoke to him. In the end, they said I could work for you because you need the help."

Oliver licked her white sneakers.

"Oliver," I complained.

Mattie blushed. "I dropped butter on my shoes this morning. I was so nervous waiting to talk to Aaron and Rachel, I became clumsy."

I started to move to Oliver to pull him away.

Her cheeks pinkened prettily. "It is fine. He is cleaning my shoes better than I can."

The dog moved to the next shoe.

I glanced over at the bakery. Rachel stood in the doorway. She waved at me and smiled. With a nod, she gave her consent.

"How about this? You can work in the quilt shop today. You will be on a trial basis, so that both of us can decide if this is a good fit."

"That's fair."

I removed my shop keys from my purse. "Okay, then let me show you around."

After walking Mattie around the store, I handed her a feather duster. "First assignment."

She laughed and went straight to work. I knew she'd do a much better job at it than I ever did. Dusting was right up there with scrubbing the toilet for me.

I flipped the store sign to OPEN. Outside a market wagon pulled to the side of the street. Minivans and buggies edged around it. Basically the market wagon was the Amish version of the pickup truck. It had a bench seat in the front, but the rest of the wagon was open in order to haul supplies back and forth from market.

Jonah jumped off the wagon and landed perfectly in the middle of the sidewalk. "*Gude mariye*, Angie. *Mamm* sent me to pick up the quilt frame for the quilting bee."

I held the shop's door open for him. "It's in the back."

Jonah nodded at Mattie when he passed her, not questioning her presence in my shop with a feather duster.

"Do you need help carrying it?" I asked.

Jonah folded the frame and grunted as he lifted it off the ground. "*Nee*. I got it." He shuffled to the open door, looking as if he might drop it with every step.

Men. Even Amish men. Outside, he lifted the frame into the wagon bed.

"Can I have a lift to the fest?" I asked. "I'm judging the watermelon-eating competition."

He chuckled as he leapt into the wagon bed and pulled a rope from under a tarp. "How'd you get that job?"

"It's the least I could do after Willow is giving me all this free publicity for the shop."

"Sure, I'll give you a ride."

"Let me grab my bag and Oliver." I walked into the store and picked up my purse and the tote bag I brought stuffed with two hundred Running Stitch flyers. With my free hand, I snapped on Oliver's leash. "Mattie, I will be back in a couple of hours."

She waved good-bye.

Jonah placed Oliver in the wagon bed next to the quilt frame while I climbed up front. He must have seen the concern on my face. "Don't worry. I tied the quilt frame down with rope. It's not going anywhere."

"I'm sensitive about Oliver right now, I guess."

Jonah hopped up into the driver's seat. "You should be." Jonah pulled the wagon to a stop to let an elderly English couple cross the road in front of us. "I heard about the fire."

"How? When?"

"This morning. The sheriff came by to ask if I knew where he could find Elijah. He knew that I was still friendly with him."

"What did you tell him?"

"The truth. That I haven't seen Elijah for the last day or so. I knew he was staying somewhere on the Walker farm, but the sheriff had already searched the farm and didn't find him." Jonah winked at me. "Mitchell seemed concerned about you while he questioned me."

I rolled my eyes. "He's doing his job."

Jonah snorted. "I don't think so."

"I don't think Mattie knows. She didn't say anything."

"It's better that way. She will know that Elijah did it, and it would only hurt her."

"It has to be Elijah?" I asked. "It can't be anyone else?"

"I doubt it." He cleared his throat. "I want to apologize for how my wife treated you on our farm the other day. It's hard for her to understand that I may have had an *Englisch* friend once who happened to be a girl. It's not a typical friendship for an Amish boy to have, so she doesn't trust it. I've told her that we were never anything other than friends."

"We weren't. Honestly, Jo-Jo, I never thought of you in that way."

Jonah flicked the reins and his horse began walking up Sugartree.

He kept his eyes on the road. "Trust me—I know."

I sat back against the bench seat, worrying over his response, afraid to ask what it really meant.

The wagon rocked as Jonah's horse pulled it from the road to the uneven grass under a large oak tree. Anna and Sarah were already there.

Sarah waved. "Jonah, what took you so long in getting the quilt frame? We need to set up."

Jonah hopped out of the buggy, and I followed. He lifted Oliver to the ground and began untying the quilt frame.

Anna squatted down to Oliver's level. "I'm glad you're okay, Oliver. I've grown attached to you."

"You know about the fire too?" I asked.

Sarah nodded so hard her glasses fell crookedly across the bridge of her nose. "It's all anyone is talking about."

My brow wrinkled. "Mattie didn't seem to know this morning. She started working for me today on a trial basis."

"*Gut*," Anna said. "The quilt shop will suit her fine. She should find something that she enjoys to do after everything she has gone through with Elijah."

"What are people saying about the fire?" I asked, knowing that Sarah would share all the gruesome details. She didn't disappoint.

"They are saying he did it because you found out he killed Joseph, and he wants you dead."

I frowned. "Actually, I have no idea who killed Joseph. Abigail provided her brother a convincing alibi. She said he was on the Walker farm."

"Abigail loves her *bruder*, but she would not lie. If she says that Elijah was on the farm at the time of the murder, then he was," Anna said.

I sighed. "That doesn't help me."

I noted the sheriff's cruiser parked a few yards away. Mitchell was already on the scene. I don't know why I was surprised by that. He seemed to turn up everywhere. I wondered if the Holmes County sheriff ever slept.

Busloads of English tourists were beginning to descend on the Watermelon Fest. Willow was right; the fest was good business for Rolling Brook. I scanned the faces for Mitchell. I found him in his uniform standing by the door leading into the barn. Hillary, the pretty black-haired woman I met at the fest meeting earlier in the week, and a little boy with the same raven-colored hair stood beside him. He laughed at something the woman said. Hillary Mitchell. That's how Willow had introduced her at the Watermelon Fest meeting. At the time, I hadn't thought it odd that she and the sheriff shared that same common last name. I should have in a place as small as Holmes County. Maybe it was his sister.

Anna shooed me away. "Go on. Jonah will set up the frame, and we will get everything settled out here. Don't you have a watermelon-eating contest to judge?"

"Yes," I admitted. Reluctantly, I walked toward Hillary and the sheriff by the barn door.

"Angie." Sheriff Mitchell nodded as I approached. "I'm glad to see you in one piece. How are you this morning?"

"Fine" was the best I could do.

Hillary touched the boy's shoulder. I guessed he was about eight. "This is our son, Zander. Thank you so much for helping with the fest. It's a bigger success than we ever expected."

Our son. So much for hoping the sheriff and Hillary were siblings. I did my best to keep my expression neutral. "The Amish came out for it. I know you were concerned about that."

She smiled. "I was. I can be harsh about them at times, I know. How is the shop doing?"

"Very well," I said.

"I'm glad." She placed a proprietary hand on Mitchell's arm. "Personally, I don't have time for crafts." The way she said "crafts" made me think she thought of quilting in the same way she regarded her son's macaroni art.

"Stop in anytime," I said. "You might be surprised by what you find."

Mitchell squinted at me. "Angie, is something wrong? Are you still upset about the fire?"

Before I could answer, Zander, who had the same aquamarine-colored eyes as his father, said, "Can we go inside now? I want to see the watermelon-eating contest."

"That's what I'm judging," I said.

He trained his blue-green eyes on me. "Really?"

"There you are," Willow cried. She wore a hot pink and dark green maxi dress. Honestly, Willow took the watermelon theme a little too seriously. She touched my arm. "Angie, are you ready?"

"Yes, yes, I'm ready." I said my good-byes to Mitchell and his family, not that any of them noticed.

Chapter Forty

Willow led me into the barn. "The contestants are eager to get started. One of them told me he hasn't eaten for three days."

I winced and resisted the urge to look back at Mitchell and his family. Why had I assumed that Mitchell wasn't married? Lots of men didn't wear their wedding rings, including my father because it no longer fit him. "I hope they like watermelon," I said.

The barn lights, which Willow promised would be installed last night, were up and the barn no longer seemed as dark as it had the evening before. All the windows were open, as were the barn doors on either side. Fifty or so people, both Amish and English, moved around the building enjoying the displays. A long cafeteria-style table ran along the south side of the barn. A baker's dozen of carved watermelons sat along the table a foot apart from one another. Metal cake pans of dry ice kept the watermelons cool and fresh in the heat. The smoke from the dry ice curved around a watermelon carved into the shape of a dragon. Beside it, a cat-shaped watermelon looked on. "Aren't they something?" Willow asked.

"They are," I agreed. "The dry ice was a nice touch."

"I thought so too. It brings an air of mysticism to the fest."

I held back a laugh. I'm sure "an air of mysticism" was just what the tourists expected when they came to Amish Country.

"The eating contest is at the far end of the barn." She pointed to the northwest corner. The barn was so large the opposite corner was a basketball court's length away. Something else caught my eye first. In the middle of the barn, there were five enormous watermelons. The largest was the size of a grown man. Several Amish men surveyed the watermelons. They knocked on them with their ears close to the rinds.

"Aren't they great?" Willow said. "I'm thrilled with the number of submissions."

I stepped in front of the largest watermelon. It had a bright blue ribbon taped to its side; "230 lbs." was written in black marker on the ribbon. "Two hundred and thirty pounds? That's more than my dad weighs, and he's a big guy."

Willow laughed.

The podium (I guess that's what you would call the platform the watermelon was on) was a tower of forklift slates stacked five high. The slates were worn and had seen better days. "Are you sure those slates can hold that monster?"

Willow waved my concern away. "No more dillydally-ing. The competition starts in three minutes." She gave me a little shove. "Get over there."

I stumbled around the giant watermelons. The one in the middle was by far the largest. The rest ranged from eighty to a hundred pounds. I wondered what the winning farmer fed the watermelon to have it grow that large. Steroids?

Willow was right. The eating competition was a big draw. Forty or so guests sat in folding chairs in front of the five anxious watermelon eaters. Another ten to fifteen spectators stood behind the chairs. Willow handed me a stopwatch. "You hit this, you say 'go,' and you hit it again when the first person finishes. That's the winner." She clapped her hands. "This is so exciting!"

I smiled at the contestants, but they didn't smile back. They were in the zone. "That sounds simple enough," I told Willow.

"Wonderful." She hooked a thumb at the contestants. "Keep an eye on them too. Make sure they really eat the watermelon. I don't want any cheaters to harm the integrity of my contest."

I chuckled. "Cheaters?"

"You'd be surprised. I bet one of them tries to pull a fast one, like tossing the watermelon under the table." She pointed at Oliver. "You better keep him to the side. He might accidentally aid a competitor by eating watermelon that falls on the ground."

Tossing watermelon? How violent did Willow think this competition would be? "I'll keep him out of range."

She tapped the face of her watch. "It's showtime."

"I thought I was the timekeeper."

"Oh no. You are running this whole thing. I'll give you an intro and then you're off."

"Thank you . . . I think."

Willow stepped in front of the contestants and held out her arm. Her blouse flowed around her like the dry-ice smoke around the carved watermelons. "Hello, every-one! Welcome to the First Annual Watermelon Fest. We have so many exciting events planned for you, and we are kicking things off with the watermelon-eating contest." She beamed over her shoulder at the contestants. "Are you ready?"

The four men and one woman nodded. In front of each contestant there was a fifteen-pound watermelon that had been cut in half, a large tablespoon, bottles of water, and a soup bowl. I wasn't sure what the soup bowl was for.

Willow beamed. "I'm pleased to introduce you to our newest member of the Rolling Brook business community, Angela Braddock."

Tepid claps came from the crowd. How long would it take for them to eat the watermelon? Fifteen minutes? Twenty?

"Angie, if you will do us the honors? By counting us down?"

I cleared my throat and used my best outdoor voice. "The competition will begin on the count of three. Ready? One! Two! Three! Go!"

I hit the on button of the stopwatch and the contestants dug into their watermelons with such ferocity I had to look away. Unfortunately, I soon learned what the bowls were for as contestants started to spit black watermelon seeds into them. Some of them didn't have the best aim, and the spectators in the front row were showered with watermelon seeds.

Oliver whimpered and hid behind a horse stall. Five minutes into the contest, the eating began to slow. The four male contestants, all built like amateur bodybuilders, groaned as they tried to maneuver their spoons. One had his forehead resting on the table.

The woman ignored her competitors and dug into the

watermelon with methodical concentration. Another ten minutes passed. Two of the men had run off in the direction of the Porta Potties when the woman held up her spoon in victory. "Done!"

I hit the stopwatch. Most of the spectators had wandered off by this point. Watching someone become sick over watermelon wasn't all that exciting. I decided if Willow held the competition next year, she would have to spice it up, like have the contestants eat watermelon while running a race. At least it would be more interesting.

Willow clapped her hands. "What a thrilling contest! Timekeeper, what is our winner's official time?"

"Twenty-four minutes and forty-six seconds."

The girl picked a seed from her cheek. "What do I win?"

Willow reached into her purse for an envelope. "You won a thirty-dollar gift certificate to any of the participating shops in Rolling Brook."

Frowning, the girl took the envelope. I would be disappointed too. Her effort deserved at least a fifty-dollar gift certificate.

Willow turned to the handful of spectators still in the folding chairs. "Please enjoy the rest of your visit to our lovely little town of Rolling Brook."

The sad remainder of the crowd dispersed.

Willow beamed. "That went well—don't you think?"

"Yep. I should go check on the quilting circle," I said. "Anna and the others should have the quilt frame up by now."

She nodded and floated away. Behind me someone tapped my shoulder. "Mind giving me a quote about the eating contest for the paper?" Danny asked.

"Tortoise wins the race again," I said, and started to walk toward the entrance of the tent.

As I expected, he followed me. "Are you going to tell me anything about the fire at your house last night?" he asked.

I wasn't the least bit surprised he knew about it. "No one was hurt, and the fire department had it under control within minutes."

Jonah pulled one of his twins off the giant watermelon in the middle of the room. The slates gave a little under the boy's extra weight but held. Jonah reprimanded his son in their language.

"What about the kerosene?" Danny asked as we stepped outside the barn.

"I don't know anything about it."

The quilt frame was up and eight ladies sat around it, quilting on their little section. Anna held court and the women nodded their prayer-cap-covered heads and laughed at the story she told in Pennsylvania Dutch.

He grabbed my arm. "Come on. That is Elijah Knepp's signature. Did he do it?"

I jerked my arm away from him. "You are the investigative reporter, Danny. You tell me."

Danny glared at me. "We had a deal that we were going to help each other."

"Yes, we had a deal until you left me stranded by the Walker place."

"Okay, I admit that was a little childish. Can we start again?"

"Danny, I don't have time for this today."

"Have you found the deed to the quilt shop? Even without Joseph around, the Walkers could still dispute your claim to it."

I ignored his question.

He chuckled. "I'll take that as a no. If you find it, I suggest you put it in a safety-deposit box at the bank. That's much safer than your aunt's methods."

I hadn't thought about that before. Would sweet Abigail try to take the shop from me?

"I don't have anything more to tell you."

"We had a deal!" He glared at me, and for the first time, he didn't remind me of a spoiled teenager. In the teenager's place was a fully grown, angry man. "Maybe you should listen to your mother and go to Texas and marry that lawyer."

"H-how do you know about that?" I'd never spoken to Danny about Ryan. I hadn't spoken to anyone in Rolling Brook about Ryan, not even Rachel or Anna.

"Is there a problem here?" Farley sauntered up to us. Despite the hot weather, he wore a three-piece suit with a pocket watch on a chain. I imagine he chose the outfit because it was in keeping with how he thought a township trustee should dress. But instead of looking the part of small-town official, he looked like a Victorian who had been dropped from outer space.

He still made my skin crawl, but in this case, I was happy to see him.

I smiled. "Not at all. Danny's asking for quotes about the Watermelon Fest. You two should talk. I'm sure you can tell him all about it, Farley."

The trustee's chest puffed out. "Yes, I can. It was my idea after all." He wrapped an arm around Danny's shoulder. "Let's talk." He led Danny away.

Danny glared at me over the trustee's arm, and I offered him a little finger wave before joining the quilting circle.

Oliver headed straight for Anna's side. I think he remembered the beef jerky from the buggy.

Rachel stood up from her folding chair. "Angie, so many of the people have stopped to take flyers about Running Stitch. They are really excited about the quilting classes."

"I'm glad," I said, hope growing in me that the quilt shop would be a success after all. "And thank you and Aaron for letting Mattie work at my shop. I know you rely on her."

She smiled. "We do, but I told my husband, Mattie needs to do something she wants right now until she can find her feet again."

I gave her a hug and waved to the rest of the ladies. "Thank you all for taking part in the bee."

"It is our pleasure," an elderly Amish woman said. "When Anna Graber calls in a favor, you jump."

Anna shook her head. "Bea, you act like I keep a scorecard."

"You don't?" The other woman cackled.

"Can you stay and quilt some?" Anna patted the top of the quilt. I could see the blue outline where she'd marked the watermelon pattern.

"I hope to. I need to go back to the shop and grab my quilting kit and see how Mattie's doing." I touched the quilt topper. "Anna, this is beautiful. Willow told me you agreed to make a watermelon pattern, but I never expected anything like this. It's a piece of art. The watermelons look like they could roll right off into the grass."

"Hush, now. It is nothing." Anna slipped Oliver a piece of dried meat from her basket. He chomped it down.

"When it's finished, I want to hang it in the shop." I didn't say so, but it would fit in the space where my aunt's wedding ring quilt once hung.

"I saw you talking to Danny Nicolson." Sarah threaded her needle. "Did he write the profile on you yet?"

I frowned. "Not yet."

Sarah adjusted her glasses. "I'm surprised. He asked dozens of questions about you. He should have more than enough material by now."

"Maybe he's concentrating on the murder story," Rachel said.

"What type of questions did he ask?"

"He wanted to know where you were from and what your background was." Sarah made five tiny, straight stitches. "He wanted to know why you came to Rolling Brook. I told him because you inherited Running Stitch from your aunt."

"Was that the end of it?"

"No. I got the impression he thought there was more to it than that." Her needle flew through the next straight line on the pattern. "He said that he was going to get to the bottom of the real story."

"That is the real story." I pivoted back toward the barn. Danny and Farley were no longer there. Had the reporter been checking up on me? Was that how he knew about Ryan?

I wanted to question Sarah more, but Martha came across the lawn to the circle.

"Martha," Anna exclaimed. "I'm so glad you changed your mind and came." She patted the seat of the empty folding chair next to her. "We have a spot for you."

I tensed up at Anna's offer. None of the quilters knew

about Martha's involvement in Joseph's death. I hoped to keep it that way, not so much for Martha, but for my aunt. Whatever she may have done to me, Martha had cared for the shop when *Aenti* needed her and I would always be grateful to her for that.

Martha clutched the handle of her basket. "I can't stay. I only dropped by to share my good news." She positioned her body to purposely cut me out of the conversation.

Rachel frowned at me.

"What's that?" Sarah asked, leaning forward. She was always ready for news, good or bad.

"I signed a lease to rent Joseph's old woodworking shop from Abigail Walker."

"You can do woodwork?" Sarah asked.

I had a bad feeling about this. Clearly Abigail had no idea of Martha's part in her husband's death.

"Of course not," Martha said. "I'm opening a quilt shop in the space. It should be up and running in a few weeks."

I gasped. "But that's right next to Running Stitch."

She sidestepped so that she could see me. "It is, but I thought Rolling Brook deserved to have an authentic Amish quilt shop in town, not one run by an *Englischer*."

My mouth fell open.

To the quilters, she said, "I hope you will all come to my grand opening in a few weeks, and I will be starting my own quilting circle. I hope you will consider joining." She nodded and went on her way.

Was Rolling Brook big enough for dueling quilt shops and dueling quilting circles? Things had not gone well for Joseph Walker's and Old Ben's dueling furniture shops, and those two buildings had been a block away from each other, not right next door.

I felt eight sets of eyes on me—make that nine, counting Oliver's. "Competition is good for business, right?" I said.

Chapter Forty-one

When Oliver and I entered Running Stitch a few minutes later, there were six customers in the store. Mattie helped a woman with red hair select an infant quilt. "This would make a beautiful baby gift for any mother-to-be." Her Pennsylvania Dutch accent was thicker than normal, as if she knew the sound of her voice would increase chances of a sale.

The woman held the corner of the mint green and periwinkle quilt in her fingers, considering it. "This is for my first grandchild. You can't help but spoil the first one, can you?"

"Congratulations." Mattie gave her a dazzling smile. "A special gift like this for your daughter would be perfect."

I slid behind the counter and began packing my sewing basket for the quilting bee. With Mattie to mind the shop, I felt free to go back. Maybe I could track down Danny and ask him why he'd been snooping into my personal life.

A woman with a variety of spools of thread approached the counter. "I love your store," she gushed.

"Quilting is such a talent. I wish I knew how. The best I can do is hem my husband's trousers."

I rang up her purchase and stuck everything into a small brown handled shopping bag. "I plan to offer quilting classes in a month or so."

Her eyes lit up. "That sounds wonderful." She waved over her shoulder at her friends. "Girls, the shop might offer quilting classes. We'd come back for those, wouldn't we?"

"Oh yes, absolutely," one gushed.

I smiled but it felt halfhearted. The women chose my shop now, but would they choose Running Stitch with Martha's authentic quilting shop right next door?

I grabbed a pad of paper from under the counter. "If you want to write down your names and e-mail addresses, I can e-mail you the class schedule when it's ready."

All five women quickly signed the paper. After they left, the soon-to-be grandma approached the counter with the baby quilt nestled in her arms. "I'll take this."

I rang her up and congratulated her on her grandchild. Finally, Mattie and I were the only ones left in the room.

"You're hired," I said.

Mattie picked up the feather duster and ran it along the fabric shelves. "I am?"

"Yes, that was a great sale."

She laughed. "That was nothing. I once talked someone at the bakery into buying five dozen cookies instead of two."

"You're a born salesperson."

"I'd like to take some of those quilting classes when you offer them."

"Great," I said as I collected my needles and thread for the quilting bee.

"Angie?" Mattie asked in a small voice.

My head snapped up. A tear slid down her cheek. "What's wrong?"

"Was there a fire at your house last night?"

"How'd you find out about it?"

"A lady from Millersburg said there was a fire in the middle of the night in her neighborhood. When she said what street the fire had been on, I knew it had to be yours."

"It wasn't my house. It was Oliver's doghouse."

Oliver whimpered.

Mattie knelt by the dog and fondled his ears. "I'm sorry, Oliver." She tilted her head up to me. "Did Elijah do it?"

"We don't know for certain, but the police think he might have done it. There was an Amish canister of kerosene at the scene."

She stood up. "Elijah," she whispered.

I set my sewing basket on the counter. "Did he ever hurt you?"

Her head snapped up. "It's not something the Amish speak of."

I took that as a yes.

"I saw him yesterday," Mattie said.

"Where? When?" My voice was sharp.

She swallowed. "At the Walker barn after supper. It was dusk."

That put their meeting somewhere around the nine o'clock hour. Long before the doghouse fire.

"I went there to tell him I couldn't see him again. I

told him I prayed about it and needed to make a change. I didn't believe *Gott* wanted us together. We both needed a fresh start. If *Gott* brought Elijah and me together later in our days, he would. If he didn't, it wasn't meant to be."

"Did you tell Elijah you were going to work for me?" I tried to keep my voice level.

"*Ya.* Should I have not told him?"

I was certain I knew who burned down Oliver's doghouse and why. Mattie didn't need to know too. "No. You did what you had to."

"*Danki*, Angie. And thank you for giving me this chance. I won't let you down."

"I'll hold you to that."

Her eyes went wide.

"It was a joke."

She dropped her shoulders in relief. "Oh."

"Since you are here, I'm headed back to the Watermelon Fest. There's a lot of interest in the quilt shop there, and I would like to go back. Can you watch the shop until we close at five?"

"*Ya.*" Her eyes sparkled.

I removed the extra set of keys the locksmith had given me the day before. "This is for you," I said, and then told Mattie about my encounter with Martha at the Watermelon Fest. Mattie smoothed her purple skirt. "How can she do it? I thought she was your friend." Mattie slipped the key into her apron pocket.

I shook my head. I didn't know if Martha ever qualified as my friend. Likely, she resented me from the moment Harvey told her who inherited Running Stitch.

"How could Abigail rent her husband's shop so soon?"

"I don't blame Abigail. She must be worried about money to lease the shop space so fast."

"If Abigail has money concerns, the community will provide for her. That is our way."

"Keep up the good work. I'll be back at five o'clock."

I arrived back at the Watermelon Fest just in time to see the watermelon roll. Children squealed as they pushed round watermelons along the grass. Parents and grandparents cheered them on from the sidelines. Jonah's twins joined in and were taking no prisoners as they rolled their watermelons around the other children toward the finish line. If the energetic crowd was any indication, the Watermelon Fest was a success—even if the crowd at the eating competition was pummeled with watermelon seeds.

Sheriff Mitchell stood with Anderson a little ways from the watermelon roll. There was no sign of his wife or son. I twisted my mouth. I knew I should tell the sheriff what Mattie had told me about Elijah. It was a clear motive for the fire in my yard.

I hesitated. I felt betrayed by the fact he hadn't shared information about his marital status with me. I wished I had asked him. I would have saved myself a lot of grief. *You are not ready for a rebound guy yet, if ever,* I reminded myself.

Even though I had not spoken of Ryan by name, Mitchell knew of my broken engagement. Would I have been as forthcoming had I known that the sheriff was not only married but had a child? Probably not.

I straightened my shoulders and marched over to the two law enforcement officers. Oliver barked softly to get the sheriff's attention and leaned into the scratch when Mitchell bent and rubbed behind Oliver's ears. I would have to give the little dog a talking-to later about who our friends were.

"Angie, I'd been wondering where you went off to."
Mitchell's blue-green eyes caught the sunlight.

Focus, Angie, focus. Don't let his aquamarine peepers cast a spell on you. A man-stealer, I was not. "I had to run back to the shop. Mattie Miller is working for me now."

"Oh." The smile left Mitchell's face.

"She told me that she broke up with Elijah." I paused. "Last night. At the same time, she also told him she was going to go work for me at Running Stitch."

Anderson cocked his head. "So, she dumped her boy-friend. What's the big deal?"

Mitchell grimaced. "It's motive. We have an APB out for Knepp, but he knows Holmes County as well as anyone. He has Amish friends who will hide him from the English police. He's not easy to find unless he decides he wants to be found."

"I have one final question."

Weary, Mitchell said, "Yes?"

"Does Farley have an alibi?"

Mitchell nodded. "Yes, he does."

"What is it?"

He shook his head. "I can't tell you."

"Fine. Enjoy the rest of the fest," I said.

Mitchell frowned. "Thank you for telling me."

I spun on my heels and walked away. I was behaving like a thirteen-year-old, but I couldn't help it. I was over men. Over.

As I wove around fest-goers, I realized I wasn't mad at Mitchell; I was angry with myself. Mitchell had done nothing to encourage my little crush. I was sure he had no idea how I felt. Thank goodness for that.

Anna patted the empty folding chair next to her, the

one that she asked Martha to sit in before she made her big announcement. "Are you down in the mouth? Is it over Martha?"

I simply nodded.

Sarah put her needle into the quilt and moved to my side of the quilt frame. "Have you figured out who killed Joseph Walker?"

I laughed. "I think I'm going to leave it to the sheriff from now on. All of my suspects have led to dead ends."

Anna snipped the end of her thread with a pair of tiny scissors. "That can only mean one thing. The murderer is someone you haven't considered."

I glanced around me. Amish and English visitors and residents walked around the fest grounds. Who was the killer? If Anna was right, it could be any one of them.

Chapter Forty-two

As the afternoon progressed, the sky became darker, and a low rumble of thunder rolled through the clouds minutes before four o'clock. A group of English children screeched, "Thunder!"

English parents herded their children back to their minivans, and the Amish did the same, only they helped their children climb into horse-drawn buggies.

All of Joseph's worries about the Watermelon Fest destroying the Amish culture in Rolling Brook had been in vain. The Amish came out for the fest just like the English had.

Beside me, Willow clicked her tongue. "The weatherman promised me no rain."

"Look on the bright side. It started after the fest was over for the day," I said.

"That's true, but we will have to get everything into the barn for the night or it will get soaked. Can you hang around and help out?"

"Sure. Mattie is back at the store. I don't think she will be too worried if I'm a few minutes late."

I helped Jonah fold up the quilt frame and carry it to

the barn. We put it inside behind the carved-watermelon table. Another volunteer packed the watermelons in coolers with plenty of dry ice to keep them cool all night.

"This place cleared out quick," I said.

Jonah stuck his bandanna into his back pocket. "Everyone wants to get home before the rain hits."

Crack! Thunder broke through the quiet.

"Did your family already leave?" I asked.

"*Ya*, they went in *Mamm*'s buggy about an hour ago."

I pushed him to the door. "You'd better go. If you don't leave now, you will get soaked."

He grinned. "Okay, okay! Sheesh, you're as bossy as you were as a kid."

"Don't forget that."

Jonah stepped out into the rain. Willow met me at the barn door. "We're all done. Thanks for your help."

"No problem."

She carried a huge carafe in her arms. "You know what's strange? Almost all of my watermelon tea is left. Hardly anyone drank it."

"Huh. That is weird."

"Do you want some to take home?" She held the carafe to me.

"Oh no, I got my fill."

She shrugged. "I think everyone is out okay."

I shot my thumb into the barn. "Oliver is in there. He's afraid of thunderstorms. I need to go get him."

"Do you need help finding him?"

"No, I should be fine. You go home before the weather gets much worse."

She adjusted the weight of the carafe in her arms. "Remember to latch the barn doors when you go."

After Willow left, I walked back into the barn. "Oliver!"

A bark came from the direction of the carved-watermelon table. I found Oliver lying on one of the largest coolers. His legs were spread-eagled to make sure his overheated belly had full contact with the cool surface.

I put my hands on my hips. "What are you doing? Are you hot?"

He barked again.

"I'll take that as a yes. Let's go home. I'll give you a nice cold bath. How does that sound?"

He jumped to the barn's dirt floor.

"Are you still set on not being my investigation partner?" Danny asked.

I spun around, and Oliver crawled back under the table, out of sight.

"Give me a break, Danny."

"We could make a great team. Someone has to catch the killer for the town, right?" He strode toward me.

Something Danny said earlier that day suddenly hit me. He told me if I found the deed not to use my aunt's methods when I hid it. Did he mean inside the quilt? Did he know? I had been distracted by his comment that Abigail might still want Running Stitch now that Joseph was gone, but standing alone in the empty barn with Danny, I realized that might have been a huge mistake. Anna's words rang in my ears. *That can only mean one thing. The murderer is someone you haven't considered.*

I'd never considered Danny as the killer.

The inside of the barn was stuffy, but I suddenly felt very cold. Had I been alone, I would have bolted out of the barn at that very minute, but I couldn't leave Oliver, who was crouched under the table.

"I realized I misspoke earlier today," Danny said. "You got me upset, and I said too much."

I willed myself to appear calm. "I don't think so. You're right, Abigail could still dispute my claim to the shop. I don't have the deed." I shook my head in mock annoyance. "Oliver, come out of there."

The Frenchie wouldn't budge. I could crawl on the floor to grab him, but that would put me in a vulnerable position.

"That's not what I'm talking about. I meant when I told you that you should put the deed in a safety-deposit box instead of using your aunt's methods."

I waved his comment away. "Oh, that. I didn't think much of it."

"Then you're not as smart as I thought. However, you would have put two and two together eventually, and that's not a risk I can take." His tone held a steel edge. "You would have figured out I knew about the quilt."

"I don't know what you're talking about."

"You know that I killed Joseph Walker. How else would I know the deed was inside the quilt or that Joseph had a key to get inside your shop?"

His sentence hovered in the air between us like one of the storm clouds rolling overhead outside.

His comment about the key gave me chills. I forced a laugh. "Why would you kill him?"

"You were my motive."

I jerked back. "Me? Why me?"

"Because I went to the shop that night searching for information about you. Joseph was already there. He'd already found the deed."

"Why did you want to know anything about me?"

"I didn't buy your story about inheriting the shop. I thought there was more to it. When I heard you and Joseph argue about the missing deed at the grand reopening, I knew there was potential for a great story there. Amish-English property disputes always grab a lot of attention in Holmes County. I went to the shop to see what else I could find on you for background. I hoped to check out the shop earlier, but you were there until past midnight." He glared at me as if I should apologize to him for delaying his break-in.

I didn't reply. Instead my mind jumped from idea to idea as I frantically tried to figure out how to get Oliver and myself out of the barn safely.

"I didn't expect to find Joseph there." He took a step closer to me. "When I found Joseph and the ripped-up quilt in the stockroom, I told him to give me the deed. I knew that it would be the perfect evidence I needed for my story. The newspaper would be fascinated by a story about an Amish man breaking into an English store. Typically, the Amish are less"—he paused—"hands-on about that sort of thing."

"How'd that go?" I asked.

He glowered at me. "Joseph jumped me and we fought. I honestly thought he was going to kill me. He's twice my size." Danny licked his lips. "So I grabbed the closest thing I could find, those fabric cutters, and I lashed out with them."

"You killed him," I whispered.

"I didn't mean to kill him, but that man was like a freight train. He was pummeling me. It was self-defense."

I took a step back and ran into the cafeteria table.

He clasped his hands together as if in prayer. "You can't tell the police. You can't. It will destroy everything that I worked for."

"You destroyed that yourself," I snapped. "The moment you stepped into my shop that night."

Danny's eyes narrowed, and his red hair had a devilish gleam to it with each flash of lightning. I knew it was only a trick of the light, but that knowledge didn't creep me out any less.

"Danny, I'm leaving now." I edged away from him. "You can leave too. You should have run away from Rolling Brook the moment after you killed Joseph."

"I couldn't do that. I had to cover the murder for the paper."

"A murder that was your fault." Did he have any idea how crazy he sounded? I guessed not.

Before I realized what he was doing, he lunged for one of the heavy serving trays that had held the dry ice. In the same motion, he hit me on the side of the head with the tray. I reached for the table for support, missed, and fell to my knees. Danny hit me a second time in the same place on the head. Oliver was barking and growling. The sounds of his barks echoing in the huge barn were like an ice pick to the side of my brain. My last thought was that Danny better not hurt my dog. Then everything went black.

Chapter Forty-three

I groaned softly, inhaling the scent of dirt, hay, and watermelon, which had been in the heat far too long. I touched my head just above my right eyebrow. It felt damp. My fingertips came away with blood. It wasn't a lot of blood, but enough to make me feel woozy.

My eyes flew open. Where was Oliver? A paw touched my hand, and Oliver's sandpapery tongue licked my cheek.

"I think it's time we went home," I whispered. Slowly, I sat up. I was still beside the watermelon-carving table. It was dark out. I consulted my cell phone. It was only six in the evening. Rain hit the slate roof like beads from a BB gun. Thunder rumbled but no longer cracked violently. The storm moved on and left the rain.

One thing was for sure—I couldn't tell my mother about this, because she would be on the next plane to Ohio to remind me this never would have happened had I moved back to Texas and convinced Ryan to marry me.

Danny must have been long gone by now. Good. Oliver and I just needed to get to Running Stitch, and everything would be fine.

"Please. Please. Don't do this," a voice resounded from across the room. "You can get away. I will turn myself in." I realized it was Danny. He sniffled.

"I don't believe you. Now you will blame the girl's death on me too. The *Englisch* system will believe you before they do me." Now I recognized Elijah's voice. "I will never have any peace again."

I couldn't see the pair, because the enormous watermelons blocked my view. I held a finger to my lips, hoping Oliver would get the picture to stay quiet. He didn't bark. Peeking over one of the watermelons, I saw Elijah had Danny tied to one of the folding chairs from the quilting bee. Elijah held matches in his hand and three canisters of kerosene were at his feet. My eyes fell on Mattie. I held the side of my head. How did she get there?

Tears poured down Mattie's face. "Elijah, please don't do this. Danny killed Joseph and"—her voice broke—"and Angie too. Run away and let him take the blame."

I'm dead? If this was heaven, I wanted a refund.

"Why should I? I have nothing to run to. You won't go with me."

"I—I can't. I can't leave my family."

He rounded on her. "You leave me no choice. I'm already going back to prison. I might as well be there for a reason that earns me respect." His beard quivered. "You don't know how those *Englischers* treat me there. I'm alone with no one who understands me. To go back would be worse than death."

You could have been with your people if you'd stopped

playing with matches, I thought. I knew better than to share my opinion with the volatile Amish man.

"Get out of here!" he yelled at Mattie as he splashed kerosene on a hay bale closest to Danny.

Danny quivered in his seat. Mattie was incomprehensible through her tears.

"Go, Mattie," I cried. "Take Oliver. Get help!"

My voice broke through her hysterics and her eyes fixed on Oliver hiding under one of the tables. Her eyes cleared. She ran for the table and scooped up the dog. Oliver whimpered and kicked in her arms. She struggled under his weight but ran for the open barn door. Elijah watched her go. He didn't want her there. He still loved her, in his way.

"I thought you said she was dead."

Danny gawked at me. "I thought you were dead."

I touched the back of my head. "Next time you try to kill someone, Danny, you should really check to make sure they don't have a pulse."

"It doesn't matter," Elijah said. "Now only the guilty remain here. This is how it should be."

Was he planning to commit suicide by fire and take Danny and me with him? I could think of twenty other ways I would prefer to go out, and since I apparently came back from the dead, I'd like to stay alive.

Elijah dropped the lit match on the hay bale, and the dry hay ignited. Panicked, Danny rocked back and forth in his chair so hard, the chair fell over and he lay on his side, putting him closer to the flames.

Elijah smiled.

I threw all my weight against the enormous watermelon, and it rocked off its platform.

Elijah was too focused on the fire and wasn't ready

when the 230-pound watermelon hit him in the side, knocking him to the ground. He cried out and the watermelon came to rest on his right hand. I winced. I'd bet three head-sized doughnuts that his hand was broken.

"Help! Angie, help me!" Danny's pant leg caught the flame, and his scream tore through my consciousness. I grabbed a horse blanket hanging on the wall and beat down the flames on his leg. I dropped the blanket and concentrated on the knots tying him to the chair.

The fire ran up the north wall of the barn like a sprinter at the Olympic Games. Soon it was on the rafters. Above us, the fire crackled and hissed.

Crack! The beam above us started to give way. The wood of the centennial barn was like tinder. Elijah could not have picked a more perfect setting for his final fire.

"Angie!" Danny screamed.

Another rafter fell a few feet from me. Hot embers shot up into my face.

"You should go," Danny said. "I'm the one who caused all this. Go."

"I don't think so."

The knots were no use. With all my strength, I flipped Danny and his chair onto its back and pulled. The back of the chair was metal and red-hot from the flame. I could feel the burns forming on my palms. Ignoring the pain in my left hand, I grabbed the back of the chair and pulled him toward the barn door. It was slow going, and more rafters fell. Inch by inch, we progressed to the door and I was able to drag him through the doorway into the rain. I pulled Danny as far away from the barn as the pain in my hand would allow. When we were twenty yards away, I dropped the back of his chair and fell to the wet grass. I heard the fire truck sirens making their way up Sugartree Street.

Even though it was only a drizzle now, the rain would help control the fire. I started to stand. Would the fire-fighters arrive in time to save Elijah? Should I go back in for him?

There was a loud crack as the center portion of the roof caved in. Inside the barn, Elijah cried out and then was silent. All I heard was sirens and rain.

Epilogue

A week later, Mattie stocked the display of souvenir thimbles in Running Stitch's picture window. "Are you sure the *Englischers* will buy these?"

Behind the counter, loading new merchandise software onto my laptop, I laughed. "Trust me. Everyone coming to Rolling Brook wants to take a little piece of Amish Country home with them."

She wrinkled her nose at a thimble with a tiny buggy painted on the side. "This isn't real Amish Country."

"Just don't tell the tourists that." I closed the laptop lid and picked up the small wall quilt. I carried it to the rocking chair by the front window. There I could quilt and watch customers as they came by the shop. I'd started the quilt a day after the barn fire. It would be my first quilt made solely by hand. I pieced together a simple block pattern and the quilting pattern on top was waves.

My quilt would never be as beautiful as one of my aunt's, but I was getting there. Rachel and Anna were great teachers. The burn inside the palm of my left hand itched. Both hands had been burned, but the left was much worse than the right. How long would my hand ache? Would there be a scar as a reminder? My first real battle wound. The emergency room doctor told me to go easy on the left hand and not use it for any fine motor skills. All quilting was fine motor skills. Thankfully, I'm right-handed. I held the fabric in my left hand and quilted with my right.

Oliver snoozed on his dog bed in the corner of the shop. "I think country life suits him, don't you?" I said.

Mattie laughed halfheartedly. "I'm going across the street to the bakery for breakfast. Do you want anything?"

"Well ..."

She gave me a small smile. "One head-size doughnut coming up, if there are any left. Rachel can't bake them fast enough."

The bell on the front door rang as the door closed after Mattie. I was happy the young Amish woman was doing so well. She had been through a lot. She put on a brave face, but I knew she reeled from Elijah's death in the barn. In time, her voice would lose its sad quality. When I didn't return to Running Stitch after the Watermelon Fest, she'd gotten worried and walked to the barn in the rain looking for me. She found more than she bargained for. I knew a small part of her still loved Elijah and most likely always would, just like a small part of me still loved Ryan. Not that I would be willing to trade in Running Stitch for a big Texas wedding, no matter how many times my mother called me and begged me to move back. In a little quilt shop in Ohio, I'd finally found what I really wanted to do. And after the sheriff searched Danny's apartment, I had the deed to prove the shop was indisputably mine.

I dropped a stitch and had to backtrack. Finding a person's passion could be dangerous too. Danny was proof of that. He let his ambition get in the way, and now he awaited trial for murder and attempted murder in the county jail. To my relief, Jessica wasn't angry at me over what became of her cousin. Last time I talked to her, she said Dodger was the pick of Cherry Cat's litter and was eager to go home with Oliver and me when he was weaned in a few weeks.

Suddenly, Oliver lifted his head and sniffed the air. "Hear a bird, boy?"

He jumped to his feet. A second later, I heard the rattle of a buggy making its way down the street. Anna's buggy pulled to a stop in front of Running Stitch. She tethered her horse to the hitching post and pulled a large brown shopping bag from the buggy.

I stood up to greet her, leaving my quilt on the rocker. "Hi, Anna."

"Gude mariye," she said as she stepped into the shop. *"Gut.* You're the only one here. I have something for you."

"For me? From you?"

"It is not from me. It is from your *aenti*. I had wanted to give it to you the day after the opening of the shop." She gave me a small smile. "But you remember how that had gone."

She handed me the bag. It was heavy. I knew immediately it was a quilt. My hands began to shake.

"Go on, take it out."

I reached into the bag and the folded quilt slid out easily. I spread it across the new cutting table I bought for the store. The quilt was even more beautiful than the one that had been ruined. It was also a wedding ring and had all my favorite colors, decidedly not Amish. It was navies, aquas, teals, lemons, and goldenrod yellows. "Eleanor planned to give it to you for your wedding."

"But I'm not getting married," I whispered.

Anna smoothed her hands over her apron. "That doesn't matter. Wedding or no wedding, she would want you to have it."

Tears gathered in the corners of my eyes. *"Danki."*

She laughed at my Pennsylvania Dutch pronunciation of the word for "thank you." "We might make an Amish out of you yet." She moved to the rocker and picked up my wall quilt. "I'm glad to see that you're quilting again." She moved her reading glasses to the tip of her nose and examined my work. "Your stitches are much better. Not perfect, but you are coming along nicely. You may grow into as good a quilter as your *aenti.*"

My chest swelled with pride and then I thought of Martha. "Do you think there is enough room in Rolling Brook for two quilt shops?"

She removed her glasses and tucked them into the pocket of her apron. "Martha will do what Martha will do. You need to worry less about her and more about yourself."

"I can't go back to Texas. This business cannot fail." I said this as a promise to Anna and myself.

"Then work hard to make sure it doesn't." She patted her silver bun on the back of her head. "Now that the business with Joseph's murder is over, you won't be seeing as much of the sheriff, I gather. I hope you won't be too disappointed."

I took my quilt from her and laid it on top of my aunt's quilt. If a side-by-side comparison was any indication, I had a long way to go to be as good of a hand quilter as my aunt had been. "Why would I be disappointed?"

She smiled wide. "I've noticed you watching him a time or two when you thought no one would notice."

I folded my quilt. "Anna, the sheriff is married."

She jerked her head back. "He is not."

I dropped the quilt back onto the table. "Yes, he is. I met his wife, Hillary. She's very pretty."

Anna laughed. "Hillary is the sheriff's ex-wife."

"Oh," I said. "Oh."

A smile spread across the older woman's face. "That changes things, doesn't it?"

The bell on Running Stitch's door rang as a troop of seven middle-aged women from the suburbs entered the shop. "What a cute store!" one exclaimed.

"I wish I could be so lucky as to own a place like this someday," her friend in the hot pink visor replied.

My chest swelled with pride. "I'm the lucky one," I told Anna. "Because the store is mine."

The Amish woman shook her head. "No, Angie, you're not lucky. You're blessed."

For the first time since I left Dallas, I thought Anna might be right about that.

Amish Quilting Tips for Beginners

By Angela Braddock, Owner of Running Stitch

The Amish live a plain life. Their homes and businesses are simple, with little ornamentation. One exception is the beautiful handmade quilts found in every Amish home. For the most part, the quilts are not held to the same standard of plainness as Amish dress or decoration because of their usefulness.

Quilting is one of the few places where an Amish woman can let her creativity take over. She has the opportunity to choose the colors and the pattern for her quilt. She may not take pride in her work because the Amish are humble people, but she will be pleased with what she has created.

Quilting began as a necessity for warmth, but today it gives Amish women the opportunity to earn extra money to supplement their husbands' income.

Here are my tips to make an Amish-style quilt of your very own.

Choosing Colors and Patterns

In the quilt shops across Holmes County, you will see a great variety of quilts, from those made with plain dark fabric to those crafted with intricate prints of flowers or even puppies. The decorative quilts are made strictly for the English. The Amish would not have quilts this flashy in their own homes.

Traditional Amish quilts are made of solid dark colors. Dark greens, purples, and blues are the most popular. The Amish choose bold color combinations for contrast. Many quilts will have black in them because to the Amish black represents joy and being chosen as God's people. The fabric of preference is lightweight wool.

When choosing your own colors, keep in mind that you need to have enough fabric of each color to keep the pattern symmetrical. Be aware of which square will fall in the center and be the focal point of your quilt. For beginners, a Nine Patch is great starter quilt.

Piecing

Use a ruler to mark the fabric before cutting. It is essential that each piece is cut accurately to avoid throwing off the entire quilt pattern. I recommend that you leave an extra half inch on all sides of your pieces when you cut the fabric so you have plenty of space for your stitches.

When cutting the wool, use sharp fabric scissors to avoid fraying. As you cut, periodically check your pieces against the others that have already been cut to ensure that like pieces are of an identical size and shape. Also check their angle alignment against neighboring pieces. The pieces should fit snugly together.

When all of your pieces are cut, piece together individual squares. For a Nine Patch quilt, you want to construct each nine patch block, which is made with nine squares of two-by-two-inch fabric, before attaching the other nine patch blocks together.

When piecing, place the fabric front side to front side, so that you see the back side of the fabric. Use straight pins to hold the pieces together as you stitch. A simple straight stitch works well for piecing.

Hand Quilting

Amish women quilt both by hand and with a treadle sewing machine. Here at Running Stitch, all our quilts are quilted by hand. It takes more time, but we believe in upholding the Amish quilting tradition.

After you have your top pieced, you will need to cut your batting, the soft middle of the quilt, and the fabric for the bottom of your quilt. Cut the bottom four inches larger than the topper, and you can use the extra fabric for binding off.

Using brightly colored thread, baste your quilt together. Basting will loosely tether the three layers of your quilt while you work. After your quilt is complete, you will remove the basting thread and discard it. That's why I say use a bright color—it will be much easier to find.

Use a template of the quilting design you would like to use. Using colored pencil, trace the template on your quilt topper. For your first quilt, I recommend sticking to one repeat quilting design, like waves. After tracing is complete, stretch your quilt on a quilt frame. You can use an embroidery hoop if you don't have a frame. Keep in mind that you will have to move the hoop often.

With your first stitch, bury the thread knot at the end of your needle in the middle of the quilt and out of sight.

Quilt using the running stitch, pulling the quilting needle down, through, and up several times through all three layers of the quilt along the penciled line. Amish women can have a running stitch nine stitches long. Start with three and add more as you become comfortable. Keep the stitches small, at least half a centimeter. Amish stitching can be even smaller than that. While stitching, use a thimble to help you push the needle through the fabric. Until you are accustomed to quilting, this will protect your finger from your sharp needle point.

Binding Off

After the quilting is complete, remove your basting thread and you are ready to bind off your quilt. Essentially you will want to create an edge to go around the four sides of the quilt. Traditionally, the Amish fold over the fabric from the bottom of the quilt to use for binding. Fold in the cut edge of the bottom fabric and fold the smooth folded edge over the top edge of the quilt. Use straight pins to hold the binding in place as you bind. A straight stitch works well for binding.

Come See Us

If you need more assistance with your quilt, stop by Running Stitch, located on Sugartree Street in beautiful Rolling Brook, Ohio. We are happy to help you in any way that we can, from picking the fabric to choosing a quilting template. Beginner quilting classes will start this fall. We hope you will join us!

Read on for a peek at another
Amish Quilt Shop Mystery

MURDER, SIMPLY STITCHED

Available now from Obsidian.

When my mother enrolled me in the Little Miss Texas Butterfly Beauty Pageant at the age of eleven, I don't believe it ever crossed her mind that one day I'd be lying in the dirt with my arms around the neck of a runaway goat.

Petunia the Nubian goat baaed and kicked at me with her sharp hooves. I shifted my body away from her reach, and one of her long tawny-colored ears smacked me in the face. Two minutes before, when Petunia had raced past me as I'd made my way to the auction barn, jumping on her back seemed like a fantastic idea. Maybe because it never occurred to me I would actually succeed in catching her. My blond curls fell into my eyes. I blew at them, but that seemed to only make the tangles worse.

The tan, white, and brown goat tried to maneuver her feet so she could stand up and make a break for it. A wild goat ride was not my idea of fun. "A little help, please!" I cried.

An out of breath Jonah Graber ran toward me and looped a leash around Petunia's neck. Dust covered his plain clothes and Amish beard. "I got her."

As I rolled off the animal, she glared at me with disconcerting goat eyes. I crawled backward on my hands and knees, jumped to my feet, and bounced off something soft. Spinning around, I saw auction house owner Gideon Nissley catch his balance. His plain button-down shirt stretched across his ample stomach.

Heat rushed to my face. "I'm so sorry, Mr. Nissley." The last thing I wanted to do was knock down the auction yard owner. This was my first day at the Rolling Brook Amish Auction. Gideon had agreed to have some of the quilts from my quilt shop, Running Stitch, auctioned off, and had offered me space in the merchants' tent to sell directly to tourists. I was the first English shopkeeper to have a spot in the auction and I didn't want to lose it.

I had my Amish friends the Grabers and the Millers to thank for my place at the auction. They vouched for me and agreed to be held accountable to the Amish community if I messed up. Seeing how I'd just tackled Gideon's goat to the ground, the auction owner might have been reconsidering his offer.

Gideon righted his straw hat on his head. "What's going on here? What's Petunia doing out of her pen?"

It was Jonah's turn to look sheepish. He flicked a bit of mud from his sandy blond beard, which fell to the second button on his work shirt. "I'm so sorry, Gideon. Petunia got loose somehow as I was moving the Kings' goats into the show pen."

Gideon hooked his thumbs around his suspenders. If anything, it made his stomach appear larger. "Now, Petunia is a *gut* goat, or as *gut* as a goat can be, but I can't have her running loose around my auction yard. What if she rammed into an *Englischer* and hurt them? I'd be the one held responsible. Those *Englischer* will use any excuse to sue me. That's why we keep her in her pen on auction days."

Did that mean he didn't consider me an *Englischer*? Was that good news?

Gideon narrowed his eyes. "How did this happen?"

"I'm not sure, Gideon," Jonah said as he dug the toe of his work boot into the dirt and reminded me of his ten-year-old self, my childhood playmate. "It won't happen again." I noticed Jonah's gaze travel over my shoulder.

All of Gideon's attention was on Jonah, so I risked peering behind me to see what or who caught Jonah's attention. As I did, Ethan and Ezra Graber, Jonah's eight-year-old identical twin sons, slunk away. The boys looked exactly like their father had at their age, and they were just as mischievous. The only problem was there were two of them. Double trouble wasn't even the half of it. But by the stony expression on their father's face, I bet they regretted goat-gate already.

Jonah's jaw clenched and he repeated, "It won't happen again."

"I should hope not." Before Gideon stomped away, he said something to Jonah in Pennsylvania Dutch. The word I recognized was *Englischer*. Me. I guessed he considered me one after all.

Petunia munched on one of the fallen leaves around our feet. Her crunching and chewing blended in with the sounds of the auction: the auctioneer calling for bids for a ram inside the barn, the mooing of the dairy cows waiting to be brought to the block, and the chatter of both English and Amish as they moved around the grounds from tent to tent and barn to barn. Holmes County,

Ohio, had several Amish auctions throughout the week, but the Rolling Brook auction was one of the largest and most successful. It was the one event in the tiny township guaranteed to attract the tourists away from the better-known Amish towns of Berlin, Sugarcreek, and Charm.

"What did he say to you before he left?" I asked.

"It doesn't matter." Jonah removed his felt hat, ran his hand through his sandy-colored hair, and set the hat back in place. I always marveled at how Amish men, despite the hard labor they did, were always able to keep their hats on. In that respect, they were kind of like Indiana Jones with beards.

"It matters to me, Jo-Jo," I said, using the name I had called him when we were children. I had been born in Holmes County and lived here until age ten, when my father took a job as an executive in Dallas. I moved back two months ago when I inherited Running Stitch from my late and beloved Amish aunt, Eleanor. "I know he was talking about me. I heard *Englischer.*"

Jonah sighed. "He said something like 'Don't make me rethink my decision about the *Englischer.*'"

I frowned. "Do you think he will kick me out of the auction? Because of the goat?"

"*Nee.* Of course he won't. You're not the person responsible. It's those *kinner.*" Jonah's mouth compressed into a thin line. "I'd asked them to make sure all the goats made it to the show pen. I don't know what got into their heads to let Petunia out. Those boys . . ."

I laughed. "You caused just as much trouble when you were their age. I think I recall your swiping fry pies from your grandmother's kitchen windowsill."

Jonah grinned. "You will have to take that to the grave. You are guilty as my accomplice." His grin grew.

"And if I remember correctly, you ate your share of those pies."

I brushed dirt off the front of my shirt. "I don't recall that part."

Jonah snorted. "Maybe we should ask my *mamm*. She will remember."

"What does your *mamm* remember?" a woman's deep voice asked.

I turned to see Anna Graber walking toward us. Anna wore a black apron over her navy dress, and her gray hair was parted down the middle and rolled into a bun at the back of her head in the Amish way. A white prayer cap hid most of her hair from sight.

"That the twins are as bad as Jonah was as a child," I said.

Jonah rolled his eyes. Why do I think he picked up that habit from me?

"Ah," Anna said. "That is true." She examined her son's appearance. "Thinking of the trouble he gave me as a child, it only seems fitting he would have twins."

"I wasn't that bad," he scoffed.

Anna tapped her chin with her index fingers. "I seem to remember some of your *grossmammi*'s fry pies going missing."

Jonah opened his mouth as if to protest, or more likely tell of my involvement in the crime, but Anna kept going.

"Emma told me Petunia had run loose." Anna patted Petunia's head on the spot where her horns would have been if they had been allowed to grow. "I see you caught her."

"Angie caught her. She tackled the goat like a football player."

I narrowed my eyes at Jonah. "What do you know about football?"

"I see the Millersburg High School team practicing when I ride by their field. You were as good as any of them."

I wondered whether his comment was more insulting to me or the Millersburg High School football team.

"You two are no better than when you were as *kinner*." Anna removed a handkerchief from her pocket and handed it to me. "This should help"—she paused—"some."

As usual, Anna was neat and tidy. I, on the other hand, looked like Pig-Pen from the Peanuts.

After wiping the worst of the dirt and dust from my hands, I tried to give it back to her.

"Oh, no, you can keep it." She adjusted her wire-rimmed eyeglasses on her nose. "Angie, I'm amazed you caught Petunia. Have you done that before?"

I brushed dirt from my jeans, which only ground it further into them. "Nope. First time." A smile formed on my face. I wrestled a goat to the ground. How many people could say that? A check for the bucket list.

Anna Graber arched an eyebrow at me. "I didn't know you knew how to handle livestock."

I shrugged. "It's been an untapped talent up to this point."

Jonah laughed. "I'll take Petunia back to her pen. After that, I'm going to find those boys."

Anna shook her head as her son led the reluctant goat away. "Those twins. I told Jonah they were punishment for all the trouble he gave me as a child, but I think they may be punishment for all of us."

I pushed my hair out of my face. A twig fell out of it. "Where's Oliver? He was with me when the goat ran by."

Fear crept into my voice, followed by guilt for just now noticing my beloved French bulldog was missing.

He usually hid when he was afraid. The auction grounds were huge, with hundreds of nooks and crannies for the black-and-white Frenchie to squeeze into, especially one as easily frightened as Oliver. A Dallas pup, born and bred, Oliver wasn't made for country living. He'd spent more of his life walking along pavement avoiding the cracks in the sidewalk than on grass. Who knew how he would react to all the new sights and smells of the auction? I prayed he hadn't wandered into the poultry tent. My ornithophobic canine would be catatonic by now if he had.

Anna scanned the auction grounds. "I haven't seen him, but I have been in the auction barn up until a few minutes ago."

I scanned the area. *Where could he be?* Amish men and women carried wares to the various tents and out-buildings. English tourists milled around and took photographs when they thought the Amish weren't looking. Red, yellow, and orange leaves fell from the maple trees and scattered around the grass and dirt paths. An Amish teenager fought a losing battle as he raked the leaves into a pile that was constantly disturbed by the chilly October breeze and the footsteps of distracted visitors who marched right through his pile. A yellow leaf landed on the brim of his black felt hat like a pointed insult. No Oliver.

"I have to find him. Petunia must have terrified him."

"I'm sure he's hiding somewhere until everything calms down. I'm going to find those naughty twins before Jonah does."

I nodded distractedly, knowing the twins would be fine. Left to their own devices, they would rule the township. I didn't even know where to begin looking for my dog.

"I know where he is," ten-year-old Emma Graber said. I hadn't even noticed the girl until she spoke. *Has she been there the entire time?* It was possible. Jonah's daughter was as quiet and shy as the twins were loud and boisterous. I guessed she was used to being overlooked with the outlandish twins as her younger brothers.

"Where?" I asked.

She twisted the end of her white apron in her hands. "He's in the bunny pen."

That couldn't be good.

Connect with Berkley Publishing Online!

For sneak peeks into the newest releases, news on all your favorite authors, book giveaways, and a central place to connect with fellow fans—

"Like" and follow Berkley Publishing!

facebook.com/BerkleyPub
twitter.com/BerkleyPub
instagram.com/BerkleyPub

BERKLEY | Penguin Random House